MW00987126

DEATH BEFORE DISHONOR

The Caldwell Series

Dan Ryan

authorHOUSE®

AuthorHouse™
1663 Liberty Drive
Bloomington, IN 47403
www.authorhouse.com
Phone: 1-800-839-8640

First published by AuthorHouse 7/23/2009

ISBN: 978-1-4490-0270-1 (sc)

Library of Congress Control Number: 2009907091

Printed in the United States of America
Bloomington, Indiana

This book is printed on acid-free paper.

Prelude

On march 4, 1861, an immense crowd was present in Washington City. Early in the forenoon
the President-elect went from the White House to the
Capitol. Between one and two o'clock, accompanied by
President Buchanan, they entered the Senate Chamber.
The two men were arm in arm. The President-elect was
pale and disturbed, while the President was cool, though
his face was slightly flushed. The inaugural address was
delivered in the presence of the Supreme Court, both
Houses of Congress, foreign ministers and members of
his cabinet.

The address was in good taste, as Buchanan had suggested. The new President declared that there was no
ground for the fears that had been expressed in South
Carolina. Southern States were not in danger from the
Republican Party. He had no purpose of interfering in
any way with slavery in those States where it existed. He
would follow the Buchanan Doctrine of 1858. In this, he
was so explicit that there was no room for mistake. He
had sworn to support the Constitution and the laws, and
nothing could swerve him from that purpose.

He so liked the changing of the cabinet members between the Pierce and Buchanan administrations, that he asked his cabinet to meet with there counterparts. There is an old tradition where the outgoing administration leaves something for the incoming. Laying on the President's desk in the Oval Office was a manilla envelop marked from #15 to #16. In the office of National Affairs Advisor, was a manilla envelop marked from #1 to #2. In the office of the Presidential Protection Detail was an envelop marked from #1 to #2. In the US Marshal's office was the same. It occurred to those of us who left the service of the fifteenth President of the United States that a number of offices had been created under his administration. The nation had been held together for four years and now great danger faced us all. For me, the possibility of returning to South Carolina any time soon was out of the question. South Carolina had issued an address to the other slave holding states, inviting them to join her in the formation of a Confederacy of Southern States. The following States called conventions and passed ordinances of secession in January, 1861: Mississippi, 9 th; Florida, 10 th; Alabama,11 th; Georgia, 19 th; Louisiana, 26 th and Texas, February 1, 1861.

On March 4, 1861, President Buchanan, his sister and his brother-in-law along with his niece and nephew left Washington on the 3:15 pm Baltimore and Ohio train bound for northwestern Pennsylvania. The president had a private compartment for him and his private secretary who had agreed to become his assistant during his retirement in Pennsylvania . His secretary had been with him for many years, was nearly deaf, but was devoted to President Buchanan and would die in his service.

His sister, Louise Buchanan Caldwell, and I got your two children, James and Ruth, settled in our compartment for the trip home to Seneca Hill, Pennsylvania. Seneca Hill was the home office for Seneca Oil Company of Titusville, Pennsylvania. Louise and I had formed this company while we were still serving in the White House as first lady and the national affairs advisor to the president in 1859. Besides the oil wells now in Pennsylvania, new coal deposits were found in the western United States. In 1859, it was estimated that the coal reserves in the United States was now equal to all the rest of the world. The oil discovered in Pennsylvania amounted to millions of dollars added to the national economy. I remembered the conversations from the cabinet meetings regarding the discovery.

"What does the discovery of oil in large amounts mean for the US Navy, Mr. Toucey?" asked the President.

"We will be able to fire our boilers with oil and not coal. Oil is more compact and lighter than coal. It means, Mr. President, that we can steam farther without having to stop and refuel."

"How will the change over to oil affect industries like the whalers in Nantucket?" to no one in particular.

"Whale oil is used to light our homes because it is so clean burning," someone said.

"The oil in Pennsylvania is a light crude, almost brown in color when it comes out of the ground. It should not take much to refine it into lamp oil," another said.

I looked around at the faces in the cabinet room and thought, maybe national wealth derived from minerals will replace wealth derived from plants like cotton. I made a mental note to write to my father in Beaufort and other *business letters.*

Trying to run a business from the White House had not been something that I would ever do again. I had placed all of my business dealings under the leadership of my trusted childhood friend from Beaufort, South Carolina. He was president of Caldwell Shipping and Trading Company. When it was apparent that James Buchanan could not keep the Union of States together, I decided to move the company headquarters to Bermuda. The election of the new republican administration ended my service in Washington City. Louise, the children and I were free to live wherever we chose. I remembered the conversations that we had regarding the relocation of the company.

"Louise, just the person I need to talk to. What does your schedule look like next week?"

"Nothing serious, why?"

"I need to travel to Titusville again and I was wondering if you would like to go with me."

"Do you want to stop by Franklin, it is only 19 miles away? I can show you the houses where James and I were born. We were not there together, but the houses are. I know all about your family history, Jason. You really have not seen where I am from, have you?"

"No, Louise, and it is time that I did. Do you trust the children with their nanny for that long?"

"Yes, they are safe here. The protection detail will not let harm come to them."

"You make fun of me for being the long term planner. I would like to find a house in Franklin that you like so the company can purchase it before we leave office."

"Do we really need a third house, Jason? The place you

bought last year in St. George is beautiful, I could live there full time."

"I know you could. You love it and so do I.. Running a business will not be easy from there. Unless...."

"Unless what?"

"Unless we have the State Department contact the British Embassy here and ask about dual citizenship so we can obtain British Passports."

"I do not understand, Jason."

"A British Passport allows us to conduct business in Bermuda as citizens. Foreigners in Bermuda pay additional taxes on everything. The house they live in, the items that they buy and most importantly the export/imports are taxed at an extreme rate. We could not afford to live in Bermuda unless we were citizens."

"You mean when we are in South Carolina or Pennsylvania, we are US citizens with US passports and when we are in Bermuda we are British citizens with their passport?"

"Exactly, we can travel anywhere in the United Kingdom as citizens also."

"I would like that, Jason."

"Alright, this is why I want to buy property in Pennsylvania. We become state residents. The children would be accepted by the people who live there and in South Carolina. It is important to me that our children have roots in both the north and south. They need to know about their mother's heritage also and not just about their father's."

"Jason, are you worried about what is happening in South Carolina?"

"Not just there, but everywhere throughout the south. They act like they want to be another country."

"Then we may be talking about trying to juggle three citizenships. Is that it, Jason?"

"Yes, in order to live our lives without fear, it will take some careful financial planning on our part. I have moved assets from South Carolina to Utah, Pennsylvania, California and Bermuda. We will be able to live a comfortable life in any or all of these locations."

1

Washington City
July, 1861

President Lincoln had sent me a letter which arrived at my home in Pennsylvania shortly after my retirement from public life and my service to President James Buchanan as his National Affairs Advisor. He had invited me to spend a day with him in the Oval Office of the White House. I answered his letter and indicated that I was not sure what I could do for him. I was no longer the advisor to the president for National Affairs. I was a private citizen and a business man. A second letter arrived and it was more revealing, he felt he needed one. On July 2, President Lincoln had authorized the suspension of the right of habeas corpus and requested my time for only one day. I boarded a train and headed for Washington.

On board the train, I still did not know what information I had that would matter to the Republican Administration of Abraham Lincoln. President Buchanan was elected in 1857 and served until March 4, 1861. It was now clear that the union that President Buchanan and I had fought to preserve had failed. On April 15, following the attack on Fort Sumter, President Lincoln proclaimed a state of insurrection. He had issued a draft for 75,000 volunteers. On April 17, Virginia seceded from the Union, the eighth and closest to Washington City. April 19, found Union troops marching to Washington City attacked in Baltimore. During the ensuing riot, fourteen people died. Lincoln then ordered the blockade of all Confederate ports. On May 6, Arkansas and Tennessee seceded from the Union. One week later, Queen Victoria recognized the Confederate States of America. One week after that North Carolina seceded.

From the White House, Abraham Lincoln could see Confederate flags flying in Alexandria and Army of Virginia campfires at night. Baltimore was ready to explode because fewer Union Army volunteers had arrived in Washington City than the 75,000 called for. When Union troops began moving into Alexandria on May 20, a close friend of Lincoln's was shot and killed becoming the first combat death. June 10, saw Confederates forces beat back a Union attack at Big Bethel. The battle of Rich Mountain in western Virginia was a minor Union victory by George McClellan. This gave encouragement to General McDowell and he moved towards Richmond in a effort to capture the Confederate Capitol. General Beauregard, General Butler's replacement at Fort Sumter, was deployed along Bull Run River near Manassas, Virginia. Here in July, Union forces were routed by Confederate forces in a battle watched by Washington residents, who had come to view the grand battle. The next day a congressional resolution was passed that the war was being fought to preserve the Union not abolish slavery. One week later, Lincoln replaced McDowell with McClellan as commander of the Army of the Potomac.

All of these events of the last four months were in my mind as I rounded a corner in the hallway of the White House and there was the Oval Office that was so familiar to me. I knocked on the door and it was opened by his private body guard, Pinkerton. I entered and was greeted by the President. "Please sit down so that we can tell you why we have asked you here."

"Thank you, Mister President."

"Admiral, you are a graduate of the United States Military Academy, class of '37, correct?"

"Yes, Mister President."

"You are a resident of the State of Pennsylvania, the State of South Carolina and Bermuda, is that correct?"

"Yes, it is, Mister President." I wondered where he was going with this.

"That makes you one of a kind and qualified to be my National Affairs Advisor. I would like you to consider the same position in my cabinet, Admiral."

"I was an advisor to the last president on how to preserve the Union. The Union is now in two pieces, both having the same constitution."

"Yes, and if I accept that, then I would be trying to locate someone that Jefferson Davis could trust as my minister to his government and someone who is still loyal to the Union, even though his background and family resides in the Southern Confederacy. That makes you unique for that position as well. But I will not accept the concept of two separate but equal nations sharing the same constitution. I am trying to readmit the seceded states back into the Union."

"I understand that, Mister President. I am not sure I am the right person for that position in your administration, however. I have a major business to run. Caldwell International has several companies that will be vital to the well being of the north in this upcoming struggle to put the nation back together. I could not move back to the White House and be able to do both things for you."

"I understand that now, Admiral. Jefferson Davis has sent a representative to meet with Mr. Pinkerton, here in Washington City. We have no idea what the topic of concern will be. Would you be willing to assist Mr. Pinkerton by attending that meeting today?"

"How can I help?

"You can listen and give me your ideas. You can represent the position of the past administration.

Whatever Jefferson Davis has in mind, I would like you to hear it and give me your reaction to it. If Jefferson Davis requires a meeting with me, I would like you to represent me. You know him from when he was the Secretary of War under Franklin Pierce. You may be able to become a roving ambassador so that you can travel on diplomatic missions between us, using your British Passport. You would be given a safe conduct through enemy lines by both Presidents."

"I do not understand, Mister President. Can I travel by ship and enter a harbor that is blockaded by the US Navy?"

"Yes, you can. You can board trains in both territories and travel between the two as you wish."

"I cannot be away from my business for any length of time and travel is a time consuming process. I wish I could help you in your choice of this special envoy or roving ambassador. If I think of someone, I will give that person's name to you."

"Have you considered the lives that may be saved by an immediate cease to the hostilities?" Said Pinkerton.

"Yes, an end now would mean two separate nations. Is that your goal?"

"No, we will accept nothing but the readmittance of the seceded states back into the Union."

"Mr. Pinkerton, I may be a little dense, but why would Jefferson Davis want readmittance? Queen Victoria has recognized the Confederate States of America as a separate nation at war with us. The Union army is outnumbered on the battle field by seasoned troops under West Point generals. I have heard that the 90 day wonders, turned and ran away at Manassas. Is that true?"

"Yes. It is true, Admiral Caldwell, they were at the end of the ninety day period." Said the President.

"What do you know, Mr. Pinkerton, that I do not? Why do you think Jefferson Davis wants an envoy from Washington City?"

"We hope that he has come to his senses. There are presently 23 states in the Union and 11 states in the Confederacy. The population of the Union is 22 million with 4 million men of combat age. The population of the Confederacy is 9 million with 1.5 million men of combat age. The economy of the regions is quite different; 100,000 factories vs 20,000, 1 million workers vs 100,000, 20,000 miles of railroad vs 9,000, $189 million in bank reserves vs $47 million."

"Well, on paper the Union has already won the conflict." I said. "To bad wars are not fought on paper, we would still be a series of British Colonies. What you do not understand, Mr. Pinkerton, is that difference does count. You are not aware of South Carolina militiamen under Francis Marion who defeated General Cornwallis and an army ten times its size. When the Confederate Army takes the field, it is composed of all 1.5 million men already trained as militia, women and children accompany there militia in the south, just like George Washington's Army. You will have to kill or capture 1.5 million men, their wives and their children in order to win a civil war. What you seem not to grasp, is that this conflict is a matter of honor. I was raised to believe that when a man lost his honor, he lost his soul. If faced with death or dishonor, men in the Confederacy will choose death before dishonor."

"Do you feel that way, Admiral?" The President asked.

"It is not what I feel, Mr. President, it is what I know. These state militias will not surrender, they will die on the battlefields. The Union army does not have 1.5 million trained soldiers from the 4 million men of age. It will take you four to five years to train that number. Every time you cross the Potomac, you will face state militias that have better trained soldiers in larger numbers than you can provide. It will not even be a close contest. You will be burying Union dead by the thousands."

"What about our superior weapons that we will carry into battle?" Pinkerton asked.

"Thanks to Secretary Floyd of the last administration, the two sides will have the same equipment. He sold weapons from US arsenals to any state militia who wanted them. We have documentation in the Department of the Navy which shows what was sold and what was given to South Carolina when I was in Charleston in 1860. Do not, for a minute, think that you will be facing untrained militia using muskets from the last war. The items given, were modern rifles like the Henry. US troops are still using Springfield. That means that 10 Confederate troops will have the fire power of 40 Union soldiers. And they already outnumber us! How can I impress upon you, Mr. Pinkerton, that the US Army is hopelessly outnumbered and outclassed on the battlefield. The only place you have superiority is on the sea."

"That is why I ordered the Navy to block southern seaports." The President said lamely.

"All that will do is stop trade with England, temporarily. I know Lord Napier, he will send HMS war ships to protect the merchant mariners from England. The only way a blockade will work is if you fire upon and sink British ships. They in turn will protect themselves and then you are at war with England over freedom of trade. You need to land marines and take control of every southern seaport, Mr. President. And the truth is, you do not have enough ships in the US Navy to do both and even if you did, you do not have marines to put on the ships. Never in the history of the United States Armed Forces has it been so unprepared to do what is required of them."

"I do not think that is the case, Admiral." Said Pinkerton.

"Mister Pinkerton, are you a trained military expert? I thought you were a City of Chicago policeman?"

"Chief of Detectives! And head of the Secret Service protection of the President."

"Well, I hope you have a private army, because you are going to need them when the Armies of Virginia, South Carolina and North Carolina sweep across the Potomac, captures Washington and arrests the President" I turned to President Lincoln and said, "Mr. President, I do not know where you are getting your military advice from, but I would fire them if I were you." I stood to leave because I thought my welcome was probably worn out.

"Admiral, do you always say what you think to your superiors?" Pinkerton said.

"Not when I was in uniform, I waited to be asked and gave them the honest truth as best I could. It would seem, Mr. President, that your advisors are telling you what they think you want to hear, not what the plain truth is. You are not prepared to fight and win a civil war. You can fight and lose in less than two years unless you make some basic changes now."

"I am listening."

" Item (1), we need to begin a war tax system to finance the war effort. The present $189 million, that Mr. Pinkerton mentioned before will not finance a large scale civil war over the four to five years that it will require. Any advisor who tells you that a war can be won in less time is either a liar or is out of touch with reality.

"Oh, I do not think we will spend $189 million on this conflict." Pinkerton interrupted.

"Mr. President, can you ask Mr. Pinkerton to leave us alone or keep his opinions to himself?"

"Are you angry, Admiral?"

"Yes, Sir. I am. You asked for advice and I am trying to give you my best estimates. Mr. Pinkerton may be your bodyguard, but he is not a military, political or governmental expert. He seems impressed that the US Treasury has $189 million dollars, so do most major companies in the US, including mine. I would not even consider going to war with the Confederacy with the worth of my company. You must begin thinking in terms of billions not millions."

"Mr. Pinkerton, will you leave us for a few minutes?"

"Oh, Mr. President, I would not advise that!"

"That was not a request, Mr. Pinkerton. Please continue, Admiral."

I watched a very angry Chief of Detectives leave the Oval Office, and said, "I am sorry, Mr. President, I can not abide fools."

"Admiral, let us start over. Just you and me. Sitting down to chat about what to get done before the roof falls in on our heads."

"Good idea, Sir. Now, where was I?"

" Item (1), we need a federal income tax. Consider it proposed to the congress sometime this week. Item (2)?"

"Item (2), General Fremonte is unbalanced, in my opinion, and needs to be replaced."

"Consider him replaced." Lincoln picked up a pad of paper and a pencil.

"Item (3), consider a Confiscation Act which will authorize the appropriation of all properties from any seceding state. I am amazed that Maryland is still with us, Mr. President."

"I have arrested and detained several Maryland citizens since July 2 nd, Admiral."

"Item (4), authorize the Secretary of the Navy to draft US citizens, former slaves and anyone else to serve, we are going to need many more sailors than you think."

"Where are we going to get the ships for them to serve on?"

"Item (5), purchase as many civilian merchant marine ships as you can find. My company has several available. Purchase war ships from any European Nation, but not England."

"Consider that in the works." He said as he wrote on the pad.

"Item (6), this is critical, replace or promote General Scott."

"Why? He is my General- in- Chief, the best brain in the military."

"He was during the last war with Mexico, he was a genius. But he is of advanced age now, he is not up to the task required of him. It will break his heart. But it has to be done."

"In for a penny, in for a pound." And he continued to write on his pad.

"Item (7), prepare for war with England, the Queen will not tolerate being cut off from the products she buys from the southern United States."

"How can we possibly fight two wars, Jason?"

It was the first time that he called me, Jason, and I thought our new President might start to make the sacrifices needed to put the Union back together again.

"Prepare for war, not fight one. You can announce to the newspapers that you are considering a civilian advisor board for national affairs. The chairman of this board will report directly to you, not to a cabinet member. I would like to be a member of that board, Mr. President. My contribution to the board will come from my contacts in Bermuda. My staff, in Bermuda, can monitor the Royal Navy Dockyards and the Admiralty in London. England fights most wars on the sea. She will fight through our blockades in order to trade with South Carolina."

"Jason, this has been one of the most productive meetings that I have had since I have been in the White House. Thank you for coming. I will prepare the announcement of the advisory board for the newspapers and I will indicate the chairman, Admiral Caldwell, now recalled to active duty for the duration of the war, has already accepted this position and has started work. How does that sound?"

"Have a copy sent to my home office, Caldwell Place, St. George, Bermuda, will you, Sir?"

"I will. Where will you get your staff?"

"You will appoint them, Mr. President."

"They will be: Commander Jerome Lewis, US Navy. Warrant Officer Thomas Schneider, USMC Master Sergeant Samuel Mason, USMC."

"You better slow down, I am writing those names down."

"You will be getting a list of ten other names from Officer Schneider, Mr. President, these men are all serving in the United States Marine Corps. Can I ask you something, Mr. President?"

"Of course, Admiral."

"Do you trust, Pinkerton?"

"With my life."

"Good, can you ask him when I am to meet with this mysterious messenger from Jefferson Davis?"

"Yes, why do you want to do that, now that you will be in Bermuda?"

"If the contact is genuine, there should not be a problem for the Confederate States of America to send a minister to either England or Bermuda. If they are serious in having contact, then we could do that in Bermuda, either Hamilton or St. George. The Government Houses have been moved from St. George to Hamilton, Sir."

"Then we should establish a US Conciliate Office in Hamilton as soon as we request permission from the Queen. You can present your credentials from me to the Lord Governor of Bermuda when you get there. That way you will have diplomatic protection, should you ever need it. I will call Mr. Pinkerton back in and tell him to set a meeting for later today in your hotel before you leave Washington. I do not want to attend this meeting."

"That is wise, Mr. President, if the contact is an assassin, he will be unable to find you outside the White House."

"Admiral Caldwell, it is an honor to have you serve your country again."

"Thank you, Mr. President. Written communication will be sent twice a week on the steamer between the Potomac Dockyards and the Royal Naval Dockyards, Bermuda. Diplomatic pouches are sealed and can be delivered directly to your office if necessary. I must admit, I will enjoy being back in St. George again. Let us hope that I am wrong and the war will end in a short time. I will resign my commission at the end of the war."

"Jason, you are a man of honor, indeed. Wait until you see if you like a diplomatic career before you offer to leave it so soon."

"Mister President, we both know that I am a warrior, not a diplomat. My reason for being in Bermuda is to keep watch on the British, report their naval movements through Bermuda and may act as a line of communication to Jefferson Davis. I will, of course, sail to South Hampton whenever you need an envoy to the Admiralty. Lord Napier is a personal friend as well as a fellow Admiral."

"I will send a White House messenger over to the Hay-Adams when we get things together on our end, Admiral. Thank you for coming to Washington and agreeing to do this for me. I will not forget what you are about to do for your country or what you have done for the past two administrations."

2

Washington City
Hay-Adams Hotel

I left the White House and walked across Lafayette Square and into the Hay-Adams Hotel. I stopped at the desk and asked for the key to my room and a telegraph pad and pencil. I had just gotten my message to Louise, James and Ruth written out when a knock on my room door interrupted my thoughts. I walked to the door, opened it and there stood Pinkerton and Ben Hagood. I must have looked confused because Pinkerton smiled and said.

"This is not the messenger from Davis, Admiral. Admiral Hagood was asked by the President to brief you on the blockade of southern ports and to sit in on the conversation with Davis's envoy. The meeting will begin when he gets here. He is staying in the Hotel."

Now, I was really confused.

"How long has he been checked in?" I asked.

"A week."

"A week?"

"Yes, he checked in right after the battle along Bull Run."

A loud knock sounded. We opened it and in walked General Butler who I had detained in Charleston last winter.

"Hello, Admiral. It is good to see you again. Mr. Pinkerton, Admiral, is it?"

"Yes, Ben Hagood, General. How do you know Admiral Caldwell?"

"He arrested me in Charleston, held me in Fort Sumter until I was released with the others on March 4 th. Now I am the personal representative of President Davis. He has sent me to Washington to meet with Mr. Lincoln, but so far all I have managed to do is spend time with Mr. Pinkerton here. Can we get started?"

"Of course," we all said at the same time.

"I am here unofficially and President Davis will not make any of these contacts public."

"Neither will President Lincoln." said Pinkerton. "He will speak only through Admiral Caldwell."

"As long as a dialog begins, my President is not concerned how it is arranged."

"I will be Minister to Bermuda from the United States. Does the Confederacy have a Minister to Great Britain?" I asked.

"We do. You know him, Admiral. He was the US senator from Virginia and a close personal friend of Mr. Davis."

"James Murray? Does he have an undersecretary for Bermuda?"

"Yes, you are looking at him." General Butler said with a smile.

"How can that be? I did not know that I was going to Bermuda until today? Do you have a spy in the White House?" I said smiling.

"No, Murray has not left Charleston and will not arrive in London until October. He will drop me off in Bermuda, after a stop at the Royal Naval Dockyards."

"The Confederacy has permission to use the docks in Bermuda?"

"Yes, Admiral. It was granted when Queen Victoria announced Great Britain's neutrality and granted us the right of 'belligerent nation status.'"

I looked at Pinkerton and then Ben Hagood, raised my eyebrows in a signal to remember to tell that to the president. "Well, General, what is your new title?"

"Minister to Bermuda and Undersecretary to Ambassador Murray, London."

"Will you be sailing back and forth, you know, to London and Bermuda? Minister Butler."

"Of course, I thought maybe we could use British vessels and travel together, Admiral Caldwell."

No one, besides the president, had called me, Admiral since I had retired until now. I liked the sound of it. "We could get many things discussed during the voyage, I hate wasting my time." I said.

"I think we have accomplished everything here, I need to get back to report to my president and then to Charleston."

"You are in the middle of Washington City, how are you going to do that?" I blurted out.

"It is surprisingly easy, when the federal troops retreated into Washington City, I just walked in with them. No one seemed to notice another newspaper reporter. I will use the newspaper credentials to take a carriage across the Potomac and then show my safe conduct from Davis and get on a train all the way into Richmond. You can travel anywhere, the situation is very fluid."

"Yes, it is. I have to ask you this. What happened after Manassas? Why not take Washington City? It was left unprotected by General McDowell?"

"Too many Generals on the Confederate side of the lines; General Longstreet , my replacement Beauregard, and General Johnson. Longstreet was still wearing his Union uniform and was nearly shot during the battle of the first day. Johnson was not even at Manassas when the battle began, he was moving his troops from the Shenandoah Valley by train. The Army of the Virginia was split between two locations and Beauregard's Army from South Carolina did most of the fighting in the center of the line the first day. When Beauregard troops were in danger of collapsing from the center on the second day, he sent a rider to the Shenandoah Valley troops newly arrived under Colonel Thomas Jackson. He asked for an immediate advancement to his center. Either Jackson did not understand or was slow in responding, because a second message was sent to him stating, 'You are standing like a stonewall. Advance. Damn it! Or I will replace you.' I am afraid that he has been nicknamed 'Stonewall Jackson'. So you see, there was confusion and failure on both sides. We had no idea that General McDowell would leave Washington City unprotected. We considered ourselves fortunate to completely defeat the federal volunteers. Our newspapers are reporting our great victory and volunteers are reporting faster than we can process them."

I again looked at Pinkerton and Hagood before I spoke. "What is your message for President Lincoln from President Davis?"

"The Confederacy has no desire to replace or become the United States of America, we are content to be the Confederate States of America. If a USA army crosses the Potomac again into the CSA,

it will be defeated as before. My President proposes that the two nations be divided along the Potomac River, North and South. The capitol of the north being Washington City while the capitol of the south already is Richmond, Virginia. Mr. Davis is moving his cabinet to Richmond as we speak. Let there be peace between our two nations. If President Lincoln agrees to this proposal, he will withdraw the naval blockades of our ports and peace will be insured. If he refuses this peace offer then we will protect the C SA with the eleven armies at our command."

"That is crystal clear, Minister Butler. Of course, we have only a verbal commitment from your government. Will there be a written version sent to the White House?"

"No, Sir."

"Alright, there will be no written document of this meeting either. I will depend upon Admiral Hagood and Mr. Pinkerton to report the offer to my president. I am leaving on the afternoon train, unless summoned to the White House. From one South Carolinian to another, can you report back to your president that he has my word, upon my honor, that if President Lincoln asks my advice, I will recommend that he accept your offer of peace."

"Thank you, Admiral, I can ask for nothing more. Good day to y'all."

The room was strangely quiet after Butler left. The three of us sat and pondered the conversation.

Ben was the first to speak. "Jason, we are in a fine mess, the President is not going to like this."

"Report it just as you heard it, Ben. Take Mr. Pinkerton with you and see the president as soon as you can. The longer we wait, the more we will forget. Why are you here, anyway? I already know about the blockade."

"The president sent a messenger with a hand written note to the Army Navy Building for me. Here, you want to read it?"

I read it. "I must have made an impression on him. This says you are to provide my transport to and from Bermuda, London and Washington City. He must feel that Washington is safe. I have my own transport, Ben. You will need every ship you have and more for the blockage"

"Thank you, Jason. I will report that to the president."

"I will need you to take the sloops and briggs that you and I bought from the Navy in '37 and have them rearmed so that they can protect themselves. Can you do that?"

"Consider it done. Send them from St. George to the Potomac Dockyards for refitting."

I turned to Pinkerton who had said very little during the entire meeting and said, "I do not know your first name. If we are going to be working closely together, I can not keep calling you, Mister."

"It is Allen, Sir."

"Call me Jason, Allen. I think we got off on the wrong foot in the Oval Office."

"We sure did, I am sorry about that. I had no idea that President Lincoln thought so highly of you."

"Do you think, he knows I am a Democrat?" I said smiling.

"Jason, at this point, it would not matter if you had two heads and came directly from the Devil!" Pinkerton blurted out.

Ben had sat long enough and had kept his opinions to himself until he could not control himself any longer. "The President already has a two-headed Devil in the White House, he is chief of his protection service!" All three of us broke into laughter.

3

Washington Post
September 1861

The mail steamer from Potomac Dockyards came twice a week to deliver the diplomatic pouch to the US Conciliate's Office in Hamilton. It passed by the Royal Naval Dockyards on the west end of the island chain and steamed into the Great Sound and on to the capital, Hamilton. The pouches and other mail from the US were left in Hamilton and the steamer entered back into the Great Sound and steamed on eastward to St. Georges, the site of the first people to set foot on Bermuda. The staff at both locations, eagerly awaited the three or four day old copies of the Washington Post. The events of this past August, as reported therein, began with the news of the congressional passage of the first income tax for the United States. Every person who earns an income will report this income to the new federal internal revenue service so that the tax to support the war can be determined and levied. "This new income tax law, along with The Confiscation Act of 1861, will help finance the effort to readmit those states in rebellion, back into the Union." This was the direct quote from the secretary of the Treasury to this reporter.

These new laws require that property owners in areas occupied by Union Forces appear in person to pay their taxes. The first property seized under The Confiscation Act has been the estate of the Curtis family overlooking the Potomac. General McDowell took the residence, known as Arlington House, as his headquarters until he was replaced by General McClellan this month. In other news of Union Generals taking command, General Fremonte has been transferred to Missouri where he was quoted as saying, " My first order shall be to declare martial law. I then will proclaim that all slaves are to be set free. After that, I intend on invading Canada since it shares a common border with Missouri."

The President's cabinet has been active this past month, also. Secretary of the Navy, G. H. Welles authorized the enlistment of run away slaves and recent freemen. Secretary Seward has announced that Queen Victoria has accepted his undersecretary, Jason Caldwell, as minister to Bermuda. Lord Napier of the Royal Admiralty was quoted as saying, "Great Britain is very aware of Admiral Caldwell's capabilities and is strongly supportive of this appointment and we look forward to his visits here in the United Kingdom."

A smile walked its way across Louise Caldwell's face as she sat at the breakfast table at Caldwell Place. "Look, Jason, the paper reports that items 1 through 4 of our national affairs advisory committee have been implemented. It does not even mention you or the committee as having suggested them in the first place. It does say that you work for Secretary Seward."

"What? That can not be right. Oh, wait, that is a newspaper article, right? They rarely get anything correct."

"It says that Winfield Scott is still the General-in-chief of the army. And look what General Fremonte is quoted as saying! You said he was unbalanced, but this is something. He thinks Missouri shares a border with Canada."

"Well, he is partly correct, because the Secretary of War sent him to Minnesota, not Missouri! Milton Fremonte has never gotten over the fall off his horse years ago. He was unconscious for over a week and when he awoke he was in a fog. Some mean spirited folks say he is still asleep, he should be retired, not sent anywhere in command."

"Are you going into Hamilton today, Jason?"

"No need. If there is anything important in the pouch Jerome will send someone over here. I think I will take James down to the beach so he can build a sand castle."

"Do you feel guilty about sitting out the war over here in Bermuda, Jason?"

"Hell, no, you and I have served our country to the best of our abilities for over twenty years. Besides the war is just underway, there is going to be plenty of action regarding Bermuda and England before it is done. I will be gone for a month at a time when things heat up. You and I should enjoy these days with the children for as long as they last."

"Oh, we have a letter from Beaufort here. It is post-marked in Havana, Cuba, but I recognize your father's handwriting. Why did it go to Havana?"

"This came on the British mail steamer HMS *Trent*. Blockade runners take the mail from Charleston to Havana and transfer it to a mail steamer. The steamer stops here in Bermuda before it reaches England."

"Open it and read it to me, Jason."

"Oh, thank God."

"What is it, Jason?"

CALDWELL HOUSE
874 Bay Street,
Beaufort, South Carolina

September 1, 1861

Dear Jason,

Trey has managed to lease the remaining family property for four years here in Beaufort. Our plans are to accept your kind offer to visit you, Louise and the grandchildren. So far, only your sister Carol remains stead-fast in remaining here. Everyone else, and I mean everyone, has purchased tickets on a "runner" to Havana. We will leave Charleston sometime next month when there is a slight storm brewing in order to make a clear escape.

Seeing not a one of us speaks Spanish, I have a letter written in Spanish which requests passage on a mail steamer bound for Bermuda. You can go ahead and find your mother and I a little cottage in St. Davids.

More later,

RHC

Your loving father

"Give this letter to Laura or Sallie to start looking for a lease on St. Davids, will you Louise? I need to get James ready for the morning on the beach."

Before I could get James packed up for the walk down to the beach, Robert Whitehall, my President for Caldwell Shipping and his wife Laura came into the dining room for breakfast. Louise handed the letter to Laura and explained what needed to be done in the next month or so. Robert and I got caught up in the status of the requests from the War Department for the purchase of some of our older merchant ships.

"What is the Navy going to do with these ships, Admiral?"

"They are going to refit them with modern deck guns, rocket launchers and motars so I can use them here in Bermuda. You need to make sure that they are stripped of anything that belongs to the company. No sense letting our fittings set in Potomac Dockyards when we can use them in our store of supplies."

"Admiral, I have no record of when these ships were purchased by Caldwell Shipping. Do you remember when or how you came by them?"

"Louise, Laura, come over here with Robert and me.

You may enjoy hearing how Ben hagood and I began Caldwell Shipping. I graduated from the US Military Academy in '37 when I was not yet 21 years of age. The Naval Academy was not split away until '44 or '45 and the Army had little or no use for the training vessels used down in Anapolis. These were ships that were used in the War of '12,but built in the later 1790's or early 1800's. Most of these were solid oak, no iron plating of any kind. The Point saw no use in keeping them around so they offered to sell them as scrap to whoever would place a bid. Ben Hagood was twenty-one years of age, so I had him write out a bid for $400.00 for a Brig named *The Providence*, never thinking that we would get it. The Providence had first seen action in 1797. No one else even entered a bid. So, Ben says, 'Your family is filthy rich why not write to your father and ask for a business loan.' Well, I did. He sent me a thousand dollars and said not to bid over a hundred on anything. Ben and I thought we at least could pay the four hundred that we owed and return the balance to my father. As a lark, Ben bid one hundred dollars on six more ships: two Brigs, called the Spitfire and Jersey; two Ketches, called the New Haven and Trumbull and two Snows called the Congress and Philadelphia. We got all six. So now, we have seven ships and no way to get them to Port Royal where I wanted to repair and work on them in order to start a shipping business."

"How did you get them to Port Royal?" Laura asked.

"A Brigg needs a crew of eight seamen and two officers. Ben and I were the officers, so we ran an advertisement in the newspapers asking for able bodied seamen who wanted to relocate in South Carolina. As soon as we had 8 sailors ready to trade work for transport we requested leave from the Navy and started sailing them to Port Royal. Ben and I left the seamen in South Carolina and rode the train back to our stations. Every few weeks we had eight more sailors and we again requested leave to transport another to Port Royal. A Brig and a Snow are the same basic ship except for how the sails are set on the forward and aft masts. A Ketch or a Sloop is a much smaller ship and has only a single midship mast."

"Admiral, my records show none of those ship names."

"I know, all of them were renamed by the Caldwell men who loved them. My father named one of the Snows 'Cold Harbor', sounds like my father and his puns! My brother, Robert, liked historical names, so he picked names of English Admirals like Somerset and Nelson."

"Jason?"

"Yes, Louise."

"How much are you selling those ships to the government for?"

"Robert, you have the figures right in front of you, tell them."

"The company sold four at $14,000.00, two at $22,000.00 and one is not for sale." replied Robert.

"Which one is that, Admiral." Asked Laura Whitehall.

"The Cold Harbor. I will never sell that ship. Too many memories for everyone around this table. Too many trips to far away places, trips to Bermuda for both Louise and me. And for you and Laura also. Just too many good times on that old bucket to ever sell her."

"That reminds me, have you heard from your brother

and father?"

"Yes, we got a letter today, Laura has it, she will let you read it. My father would like to 'let', as the English call it, a small cottage near you and Laura over on St. Davids. Do you still like it over there? No trouble getting to work over here every day?"

"No, Sir. We love our place. We made an offer to buy it. We should hear soon from the owner. When the war is over, we would like to keep it as retirement home." Laura said.

"We have done the same thing here and I think we will enjoy having a place away from Pennsylvania when it comes winter time." Louise said.

"Laura, have you found places for Tom Schneider's and Sam Mason's families yet?" I asked.

"Yes, I found two places in St. Davids and two places in St. George for them to look at when they get here."

"Where are you going to put Admiral Hagood when he is in Bermuda?" Louise asked.

"Ben and any of his family are getting our old quarters here in the Inn, while the ten single marines are going to use the cottages here at Caldwell Place. The cottages are not modern, but they will do until they find something better."

"How did Jerome Lewis and his family like the house in Hamilton that Laura found for them?"

"They have not complained about being away from St. George. When the entire detachment is located here in Bermuda, they will be scattered all over the islands. Thank you, Robert and Laura, for taking on the extra work load. Louise and I really appreciate your work."

"Hey, there is a war going on!"

4

Bermuda Station
Caldwell Place

Everyone finished breakfast and I located James playing on the lawn outside one of the cottages which dotted the grounds of Caldwell Place. "James," I yelled. "Want to go down to the beach this morning?"

"Yes, Sir. Can I tell Sallie to pack us a lunch?"

"Sallie is busy this morning, why not ask Mommy to pack us a lunch and bring Ruth along?"

In an hour we were packed and ready to get on a carriage for the short ride down to St. Catherine's beach. The driver looked at the two adults, two children and related gear and said,

"I will need 50 pence instead of the usual 25, Admiral."

I paid him and we were on the beach in a few minutes. "Pick us up in two hours if you can, there is an extra 50 pence in it, if you can."

He smiled and said he would be right here in two hours. We walked to a smooth, sandy spot and put up a small umbrella for sun, sat the picnic basket down and got both children covered with skin cream of some sort that Louise had brought with her. James built his sand castle and Ruth ran in and out of the water, too many times to count. James then said, "Daddy, can we play our drawing game in the wet sand?"

"Sure, find me a stick and I will test your memory of old fashioned sailing vessels of the Revolutionary War."

"Which one is this?" I asked after I drew a three masted, three decked outline which had sixteen sails set off the masts.

"That is a Ship of the Line, it had 60 to100 cannon and a crew of 3 to 5 hundred."

I wiped out the sketch and started another. I had only gotten to the double masts and James cried, "Two masts, that is a Snow, Brig or Schooner, Daddy."

"The placement of the masts will tell you which one, Son."

"Let me see, how many decks are there?"

"Oh, that would make it too easy! Let me draw you some sails."

"It is a Schooner! See that large single sail off the aft mast, Mommy."

"Yes, I do. How do you know that is not a Brigantine. It had a single large sail on the aft mast, also."

"'Cause Daddy never draws a Brigantine, he says the forward sails are a mess!"

We all enjoyed a laugh together. I pulled my pocket watch and said, "It is time we started back if we want to catch the carriage up Rose Hill and back to Caldwell Place. The kitchen will have the lunch crowd finished and they can fix something for us."

The carriage was waiting for us and we loaded our beach gear and headed up the Duke of York Street until we reached Rose Hill, turned right and rode up the steep hill to Caldwell Place. As we pulled into the portico, Sallie stuck her head out of the front doors and said, "You have guests from the United States." We met the detachment sitting in the dinning room finishing their noon meal. When Tom Schneider saw me, he jumped up and out of habit yelled, "Officer on deck."

I laughed and told him and the rest of the detachment to sit down, I was not assigned to the Navy, I was a trusted member of the State Department. I shook each of the men's hands starting with Sam Mason and ending with Tom Schneider. They all looked seasoned, fresh from a short ocean voyage.

"How did Admiral Hagood arrange to have you Marines sent here so fast?"

"We got our orders from the White House, Sir. Admiral Hagood says to give you his best, the *USS Providence* has been recommissioned and ready for action. It is in St. George Harbor. He saw us off from the Potomac Dockyards in the Providence."

"Did he indicate when your families would arrive?" Louise asked.

"No, he said that the paperwork was in the mill and that they would follow in a few days, Ma'am."

"I will go and tell Laura to expect the families in a few days, then."

"The cottages that you and your families will be staying in are spread around the grounds of this old golf course. You are standing in the former club house. You and your wives have kitchens in the cottages, but you are welcome to eat meals here in the dinning room whenever you like. I have never been a foreign diplomat before and I am sure that you may have a new experience as well. You all know Commander Lewis, he and his family are located in the US Conciliate quarters in Hamilton. It is a short train, a trolley actually, ride from here. You will all have to catch it this afternoon to report in there. Commander Lewis will have your work schedules for you sometime today. There is quite a bit of responsibility with being a Marine assigned to a foreign office, especially this one. I know each one of you. I requested the President to assign you here. We have to not only protect the people serving inside the Hamilton Office, but our families here at Caldwell Place. Our primary mission is to monitor the goings and comings of the Royal Naval Dockyards on the west end. If England tries to enter the war on the side of the Confederacy, they will go through here in great numbers on ships of the line and troop carriers."

"Admiral?"

"Yes, Tom."

"Does someone have our cottage numbers for us so we can dump our gear and get into civilian clothes?"

"The only Marines in civilian clothes will be those close to the dockyards, watching and reporting. Always wear a dress uniform when on duty in Hamilton. You can leave your dress uniforms in Hamilton, if you like. The natives will come to respect the US Conciliate as US property if we make a show of protecting it. Always travel to and from Hamilton in uniform and when on duty. Off duty, is civilian all the way, be comfortable."

"Can we dump our gear?"

"Yes, Sallie Trott is the manager here at Caldwell Place. She has the cottage closest to the club house. Her office is there and she will have your cottage assignments. Sam and Tom will you stay behind and let the detachment find Sallie?"

"What is it, Sir?" Sam asked after everyone had left the dinning room.

"I am not sure we have enough Marines to do everything the President wants done here. I did not want to mention this in front of the men, but we are going to be stretched really thin to do this. We have to find a contact inside the Royal Naval Dockyards to get current information. I will leave that up to you two. You have done this before, remember the Resolute Matter?"

"Aye, aye, sir!" They both said with a smile.

"Tell the men not to call me Admiral. The natives here in Bermuda do not need to know that we were once a smooth running military unit. Sir is alright and Minister is fine. But try to keep the military courtesy to a minimum."

"Got you, Sir."

"Good, now think about how you want to make contact with someone who can help us inside the Dockyards of the Royal Navy. It should be someone who is not happy with his or her level of responsibility and will trade information for US gold coin. You both will carry a money belt full of coin, so let us see what the greed of an Englishman can get for us. You two are the only ones of the guard detachment that will have this task. Go slow, do not take chances with the British system of justice. Report only to me or Commander Lewis. No one else."

"Will we have to stand guard duty in Hamilton,

Sir?"

"No, your assignment is information gathering only. Are either one of you familiar with a simple substitution code for sending messages to Washington?"

"No, Sir."

"Let me explain then. Every day diplomatic pouches are sent to Washington from Hamilton. They contain letters, orders, and coded information. A coded message has a key. I will write something on this piece of paper so you can watch." I lettered the following name.

GEORGE JEFFERSON WASHINGTON 123456789

This is the key. Under each of the letters in this name I will write the alphabet.

GEORGE JEFFERSON WASHINGTON 123456789
a b c d   e f   g h I j   kL   m   n o p q r s t u v

Notice that WXYZ do not have a substitute code, so our messages will not contain those letters when we send them, just leave blank spaces. So in the diplomatic pouch when we have really something of military value to send to Washington, such as "British troops arrived Bermuda." We would send that as:

E5WMW6K M52236   G55W9JR   EJ5T8RG

"You both will be sending coded messages from Hamilton to Washington on a regular basis as things heat up here in the middle Atlantic."

"And we thought this was going to be a baby sitting operation," Tom said.

34

"No, the success of the US Naval Blockade depends on us keeping the British off the Navy's back. And to make things worse, General Butler will arrive to set up a foreign office for the Confederates which will try and get the British come into the war on the C.S.A. side."

"The General Butler we arrested in Charleston?"

"The same, he is now Minister to Bermuda for the C.S.A. We need to monitor his activities while he will try to monitor ours."

"Sounds like a cat and mouse game, Sir."

"That is what life in Hamilton will be for the twelve of you men that have just arrived. Commander Lewis has been running the entire operation until today, he will be very happy to see you men report to him."

Tom and Sam left the dinning room to find their cottages. They stored their gear and got into clean uniforms. Shortly we were all walking to the St. George train station. We waited for the next train and caught some interesting glances from the townspeople. We got off the train in Hamilton and walked to the US Conciliate Office. Jerome Lewis was ready to have his Marines report for duty.

"Gentlemen, welcome to Bermuda and the US Conciliate's Office. It is good to see everyone again. I have work details for each of you. The front gate should be guarded at all hours of the day. If we use 8 hour shifts, then the day is divided into three parts. We will need two uniformed personal on each shift so that means 6 of you men will have front gate duty. That leaves only four to roam the grounds and inside the building for security. I know it will be extra work because we are short handed here but I have worked out the following schedule. You will work 8 hours, sleep 8 hours inside the building here and have 8 hours of free time every day. The schedules are rotational so that you can have days off. In that way we will try to fool the public into believing that we have a full company of Marines here."

"Commander Lewis is the assistant undersecretary here in Bermuda and you report directly to him." I said. "Warrant Officer Schneider will be available most of the second eight hour shift to answer any questions you might have. Master Sergeant Mason will be available most of the third shift to do the same thing."

"Minister Caldwell has an office here in this building and in St. George. If I am unavailable for any reason, you can contact him in an emergency." Said Jerome.

"Yes, remember, we function as a protection detail with things handled at the lowest level possible. We are here to protect the war secrets of the United States as well as the personnel and families of everyone assigned to this State Department Outpost. We need for everyone to get some rest, I know you traveled several days to get here. Your assignments can wait twenty-fours, is that correct, Commander Lewis?"

"It is Minister. I would like to visit with each of you as you leave the building today. Let us begin with Corporals Wilson and Clemens please. As they leave, Simmons and Farley are next. Then Smith and Wallace, Norwich and Olsen, Saunders and Marlin. That is the rotation that I have set up and I want to make sure that it runs smoothly."

Tom Schneider and Sam Mason looked at me and nodded their heads. We walked into my office and Tom said, "I wish we had some of the patrolmen who joined the US Marshal's Office here on this. These young Marines are going to be fine on guard duty, but they will not work on under- cover assignments."

"I was just thinking the same thing, Tom. Let me get a request off to the White House and see if Allen Pinkerton can find us some policemen."

"Sam and I will start finding out where the British Marines and officers go for rest and recreation. If we find anything out in the next few days, we will let you know, Admiral." "I mean, Sir."

In less than a week, Tom returned with the following information. "It seems that the pressed seamen are not ever released from the dockyards. We found out from talking to an officer at the 'Country Squire Pub', that the makeup of an average crew of a royal naval vessel is 75 men. Fifty percent of these are pressed seamen, twenty-three percent are volunteers, fifteen percent are from jails and twelve percent are foreigners. That means for every ship in the dockyards, thirty-seven are held and not avail-able to us for gathering information."

"Where is this Country Squire Pub?"

"It is close to the dockyards in a place called 'Mango Grove', that is in Somerset, Sir".

"Who was this officer?"

"There were two officers that we talked to; both Lieutenants, A. J. Schmidts and Horatio Farnsworth. We learned that Farnsworth was demoted from an Admiral's Aide, a major, I think."

"He sounds like he might have some useful informa-tion if you go slow and let him tell you what he knows. He might try to impress you with his experience as an Admiral's Aide."

"I think so too, Sir. The other one feels he is not being used to his fullest capacity. He is a marine but he never gets on a ship. He can use one of the those new underwood typewriters so he types letters and communications all day long."

"He could be a gold mine of information, Tom. I wonder if he remembers anything that he types and would like to impress you or Sam with what he knows? What is your cover when you see these officers?"

"We are both are AWOL seamen from a Confederate ship that stopped at the Royal Dockyards last month."

"Be careful with that cover, you could wind up as pressed seamen on an outbound vessel."

"We are careful, always together and armed to the teeth. The Brits are looking for easy pickings, Sir. We will be fine for a few more visits anyway. By that time, the additions from Pinkerton can take over that part of the operation."

"What do you think of having them sail directly into the Royal Naval Dockyard as survivors of a running gun battle with a US Naval vessel. This Confederate vessel could be a blockade runner whose captain and most of the crew have been killed, say, only five or six survivors. These members would not know anything about passwords or agreements with the Royal Navy. They would just be requesting aid. How much information could we get about British plans to run through or destroy the blockade of ports?"

"I can code up a message and send it through the State Department to Admiral Hagood for his reaction after I talk to Commander Lewis. The Commander always adds things to my plans to make them better, Sir."

"Commander Lewis and you are two of the best idea men I have, Tom. Do not tell him it was my idea, let him develop it for us. He will put on the necessary touches here and there that will make it viable. How do like Bermuda so far, Tom?"

"Better now that Beth and the kids are here. We really like the house that Laura Whitehall found for us in St. Davids. But I can not get an answer from her on how much rent we owe her."

"The house is part of the per diem expenses forwarded from Washington, Tom. All you need to buy is food for the family. All other expenses should be paid through the Conciliate in Hamilton."

"Thank you, Sir."

"Because you are on duty for eight hours a day and sometimes have to sleep inside the building, you will be given an increase in your normal Navy pay also. Commander Lewis went through all that with you and Sam, right?"

"Yes, Sir."

"Anything else that we need to talk about?"

"No. Sir."

"Good, then get out of here and get back to your family on St. Davids."

"Aye, aye. Sir."

5

The Trent Affair
October 1861

The night of October 11, 1861, was dark and the sea was boiling. Rain came down in sheets as a Confederate blockade runner slipped out of Charleston, South Carolina, carrying Robert Hays Caldwell the second and his son "Trey" along with their families. They had purchased the last available spaces on the run to Havana, Cuba. The cabin spaces had been reserved for Confed- erate foreign ministers, James Murray and John Butler. Robert knew John Butler. He was a general in the State of South Carolina Militia. He had no idea that James Murray was a Virginia lawyer who had served in both houses of congress before he was appointed as Ambassador to England by Jefferson Davis. Before the cruise was over, however, he knew that James Murray was a tobacco-chewing, swearing, staunch states' rights Democrat who had drafted the Fugitive Slave Act of 1850. He also knew that Murray was a close person- al friend of President Davis and had served on the US

Senate Foreign Relations Committee with him, because the man never stopped talking about himself. There was another foreign minister, David Slidell, bound for Paris after Havana, but he kept to himself. Trey had talked with him some and found out he was a US Senator from Louisiana before the war, but he had a New York accent and Trey doubted he was telling the truth.

Robert Hays Caldwell II was 64 years old when he decided to leave his home in South Carolina and board the runner to Havana. If the war lasted the four or five years as his son, Jason, had suggested, he hoped he would live long enough to return home. He and his wife, Mary Elizabeth, had five children, two had died in infancy and three had grown to be his pride and joy. He had not talked to any of his children about how or where he was to be laid to rest, but he hoped that he would be laid beside his babies in the Beaufort St. Helena Church yard whenever the time came. His daughter, Carol, and her husband had stated flatly that they would not leave Beaufort no matter what her brother, Jason, said. It was typical of a brother and sister.

He hated to have his family separated but he also trusted Jason's judgement. Ever since '37 and his purchase of surplus ships to start a shipping business in Port Royal, Jason had made one good judgement after another. Jason and Louise had said to leave Beaufort with no luggage. Do not give any indication that it was anything other than a weekend trip to Charleston. Each of us carried a small overnight bag, even the grandchildren. We arrived in Charleston and stayed at the Planters Inn. Trey had gone down to the harbor to find the cutter to Havana. He found it and asked what date the runner

41

would try to get out of the harbor. The first mate said as soon as the weather gets stormy, we would leave at night and have the best chance of getting through. If we were stopped, then we would be fined and returned to the harbor to try again later. It seemed rather ordinary and not at all unusual. He had already sold the three private cabin spaces, but there was room below decks among the cargo for bedrolls for all the Caldwells. So, Trey paid a retainer and started checking every afternoon until the eleventh, when the first mate indicated that we would try to go tonight.

We boarded the boat in the driving rain, flashes of lightening frightened the grandchildren while the smells coming from below decks did not seem inviting. We had not gotten the beds rolled out before the boat began moving. The captain had a full head of steam and he was not waiting around for a patrol boat to spot us leaving the docks. Blockade runners were primitive vessels in '81. We relied on the darkness of night, with all ship lights extinguished, a rain storm to block the moonlight and the cloud of steam produced by the ships boilers. It was several hours before a crew member came below and said we were in international waters. We were to try and get some sleep. He would return at sunrise.

Passengers were not usually allowed on deck when making the short run to Havana, but the captain relented and let the men only come up on deck to stretch their legs. After they had some exercise, they could return and the women could do the same. No children would be allowed on deck. We spent the time in shifts and said we would never try this again. It was a beautiful day when we entered Havana. James Murray announced that he and the other two ministers, Slidell and Butler, would board HMS *Trent,* the mail steamer, bound for London and Paris. The rest of us could wait for the next ship to Bermuda. Mary Elizabeth announced that she thought that was an excellent idea.

"Robert, he is an awful person and I do not want to spend another minute with him. Use your Spanish language letter and see what cabin space is available to Bermuda. Otherwise, I would enjoy staying in Cuba for a few more days."

Robert had lived with Mary Elizabeth for 45 years and knew that when she said something, she meant it!

"Trey and I will look today. But before we do that, we need to find the nicest hotel in Havana. Then you, Mariann and the children can have baths. We need to buy new clothes and become civilized again."

"Thank you, Robert. You need a bath also!"

We found two carriages and managed to communicate that we needed a hotel, "Casa del Resort, Amigo." The driver nodded his head and instructed the other carriage driver to follow and we headed for our place of reorganization as Mariann called it. We gave the drivers a US gold five dollar coin. By their reactions we knew that we had overpaid them. They carried our hand luggage inside the hotel lobby. One of the drivers could speak a little English and asked if we had "Del Casa Reservacion?" We shook our heads no, trying to indicated we had just come for the United States. He walked to the desk and spoke to the desk clerk, showed him his five dollar gold coin and returned to us. He says that for another gold coin you can stay two days at this hotel. "Gratias, Amigo."

The next day Robert Caldwell II showed his letter

of introduction to the Harbor Master and found cabin space on the next ship to Bermuda. At about that time, the HMS *Trent* was approached by the USS *San Jacinto*. The San Jacinto was a first class steam powered sloop. It had 13 guns and weighed 1446 tons when it was built in 1850 at the Brooklyn Ship Yards. When the Trent did not stop, the San Jacinto captain ordered two shots fired across the Trent's bow. The US and England were not at war and this was a flagrant violation of international maritime law. Captain Charles Wilkes demanded that a Mr. Murray and Slidell be placed on his ship for transport to Boston. They were being arrested for treason. The was no arrest warrant and the captain of the Trent was outraged.

"This will be reported as soon as we land in the United Kingdom."

Murray and Slidell were taken to Boston and jailed while the Trent sailed on to Bermuda.. The US newspapers rejoiced over the capture of Confederate diplomats, but none indicated how Captain Wilkes knew that the diplomats would be on that ship in that location. Congress passed a resolution thanking Captain Wilkes for his actions while Queen Victoria had a different reaction. She sent a message to Abraham Lincoln via transatlantic cable.

> YOUR GOVERNMENT HAS DETAINED
> A MINISTER TO GREAT BRITAIN.
> UNDER INTERNATIONAL LAW, YOU
> WILL RELEASE HIM IMMEDIATELY
> WE SHALL DETAIN YOUR
> AMBASSADOR IN LONDON UNTIL

MR. MURRAY
ARRIVES HERE IN ENGLAND.
LORD PALMERSTON FOR HER
MAJESTY

When HMS Trent stopped at the Royal Naval Dockyards in Bermuda, The captain of the Trent reported the arrest of Ministers Murray and Slidell. Minister Butler reported his credentials to the Lord Governor at Government House, Hamilton, and walked to the US Conciliate Office. He was angry and shaken at the removal of Murray and Slidell. He would lodge his own complaint with the US Minister to Bermuda, Jason Caldwell. How had the Captain of the San Jacinto known to stop the mail steamer and why had he escaped arrest? It had to be Slidell, he must be an informant. He was stopped at the front gate to the US Conciliate by two armed US Marines in dress uniform.

"Can I see your credentials, Sir?"

He handed a copy to one of the guards and said, "I must see Minister Caldwell on a very important matter."

"You may see his deputy, assistant Minister Lewis."

"Fine, let me in and I will see him."

A few minutes later John Butler, former General of the South Carolina Militia was cooling his heels in an outer office waiting to see Jerome Lewis. He was not used to treatment like this, the longer he waited the angrier he got. When a secretary admitted him to see Mr. Lewis his was livid. "Where is Jason Caldwell?"

"Admiral Caldwell, Under Secretary of State and Minister to Bermuda is not in at the moment. I am his assistant and have his full authority to act in his absence.

Can I be of help, Minister Butler?"

"Yes, I would like to give an eye witness account of an abduction of two foreign ministers upon the high seas."

"Who were these foreign ministers?" Jerome Lewis asked as he reached for paper and pen.

"James Murray, Ambassador to Great Britain and David Slidell, Ambassador to France."

Jerome was taking names and information and as he wrote, he asked. "These two Ambassadors were in transit from where to where?"

"Havana to London and Paris."

"And how were they taken?"

"The USS *San Jacinto* was captained by a Charles Wilkes and he fired upon the HMS *Trent.*"

"The same Captain Wilkes who was the first American to sail around the world! This is incredible. He must be nearly 70 years of age. I doubt that this is accurate, Minister Butler. Perhaps a privateer posing as Wilkes boarded the Trent. Did you see this man who said he was Captain Wilkes?"

"Yes, I did."

"Did he look 70 years old to you?"

"No, he did not."

"Alright, I will report this to our State Department after Minister Caldwell gives me his permission. I would suggest that you accompany me when I report to him. Do you have the time?"

"I would be delighted to see Jason, again."

"You know him?"

"Yes, the first time was in Charleston when he arrested me and held me unlawfully for five months. The second time was in Washington City, where I met with

Admiral Hagood and a Mr. Allen Pinkerton."

"The President's bodyguard?"

"Yes, and I believe that Admiral Hagood is the Atlantic Fleet Commander in charge of the Union Blockade of Charleston Harbor among others."

"You are well informed, Minister Butler. Have you just now docked at the Royal Naval Dockyards?"

"Yes, why?"

"You must be exhausted from your ordeal. Why not meet at the C. S. A. Embassy here in Hamilton? Do you know where that is, Minister?"

"I have a street address, I can find it."

"Do you want to meet later today, or would tomorrow be better for you?"

"I would like some action on this matter today, if possible."

"We can meet you at your embassy in three hours. The train schedules are accurate here in Bermuda. I will leave immediately and contact the undersecretary, that will take anhour, the return trip another hour, three hours would be about right."

"Tell the Admiral that I was traveling with his family and I would like his attention to this matter at his earliest convenience. People traveling from the Confederacy on neutral nation's ships should not be attacked in international waters. We must put a stop to this at once."

"I understand, and agree completely, Minister Butler. I have notes on the matter and we will find a solution as soon as possible."

"Thank you, Mr. Lewis, you have been most courteous and helpful. You are not a southern gentleman by any chance, are you?"

"Louisville, Kentucky, Sir."

"Close enough, see you and the Admiral in three hours."

6

CSA Embassy
Hamilton, Bermuda

In three hours, Jerome Lewis had sent a message with one of the roving marines to alert me that a meeting was going to be held in the C. S. A. Embassy at 4 pm. The St. George train had delivered me promptly to Hamilton and I had walked to my office, picked up Jerome and we were walking to the C.S.A. Embassy while we talked. "Did he say why my family did not come with him on the HMS Trent?"

"No, Sir. He is too shaken to be diplomatic, maybe the three hours will help him get his poise."

"He thought he was absolutely safe on a British ship. I would assume the same thing. I wonder what really happened?"

We were on the steps of the Confederate Embassy next to the Government House, Hamilton.

There were no formal gates to enter, no guards of any kind to stop our progress. We tried to open the doors, but they were locked and a small sign said ring the bell.

We did. John Butler opened the door in his shirt sleeves and said, "Good to see you again, Admiral. Come inside please. I assume your assistant here has told you what happened?"

"Yes, what a deplorable act."

"Almost as bad as kidnaping a sleeping General from his bed in Charleston." He said with a smile.

"I had an arrest warrant, General. And you were a citizen of the United States then." I said smiling.

"Yes, I do not understand how the San Jacinto found us, Admiral. Can you tell me what you know?"

"Of course, Mr. Lewis gets a weekly briefing on all USS ships and their stations. One week ago the San Jacinto was on patrol off the coast of Africa. I doubt it was the San Jacinto that stopped you."

"Mr. Lewis has indicated the same thing earlier today. The man who claimed to be her captain was not the right age, we know that."

"What about the ship itself? I play a game with my son where I draw an outline of the ship and he tells me the class of ship. Do you think you could draw an outline of what the ship looked like?"

He reached over on his desk and got a pad of paper and a pen. "I am an army general, not an admiral, so excuse the crudeness of my artwork." He handed it over to me.

"That is a steam powered sloop alright." I said as I studied his sketch. "Did you see any markings or was this at night?"

"No, it was in broad daylight. There was lettering along each side which said USS San Jacinto."

"Give us enough time to contact Washington and

find out what they know. Mail ships are back and forth, both British and US, so it should not take very long. Have you notified Richmond?"

"Yes, I told the British captain of the Trent to have the Royal Admiralty send a transatlantic cable to Canada and have them forward it to Richmond."

"So, Richmond is unaware of what happened because the Trent has not reached England." I said.

"Yes, I suppose so."

"The first thing I think we should do is figure out a way to send messages directly to Richmond. Does the telegraph still work between South Carolina and Richmond?"

"Of course, we can send and receive telegrams anywhere inside the Confederacy. Richmond and Washington City are very close and we cannot communicate between them, but we can send a telegram to Texas and get a reply in an hour. What a situation!"

"What if we figure out a way to communicate with someone close to the Confederacy? Say Havana or Mexico City?" I offered.

"The British mail steamers make frequent runs between Bermuda, Canada and Cuba. I can send a message to Havana and have a runner try to take it into Norfolk" He said.

"Do that. You can indicate that you have talked to me and I am cooperating fully. We will have additional information in a few days, but I would not wait, Richmond needs to be notified."

"Good suggestion, I will do that, Admiral."

"Commander Lewis said you were traveling with my family?"

"Yes, we shared the same runner out of Charleston. When we got to Havana, the Trent cabin space was sold out and your father checked into a hotel."

"It was probably a good thing, seeing what happened to you. Do you have any idea why they took Slidell and Murray and left you aboard the Trent?"

"I have thinking about that. May be they wanted the kidnaping reported as soon as the Trent docked in Bermuda."

"Of course, how stupid of me, the captain of the Trent would report to the British and you would report to Richmond. The only people in the dark are in Washington. They have created an inter-national incident so that England will give the Confederacy more than just recognition of nation status. I wonder who, they are? I doubt very much if the US would do this, they can only be losers in this affair. I will refer to this as the Trent Affair in my communication." Said Jerome Lewis.

"Welcome to Bermuda, Minister Butler. This is going to be a very interesting time to be in the middle of the Atlantic Ocean, I think. Well, Commander Lewis and I have some messages to send. I will, of course, let you know what I find out about the Trent Affair. We should know some of the answers within a few days. Do you know where the San Jacinto was headed?"

"The man posing as the captain said he was taking them to Boston. That is all I know."

"Thank you, we will start there. And, feel free to visit me here in Hamilton whenever we can be of assistance to you, Minister Butler."

7

USA Conciliates Office
Hamilton, Bermuda

We left Butler's office and headed down the street to the US Conciliates Office.

"Do you think he has told us everything, Admiral?"

"Yes, it is just as big a mystery to him as it is to us. If this Captain Wilkes or whoever was stupid enough to land in Boston then we will find out something immediately. When we get back to the office, I will let you send what we know to the State Department, President of the United States through Secretary Seward. That way if Seward or someone tries to bury the information, we will have a copy in our files. We need to send a blind copy of the information to General Butler. At this point we are seeking information and clarification only. There is no need to send secret coded messages in the dark of night."

"I agreed, Jason. This will blowup for whoever ordered this action. I can not imagine a ship's captain doing this on his own. How did he know that there were

Confederate Diplomats on that particular ship at that particular location?   I doubt we ever find out what started this or why, the coverup has already started."

"It will take several days for a response from Washington. Why not try through the US Department of the Navy, also? I will send a personal to Ben Hagood and see if he knows or can tell me it he knows."

I left Jerome to get to work and I walked to the train station in Hamilton to catch the last train to St. George. Five days later we got our response from the State Department in the sealed diplomatic pouch.

TO: Mr. Jason Caldwell, Chairman National Affairs Committee

FROM: Secretary Seward

SUBJECT: Receipt of eyes only President, through the State Department

The White House has no information to share with you on this matter at this time.

Inquires are being made to location and recent actions of USS San Jacinto. White House not aware that Confederacy was planing to send diplomats to England until transatlantic cable from Lord Palmerston arrived. Copy attached.

In the regular mail pouch we received the following personal from Admiral Hagood.

Jason,

Got your inquiry about our Spanish friend not being at home. That is true. He had to return to Cuba to see his sick Aunt Maurry. I understand that the doctors in Cuba could not help her and she was sent to Boston General Hospital for observation and isolation until the sickness is identified.

Glad I could help.

Ben.

PS I have enclosed some newspaper articles on another unrelated topic

When Jerome showed me the items in the two pouches, I said. "Contact General Butler and let him read this first response and the attached cablegram. The fact that Lord Palmerston has placed our ambassador under house arrest, may give him cause to pause and communicate this to Richmond. Do not show him Ben's personal. What that tells us is that the Navy was instructed to take Murray and Slidell but leave Butler so he could get to Bermuda to open the lines of communication. Some- one did not think this through very carefully. The President can suspend the right of habeas corpus on US soil, but not on the high seas or anywhere in the Confederacy.

He still thinks the southern states are states within the Union."

"Look at these London Times press clippings, Jason. 'If Captain Wilkes is typical of USN officers then the entire breed from the Northern United States can be judged. They are an uncivilized nation built on a foundation of vulgarity and cowardice.'"

"Here is another from The London Daily. 'Perhaps Secretary of State Seward thinks that war with Great Britain will bring the seceded states back to the Union'."

"Here is a quote from the Washington Post. President Lincoln has said, 'One war at a time.'"

"There must be twenty clippings here, Jason."

"Yes, the British business world is upset. They are frustrated by the Union blockade. Lord Palmerston is playing to the fear and frustration. In this article, he says that the Admiralty is sending 8000 troops and 40 ships to rescue the diplomats. Read that as an attempt to smash the blockage of southern ports."

"Do you think they will come through Bermuda?"

"Yes, I do. We need to start to squeeze the two officers that Tom and Sam have found and try to get information to Washington as soon as we can."

Tom Schneider and Sam Mason began their vigil at the Country Squire. They met with the two contacts separately on several occasions buying drinks and making small loans of gold coins.

"It is about time that England comes to our aid. The blockade is a joke, it needs to be removed by force. From what we have seen, the Royal Navy can sweep the blockades away from our Confederate ports any time they choose." Tom said.

"The Admiralty has warned us to expect heavy ship traffic through the dockyards starting November 1. We cannot process that many ships at a time so they will come through in groups of twenty. It will take us a month to pass through 40 ships and 8000 marines. Of course, most of the ships are fast cutters to run through the blockades at Charleston, South Carolina. If they are successful there they will open Norfolk and a pathway to Richmond with the 8000 marines." Lieutenant Farnsworth proudly announced. Tom made mental notes and stopped off to see Commander Lewis on his way home to St. Davids.

"Commander Lewis, Sam and I have nearly the same stories from the Lieutenants Farnsworth and Schmidts. They have been put on alert to receive a small fleet for refueling and provisioning. The fleet consists of 38 vessels. Two ships of the line will serve as escort, each have 150 guns. Our largest ship of the line was the Pennsylvania with 120, it was captured on station in Norfolk harbor. The rest of our ships all carry 84 guns. So we will need four vessels to match that number of guns. There are no Frigates in the English fleet, so that is helpful. They are to receive eight first class steam sloops, all screw operated, no side wheelers. They are to expect eight screw, and eight side wheelers of second class sloops, ten third class steamers and four steam tenders."

"Excellent work. We need to send a coded message for the outgoing diplomatic pouch. Make it simple. Say, confirmed from multiple sources; a number of blockade running vessels on route to Bermuda; escort consists of two men-of-war. Number of marines on board ships unknown. Will report ships as they arrive. Will report number of troops as they pass through. Early indication is Charleston Harbor – not Boston. Repeat not Boston. Can you do that for me, Tom?"

"That is a long coded message, Sir. Will you review it before I type it up?"

"I will, but I doubt you will have any trouble with it. I will put it on tomorrow's mail steamer so the Admiral can make last minute changes if he likes. Has his family arrived in Bermuda?"

"Yes, they are all at Caldwell Place. You should see the dining room over there, it is a three ring circus. These cousins have not seen each other for two years! His father looks ten years younger. The blockade running must have stirred up a few juices."

"Good, the Admiral is a strong family man. I am glad that he got his family out of South Carolina."

"The Admiral takes care of all us, Commander. Did you know that he tried to hire us as company men after we finished the operation last winter in Charleston?"

"What did you tell him?"

"I told him that I would go wherever the Navy sent my unit as long as you were the unit commander. If the Navy did something stupid and split up the unit, then I would see him in Pennsylvania."

"I think we all think along the same lines, Tom. Since the Republicans have taken over the White House and therefore the military, it has been like a basket upset. The newspapers report how many army officers went with the Confederacy, but no mention is given about Navy transfers. Last year when we were in the White House, there were ten ships of line in the entire Navy, four of those were in Norfolk harbor and were taken when Virginia seceded. There were ten Frigates, three were in Norfolk.

There were twenty Sloops of War, we lost four of those. There were three Brigs, we lost one. And the list goes on, 30 to 40 per cent are now Confederate Navy vessels. The shipyards of the Confederacy are building full speed, especially Jacksonville."

"I had no idea, I knew we lost some to Florida and Virginia. How does this affect the blockade of southern ports?"

"We are making progress in the Gulf and up the Mississippi, but it is slow going. The blockade is along the east coast, nothing in the Pacific. No ground troops have taken harbors or ports away as of yet. If that happens, then we have a chance to win."

"What if this British fleet descends on Charleston?"

"If they can run off the blockade vessels and land 8000 marines, then the Confederacy will hold the city and harbor for the entire war. More importantly, the British might try to do this again in Norfolk."

In the last week of October, we received several reports in Hamilton via the mail steamer from Washington. The first was the after action report of the Battle of Ball's Bluff near Leesburg, Virginia. President Lincoln could not get his newly appointed General of the Army of the Potomac to leave Washington City and cross the river into Virginia. The Union Army was close to 200,000 by late October, but General McClellan was unwilling to cross and engage the Confederacy. Lincoln's close personal friend was senator Edward Baker from Oregon. He also was a colonel in the army reserve, having served in the war with Mexico. Lincoln had confided in him that he was disappointed in the lack of progress towards the prosecution of the war across the Potomac. He offered Baker an appointment as a brigadier and command of a small brigade, 1700 member reconnaissance force. Lincoln was convinced that the Confederate line was porous and could be penetrated. He encouraged Baker to find this opening and report it to McClellan. On October 21, Baker lead his brigade from Maryland to Virginia. At the river's edge, they found a swollen river from fall rains and a hundred foot high bank on the Virginia side of the river called Ball's Bluff. Baker sent his men up and down the Maryland side looking for any available boats to ferry his men across. They found three boats. In dozens of trips back and forth, good fortune seemed to smile on them as all 1,700 were ferried across safely. The way up the bluff was a narrow pathway with Virginia sharp shooters killing every fifth man who plodded up the bluff side. When eighty percent of the force reached the top, they found themselves on open ground and confronted by four Confederate regiments. Baker was killed in the first volley. In a frenzied panic, the force raced backward and fell to their deaths at the bottom of the bluff.

The second report was even more incredulous. Lincoln replaces Winfield Scott with the General who refuses to fight across the Potomac and prefers to "protect" Washington, General McClellan. "Jerome, have you read this?" I asked.

"Yes, it is what you recommended, Admiral."

"I know, but Scott at least has a brain. I am not sure about McClellan. He lacks the will to lead his army against the enemy."

"Then you do not want to read this last report, Admiral."

"What is in it?"

"An assessment of our undercover work regarding English intentions in either Norfolk or Charleston."

"Go on."

"The War Department, in particular the Secretary of War, has informed us that we are in error. The war department has just ordered 2,300 tons of gun powder from Great Britain. Why would they sell us gun powder to kill their troops if they were planning an attack?"

"I cannot abide fools, Jerome. The man has 'ordered' not received gun powder. Now England knows that we need gun powder for the ships on blockade! What an idiot!"

"What do we do now, Admiral?"

"Report how many Royal Navy ships are re-supplied in November, where they are headed and the number of troops aboard. What else can we do?"

"We could send a blind copy to Admiral Hagood, after all, it is his men that will die on the blockade ships because of the lack of gun powder."

"Thank you, Jerome. You are always one step ahead of me."

8

Royal Naval Dockyards Bermuda
November 1861

November 1861 found the Royal Naval Dockyards crowded with British shipping. From captured French luggers used as troop transports and supply ships to sloops, frigates and two ship of the line came the shrilling of whistles and stamp of feet as the crews of more than 40 vessels settled down to the day's routine. In the cabin of HMS *Revenge,* Admiral Lord Willingsworth studied the charts of the waters off Norfolk Harbor. For "Black Billy," as his seamen called him, had been given the task of smashing the North American blockades, first at Charleston and then Norfolk. This was to be punishment for the kidnaping of an ambassador to Great Britain that was held in Boston. Why he was not attacking Boston was unclear to him. Lord Palmerston had been very clear that the action was to take place unless the diplomat was released and Black Billy considered his role as the one to rattle the saber and show the Union Jack. He was positive that a war with America was not about to happen. His task force was too small for such action, but it was the right size to send a serious message to both the North and South. To the North, it would indicate that England would not tolerate the interference with free trade and to the South it would indicate that they were a separate nation, an equal trading partner. The violation of international maritime law had been the excuse necessary to begin the operations he was sent to complete.

Suddenly a tremendous explosion jarred the dockyards out of its morning routine activities. Those nearest the explosion saw a tall column of water collapsing into a large cloud of gun powder smoke. No sooner had this occurred before several smaller bangs were heard off the stern of HMS Revenge and HMS Rapier. In an instant the dockyards was in an uproar. Drums beat to general quarters as the Queen's ships prepared for action. Men were heard yelling, "search for mines, get the divers under the hulls, move, move." Officers shouted orders to fire the boilers, prepare to get under way. Other ship captains that were aboard, cut mooring lines and started to drift into quays and wooden pilings. With that many ships in such a small space, more damage was done in one hour by ship collisions than the United States Navy could hope to accomplish on the high seas.

The chaos in the dockyards was seen from a hillside less than a quarter mile away. Tom Schneider and Jerome Lewis had been in the Royal Navy Graveyards since before sunrise. They had brought a picnic basket filled with sandwiches and other snacks. It also contained two spy glasses, a map, a train schedule, pen and paper. As they sat with their backs to grave markers, glasses to their eyes, they were enjoying what was unfolding below them.

"The stupid bastards brought the entire fleet into the dockyards. Just like Admiral Caldwell said they might. This will teach them a lesson." Tom said.

"There was absolutely no need for all that destruction. Look, Tom, that tender was literally torn apart by that steam powered sloop screws."

"The damage done to the dockyards is as great as anything done to the ships. Look at all the secondary explosions and small fires that are everywhere. Smoke will soon block us from seeing much of anything. We had better start writing down which ships are damaged and those that have left the dockyards under their own steam."

Notes from observation team 11-17-61

2 Man-of-war damaged by small mines, blown steerage - still in docks.

6 steam powered sloops left docks - now in Great Sound anchored.

2 steam sloops afire, minor explosions below decks, assume boilers out.

4 steam tenders destroyed by collisions with sloop screws - below water.

8 second class sloops took out several docks and themselves in panic to get out of dockyards.

8 side wheelers left dockyards and are
steaming east for St. George.

10 French luggers are still tied up and did
not get damaged in the melee.

The raid on the dockyards had been planned after Admiral Caldwell said something should be done to give Admiral Hagood some time to respond to the threat. He said he could not know how the delay was caused but offered any equipment we might need, including a Bushnell Turtle, from his dockyard in St. George. Jerome Lewis had heard of the submersible repair device, but he had never seen one until he and Sam Mason had seen it in St. George.

"We will need to construct small charges that will destroy the two escort vessels steerage. No deaths, just confusion and fear. Do we have everything for that?" Jerome Lewis, master planner of chaos, and assistant minister to Bermuda was making a list of needed materials.

"Yes, Sir. Good swimmers can place these charges, why do we need the Bushnell Turtle?"

"For the main event, Sam. There is an empty prison hulk right in the middle of 40 ships. If we can either set it afire or blow it up, the resulting chaos might be interesting!"

"So, how do we blow it up?"

"We use the Admiral's turtle. A bushnell turtle was last used to blow up a man-of-war in New York Bay."

"When was that? I never heard about it."

"It was a little before your time, Sam, it was September 7, 1776."

"Oh. No wonder I never heard about. Who is going to operate the turtle?"

"You have two weeks to learn how to master the craft. You can start by studying these diagrams the Admiral gave me. See here is a cutaway view of the turtle. The two clam shell sides are seven feet long and it looks about six feet in diameter when it is closed. Tom will not fit inside the turtle, but you are just the right size. You have to master the hand cranks for horizontal and vertical propellers."

"When do I master the controls?"

"You will be here in the Caldwell Shipping docks until you do. Do not report for duty in Hamilton until you can prove to me that you can navigate the turtle as well as use the attachment auger, foot operated rudder and ballast pumps. I do not want to let you into the Royal Dockyards so you can drown in this oaken bucket."

"Aye, aye, Sir."

Every day of the first week, Sam practiced on the water's surface around the wooden docks of Caldwell Shipping Company. He sat on the pilot's seat and looked through the tiny portholes of the conning tower. The tower was about as tall as his head. Snorkel tubes extended above the tower about six inches, so there was fresh air until you had to submerge. It was fun trying to learn how the propellers and rudder worked. He bounced off of and bumped into every wooden piling in the dockyard. Finally he tried to submerge by cranking the intake valve by his right foot. Water came into a holding tank and the turtle sank below the surface. The snorkel tubes closed and he could stay under about thirty minutes before the air became fouled. His depth was shown by a vertical glass tube, closed at the top and leading to the water outside through a brass, water tight fitting. Any increase in water pressure forced the column of water upward, any decrease dropped the level of the water in the tube. As a safety precaution a 200 pound lead keel could be released from inside the turtle, counteracting any tendency to sink. This was also the anchor, since it was fastened to a rope.

The second week, Sam practiced attaching the mine. He would navigate to a wooden platform in the water, submerge one foot and propel himself under the platform. He then practiced the use of the metal auger. This was very tricky since the turtle tended to settle down when the auger tried to fasten itself to the wood. But with practice and patience he mastered the attachment of the egg shaped wooden cask containing the powder charge of 250 pounds and a clockwork timing device. When the mine was released from just above the rudder on the turtle, it floated to the bottom of the practice platform and became inverted. This set the timing device for one hour. Sam needed to get way to a safe distance in that hour. After that, a flint gunlock set off the charge.

In the early hours of November 17, 1861, the turtle was dropped from a Caldwell Sloop that was passing into the Great Sound, adjacent to the Royal Naval Dockyards. The sloop continued on into Hamilton and tied up at the wharfs. Sam was like a floating child's top until he managed to get some water into the ballast tank and the turtle settled to the depth of the conning tower. It was past sunrise, but just barely. His heart was pounding while he turned the hand crank of the horizontal propeller. The turtle edged into the middle of the vessels tied up inside the dockyards. He spotted the old deserted prison hulk and propelled himself towards it. When he was along side, he again turned the intake valve and slipped below the surface of the water. He watched his depth gage and maneuvered under the hull. He released the auger and placed it for attachment. Slowly he turned and the metal bit caught and the attachment bolt was firmly in place. He pulled the release level for the mine and prayed that his fellow marines had built an accurate timer. He did not wait for the mine to float up and invert. Instead he placed both hands on the horizontal propeller and turned as fast as he could. He would need to blow some water out of the ballast tank so he could rise to the surface and get his bearings. As he pumped the ballast tank, he slowly rose and broke the surface. He wondered if the two marines assigned to place the charges on the escorts had been successful. If they were unable to place the charges then all his work would be for nothing. He followed the sea walls out of the Royal Navy Dockyards and entered the Great Sound. He kept as near to the shore as he could. There was a waiting fishing boat to pick him and turtle up a quarter mile away. He kept turning the horizontal propeller and praying.

"Please, God, get me safely out of this machine so that I can see Rachael and the children once more before I die."

He found the fishing boat waiting and had cracked the hatch to crawl out when he heard the first giant explosion followed by two, then two more bangs.

"We had better get that turtle secured and towed back to Hamilton before the British figure out what happened here." Said Timothy Saunders.

An hour later, they were tied up beside the Caldwell sloop and began the loading process for the return to St. George. Sam left them to continue and walked to the US Conciliate Office across from the Government House in Hamilton.

"Reporting back, Sir." Sam said.

"You mean reporting in. I have no idea where you have been Sergeant Mason or what you may have done on your two week leave." I said with a smile.

"Are Tom and the Commander back?"

"No, they will ride the train back and it will take longer than your boat ride."

"I heard the explosion go off, Sir. I have no idea if blowing that deserted hulk did any good or not."

"We will be getting a report from our observers soon, Sam. Be patient and hope that the escorts are held up for repairs four to six weeks."

The next day we prepared and sent our messages on the outbound mail steamer to Washington.

TO: Eyes only President of United States

THROUGH: Secretary of State Seward

FROM: Jason Caldwell, Chairman National Affairs Committee

SUBJECT: Delay of English Naval Fleet

It has come to our attention that an accident has occurred in the Royal Naval Dockyards, November 17. A British prison hulk apparently exploded from the ignition of methane gas. Nearby vessels were damaged and are now under repair. Of the forty ships in the invasion fleet, 4 tenders were destroyed beyond repair, 8 sloops are now in St. George Harbor under going repairs by the Caldwell Shipping Company. The Caldwell Company assures me that the repairs cannot be made before six or eight weeks.

Two escort vessels are currently under repair in the Royal Naval Dockyards. But this will also take some time, since the dockyards are also under repair. Numerous fires were caused by flying debris from the hulk. Most were extinguished in a matter of a few minutes but one could not be brought under control until it had destroyed a repair bay and ship's hoist. The repairs to the steerage of the escort vessels will now have to be made by "Careening" instead of hoisting the vessels, this will cause a delay in the repair process.

It is the advice of this committee, that the actions that caused the formation of this fleet, be removed by the prompt release and return of the diplomats held in Boston. I would be available for the assignment of personal envoy to return the English diplomat in question. A letter, from the President, recognizing that he had been taken illegally would make my mission somewhat more palatable to the British. Awaiting your response

We also sent the following to the Confederate Embassy, Hamilton:

TO: Minister Butler

FROM: Minister Caldwell

SUBJECT: Disaster at Royal Naval Dockyards

Please be advised that repairs on eight of the vessels damaged on November 17, last, are currently underway at Caldwell Shipping Co., St. George Island, Bermuda. Docking space is also available for Confederate ships that would normally be repaired at the West End. I have informed my government that all repairs to the English vessels shall be made in a timely manner and that the holding of the Confederate diplomats would only bring further reprisals from Great Britain.

I proposed the diplomats being held in Boston be released to you and me. If it is agreed upon in principle, could you get permission to travel with me from Bermuda to Boston and then on to London via the port of South Hampton? Awaiting your response

It was now time to send a personal to Ben Hagood.

Ben,

Jason here, just wanted to let you know that the foreign group of travelers will be delayed. The two guard dogs are unable to proceed at this time. Estimates are a month to six weeks, if this time estimate changes, I will update you.

Jason.

The incoming mail had some interesting after action reports. They began with another account of a defeat for Union forces. The morning of the 7 th a group of 3000 Illinois volunteers under Colonel Grant floated down the Mississippi River in barges from their camp in Cairo. Here,

Grant's forces met a smaller group of Confederates and they pushed them back down the river and into Belmont, Missouri. Here they over ran the camp and started looting the Confederate supplies when they came under heavy artillery fire from a hill across the river. These troops were commanded by General Polk, a West Pointer. Now Grant was faced by twenty-seven hundred troops who began crossing the river towards him. The troops who he had temporarily pushed down the Mississippi turned and advanced. This caught Grant's outnumbered troops in a pincher movement. Grant ordered his troops to retreat to the barges for a quick return to Cairo. He was forced to leave his wounded and the captured Confederate supplies. Grant was fortunate to escape with his troops and his life. General Polk could see Grant and offered his sharp shooters $100.00 if they could bring him down. Grant dived into the bottom of the barge and hid from sight. Unconfirmed reports are that Colonel Grant was drunk at the time of the engagement.

"Well, at least Grant is willing to engage the enemy." Said Jerome Lewis as he read the report.

"Too bad he has to find courage in the bottom of a bottle." I replied.

"Maybe we should find out what he drinks and send a bottle to General McClellan." Jerome was smiling.

"Lincoln has said, 'One war at a time', maybe he is letting McClellan hide in Washington until all the east coast seaports are either captured or contained by blockades." I offered.

"The press likes to cover land battles, they do not like sea engagements. It is hard to send a telegram from a location at sea. The war will be won by which side has the most effective Navy. So far, we control the sea lanes everywhere. The rivers are another matter. Lincoln should let Grant clear the Mississippi and Ohio rivers of all Confederate forts and gun boats. I like Grant, he goes to battle in barges or gun boats, he is really a marine in disguise!" Jerome was laughing now.

"You may have something there, Jerome, Firm it up and I will let you send it off as an official suggestion from the committee, which reminds me I must send out some missives for the rest of the committee to read, agree with or vote no. I am heading to my office to construct the first set of letters to be sent on the next mail steamer. If you need me, you know where to find me."

The committee members were all captains of industry or financial firms in the northern United States. President Lincoln had written to each and asked for their service for one year. Those that accepted became my committee list. Because they were located across the country, I wrote whenever I needed to bring matters to their attention. I took out the list and began to write the letters to the following:

Asa Parker Mansion
122 Penn Ave.
Scranton, Pennsylvania

John Nesbitt
1311 Redwood Way
Sacramento, California

Henry Huttleson Rogers
One Wildon Ln.
Titusville, Pennsylvania

John Peirpoint Morgan
550 Park Ave.
New York, New York

Henry Brooks Adams
1100 Commonwealth Ave.
Boston, Massachuttes

Amos J. Stillwell
22 Post Fort Rd.
Des Moines, Iowa

George Hiles Wisconsin
349 Elm St.
Madison, Wisconsin

Simeon Brock
1101 High St.
Camden, Maine

Isaac Norris
11 Cardinal Gannon St.
Erie, Pennsylvania

Jason Caldwell, Chairman
Seneca Hill
Titusville, Pennsylvania

The letters would all be the same and I began to put my thoughts into writing:

November 18, 1861

Committee member name

Street Address

City and State

Dear _____,

It is time again to convene our committee by mail. In the near future, I am hoping that the President will find the time to sit down with us in the White House. The committee can reach Washington by train with the exception of John Nesbitt and myself. We will need some advanced notice in order to plan an ocean voyage. If an emergency meeting is ever called, I will send my proxy via Admiral Hagood of the Army Navy Building. John, if you could select a proxy also, that might be helpful.

The matter to report today is the progress towards the solution of the Trent Affair. The British fleet to remove the blockades of Charleston and Norfolk has been held in Bermuda for the next six to eight weeks. I have requested that Minister Murray be released to me for transport to London. This half- baked idea of detaining Confederate Diplomats has caused a great deal of strain on US Navy resources. We have only 42 ships at the present time to maintain the blockade of the southeastern coast line. The gulf effort is progressing, but the number of Confederate ships outnumber us in this region. We should recommend to the President the following:

1. Promote US Grant to Brigadier.

2. Order him to engage all Confederate forts along the Ohio and Mississippi.

3. Recruit US Marines to serve on Grant's barges and gun boats.

I was about to finish the form letter when Jerome stuck his head through my office door and said, "Your family is here to see you, Minister."

"Tell them I am on my out!"

Louise, James and Ruth had brought everyone to Hamilton shopping. My father was insistent that he needed a suit of clothes. Mother had shopped in St. George with Laura and Louise and had found most of the things that she needed or wanted. We all walked down to front street so that father could either buy off the rack at Trimminghams or get measured at a tailors shop. Trey and Marriann and the three children tried to buy Trimminghams out of stock. I was happy to see everyone enjoying their time together. Louise said, "What is the matter, Jason?"

"Trey, Louise and I are going upstairs to the tea room here at Trimminghams. Can you or Mariann watch James and Ruth?"

"Mariann will take them with the girls to try on dresses."

"None for James, please!"

When we reached the third floor, we slipped behind chairs and ordered a pot of tea. "I may have to go to London, Louise. I would like you to go with me."

"Can the children go, too?" She asked.

"Let me tell you what it is about, then you can decide. I think that President Lincoln is going to release the Confederate Diplomats held in Boston."

"He is going to release them to you, if you agree to take them to London, is that it?"

"Exactly, he has written a letter of apology to Queen Victoria and he wants it hand delivered by someone she has met and trusts. I can answer any questions she might have."

"How are you going to get them?"

"I think Ben will send a steam powered sloop or larger vessel if he can find one not doing blockade duty. He will pick us up in Bermuda, return to Boston, pickup the diplomats and then head for South Hampton."

"Could you change his mind?"

"About what?"

"I would like for the whole family to leave Bermuda in the Cold Harbor and sail to Boston. Your family needs to feel like they are not trapped on this island. Your Mother and Father can really shop in style. James and Ruth can stay in Boston with Trey's family or with Grandma and Grandpa. I will write to my brother at

Wheatland and see if he can come to Boston by train and meet us. I think he would like to go to London again. He could even smooth over some of the rough spots created by that Republican in the White House."

"No wonder I married you, Louise. This can be our December Christmas presents to each other. I missed last Christmas by being away for your brother. If we can work out the details, I would enjoy this very much." I bent over and kissed her on the lips.

"Jason, control yourself, we are in public!" But she was giggling again like she always did.

We returned to the Caldwell family shoppers and my father announced, "We have way too many packages to get on a train. Let me hire a carriage and a wagon to get us back home."

"Home, father?"

"Yes, Jason, this is home now. My family around me and a wonderful climate to live in. What more could a man ask for?"

"How about a shopping spree to Boston?" I asked.

"Jason Caldwell, do not tease about something like that!" My mother said.

"I am not kidding, I may be sent to Boston on business and there is plenty of room in the Cold Harbor for any Caldwell who would like to tag along."

"Would we spend December in Boston?" My father asked. "No thanks, on that one."

"Oh, Robert Caldwell, you are such an old fuddy duddy. Think, snow for Christmas!" Mother said. Everyone began to talk at once. "Wait, wait. I do not even know that I am going. I will find out as soon as the mail steamer gets back from Washington."

"When will that be?" Mariann said. "I have lots more things to buy before I get on another ship!" Everyone laughed as my father returned with a carriage and drivers in tow. "Children do you want to ride in the wagon with the old 'fuddy duddy'?" They piled in around the packages and Grandpa sat next to the driver. The adults climbed into the carriage and we headed for home.

9

Solution of Trent Affair
Bermuda Station

The next day in Hamilton the mail pouch came into the office and we opened and read the following:

TO: Jason Caldwell, Chairman National Affairs Committee

FROM: Secretary Seward

SUBJECT: Receipt of eyes only President, through the State Department

The White House approves your plan to return Ministers Murray and Slidell.

You will proceed to Boston to meet Admiral Hagood at your earliest convenience.

Admiral Hagood will pass to you a letter from the President to the Queen. USS

Intrepid released from blockade duty to transport

diplomats to London and Paris.

A transatlantic cable sent this date to the Queen informing her of your arrival at South Hampton. Copy attached.

In the regular mail pouch we received the following personal from Ben Hagood.

Jason,

Ben here, got your inquiry about meeting in Boston. Sounds good to me. I will be traveling with you so I can eat humble pie for the one who approved the snatch of the diplomats. I am to personally apologize to Lord Naiper for the Trent Affair.

See you in a few days. Oh, I have been asked to request that you bring your formal naval uniform in as much as the President has been granted permission from the US Senate to promote you to Rear Admiral.

Ben

I stood looking at the personal and laughing. "Ben is up to his old tricks again, Jerome. He thinks I will fall for that old trick?"

"I do not think so Rear Admiral, here is a message from the Army Navy Building with a copy of the resolution from the Senate. It says for meritorious service to the Navy on November 17, 1861, you are hereby promoted to Rear Admiral in the United States Naval Reserve on

Presidential assignment in Bermuda. It does not say you are retired. This means you are now back in the Navy! Congratulations, Sir."

"Congratulations, my ass. Lincoln did an end run on me. I will write and process my retirement papers again if necessary."

"I think the President is trying to protect you on the trip to England, Sir. If you traveled as a diplomat the Queen might hold you like Lincoln held her diplomat. But holding a Rear Admiral and a Fleet Admiral, like Ben Hagood, would be next to impossible."

"I will think about that, Jerome. But returning to active service is out of the question. I will not raise a hand against my native state."

The next day, I sent the following information to the Army Navy Building.

TO: Fleet Admiral Hagood, Army Navy Building

FROM: Chairman National Affairs Committee

SUBJECT: Commission in United States Navy

As a voluntary member of the State Department, I thank the Senate for the rear admiral title. Would you please pass my appreciation to the Secretary of the Navy and have him bring to the attention of the President that I am a retired Vice Admiral. I am not a member of the reserve. If a mistake has been made, then I hereby retire again from the Navy.

My chairmanship duties for the President ends at the end of the war, and I look forward to returning to private life and to being the full time chairman of the board for Caldwell International.

I left the office early to return to St. George. "Had I done the right thing?" I thought. What role was I playing in the civil war that was tearing families apart? I had used my best judgement on not violating my oath as an officer in the United States Navy when I was on active duty. Now that I was retired, how did I feel? The train stopped in St. George and I was still pondering the thoughts as I walked up Rose Hill and into the front doors of Caldwell Place. There was not a sound of any kind in the office wing, everything was closed and locked, that was strange. I headed to the main dining room to find the entire extended family sitting around a large table, tears streaming down their faces.

"What happened?" I asked.

"Oh, Jason, your father just got a letter from Beaufort. Your sister, Carl and the children have been killed."

"Killed, what happened?"

"Carl was assigned to Fort Beauregard. It was bombarded by the Navy Warships when they invaded Port Royal. All the Fort's Officers and families were killed when their living quarters were hit by heavy mortar fire."

I held Louise for a long time and wept. I looked over at my father and brother and said, "Thank God, you came to us." They both could not speak, they just nodded their heads in agreement.

10

Christmas in Boston
December 1861

Christmas is a special time of year, a time for family gathering and celebration. This year the death of my sister and her family hung like a cloud over the rest of us. My father and mother said they would like to stay in St. Davids for Christmas. Trey and Mariann said they did not feel like going anywhere either. They would like James and Ruth to celebrate with them while Louise and I were gone to Boston for a few days. I suggested that the Whitehalls and Caldwells move into the Inn so they could all be together and they agreed. My father pulled me aside and said, "Please do not go to Europe, come back to Bermuda when your business is finished in Boston."

"I will make the necessary arrangements with the White House, do not tell anyone this yet, but Louise and I will try to be here for Christmas, if we can."

"Thank you, son!" He held me close and it reminded me of James Buchanan's embrace in the parlor at 353

Bay Street. Another time and another place, ages ago, it seemed now. Louise had not written to her brother, she would instead take a train from Boston to Wheatland if things took more than a few days to accomplish. I contacted Captain Jacob of the *Cold Harbor* to see what day he could leave St. George. He indicated that it was now December and anytime would be fine with him. I told him to prepare to leave in two days and returned to Caldwell Place and told Louise to pack. I needed to get on into Hamilton and send off the mail for the White House and Army Navy Building.

"Jason, are you all right, you look pale?"

"Yes, I have been fighting with myself about a decision that I must make." I left her to pack and I boarded the train for Hamilton. It arrived an hour later and I walked to my Office to visit with Jerome Lewis.

"Jerome, I have made a decision. You were right. It does not matter if I am a member of the US Navy Reserve or not. Because the task that I have undertaken requires me to function as a Rear Admiral on active duty. I cannot continue to walk a fine line between serving the country that I love and not harming the State where I was born. All that changed with the invasion of Port Royal and the deaths of my family members. I advised the President to invade each seaport and harbor along the southeastern coast. Her death was caused by my advice and recommendations."

"Admiral, on November 7, 1861, Captain Samuel Dupont caused the deaths of your family by ordering the attacks on Fort Walker and Beauregard. You are not to blame for the deaths of anyone. I cannot remember a time that you ordered anyone killed, it is not in your nature to do so. You, can not take the responsibility of your sister's death, Sir. It will destroy you."

"Maybe you are right, Jerome, but the way I feel now, I cannot ever set foot in Beaufort again."

"Admiral, you need some time off, go to Boston. Let me write the communications for the mail pouch and you can read and sign them. Do you still want me to be acting minister to Bermuda in your absence?"

"I have thought about this some, Jerome, you are ready for a promotion. How would you like to be an Admiral's Aide, Captain Lewis?"

"Captain? Admiral's Aide? Are you out of your mind, Sir? I am a policeman!"

"That was a long time ago, Jerome, you have been my aide for a year now. Let us get the paperwork off to Washington."

I signed and we sent the following:

TO: Secretary of State Seward, the White House

FROM: Rear Admiral Jason Caldwell, Hamilton, Bermuda

SUBJECT: Changes in schedule for returning ministers Murray and Slidell

Due to deaths in my family, I will be unable to accompany Admiral Hagood in his delivery of ministers Murray and Slidell to their posts. I would like your permission to return them to Bermuda with me. Minister Butler here in Bermuda is undersecretary for Great Britain and will accept their release. He will then inform London and Paris of the transportation arrangements to their posts. This is considerably easier than taking needed ships from the blockade effort in order to take two people to Europe. Awaiting your response

TO: Secretary Welles, Army Navy Building

FROM: Rear Admiral Jason Caldwell, Hamilton, Bermuda

SUBJECT: Promotion of Commander Jerome Lewis

Please disregard any communication that you may have had with Fleet Admiral Hagood. I am delighted to be promoted to Rear Admiral. In that regard I would like to name commander Jerome Lewis as my aide. The problem is the rank of Lewis, he is a commander and most admirals have a captain as their aide. He has served in that capacity for over a year and deserves promotion. I have named Jerome Lewis as my aide effective today.

TO: Abraham Lincoln, President of the United States

FROM: Jason Caldwell

SUBJECT: Membership changes on the National Affairs Committee

I regret to inform you of the death of John Nesbitt in California. You should consider a replacement before we meet in Washington. By this time, I am sure that you have been notified of my acceptance back into the USN reserves by Secretary Welles. I hope that this promotion to Rear Admiral will not affect my serve to Secretary Seward in the State Department. In times of war an overlap in service can sometimes be helpful.

In any regard, I look forward to your assignment and I serve at your pleasure. You have my full and undivided support of the war efforts made to this date.

I left Jerome with the mail and walked to the C S A Embassy. I rang the bell and a woman answered the door. "Is Minister Butler in?" I asked.

"Yes, who shall I say is calling?"

"Admiral Caldwell."

"Jason, I am so sorry to hear about your sister and her family." John Butler greeted me with a genuine sadness in his eyes.

"Thank you, John. Do you have news of what has happened in Beaufort? We have had only the one letter informing us of the deaths."

"Yes, come in and I will tell you what I know." He handed me a letter from his aunt in Beaufort.

November 12, 1861

Dear JB,

I have some terrible news from Beaufort. It was over run and captured by Yankees. General Dunavent's regiment was camped between Port Royal and town. They could hear the heavy mortar rounds explode in the water. Every man under sixty was asked to go to the two forts, Walker and Beauregard. Some of the officers took their wives and families with them thinking they would be safer there than at home in Port Royal. A terrible tragedy occurred at Beauregard when the one of the war ships hit an officer's quarters and destroyed the building and everyone inside.

Most of Dunavent's men survived but the folks in Beauregard were never found. A few body parts were buried in the Port Royal cemetery yesterday. The marker just says defenders of Fort Beauregard. The next day, the war ships came on high tide and are now tied up in Beaufort opposite Bay Street. Several of the Caldwell Mansions have been seized under the Confiscation Act. A general is living in one and rest are hospitals for Union wounded.

I did not read any more of the letter, I thanked him and said, "I will be leaving in two days to bring Minister Murray and Slidell to your embassy. Will you accept their unconditional release?"

"Of course, Jason. How are you getting to Boston?"

"I will use a Caldwell ship, probably the Cold Harbor. There are no USS ships available, they are all active on the blockade of C S A harbors, as you well know. They have not stopped the faster C S A ships that you have been building in Florida. I hope that you can continue to carry mail pouches to Norfolk and then to Richmond, John. I am so sorry that this war will be one of blockades, fort seizures and starvation. No one should have to suffer for politician stupidity."

"I could not agree more, Jason. I no longer think the war will be won in a year or two by the C S A. There will be no winners, only those that lose less."

"Well put, John. You are becoming a diplomat instead of an army general."

"Not a diplomat, Jason, only a realist."

"Do not let Murray hear you say that, John. He is bound to be angry over his illegal detention in Boston and he will want revenge."

"Yes, I do not envy the trip back to Bermuda with him bending your ear. Could I be of any assistance to you on the voyage up or back?"

"I think that would be a very good idea, John. That way the newspapers will report that they were released to a C S A representative in Boston. I can stay in the background."

"What is the date and time of sailing, I will be on the docks in St. George, an hour before."

"I will have my aide drop off a note to you, John."

I left John Butler with a better feeling than I had felt for several days and I realized that it was talking to someone from home that made me feel that way. The war would rage on, but people you knew would remain the same or disappear from your life forever. I realized that my function for the US Government would be one of trying to shorten the war wherever possible.

We left St. George Harbor on December 12, 1861, and headed north by northwest until the windy weather drove us below decks and into our cabins. Louise and I were in the captains quarters below the Poop deck. The captain had moved to the first mates cabin off the quarter deck, the first mate bumped the tiller's mate and so on. John Butler was given the guest cabin under the forecastle deck. It was a two day trip by steamer, but the Cold Harbor was built in 1797 and it was a sailing vessel from times past. It was quiet on deck, only the sound of wind in the sails. Louise and I bundled up in coats and sat in deck chairs and just enjoyed the time alone.

We entered Boston Harbor on December seventeenth. We were met by a representative of the Navy, a Commander Whitsill. He saluted sharply and then handed me a garment bag that he had carried down to the docks. "A present from Admiral Hagood with his compliments, Sir. He would like you to wear this during the handing over ceremony."

"There is going to be a ceremony?"

"You know the Navy, Sir. I will wait for you to change before I escort you and General Butler off your ship, Sir."

I returned to our cabin and said, "A present from Ben Hagood."

"What is it, Jason?"

"Probably a joke, knowing Ben." I pulled the garment bag open and there was a brand new dress uniform for a Rear Admiral. "So much for staying in the background."

"Put it on, I want to see how you look, Admiral. Can I see your 'rear', admiral?"

"Yes, while a drop my pants and get into this thing."

Twenty minutes later, I was top side and found the Commander and John Butler. Butler smiled and said, "You look splendid with three stars on your shoulder, Jason. I would have worn my one star if I had known this was a masquerade party." He was smiling from ear to ear.

"This is not my idea, General. A friend of mine is returning a favor, when he got his first star, Louise took him to a tailor and had a dress uniform made for him. He has waited a long time for this."

"You deserve to be recognized for your service to your

country, Jason."

"Thank you, John. So do you!"

"Where are you taking us, Commander Whitsill?" John Butler asked.

"To Boston General Hospital, Sir."

"To a hospital?"

"Yes, Sir. Both men are ready to be released, all you have to do is sign them out."

"Good, I want to be home for Christmas not stuck in Boston, God Damn, Massachusetts." He said.

The Commander led the way and we left the ship and got into a carriage headed for Boston General Hospital. The newspaper reporters were everywhere when we arrived and stepped out of the carriage. They all asked questions at the same time. I said nothing while John Butler was in his element, he answered questions in a direct way. He said he was the representative sent by President Davis. Yes, they would be released today. No, the foreign ministers were not spies, they were on their way to London and Paris. Yes, it had been nearly two months since they were detained.. No, he did not know when the ministers would arrive in London.

We broke away from the reporters and headed into patient receiving. Here we met a doctor who took us to the mental ward. We passed through locked doors and into a hallway marked patient holding. There sat David Slidell and James Murray. Murray jumped to his feet and ran to Butler and hugged him.

"John, you have finally come to rescue me from this hell hole of a place!"

"Actually, Admiral Caldwell here rescued you. I am here to accept your release and to certify that you have been well cared for."

Murray was about to moan and complain again when David Slidell rose to his feet and said, "Admiral Caldwell, on behalf of the Confederate States of America's, Paris Embassy, I thank you."

"You are most welcome, Minister Slidell. On behalf of my government, I apologize for any mistreatment that may have befallen you. Commander, the ambassadors have luggage, you will fetch it for them."

"But, Sir. The handing over ceremony is to be ....."

"There will be no 'handing over ceremony', Commander. These two men are foreign diplomats not criminals."

"I do not know, Sir. I have my orders."

"Were they given to you by a three star Admiral commissioned before 1837?"

"No, Sir."

"Then my orders stand, ya here?" I realized that the madder I got the more pronounced my southern accent became. John Butler had a grin on his face.

"But, Sir, the reporters."

"General Butler here is an expert on handling reporters. Doctor, do have anything for the General to
sign before we leave?"

"No, Sir."

"Good, then we are on our way back south. Commander find the bags and meet us on the docks."

The four of us walked out of the mental ward, through the hospital patient receiving and out the front doors. I did not look back, the carriage was still waiting, we got in and started for the docks.

"I was kidding about getting home for Christmas,

Jason."

"I think that is a very good idea, John. I cannot abide fools or the messes that they create."

Neither Murray or Slidell had said a thing until James Murray said, "Admiral, were you a captain in the Army Navy building when David and I were in the Senate?"

"Yes, Sir. I was. Navy Intelligence."

"Do you have any idea why we were detained, Admiral?"

"Not a clue, Ambassador. All I know is that I was given the job of cleaning up the mess."

"Sometimes you have to create a mess in order to cleanup another, right Admiral?"

I glanced over at John and said, "I did not give any orders to destroy any British property anywhere in the last year, General."

"Well orders or no, it worked and I thank you on behalf of President Davis."

"As one South Carolinian to another, John, you can report to your President that Jason Caldwell will never raise a hand against his native state. That is more than I can say for the United States Navy."

We were now on the docks and in a few minutes, Commander Whitsill appeared with two very large suitcases. We walked up the gangway and I shouted to Captain Jacob, "Permission to come aboard captain."

"Permission granted captain."

"He called you captain, Admiral." Murray said.

"That is correct, I own this vessel. It is part of my commercial fleet. I was a ship's captain long before I was a captain in the Navy. Captain Jacob there trained under me when I was his captain and he still thinks of me as his captain."

"Oh, that, Caldwell." I could hear the items falling into place for Murray.

"Gentlemen, we will be getting underway shortly. I will have your bags taken to your cabins, they are next to General Butler's. You might want to refresh yourselves before dinner, it will be at six bells." I walked away towards the captain's cabin to find Louise.

"What happened? Why are you back so soon?"

"Every thing was in order and we came right back here to avoid newspaper reporters and so that I could get out of this monkey suit."

"Oh, Jason. You look so good in that uniform."

"I bet you say that to all the sailors you meet!"

"Just the ones I find in the White House."

"We have had quite a marriage, my love, I was lucky to find you!"

"I feel the same way, Jason."

"What would you like for dinner? I told the three gentlemen to expect a light supper at six bells. I am on my way to Hop Sing and give him the dinner order."

"Tell him no onions!"

"Very good. When I return, we can go top side and see the lights of Boston, it is getting dark."

"The lights of Boston?"

"Yes, I have been told that they have gas lamps throughout the city, just like London. Did you find the gas lamps in London interesting when you were their with your brother? You had better bundle up, it is getting cold."

I left the cabin and headed for the galley where I would find our Chinese cook, Hop Sing. The captain's cabin is at the aft and the galley on the *Cold Harbor* was down one deck and behind the fore mast. I found Hop Sing and asked him if he had found anything in Boston Harbor that was fresh.

"Yes, captain, I found plenty of sea food for sale right on the docks."

"Did you find any shrimp or lobster?"

"Yes, captain, I got plenty of both."

"We have two additional guests for dinner at six bells, can you prepare one of your famous shrimp and lobster dishes?"

"In the main salon, captain? At six bells. It will be done, Sir."

"Thank you, Hop Sing. You are a wonder, I can always count on you to impress my guests."

He was beaming as I left the galley and looked for Louise on the top side. I found her talking with James Murray and David Slidell. They had been viewing the street lamps glowing throughout the city of Boston. "Can anyone join the viewing?"

"Hello, darling, I was just telling the Ambassadors that I spent several years in both London and Paris and the lights of Boston can surely compare. Did you know Ambassador Slidell can speak French?"

"No, I did not. Louise can speak excellent English, not like mine, Russian and French. I feel like my military education was lacking when they did not give us at least Spanish. I needed that during the last war."

"You were in the Mexican War, Admiral. I did not know that." James Murray said.

"Yes, I was a Fleet Admiral's aide in the Gulf of Mexico. That seems a life time ago, now. What did you do in the last war, Ambassador?"

"I was elected to the House of Representatives and

that way I missed the war altogether. I wished I had served, I heard Winfield Scott was something of a genius."

"He still is, Lincoln should keep him as an advisor. He is so angry at being forced to retire, he will not be of any help to the President."

"Scott's been replaced?"

"Yes, that happened when you were detained, Ambassadors. That is news to you, I forgot."

"Gentlemen, if you will escort me to the main salon, I would be most grateful, it is getting cold up here. Jason has refurbished the Cold Harbor after it was built in 1797. He had the Stern Galleries converted to large dining room. The deck to overhead windows provide a magnificent view from astern. We can continue to enjoy the light of the city and have warm drinks if you like."

"Mrs. Caldwell, allow me." David Slidell offered his arm and they walked ahead of us. We went down one deck and knocked on John Butler's cabin door. He joined us and we found our way aft. The main salon was warm, out of the slight breeze, and the window wall was aglow from the city lights. The ships bell began to toll, it stopped at six. Hop Sing threw open a side door and stepped into the salon and said, "Captain, the seafood surprise is ready to be served."

"Thank you, Hop Sing, we may proceed. Would you ask one of the cabin stewards to come in and take the drink orders?"

"As you wish, Captain." He disappeared and a young man in a starched white uniform appeared with a pad and a pen.

"Ma'am, what you like before dinner?"

"A white wine with dinner, for now bring me a hot chocolate!"

"Ambassador Slidell?"

"The same, thank you."

"Ambassador Murray?"

"That would be wonderful!"

"Ambassador Butler?"

"I hate to be different but could I have some southern comfort?" The cabin steward looked at me for guidance.

"That would be some my finest sipping bourbon.. I will have the same, Won Sing."

"Jason, I am beginning to like you more and more. When you arrested me, I thought you were the devil himself."

"Well, John, I was supposed to put the fear of God into you so that you would not fire on Fort Sumter 'till I was out of the White House." We both laughed as the drinks were rolled in on a cart and handed to us. "Louise, will you show us the seating for dinner? We do not want Hop Sing's special to get cold."

The *Cold Harbor* was still tied to the Boston Docks as we feasted on a culinary delight known as the 'Hop Sing Special'. It was a five course affair, equal to anything I had ever eaten in the White House. After dinner I asked John Butler if he had arranged for the London and Paris trips. He replied, "Yes, Jason, I have and I want to warn these two gentlemen on my right that the food on a British mail steamer is nothing like this!" Everyone laughed and I said, "Yes, my family found Hop Sing and his family stranded in Charleston a number of years ago. Now they are part of the crew of the Cold Harbor, my father likes his creature comforts, so we remodeled the entire ship for family business use only. It really should be replaced with a steamer, but the romance of travel will be lost. I will use a steamer if speed is essential, otherwise, I like the quiet of a sail boat and the safety of the last century Snow Architecture."

"You lost me there, Jason, I am a general, a real land lubber, what is a Snow?"

"I wish our son, James, were here General Butler, he and Jason play a game of Revolutionary War ship identification." Louise said.

"Yes, I know, Jason and I have already played that game, that is how we identified the San Jacinto."

"Now all the rest of us are lost." Louise countered.

"Right after the Trent Affair began, I drew an outline of the Sloop that stopped us."

"The Trent Affair?" Both Slidell and Murray said.

"Yes, that is what the newspapers called your detentions, you are both famous." John Butler reached into his breast coat pocket and took out a folded newspaper article from The Boston Globe, he began to read:

Captain C. Wilkes commander of the scientific expedition around the world in 1842 to 1843, and now captain of the USS *San Jacinto* recalls the arrest and detention of commissioners James M. Murray and J. David Slidell. My orders were to intercept the *Theodora* on route to Cuba from Charleston. I waited for the intercept, but by the 26 th of October, I realized that I had missed them. I then went into Cuba for a re-supply of coal and learned that Messrs. Slidell and Murray, with their secretaries and families, would depart on the 7 th of November in the English steamer Trent for Bermuda on their way to England.

"I made up my mind to leave Havana and find a suitable position. On the morning of the 8 th, her smoke was first seen; at 12 our position was to the west ward. We beat to quarters and orders were given to Lieutenant Fairfax to have two boats manned and ready to board her. He was to take Messrs. Slidell, Murray, and Butler prisoners and send them immediately aboard."

"The steamer approached and hoisted English colors. Our emblem was hoisted and a warning shot fired across her bow. She maintained her speed and showed no disposition to heave to. Then I fired another shot and this brought her to. I hailed that I intended to send a boat to board and Lieutenant Fairfax, with his armed men in two boats left to do so. The captain of the steamer declined to show

his papers and passenger-list, force became necessary. Messrs. Slidell and Murray were located, but Butler was not found. Their wives were offered my cabin on the San Jacinto, but they refused and remained on the Trent. They and their luggage were then taken aboard. The Trent was suffered to proceed on her way to Bermuda.

It was my intension to take possession of the Trent and tow her to Key West as a prize for resisting the search and carrying these passengers, who had no federal identification, no passports. But the large number of passengers on board bound for Europe, who would be put to great inconvenience, decided me to allow them to proceed to Bermuda. We then proceeded to Hampton Roads and after taking on more coal and reporting to the Navy Department, I continued on to Boston. I handed over the prisoners to the commandant of Fort Warren.

Gideon Welles, Secretary of the Navy, approved Captain Wilke's course in the following quote: "I congratulate you on your safe arrival and especially do I think you have done a great public service . The two individuals that you have detained have been conspicuous in the conspiracy to dissolve the Union and it is well known that when seized by you they were on a mission hostile to the government and the country. Your conduct in seizing these public enemies was marked by Naval intelligence and has the emphatic approval of this department."

"We really have been out of touch, what else has happen?" Slidell said.

"I can fill you in on the Federal side, if John will give you the Confederate?"

"Everything that I have is either classified, or of no great importance. But I would love to know what the Federal side thinks is important the last two months."

I laughed and began a run down of all the defeats for the Army of the Potomac. I did not mention the actions of the United States Navy and Marines in South Carolina because John Butler had the same sadness in his eyes and a pained look on his face. I finished with, "And that is all I know about current events in the last two months." As the last word came out of my mouth, I could feel the ship start to pull away from the docks.

"Gentlemen, we have a begun our trip south. Everyone and everything on the Cold Harbor is at your beckon call. If you need anything during the night, there is a steward on duty, just pull your bell cord and he will answer. Until then, you are free to move about the ship. She is 175 feet long and 40 feet in beam so you will not get very far if you like to walk and explore. The lower holds are for cargo we have unloaded some in Boston and some remains. Above that are two passage ways in which you can barely stand. It is a working space for ropes, metal cables, capstans, tiers, winches and what not. It is definitely not a place for dress clothes. There are two main decks above that and you are welcome to explore anywhere you like. Meals can be brought to your cabin or you can eat with Louise and me here in the main salon. The meals are plain, not fancy like tonight, there is also a crew salon, where you will find coffee and snacks nearly any time of the day or night."

"Louise, have I missed anything that they should know?"

"Only that Captain Jacob is really in charge, not my husband. If he gives you an order, it is for your safety and well being, follow it explicitly. That was really hard for me to understand when I first

sailed on the Cold Harbor." She said with a smile. "The Cold Harbor is the safest ship I have ever traveled on and it will get us home even through a hurricane."

"Louise, we need to give these Confederates some time alone to get caught up with what they have missed in last two months. Good night, gentlemen."

We retired to our cabin and Louise said, "What did you think of David Slidell, he is an interesting man."

"Stay away from him, he probably pinches!"

"His French is better than mine and I do not think he is from New Orleans as he claimed. Can you find out more about him, Jason. He may be a Yankee spy."

"Oh, Louise, you are as bad as John Butler, that is what he thinks."

"He does? What do you think James Murray thinks?"

"James Murray only thinks about James Murray." I said with a smile.

The next morning we did not see our three guests in the main salon. Noon came and went and still no sign of them. "Do you think we should go to their cabins and check to see if they are alright?"Louise asked.

"I will have one of the stewards knock and say he wants to change the bed linen, he will report back if anything is a miss."

In a few minutes the steward returned and said all three were sound a sleep. " They look healthy, they rolled over when I opened the cabin door but did not awake."

"Thank you, Won Sing."

"Jason?"

"Yes, Louise?"

"Why not go back to our bed and change our linens?"

Sea air always had this affect on Louise and I made a mental note to sail with her more often. We awoke in the middle of the afternoon, got dressed and took a walk on the open decks. We stood by the Hammock Rail and gazed out to sea. "Jason, do you think we will always be in love?"

"It took us thirty-eight years to meet. A year to get to know each other. We got married at sea. We had our honeymoon aboard ship. I think if I can keep you at sea we will last fifty years. What do you think?"

"I think fifty-five!" She stood close and I wrapped my great coat around both of us. "Jason, do you want to have another child?"

"We can see if we can find a children's home in Bermuda, if you like."

"We will not need a children's home, Jason."

"Why not? Do you want to get a child from Pennsylvania?"

"No, we will get it from me! I want to call her Carol."

"And if it is a boy, we will call him Carl."

11

Lincoln's Council of War
January 1862

On January 11, 1862, President Lincoln contacted his National Affairs Committee and requested that they meet with him in the White House. Jason thought that the President had finally decided to meet the committee in person, instead of dealing with only him through the State Department. He was wrong. Three days earlier a group of Republican Senators had met with him in the White House. They were critical of Lincoln's conciliatory manner toward the seceded states of the South. In particular, they doubted that General McClellan was the correct choice for General-in-chief. He was a democrat, he had a slow pace in moving across the Potomac, and he was unconcerned about the defeats at Bull Run and Ball's Bluff. They indicated that Lincoln's assumption of dictatorial powers and the arrest of Maryland citizens was un-American. They told him that they saw no choice but to provide a Congressional Joint Committee on the Conduct of the War, to oversee the president to root out corruption and inefficiency in the Union Army and Navy.

Lincoln indicated that such a committee already existed, would they like to join the National Affairs Committee? They indicated that they would like to appoint three nonvoting members for coordination with their committee. Lincoln said that would be alright if he could appoint nonvoting members from the National Affairs Committee for coordination, also. It was agreed that Franklin Wade would serve as Chairman, Joint Committee and nonvoting member of Jason Caldwell's Committee. Zachariah Chandler and George Julian would also serve. Lincoln appointed Jason Caldwell, JP Morgan and John Nesbitt, who he had forgotten was deceased and he had not yet replaced.

When Jason Caldwell received this information in the diplomatic pouch, he wrote to the Secretary of State, Seward. He explaining that he would not accept the three members of the Joint Congressional Committee as oversight to his committee. His committee reported directly to the President and he would resign before he accepted them. He also indicated that he would poll his committee, but he doubted anyone would want to serve with or on a Congressional Oversight Committee. He also suggested that the President ignore the committee and get on with the prosecution of the war. He further stated that the so called corruption of the war department could

be solved by the removal of the Secretary of War, Simon Cameron. "He would make an excellent Ambassador to Moscow!" wrote Admiral Caldwell on January 17, 1861. "It is also time for the President to decide how he wants to divide and conquer the Confederacy. The fastest way to end the war is to split the Confederacy into two parts. The western commander should seize the Mississippi River and all the forts along it. New Orleans should be taken by the Navy. The Navy should supply gun boats and marines for the western commander. The most capable General for this is US Grant."

"My committee has suggested that the eastern commander should cross the Potomac and march towards Richmond. If Richmond is taken, then the Confederacy will have to move its capital and the government will be thrown into confusion. The committee also suggests that the General-in-chief should not be the eastern commander. If General McClellan is unable or unwilling to accept direction from the Commander-in-chief of the Armed Forces he should be replaced with someone who understands who is in command."

The following message arrived from the State Department:

TO: Rear Admiral Jason Caldwell, Bermuda Station

FROM: The Department of State and The White House

SUBJECT: Receipt of eyes only President, January 21, 1861

The White House has indicated to Senator Wade that no members of the National Affairs Committee have agreed to serve as nonvoting members of his committee. And further that no Congressional members will be accepted on the National Affairs Committee. The President has therefore stated that he will not accept any over sight from Congress. The separation of powers stated in the US Constitution clearly set the military guidance with the Administrative Branch of Government.

He, therefore, has made the following appointments without congressional approval:

1) Simon Wade appointed Ambassador to Russia,

2) Edwin Stanton appointed Secretary of War,

3) General Halleck western theater commander of the Army,

4) Admiral Caldwell western theater commander of the Navy,

5) General-in-chief has been absolved, theater commanders report Secretary of War,

6) George McClellan appointed eastern theater commander of the Army,

7) Benjamin Hagood appointed eastern theater commander of the Navy.

You will report to the Gulf of Mexico to assume your command within thirty days. Assistant minister Jerome Lewis will maintain his station on Bermuda and report to you. You are to return to Bermuda as soon as the western naval operations are complete.

I sat and read the message again. "Well, Jerome, my big mouth just got me in trouble again."

I handed him the message. He read it and said.

"Your newly pregnant wife is not going to like this depending upon how long the capture of the Mississippi takes."

"The sooner I get started, the sooner I can get back to Bermuda." And we sent the following:

TO: Gideon Welles, Secretary of the Navy, Army Navy Building

FROM: Rear Admiral Jason Edwin Caldwell, Bermuda Station

SUBJECT: Assuming Western Theater Command, January 27, 1862

I will need sea transport from Havana, Cuba to New Orleans. Request the USS San Jacinto if it is on station the above date. I would like orders for Flag Officer Andrew H. Foote to contact General US Grant on the upper Mississippi to coordinate his flotilla consisting of the USS Cincinnati, Essex, Carondelet, and De Kalb plus the wooden gun boats Conestoga, Lexington and Tyler. Foote is to place his marines under Grant for land action against Fort Henry on the Tennessee River. This action should commence on or before February 10, 1862. If action is delayed for any reason, appoint Flag Officer John C. Halston as his replacement.

Following the fall of Fort Henry, which is little more than a pile of dirt, the Navy units are commanded to proceed to Fort Donelson. This Fort is commanded by the former Secretary of War, John Floyd. Please relay to General Grant that Floyd is a coward, demand his unconditional surrender. He is to be arrested on a federal warrant and taken to Washington City to stand trial for treason under the Buchanan Administration.

Following the fall of Fort Donelson, the Navy will proceed to Nashville and capture the store of supplies contained in that city. This action should be completed by April 1, 1862. If General Grant is in disagreement with any of these objectives, then the Navy support is to be withdrawn. The Navy in the Western Theater will support only those Army Generals who will advance and capture.

New Orleans will be attacked after the Tennessee campaign so that Commodore Foote can proceed down the Mississippi towards New Orleans. I would like orders for Flag Officer David Farragut to proceed into the Gulf of Mexico to meet me at or near the Mississippi Delta. While David is over sixty years of age, I have served with him in the gulf in the last war, he knows how to break through the Confederate Naval lines and sail up and into New Orleans. If action is delayed for any reason, appoint Commodore David Porter as his replacement.

I leave Bermuda for Cuba aboard the Cold Harbor. When in Havana, I will be able to send and receive mail by steamer. I will report success or failure of missions as soon as possible, after actions will be sent by ships pouch. This means that you will probably read about the success or failure of these actions in the newspapers before you receive my reports. It is important to note that the success of these actions will be the efforts of Admirals Foote and Farragut, only the failure will be my fault for not planning and executing the mission in a timely manner. The ship yards in New Orleans are constructing modern steel plated battleships that will destroy the Union Navy if this is not captured or destroyed.

"Jerome, please copy the Secretary of War, Edwin Stanton and Secretary Seward, eyes only the President."

"Admiral?"

"Yes."

"Good to see the warrior again, Sir."

"Let us hope that my wife feels the same way, Jerome. I need to be back by late May or early June or I will miss the birth."

"Sir, you are the Western Theater Commander, you can come and go wherever and whenever you like. No one can question your actions unless he is the Secretary of War."

"Good point, Jerome, see you in May then."

Captain Jacob had me in Havana a day before the San Jacinto pulled into port. It was February 10, 1862, and I needed to get to New Orleans before the action started on the Tennessee River. The new captain of the USS San Jacinto said he needed to stay a week in Havana. I replied, "We leave in two hours. If you are unable to comply with my orders than your executive officer just became the captain of this ship." His eyes grew wide and he said, "Aye, aye, Sir."

"Tom, you and Sam get your gear aboard. I will handle getting the ten little Indians on board. We had become accustomed to calling the marine guard detachment in Bermuda the ten little Indians. They had served with distinction until Allen Pinkerton had sent us ten policemen to replace them last year. Now they did odd jobs for Jerome or me as we needed them. I figured I would need all the help I could get to start fires under Navy butts from here to the upper Mississippi.

The cruise from Havana up into the Gulf was uneventful and we linked with Admiral Farragut in three days. I transferred my flag from the San Jacinto onto

Farragut's Ship of the Line.

"Permission to come aboard?"

"Permission granted, Admiral Caldwell", David Farragut returned my salute.

"What is the status of Commodore Foote's forces on the Mississippi, Admiral?"

"They have linked with Grant, the iron sided Cincinnati, Essex, Carondelet and De Kalb should be fine but there are a pitifully small group of gunboats with too many marines crammed on board. If any of the boats are hit, there will be a great loss of life."

"I feared as much, in my orders to Commodore Foote, I suggested taking any small boats that he could find along the Tennessee under the Confiscation Act."

"Well, he must have done that, because Fort Henry has fallen and so have several newly constructed ones between Henry and Donelson. As you indicated they were poorly defended and Foote has a large number of captured and wounded enemy that are slowing him down."

"How often do you send and receive the mail pouches?"

"Everyday since the campaign began, Admiral."

"Excellent, how soon can a message reach Foote?"

"I would guess more than a month while the fighting is current, after that a message should find him in a couple of weeks."

"The Navy needs to do something about communications, the time required is ridiculous." I looked at David Farragut and he was smiling. "What?" I said.

"I remember an Admiral's Aide in the last war saying the same thing right here in the Gulf. It has not improved a whit, has it!"

"No, Sir. It has not. I still need to get a message off to Foote to congratulate his taking of the forts before Donelson."

As I sat down to write, Foote was advancing on Fort Donelson with his iron clads, gun boats and towed boats full of marines. Fort Donelson was not a quickly constructed pile of dirt and the stone walls stayed intact while the iron clads could not make any penetration. The cannon fire from the fort put the Essex out of the fight with 42 killed. In sharp fighting, Foote's marine force was driven backward as General Grant watched through his field glasses. He ordered a counterattack by his army forces, this caught the confederate defenders out in the open and sent them reeling back into the fort. These Confederate forces were led by General Gideon Pillow and when he reported what had happened to the fort commander, John Floyd, he was shaken. Grant knew Pillow was a political appointee and Foote knew that an arrest warrant waited for Floyd. As Grant and Foote discussed how to take the fort with their combined forces, two things happened. Nathan Forrest, a Confederate cavalry officer ordered his men to mount and break through the lines to protect the supply depot at Nashville. During this action, both Floyd and Pillow deserted in the face of the enemy to save themselves. Command now rested with Simon Buckner. He decided to request the terms of surrender from the combined Union forces.

General Grant replied with the following which was to make him famous: "Sir: Yours of February 16, 1862, proposing armistice and appointment of commissioners to settle terms of the capitulation, is received. No terms other than Unconditional Surrender can be accepted. I propose to move immediately upon your works." The fall of Fort Donselson was front page news and the reporters decided that Grant's initials stood for Unconditional Surrender. General Buckner was quoted as saying the initials stood for Unchivalrous and Sanctimonious.

Foote and Grant now had thousands of prisoners, some able bodies and some wounded. The wounded were loaded onto the boats that the marines had towed to battle in and the marines joined the army of Grant for the march to Nashville, last objective in the northern Mississippi campaign of 1862. The able bodied prisoners were told to march between an armed federal troop. Grant ordered his men to cut willow branches from the Tennessee river banks and the Confederates carried these like rifles. From a distance the army looked twice its size. On February 25, 1862, Grant's army approached the city of Nashville. When scouts saw the size of the army, they surrendered without firing a shot. The campaign of the northern Mississippi was over for Grant. He took the supplies stored there and locked the confederate prisoners in the empty warehouses. Foote continued down the Mississippi towards New Orleans.

On board the USS Hartford, flag ship of Farragut's fleet of seventeen ships, Jason watched as, Farragut, veteran of the War of 1812, the Mediterranean and Mexican Wars led his fleet into one of the greatest naval battles of the Civil War. Before the engagement of the Confederate defenders they faced numerous obstructions, including fire ships, these were barges that were piled with wood and set ablaze. A large iron chain was strung across the river from Fort Philip to Fort Jackson on the other side. For six days and nights these forts were pounded by mortars from flat bottom barges by Commodore David Potter. They were reduced to rubble. As Farragut's fleet advanced, he commanded six sloops of war, sixteen gun boats, twenty mortar barges and five other vessels. He continued to pour cannon fire into the fifteen Confederate ships which lie in wait. When it was over, Farragut had run the gauntlet of the forts and opposing fleet with the loss of only one ship, 37 men killed and another 147 wounded. This was less than the losses of Foote on the upper Mississippi.

On the morning of April 25, 1862, Farragut's ships steamed into a defenseless New Orleans. Jason stood on board to see and later write, "desolation, ships and steamers destroyed all in a common blaze, along with 20,000 bales of cotton, coal and cord wood. The *CS S Mississippi*, stood in the ship yards uncomplete, its iron ribs like a decayed animal dead upon the prairie." General Benjamin Butler stood beside Jason and said, "I will be in the unfortunate situation of having my forces try to occupy New Orleans."

"Yes, your job will be to seize the US Mint and the rest of the land objectives outlined from the War Department. Yours is the real job of the capture of New Orleans. I will leave my detachment of marines and you will decide when it is safe for them to advance up the river to meet Foote."

I handed him a letter from the White House similar to the one President Buchanan had made for me to use in Charleston. He read it and said, "I think Officer Schneider will be telling me when he is ready to leave for the meeting with Commodore Foote!"

THE WHITE HOUSE
Washington, City

January 15, 1862

To whom it may concern:

Rear Admiral Jason Edwin Caldwell and Warrant Officer Thomas Q. Schneider, USN, in connection with their mission for me, will travel to such places at such times as they feel appropriate, accompanied by such staff as they desire.

Warrant Officer Schneider is granted a Top Secret/ White House clearance, and may, at his option, grant such clearance to those he meets on my behalf.

US Military and governmental agencies are directed to provide Officer Schneider with whatever support he may require.

A. Lincoln

Abraham Lincoln
President of the United States

"Officer Schneider is unique, I trust him with my messages and orders for Commodore Foote. I have left my orders for Admiral Farragut to split his fleet, the sloops of war will stay here in New Orleans for your protection, the gun boats and other vessels are to proceed up the Mississippi to join with Commodore Foote."

12

Return to Bermuda
May 1862

On May 10, 1862, Sam and I boarded the USS San Jacinto for passage to St. George, Bermuda. I had sent my after action reports, but the newspapers were full of the accounts of the western campaign. I doubted that my reports would cause much of a stir. When the USS San Jacinto docked in Bermuda, Sam and I stepped onto the pier. The San Jacinto pulled quickly away knowing its reputation among the British. We were greeted by our families, even Louise who looked like she was going to have twins. I put my arms around her and held her close, not wanting to hurt the baby.

"Give me and her a hug!"

"I do not want to start labor."

"I am fine, the doctor at the hospital in Hamilton says I am healthy as a horse, he says we should have more children."

"No, Louise, three is enough, just as your brother said it was!" We both laughed at this shared memory.

Louise could not walk very far before she had to sit on a bench and rest, but we made it to the square in St. George and caught a carriage to Caldwell Place. We kissed for a long time. "Oh, Jason, we are going to be so happy with our family here in Bermuda." She put her head on my shoulder and fell asleep. We stopped under the portico at the Inn and another crowd of people were there. I thanked them all for coming and put Louise in her bed for a nap. I returned to the dining room to find Jerome Lewis waiting for me.

"Hello, Jerome, there are 42 rooms in this place and you decided to rest here?" It was a running joke from our White House days and Jerome smiled and said, "I brought some after actions for you to read. I think you will find them interesting."

"Did you summarize them for me, Jerome, I am too tired to read them all."

"I did, the page on top is all you need to read for now."

AFTER ACTION REPORTS: January - May 1862

1-11 Lincoln calls for a Union offensive in General War Order No. 1

At the request of the President, General McClellan made a plan of operations. It was his belief that the decisive struggle would be fought in Eastern Virginia. He drew up a plan of support for his efforts to take Confederate forces away from Virginia to defend the western area along the Mississippi. He urged that western Virginia be allowed to break from Virginia and form their own free state, which would support the Union. Likewise he urged eastern Tennessee to break from western to form another support area for the Union. He urged a military campaign along the Tennessee and Mississippi rivers. He suggested that all Confederate strongholds along these rivers be seized and held. Troops should be sent to West Virginia, Baltimore and Fort Monroe should be occupied with a sufficient force kept within call of Washington to hold it secure. By capturing the cities of Richmond, Charleston, Savannah, New Orleans, Montgomery, Pensacola and Mobile, the Confederacy would be driven to the wall and would see the hopelessness for further resistance.

2-13 West Virginia Constitutional Convention is formed seceding from Virginia

By this action, federal troops had taken command of West Virginia and had driven all Confederate troops from the state. The Confederacy responded by sending General John B. Floyd to reinforce General Wise at Lewisburg, on the Greenville River. When General Floyd faced federal forces in the field, a ten hour battle killed seventy-five per cent of the troops he commanded. During the night he fled the field. The remnants of the forces driven from West Virginia had been gathered at Monterey and were placed under the command of General Robert Lee.

2-16 Fort Donselson surrenders (this is what you sent to Washington).

2-25 Nashville surrenders (this is what you sent Washington)

3-9 Battle of Hampton Roads considered a moral victory by Admiral Hagood

While you were commanding in the wester theater, a battle between the Monitor and the Merrimac occurred near Norfolk Harbor. The Merrimac sunk one Union vessel and nearly destroyed several others before being badly damaged itself. It was rechristened the Virginia and then sunk to prevent capture.

3-11 General McClellan is demoted in rank

The reshuffling of command results in a demotion/ promotion for McClellan. He is no longer general-in-command, because he refuses to see the big picture coming from the White House, he is given command of the eastern theater- Army Operations.

4-4 McClellan begins Peninsular Campaign, advances between James and York rivers

In its first major offensive, the Army of the Potomac advances toward Yorktown on the peninsula between the James and York rivers. Little or no resistance encountered.

4-7 Grant wins at Pittsburgh Landing, Tennessee (Shiloh)

Two days of furious fighting and tremendous casualties (Federal: 1,735 dead, 7,882 wounded and out of action for rest of war, 4,044 missing and assumed dead; Confederate: 1,728 dead, 8,012 wounded, 959 missing) end when Grant forces General Beauregard to withdraw after the death of the commanding Confederate General Albert Sidney Johnston.

4-7 Island Number Ten, falls to Foote on Mississippi, Union controls Upper Mississippi

Before meeting Grant at Shiloh, General Johnston

left a force to defend Island No. 10 (an earthworks fort). A combined land and naval attack was made by Commodore Foote. Commander Walke, of the *Carondelet* volunteered to lead the attack. The *Pittsburg* pounded the batteries of the fort taking out two ten inch columbiads, four eight inch guns, five thirty-two pounders and five sixty-four pounders, 5000 men surrender to Foote.

4-10 Fort Pulaski outside Savannah falls to General Gilmore of eastern army command

In less than two days, the imposing masonry structure near the mouth of the Savannah river is reduced to rubble, there were no Confederate survivors.

4-10 Lincoln signs a congressional resolution to free slaves in Washington City

4-25 New Orleans falls to Farragut, he proceeds up to Natchez (this is your report)

5-4 McClellan occupies Yorktown, Virginia

5-12 Natchez falls to Farragut (this is your report)

5-14 McClellan stops five miles from Richmond, says he faces overwhelming forces

"It appears that there is a war on more than one front, that will shorten the war, the south is not equipped to fight on two fronts."

"Do you think Washington will realize how close they came to having the CSS *Mississippi* and her sister ships destroy the blockade, Admiral?"

"No, they probably think they can fight them to a standstill like at Hampton Roads. We will never see wooden ships built for the Navy again, an era has passed. Just like steam engines replaced the sail, steel has replaced the wood building, except for pleasure craft."

"What do you think your next assignment will be, Admiral?"

"The Mississippi River is in Union hands except for Vicksburg. It may take General Grant some time to completely split the Confederacy into two parts. I am sure that the Secretary of the Navy will want a plan other than a 'siege and starve them out' plan. Foote should be able to patrol the river north to south if we can find him enough gun boats. I assigned Tom and his detachment to a tour of duty with Foote. I will send a letter through Secretary Welles asking if he needs extra officers and plans for the seizure of docks on either side of the river within the Confederacy."

"What if something happens involving England again?"

"That would be Ben Hagood's decision, it is in the eastern theater of naval operations."

"Do not tell Louise this Jerome, but I am home only for the birth of our baby. I may have to return to Washington to command the western theater of naval operations soon."

"Your secret is safe with me, Sir."

"When the baby is born and the war is under control, we might move back to Pennsylvania and I can take long weekends by train. I have to wait and see what the Secretary of War has in mind."

I sent the following to the Secretary of war:

TO: Edwin Stanton, Secretary of war, the Army Navy Building

FROM: Jason Caldwell, Commander Western Naval Theater

SUBJECT: End of naval campaign to free Mississippi and Tennessee River Basins

At this time both rivers are in control of USN surface craft. This does not mean that there is no Confederate boat traffic. My standing orders are to capture or destroy any Confederate vessels that our patrols contact. All shore batteries have been silenced except Vicksburg, Mississippi. As of this writing the city is surrounded by the Army under General Grant. The river is blocked so no supplies can reach the docks. Office Schneider and his detachment have penetrated the city and report that they can last only a matter of weeks. His last report is attached for you reference.

I wish to recommend the following officers for meritorious service to their country:

Admiral David Farragut: I continue to be amazed by what this flag officer has done in the last few months: the absolute destruction of the Confederate Fleet in the Gulf, the capture of the cities of New Orleans, Natchez, Memphis and finally Vicksburg.

Captain Andrew Foote (acting Commodore): the capture of Fort Henry, Fort Donelson, the city of Nashville and the siege of Vicksburg. I recommend that his first star be awarded with the removal of the acting Commodore status.

Brigadier General US Grant: I am directly opposed to the recommendation from General Halleck. Grant is functioning at the level of a three star, not a one star. I recommend that he be promoted to the rank of Major General and transferred to the eastern theater of operations for the Army. He wins battles! He does not coddle the enemy, either they surrender or he kills them - that is what war is in its simplest terms.

Warrant Officer Thomas Schneider: The United States Marine Corps has no finer officer than this man. I desire that this officer be promoted so that he can become an Admiral's aide, he has functioned in this capacity since my assignment as western naval commander.

Captain Jerome Lewis: This officer is presently the acting foreign minister to Bermuda, it is time to promote him for his service in this capacity. The acting should be removed so that he can become the foreign minister. A joint recommendation from you and Secretary Seward to the President should accomplish this so that I may focus my full attention upon the war effort.

Three weeks later the following was received from Secretary Stanton:

TO: Rear Admiral Jason Caldwell, USN

FROM: Edwin Stanton, Secretary of War

SUBJECT: Recommendations from the President to the Congress

At this writing the following are awaiting Congressional Approval:

1) Promotion of US Grant to Major General United States Army, commander western army

2) Promotion of David Farragut to three star flag officer, commander western naval theater

3) Promotion of Andrew Foote to two star flag officer, commander western naval theater

4) Promotion of Jason Edwin Caldwell to four star flag officer, assignment Army Navy Building Undersecretary of the Navy

5) Promotion of Thomas Schneider to Captain USMC and Admirals Aide, Washington City

Under separate cover from the State Department, you should receive notification of the appointment of Jerome Lewis as foreign minister to Bermuda. You are hereby ordered to report for duty three months after the birth of your third child in Bermuda.

PS

Jason, you have performed your duties and have succeeded beyond our hopes and dreams here in Washington. Congratulations on your appointment and I will see you when you report here.

Ed Stanton

13

Davis's Council of War
June 1862

In Richmond, President Davis was frustrated. The Confederate armies were successful in many of the battles fought to date. The Confederate navy was another matter. When the war began, there were only ninety vessels in the United States navy, and of these, twenty-seven were out of commission. Twenty-one vessels were unfit for service, leaving only forty-two in commission. Of these forty-two only eleven carried one hundred and thirty-four guns, were in northern harbors. The rest had been scattered around the globe or were in southern harbors. The total number of officers of all grades in the navy, August 1, 1861, was fourteen hundred and fifty-seven. Three hundred and twenty-two officers resigned and entered the service of the Confederate Navy.

By July, 1862, President Davis now understood that the war would be won or lost by his navy. He ordered his government to begin at once to replace its naval power lost at New Orleans and Hampton Roads. Merchant vessels were bought from England and converted into war vessels. Construction was begun on eight additional sloops-of-war at the Jacksonville, Florida ship yards. Numerous contracts were let in Mississippi and Alabama for heavily armed gun boats. These were known as the "ninety-day boats", because they were begun and completed in that period. The same vigor was shown in the building of "double-end" side wheelers for river and ocean service.

As he addressed his council of war he said, "We have all learned of the glorious record of 'Old Ironsides' from our history lessons. Let us build the same kind of war vessels and place men of honor to serve upon them. Nearly all of the ports within the Confederacy were taken by us in 1861. Let us now pledge to retake those taken from us. Let us begin the process with Fort Pickens in Florida. I am today ordering General Anderson to capture the town of Santa Rosa, a mile distant. He will approach from land while the remaining Gulf fleet will attack from the sea."

"If that is successful we shall take Fort Hatteras and Fort Clark with our surviving Atlantic Fleet. I have given the mission of the recapture of Charleston via Beaufort to Admiral Josiah Tattnall.

What I need from each of you here today is the following:

Vice President Stephens, I would like to raise the capital for a new navy via foreign contacts, begin with England, France and Russia.

Secretary Toombs, I want you to visit the countries that agree to loan us funding for the rebuilding of our navy, thank them and get their advice on how to improve our foreign trade.

Secretary Memminger, I want you to replace the assets lost at New Orleans, see if we can interest anyone in the western states to help us.

Secretary Walker, continue with the ground campaign by allowing our Generals to cross the Potomac and fight the Union armies in Pennsylvania, Maryland, West Virginia or anywhere we have the advantage. It is no longer a defensive struggle on our part, we must crush the Union and replace it with our own.

Secretary Mallory, it will be your job to oversee the rebuilding of the Confederate navy and the undermining of the Union navy. Send your naval combat troops to destroy Union shipping in northern ports. Ask for volunteers to move into northern harbor cities so that they can report the activities of the Union navy.

Secretary Reagen, try to improve our ability to send timely commands from the battlefields to the government and return.

Attorney-General Benjamin, appoint a committee to increase the borrow limit authorized by our congress from $15,000,000 to $30,000,000 and to accept another 100,000 volunteers. We need to conscript another 100,000 before the end of the year."

The room was deadly quiet, usually a cabinet gathering was loud and opinionated during its several hour duration. "Mister President?"

"Yes, Secretary Walker, you have a question?"

"Why should we fight so far from home? The Army of the Potomac is led by an idiot! Why not let him come up into Virginia as far as he wants and then crush him? He left Washington by ship to land at Jamestown with a modest size infantry and no naval support. He could have come straight down through Alexandria, Virginia, and captured Richmond months ago. We should hope that the Union forces are led by party Generals who would rather be in a Washington parade. We have seasoned Generals who have graduated from West Point who lead our armies. Lincoln is not a military man, he is a lawyer and a do-gooder. People who have been around him for any time will tell you he is an idealist, but has no practical knowledge on how to get things done. I would consider your idea of invading the north, ill-conceived and if you continue with this, I will resign my office. Let them come to us. We can kill them in familiar surroundings easier than we can travel hundreds of miles. The death rate at Shiloh proves that the leadership of the north cares nothing for the lives of their soldiers."

"Does anyone agree with Secretary Walker?" Jefferson Davis asked.

A chorus of seven voices said, "I do Mister President."

"Mr. President, as your Secretary of the Navy, I would advise along similar lines for the time being. We need to construct more vessels and then attack, but not to retake ports that we have already lost. We need to be thinking about how we can protect our rivers and trading ports. Why would we want to sail up the Chesapeake and fire upon the White House as the British did in 1812? Let us concentrate on building blockade runners to get our products to market in England and France."

"I agree, as your Vice President, I should be trying to encourage the Europeans to assist us through a lend or lease of war materials, ships, armaments of all types. We can buy ships faster than we can build them."

"Wait, wait, I see your positions and you can do all that besides what I have suggested. The biggest mistake in my life was not letting Stonewall Jackson take his army from Manassas into Washington City to arrest Lincoln and end this mess a year ago. Look what Jackson did this March in the Shenandoah Valley. As a result, the Union army fled across the Potomac to protect Washington. The Union army is still unled and disorganized. It will crumble if attacked and pursued across the Potomac."

"We understand you are upset about the failure in the Mississippi and Tennessee river campaigns, Mister President. Our Generals there were political appointments, Floyd has turned tail and run in the last two engagements, he should be arrested and court marshaled along with that Pillow fellow."

"We have no need to panic, at this point the war has progressed according to our schedule, we do not need to upset that schedule by trying to recapture what the Union forces have done. Why not meet again in a few months and evaluate what we have accomplished?"

"You have given me new confidence. I shall not attempt to undertake the winning of the war single handed!" Laughter followed the President's comment and peace was restored to the council. "I would like to consider our contact in Bermuda. One year ago, I sent General John Butler through the lines at Manasses to contact the White House and offer our hand in friendship and peace to Mr. Lincoln. He never spoke to Mr. Lincoln, he could not get anyone other than his body guard to respond. I think Lincoln wanted to deny the offer from us. John Butler did meet with his National Affairs Advisor, an Admiral Caldwell, who was born in

Beaufort, South Carolina, and graduated from West Point. Caldwell is now the foreign minister to Bermuda where John Butler is now our representative to Bermuda. As you may remember, from the Trent Affair, that it was settled by the intervention of Caldwell and Butler. They have maintained a friendly and cordial working relationship ever since. With your permission, I would like to use that relationship to our advantage. Minister Butler can inquire if Caldwell has any contact with Lincoln through the department of state. If we draft an offer of an armistice between our two nations, maybe Lincoln will consider it this time."

"An armistice would give us time to rebuild our navy and recruit infantry for our armies, Mr. President. That is an excellent idea. Even if Lincoln rejects our offer again, it still slows down their efforts to create new free states, like West Virginia. It concerns me that we may will be two nations which have divided states like; North & South Missouri, East & West Tennessee. We still have slave holding states which have not joined the Confederacy. We should approach Maryland and the others to see if they would consider joining us if an armistice is signed." Secretary Toombs said.

"I agree, we should send representatives to the western territories to see if they would like to consider statehood in the Confederacy. Utah is still not accepting federal troops on their soil. That might be an area that we can tap for funding." Secretary Memminger said.

"Yes, I like all those ideas, begin at once to explore them gentlemen. I will contact Minister Butler through the normal channels and have him meet with Caldwell in Bermuda." President Davis was smiling for the first time in several months.

He left the council of war meeting and sent the fol-lowing instructions to Bermuda through the blockade at Norfolk:

CONFEDERATE STATE OF AMERICA

Office of the President

Richmond, Virginia

June 14, 1862

Dear General Butler:

Begin the discussions with your contact in Bermuda for an armistice with the Union. The war council has approved the following guidelines:

1) immediate cease fire to go into affect July 4 th, 1862 (seems an appropriate date),

2) withdrawal of all troops from western Virginia and return of property to State,

3) removal of all enemy forces from each nation (includes harbors and rivers within state boundaries),

4) failure to accept this offer, changes our position from defensive only to an offensive position whereby we will march on Washington City.

Jefferson Davis

When this missive arrived in Hamilton, John Butler was overjoyed. He needed to meet with Jason Caldwell as soon as possible. He called his secretary into his office and said, "Did I hear that Louise and Jason Caldwell had a baby girl?"

"Yes, Sir. She delivered a baby at the Hamilton hospital last week, I think it was the seventh of June. I sent a note of congratulations for you. I know how much they both mean to you, Sir."

"Thank you, Petterson, you take good care of me. I need to walk down to front street and get a baby gift at Trimminghams for them. After that I will catch the train to St. George and walk on up to Caldwell Place and deliver it."

"Very good, Sir."

"I will gather up a few papers and be off, see you tomorrow, Petterson."

He closed and locked his office, bought a small baby thing that the clerk in Trimmingham's said was in fashion and he caught the train for Caldwell Place.

"Hello, Mrs. Whitehall, I hope I am not interrupting your business day. I have a small gift for Mrs. Caldwell and the baby. Is she at home by any chance?"

"Yes, Mr. Butler, baby Carol and the Admiral are with her in the nursery. Let me go and tell them you are here." She disappeared down a hallway and was gone for a few minutes and returned with a smiling Jason Caldwell.

"John, how good of you to call. Louise is nursing the baby, but she will meet us along side the swimming pool when she is finished and the baby is asleep." He motioned for them to exit through a set of french doors onto the pool deck.

"Have a seat John. What really brings you to see us?

You are a bachelor and not really into babies are you?"

"I must confess that you read me like a book, Jason. Of course, your joy in fatherhood can not be appreciated by a bachelor, but just seeing your face just now leads me to believe that you have never been happier."

"You are absolutely correct, my friend."

"We are friends, are we not, Jason?"

"We are."

"Then as a friend, I would like you to send this letter directly to the President of the United States."

I took the letter and read it. "Do you think this is a genuine offer of peace? Or is it a ploy to buy more time to rebuild the Confederate losses?"

"I am sure it is both. The south is exhausted with the effort required to defend itself from attack. If an armistice is put in place, both sides will rebuild and the conflict will continue again at a much larger and frightening scale. The battlefield at Shiloh had 19,357 men from both sides laying dead or in the process of dying when we took the body of General Johnston and withdrew. The reports that were given to me is that the ground was covered body to body, the results of hand to hand combat. When and how will all this end, Jason?"

I shook my head that I did not know and said, "I have been replaced here in Bermuda, John. Jerome Lewis is now your contact for peace talks. Do you want to show this offer to him?"

"No, Jason. We need to decide how to get this directly to your president."

"You are afraid that it will be buried in the State Department?"

"Yes."

"Is time critical? Can I hand carry this to my president?"

"Oh, Jason, that would be wonderful!"

"Did you make a hand written copy of this for your files? Can I carry this original?"

"Yes."

"Well, then can I offer you some southern comfort?"

"Yes, you can."

I got up to go into the dining hall and find two glasses when Louise walked over and gave me a kiss. "Thank you, Daddy."

"For what?"

"You know what for, she is asleep in her crib. The nanny is with her. I wanted to see what John brought for her."

"He is pool side, I am trying to find a bottle of bourbon to fix him a drink."

"I will be thanking him for his thoughtfulness, bring your drinks out when you finish."

I did and we had an enjoyable afternoon catching up on the changes in our lives. We told him that we were not looking forward to life in Washington City again. We would be opening the house at Seneca Hill for the household staff, Louise and the children. I would have to ride the train back and forth to Washington. I had no idea what an undersecretary did. We hoped that he would continue to write to us, mail still passed from Bermuda to the Union. We told him that we had lost our homes in Beaufort, they were now government property, they might be returned as I had already petitioned the war department that they had seized property of a serving United States Admiral. I was told that the house at 353 Bay Street did not belong to me. It belonged to someone named Louise Buchanan. He laughed and said she did not need another house at the moment.

14

Caldwell Place
September 1862

We were scheduled to leave for my service at the Army Navy building in Washington on September 7, 1862. I planned on meeting with the president as soon as I arrived. My extended family decided to stay in Bermuda. My mother and father were looking for a larger house on one of the islands that dotted the Great Sound. Their house, that they had purchased in St. Davids was for sale. I did not know if they would ever return to South Carolina. Their fortune was safe in the Bank of Bermuda and they had applied for British citizenship. My brother, Robert, was another matter, he was restless and wanted to see the war damage in Port Royal, Beaufort and on Pollawanna plantation. He did not want to be a British citizen and I understood that. I could work out my frustrations with the war by trying to do something to stop or shorten it. He could only sit and wait for it to end. I decided to talk to him and I walked to his living quarters in Caldwell Place.

"Robert, I need your help."

"Sure, your departure date is coming, need help with the sea trunks?"

"Not that kind of help. I want to start a new venture here on Bermuda."

"A business, you know I am not good with that, you and father always did the business at home."

"No, it is not a business with a lot of paper to shuffle. Robert Whitehall is my paper shuffler here in Bermuda. I want to start to raise crops here in the islands."

"What kind of crops?"

"They have to import almost everything they eat here, Robert. What would you think of renting or buying as many small plots of land as we can find to raise produce (fruits and vegetables) for sale here?"

"That makes good sense to me, Jason. We can always import those that will not grow here. First I will have to make test beds here on Caldwell Place. I need to take soil samples and have them tested for contents. I can check with the southern chain of Carribean Islands to see what grows well there, maybe we can grow bananas, that would really be something! I need to walk down to St. George and talk to the green grocer there and see what he orders and from where. Then I can ask him if he ever considered buying from someone local, like me. Jason, can I use Caldwell shipping to start bringing in some produce before we start to plant? I am going to need field hands here. Boy this is really going to take a lot of my time."

He was talking to himself by this time, I had gone looking for Louise, with a smile on my face. I was going to tell her how the Caldwell Produce Company of

Bermuda was formed and to look for the Caldwell label when purchasing her fruits and vegetables.

The last communication from Washington informed me that between June 26 and July 2, Union and Confederate forces fought a series of battles: Mechanicsville, Gaines Mill, Savage's Station, Frayer's Farm and Malvern Hill. On July 2, 1862, the Peninsular Campaign was finished and so was McClellan. On July 11, 1862, he was demoted and replaced by General Halleck for the Union forces. In August, Union General Pope was defeated at the second battle of Manasses. On August 29 th Union General Fitz-John Porter was defeated and General McDowell began the defense of Washington. Jefferson Davis's fears were calmed and a replacement Confederate Navy was never formed.

15

Army Navy Building
September 1862

It was strange returning to the building where I started my career with Navy Intelligence so many years ago. Gideon Welles was there to greet me and we sat in his office and talked about what he expected the Navy's role to be for the remainder of the war. I did not say much until he finally said, "Admiral, what is wrong? You seem to be somewhere else."

"Yes, Sir. I would like you to read this and tell me what you think." I handed him the letter that John Butler had given me to hand deliver to the president.

He read it and said, "This is dated three months ago, why have you not forwarded it to the president through the state department?"

"It is written to John Butler, the minister to Bermuda. He gave it to me to hand deliver to the president. He was afraid that it would be ignored inside the state department."

"I do not follow you, Jason."

"The one and only time I have met the president he asked me to go over to the Hay-Adams and meet with John Butler, Allen Pinkerton and Ben Hagood. The president said that an envoy from Davis was waiting to talk to an envoy representing the Union. Mr. Lincoln chose me as his envoy."

"When was this?"

"July 1861, right after the first Battle of Bull Run."

"How did a Confederate get through our lines and into Washington?"

"There were no lines of defense, anyone could have entered the city without any security check what so ever. I believe that the south sent a number of people into Washington and they are still here sending information to Richmond."

"Incredible! You know this for a fact?"

"Yes, John Butler was one of them."

"We need to get this information to the president as soon as we can, it would appear that a general invasion of the north may be upon us. Are you aware that Lincoln has replaced General Pope who was defeated at Bull Run with McClellan?"

"No, I had not heard that." We stood to walk to the White House and contact the president's scheduling secretary.

"Jason, this does not change why you were brought to the Army Navy Building to work for me. Even if the president will not see us, we have important work to be done. The Secretary of War was very impressed with your battle plan for the Mississippi and Tennessee river basins. It was the best use of land and sea assets I have ever seen. You have a knack for this, mind telling me how you came to use the Navy marines off the ships?"

"President Buchanan felt that the marines were underused, they should consist of a ground force controlled by the Navy. In the eight years that I served under Presidents Pierce and Buchanan, I used a detachment of marines wherever I went. I can not remember of any action that I have been involved in that has not included marines used as group forces. In fact, my service record shows that most of my combat experience has been on the ground, not the sea. I believe that ground forces should be moved from place to place by water, not marching for days or even weeks to get to the battlefield."

We had cleared the guard stations and were admitted to the White House. "I suppose that Allen Pinkerton will want to sit in on this?" I said.

"Allen is not at the White House, he has been assigned other duties." Gideon Welles was smiling.

"Two to see the president, Mr. Ambrose."

"What day, Mr. Welles?"

"Today, Admiral Caldwell has a letter from Jefferson Davis."

"The President of the Confederacy, Davis?"

"That is the one."

"Can I take the letter into the oval office and let President Lincoln read it and decide when he wants to see you?"

"Of course." I said. I handed the letter to him and we sat on some very small chairs that were not comfortable.

"It seems that these chairs do not encourage people to come and 'camp out here'."

I smiled remembering that Franklin Pierce had selected these chairs for the very reason stated. Mr. Ambrose returned with the letter and handed it to me.

"The President has told me to tell you that this was a very interesting letter and if Jefferson Davis would compose another up-to-date letter and send it to him here at the White House, he would read it."

"Read it?" Gideon Welles said.

"Those were his exact words Mr. Secretary."

"Can you tell him a former member of his National Affairs Committee has recommended that he try to begin a conversation with Jefferson Davis." I said.

"The president knows that you are with Secretary Welles, Admiral. He will deal directly with Mr. Davis, not through anyone else. His decision is final, gentlemen. Good day to you both."

We looked at each, shrugged our shoulders and began walking back to our offices. "Has he always been this unavailable to his cabinet members?" I asked.

"Since the death of his friend, Senator Edward Baker at Ball's Bluff, he has been depressed. He has shut most of us out of his inner circle. The only time I see him is in cabinet meetings."

"I had no idea that things were that bad here in the White House, Gideon."

"That is another reason that I asked you to resign from his advisory committee and get away from the Department of State. A hand full of men will save the Union and right now Abraham Lincoln is not one of them. Unless he can get control again, he will just react to things, not cause them to happen. I worry for sake of the Union. The armies of the Confederacy can sweep across us on land whenever they please unless a few army officers and the Navy stop them."

"My God, I had no idea!"

"You are a welcome sight here for those of us who work in the Army Navy Building, Jason. Secretary Stanton wants to greet the man who planned the Mississippi campaign, he wants to pick your brain on how to stop the Confederate invasion that is sure to come, now that Mr. Lincoln has closed the door on Jefferson Davis."

By this time we were back at his office and he said, "I will take you to Edwin Stanton's office, Jason. I think you will find him like a breath of fresh air. He has changed since he was in the President Buchanan lame duck cabinet"

"Good morning, Ed. I have Jason Caldwell with me, can we have a minute of your time?" He said as he stuck his head into Stanton's office without bothering to stop at the secretary's desk or even knock on his door.

"Yes, come right in. I want to see this four star Admiral of ours! It is good to see you again, Jason."

He held out his hand across his desk and grabbed mine with a very firm grip. "Sit down, sit down both of you. You do not look like you breath fire and spit death, Admiral."

"Sir?"

"When I asked Commodore Farragut to command a strike force into Norfolk Harbor, he refused saying he would not raise a hand against his home state. He did say, 'I would be happy to serve under Jason Caldwell who was my aide in the Mexican War. He breathes fire and spits death! Once his mind is made up, the enemy is either dead or captured. He is the Ulysses Grant of the Navy.' "

"So that is how my request for David was answered in such a short time frame. You both should have been with me at New Orleans and seen how David Farragut is still the best Admiral in the Navy."

"A mutual admiration society, he says the same thing about you!"

"So, can I use him again, if it is not in Virginia?"

"Sure, what did you have in mind?"

"I have not discussed this with Gideon, so maybe we should talk first."

"You can tell Ed, anything that you would tell me, Jason. We actually like each other. Not like the last two Secretaries of the Navy and War under the last administration. Speaking of that, did you know that John Floyd was finally arrested?"

"Yes, I heard that Jefferson Davis had ordered a court marshal."

"Now tell us how you would use David Farragut if he was not the commander in the west."

"I think the next several battles of the civil war will be fought in the north. The information that I have says that Davis must act quickly to end the war before we get midyear, 1863."

"Where did you get this information?"

"General Order: 191, from his minister to Bermuda."

"We have a copy of that from Pinkerton. Go on."

"That means he will rely on his army, not his navy. They will have long marches to get to the battlefield. I suggest that we put a smaller land force near the water as bait and maybe a Confederate General will try to attack them. We can bring both our naval fire power and marine corps to trap them and destroy the invading armies from the south."

"Interesting. How can we do this?"

"Station the armies of the north near a river or the ocean. If the south wants to dance, they will have to find us. We choose the location of all future battles. Under no conditions should we ever have another engagement without Navy involvement. Our only victories to date have been with navy coordination or command. We will be defeated whenever we have to fight single handed (army alone or navy alone), look at what happened to Ben Hagood at Hampton Roads when the navy went alone into battle, look what has happened when the army is left on its own. Fight with both hands."

"My God, Gideon, no wonder you wanted this man! From this day forward the standing orders from the White House should be, Army, where is the Navy? Navy, where is the Army? Simple, yet affective, both branches fight together." Ed Stanton was smiling.

"Well, planning is the key to any military operation, that is why I want David Farragut or Andrew Foote to plan the battles that we fight in the west. I think they will see action in Kentucy next, maybe while Ben Hagood sees a campaign in Maryland."

"Kentucy, first. Why, Kentucy?"

"I think that Davis will send the remainder of his Tennessee forces under General Bragg, into Kentucky, then swing east to invade western Virginia. We can wait until he reaches Virginia or set up an ambush along his route of march. Navy intelligence should fine out for us the probable dates and locations. I would guess late September or early October."

"Now Maryland, when and where?" Stanton asked.

"Again, it is my guess that the remainders of several armies will be joined under the command of General Lee to cross into Maryland along the upper Potomac anywhere from Sharpsburg to Brunswick. Again, armies do not move in a vacuum, as soon as there is movement naval intelligence can send word to us to set the trap. We will need many more gun boats to patrol the upper Potomac and transport the marines into fighting position."

"You mean, set our spy network run by Pinkerton to watch Generals Bragg and Lee?" Stanton quipped.

"Exactly. Whenever they move, we will know, dates and directions of march." I replied.

The discussion went on for two hours, Edwin Stanton's focus and concentration was amazing. "Admiral, you have given us your thoughts for the remainder of 1862. Any guesses on '63?" Asked Gideon Welles.

"God willing, the war will be over after the invasion of the north is crushed." I answered.

"Then I will inform the White house that the three of us expect a Confederate attack north and east from Tennessee and across the upper Potomac River into Maryland. This will be supported by our reports from intelligence agents in the field." Said Stanton.

"Why the three of us? Why not include General Halleck, he is the only four star at the present time in the Army." I said.

"And at the present time, he is the only one who is inside the inner circle of the president. I would not be surprised if he was meeting with the president and that is why he would not let us in the oval office today." Gideon Welles said.

"We need to tell you who we think the president trusts and who is in the circle. It does not leave this office, Jason, understand?" I shook my head yes and sat forward in my seat.

"We think he is taking his advice from a small group of generals headed by Halleck. Pinkerton is the spy master and he listens to him. Whenever the two sources confirm current or future events, the president reacts with general orders from the White House."

"There is no cabinet level input?"

"If the cabinet was uniformly opposed to something, in a cabinet meeting, then the president might change his mind. But none of us sitting in this office will see him on a day-to-day basis, he will not consult with or send for us on an individual basis for consultation. General Halleck sits in on every cabinet meeting as my undersecretary, even though he is not. He is an automatic consensus vote for Lincoln's positions on agenda items. You will attend the next cabinet meeting as Gideon's undersecretary to see what the reaction is from the president. We hope that he will see you as another consensus vote. What the two of us would like is for you to speak your mind, just like you have done in this meeting. Can you do that?"

"Be honest, tell the truth, try to bring the president out of his depression, yes I can do that."

"Thank you, Jason, that is the reaction that we hoped for."

"We should let Admiral Caldwell get back to his office, Ed, he has not even unpacked his things and found a billet for his aide. What is your aides name, Jason?"

"Captain Thomas Quintin Schneider of the United States Marines, Sir."

"I should have guessed that one!" replied the Secretary of the Navy.

As we walked back to Gideon's office he said, "What else do you need to begin work, Jason?"

"Several items, we must improve the speed of communication within the military. We can no longer rely on paper messages that take days or weeks to deliver. I will pay for and have installed private telegraph monitors in my office, your office, Ed's office. I already have one in my office at Seneca Hill. I will hire morse key operators for a 'basement' station here in the Army Navy Building. Right now we send and receive telegraph messages through the White House 'basement.'"

"Telegraph monitors?"

"Yes, I first saw them five years ago in Council Bluffs, Iowa. General Dodge, who I think is inside the circle with the president by the way, had one installed from the railhead to his home office. It looks like a stock market ticker and translates morse code to a small strip of paper."

"Do it. We do not need permission from the White House if the monitors are property of Caldwell International. Thank you, Jason, you have no idea how this will help me. I can send messages via the key operator from our building to whomever can receive them."

"Yes, you can send back and forth to London, if you like. I visit with Lord Napier at the Admiralty on a regular basis."

"You do?"

"Yes, that is why I know that the 8000 British Marines have not returned home. They have left Bermuda, I know that. The British ships of the line are still in Bermuda. They are waiting to get an order from Jefferson Davis to enter the Chesapeake and sail up the Potomac to burn the White House again, I am sure of it."

"You mentioned several things, what else do you need?"

"I will need the freedom to move around. I can not be effective locked inside an office here at the Army Navy Building. After the telegraph station is installed here, I will monitor things on a hourly basis. I will of course be available for cabinet meetings and other functions, but I plan to work from my office at Seneca Hill, not the office here.My aide will be sitting behind my desk here and he will keep me informed. I trust his judgement. And as you become familiar with him you will find that he functions exactly as I do."

"What if that is not satisfactory?"

"Then my career as an undersecretary has been one day long!"

"I am not sure about this, Jason."

"Why not think about it? I will return to my office and have a letter of resignation written for you, I will not date it. You keep it in your office and when my service is not satisfactory you can date it."

"That would be satisfactory, very satisfactory indeed. I am going to do the same thing and give it to the president, I am tired of sitting outside the circle. I either want to be part of the future of this country or I want to leave the future to someone that the president trusts."

"You can always come to work for Caldwell International, I know the boss!"

In two days the telegraph station for the Army Navy Building was up and running. I sent a test message to myself before boarding a train for Seneca Hill. I welcomed Tom to his new office and asked him if his family had arrived from Bermuda. He indicated that they were in transit on a Caldwell ship. On September 17, I received the following message from Tom:

Admiral, Union forces under McClellan met Lee's army in Maryland at a place called Antietam, not far from where you predicted. Admiral Hagood's gunboats produced one of the bloodiest single days of the war so far. He estimates 23,000 dead or disabled from grape shot and mortar shells. Lee has retreated back into Virginia. We doubt he will be back. We followed your plan and the advanced information contained in the Confederate General Order 191 to pinpoint enemy strength and weaknesses.

Thomas Quintin Schneider, Captain USMC

Being at home with Louise, James, Ruthie, and baby Carol was a Godsend. I found that I loved family life, especially Ruthie. She was talking a blue streak. She would run to my side and scream, "Up, daddy, up. Then she would whisper in my ear that James had hit her on the arm."

"Does it hurt? Show daddy where he hit you. I cannot see anything. Do you want me to kiss it and make it better?" I would and then sit her down to run and tell her brother James, "Daddy fixed it for me and he says if you ever hit me again, you are in BIG trouble."

Louise would then look at me and say, "I have an ouchy, daddy, can you kiss it for me and make it better?"

"Sure, where is it? No, I cannot kiss that in front of the children." And we would both burst out laughing. I found I liked being a husband and a family man.

On September 23, I received the following:

Admiral, under separate cover I am sending the preliminary text of the Emancipation Proclamation.

It will take affect on January 1, 1863.

Thomas Quintin Schneider, Captain USMC

On September 27, I received the following:

Admiral, thought you might like to know that your General Butler, the one in New Orleans, not the one in Bermuda, has just formed the first officially recognized Negro regiment. Blacks have volunteered at a rate not seen prior to this date.

Thomas Quintin Schneider, Captain USMC

These three telegrams proved that the system I had set up for communication was working. I replied to all three and sent separate congratulations to Admiral Hagood and General McClellan. There were no more messages until October 8.

Admiral, a second Confederate invasion of the North under General Braxton Bragg has been checked by Union General Don Carlos Buell at a place called Perrysville, Kentucky. Same battle plans were used. River gun boats caused second most casualties in the civil war. Bragg retreated.

When the Army Navy Command suggested that General McClellan not pursue Lee back into Virginia and be caught away from naval gun fire support, he was dismissed from military service by the president. He was replaced by Ambrose E. Burnside, an inside the circle, General. George McClellan sent me the following letter:

November 15, 1862

My dear Admiral:

Working with you these past two years have given me an insight to what our military needs are going to be in the next few years and beyond the civil war. Lincoln has a small group of advisors, as you well know, we were not part of the inner circle and, therefore, unable to reach him with what would work on the battlefields of our nation.

I have thought about this since leaving the military and I will form a committee to seek the nomination from the Democratic Party to run for the White House. I would be honored if you would run with me. Lincoln cannot be allowed to remain in the White House and prosecute the war in the way that he has. The confederacy should not be allowed to exist another day. The reconstruction of the war torn south must begin immediately.

I await your decision before I form the committee.

Faithfully yours,

George Mc Clellan

I responded with a personal letter and a letter of credit for $100,000.00.

In December I received two messages:

Admiral, December 13, 1862, General Burnside, without naval support, crossed the Potomac and attacked the Confederate fortifications at Fredericksburg, Virginia. He was routed with large Union casualties.

Thomas Quintin Schneider, Captain USMC

I responded to both Stanton and Welles asking if the inside circle was really that INANE!

Admiral. Admiral Foote reported on December 31, 1862, the Battle of Stone River, Tennessee, is over. Combined naval gun boat and army artillery fire has caused 25,000 confederate dead or disabled for the remainder of the war.

Thomas Quintin Schneider, Captain USMC

I responded to both Stanton and Welles asking when will they understand, it is a matter of numbers!

A one line response came back from the Army Navy Building.

Not this year!

16

State of the Union
Washington City, 1863

It must be admitted that the state of the Union had seen substantial progress during 1862. The important victories were Mill Spring, Forts Henry and Donelson, Pea Ridge, Shiloh, Fort Pulaski, Corinth, Roanoke Island, New Orleans, opening of the Mississippi River, Seven Pines, Antietam, Perrysville and Stone River. The Union lines had been extended across the entire State of Tennessee and it was out of the fight. Ben Hagood's blockade of the southern ports was becoming more rigid with the sinking of the following ships trying to run out of Charleston; Osiris 10/61, Peerless 11/61, Governor 11/61, Rattlesnake 3/62, Experiment 4/62, Samuel Adams 4/62, Edwin 5/62, Nellie 5/62, and Minho 10/62. There had been a vicious outbreak of the Sioux Indians in Minnesota, but troops were sent and quiet was maintained.

But the truth was that the suppression of the rebellion was no easy matter. In January, 1,300,000 volunteers had been called for, the number of vessels in the US Navy was now 600 and the war expenses now reached the total of $3,000,000 a day. Just as I had predicted to President Lincoln in July of 1861, a year's cost was now one billion, ninety-five million dollars. After both invasions of the north had been turned back, President Lincoln issued the Emancipation Proclamation.

In 1863 the government issued paper money in bills, which became known as "greenbacks", because of the color of the ink with which the bills were printed. These bills became legal tender. But because of the need for vast sums to pay war debts, the price of gold rose quickly to 285 dollars a troy ounce. This made the paper dollar worth about 35 cents in gold. Caldwell International had a huge inventory of paper bills because the gold coming out of Nevada was exchanged for paper money. A large portion of the war debt was paid by war bonds, a form of loan with interest to be repaid by the government. To aid in the sale of bonds, the National Banking system was established and Caldwell International now owned; two national banks, seven state banks, one territorial bank and one foreign bank. I figured with my net worth, I could finance about a week of the war.

I struggled with the duties of the undersecretary of the Navy. There were four Union Army Navy forces in the western theater of operations. Rosecrans/Foote near Murfreesboro, Tennessee, Grant/Farragut near Vicksburg, Mississippi, Banks, who had succeeded Butler in New Orleans and a fourth was in Arkansas, where the confederates were comparatively weak.

So far this year, the Union armies in the western theater alone had taken over 80,000 prisoners, including three major generals, nine brigadiers and about a hundred thousand pieces of military hardware. Grant summed it up best by stating: "The engagement of the enemy in five separate campaigns; (Chancellorsville, Vicksburg, Gettysburg, Chickamauga and Chattanooga), the occupation of the entire states of Mississippi and Tennessee, and the elimination of troops and materials to equip two Confederate armies have fallen into our hands."

Of all the records kept in 1863, the battle of Chickamauga was the most costly to the Union. The percentages of losses was greater than those incurred by the British army in a hundred years, including those of Waterloo and the entire Crimea War. Thirty regiments, composed of western soldiers, lost fifty percent. This percentage was more than fell in the "Charge of the Light Brigade" from British failed efforts.

Of all the records kept by the confederacy in 1863, the battle of Chancellorsville was the most costly to the south. The percentages of losses were greater than those of the Union at Chickamauga. Lee was unable to replace these losses suffered in May, before he met General Meade at Gettysburg on July 1, 1863. On November 19, 1863, Lincoln visited the battlefield and delivered his memorable "Gettysburg Address." The outcome of the war was no longer in doubt. But a strange thing happened in Washington City. General Halleck suddenly resigned and George Meade replaced him as commander of the Army of the Potomac. The inner circle was drawing ever smaller.

The President seemed less depressed and he ventured out of the White House as far as Gettysburg in Pennsylvania and around Washington City he was seen on a regular basis. He would often walk over to the Army Navy Building and talk to either his Secretary of War or his Secretary of the Navy depending upon which could answer his question at that moment. He walked into the undersecretary of the Navy in late November and asked to speak to whomever was in charge.

"The Admiral is not here, Mr. President, he is at sea with Admiral Hagood." Answered his aide, a captain in the marine corps.

"Well, tell him to stop over and see me tomorrow, will you?"

"Sir, I have no way of reaching him, he is at sea, on a ship somewhere between here and Cape Hatteras, North Carolina."

"What are they doing there? Who gave that order?"

"You did, Sir. War order no. 157. I have a copy of it right here, Sir."

"Never mind, if I gave an order, then I gave an order. Tell the Admiral that I would like to see him as soon as he returns to his office."

"Aye, aye, Sir."

"What did you say?"

"That was, Yes, Sir. In the navy, Sir."

"Well, you are not in the Navy, you are in the Army Headquarters Building, Washington City, USA."

"Yes, Mister President."

"Thank you, that was better. What did you say your name was soldier?"

"I am in the navy, Sir."

"Then what are you doing in the Army?"

"Just visiting, Sir."

"No wonder we are losing......" And the President collapsed onto the floor of Tom Schneider's office.

Tom rushed out of his office, crying, "Someone get the White House doctor." A clerk heard the cry and ran into the hallway and found a messenger to send to the White House to find the President's doctor. By the time that the doctor arrived, the President was sitting up and shaking his head.

"Did you faint again, Mister President?" The word 'again' was not lost on Tom Schneider.

"Yes, I must have. Where am I?

"In the Army Navy Building, Mr. President."

"Oh, yes. I came to see Secretary Stanton, but he was not in. So I was looking for Welles."

"This is not Secretary Welles' office, Mr. President. It is down the hall. Do you feel dizzy?"

"No, I am fine. Help me up and I can find Welles' office."

He was helped by his doctor and they left for Welles' office, Tom grabbed a pad of paper and

began writing down what was said so he could tell the Admiral what happened. He finished his notes and walked down the hall to see if Secretary Stanton was in his office. He was there.

"Excuse me, Sir."

"Yes, Captain, what can I do for you?"

"Have you been in all morning?"

"Yes, why?"

"Did the president find you? He was looking for you or Mr. Welles."

"No, I will go down to Welles' office with you, Captain."

They walked down to Welles' office and asked, "Did the president find you a few minutes ago, Gideon?"

"No, I have not seen him, what happened, Tom?"

"He fainted in my office, Sir." Tom related the conversation as best he could remember it without his notes.

"He gets confused right before he faints. They are really small seizures, his doctor says they come on when he is under a great deal of stress. Something must have happened or someone has resigned that was part of the inner circle."

"Ed, it must be either Burnside or Meade who has called it quits, either one could trigger a seizure."

"For the sake of President Lincoln, let us hope it was both and we can convince him to appoint General Grant!" Said Tom Schneider without thinking. Both of the Secretaries glared at him.

"I am sorry, Sirs. I should not have said that."

"It is alright, Tom, we were thinking the same thing."

Tom retreated to his office and checked his calendar to see when the Admiral indicated he would return with Admiral Hagood. It would be just before Thanksgiving a new holiday that he and his family would be celebrating this year in Seneca Hill, Pennsylvania. He would try to remember to tell the Admiral how the president had acted and what was his last that he had said just before he fainted. Was losing or was it choosing something, he could not remember. He went home that night still bothered by what had happened, even though the cabinet members seemed to think that is was a common occurrence whenever the president was under extreme stress.

The train ride from Washington City to Pennsylvania was enjoyable for his wife Beth and the two children;

Tom Jr., called JR and Emily Schneider. They had not seen the northwestern part of Pennsylvania before and the train ride was exciting for the children. Tom was met at the train station by a carriage from Seneca Hill and in a short while they were traveling on country roads that twisted through that part of Pennsylvania. They came over a rise and spotted the house on a hill. It looked like a mansion to Tom. It had giant white columns in front and a huge wrap around porch that had several french doors that led into different rooms on the ground floor. A side carriage portico was towards the right hand side of the first floor and the carriage stopped here to unload passengers and baggage. Louise Caldwell and her son James were waiting on the porch to welcome them.

"Tom, Beth, it is good to see you again." She hugged them both and smiled at the children. "James do you remember Emily and JR from Bermuda?" She asked.

"Yes, ma'am. Hello, JR, want to see my pony?" And they were off running towards a stable at the rear of the house.

"Emily, you are not going to believe how much Ruthie is talking now. If she bothers you, just tell her to leave you alone." This was said just as Ruthie came bounding out of one of the french doors and ran into Beth Schneider and fell to her knees.

"Sorry, Mrs. Schneider, I was trying to hurry and beat daddy and baby Carol out to see you." Jason Caldwell came through the open doors carrying a beautiful seventeen month old baby girl who looked exactly like her mother.

"Oh, my. She is the image of her mother!" Said Beth.

"Thank God." Said Tom and everyone laughed.

"Admiral, we sure wish we were going with you and your family to Bermuda this Christmas. We miss your brother and especially your father."

"I will tell him you said hello, Tom."

"When you get to be an Admiral, Tom, maybe you will take us somewhere special for Christmas." Beth said teasing.

"Marines do not have admirals, we have generals just like in the real army." Everyone laughed. "Besides I need to make major before we dream of anything more."

"You will, Tom. I think your performance in the Army Navy Building will get you that promotion."

Tom looked pained and said, "Admiral, can I talk to you in private?"

When he had finished telling Jason everything that was written on his notes, Jason said, "That explains several things, Tom. The president seemed as normal as you and me when I met with him in July of '61. I have not seen him since. He is avoiding all kinds of stressful situations and being around me would be extremely stressful because I tell him that his military advisors are addle minded."

"Admiral?"

"Tom, when we are alone, you can call me Jason."

"I will think about it, Admiral." I began to laugh. "What is wrong, Sir?"

"That is always what I used to tell Louise's brother when I was in the White House."

"I remember, Sir. I made a small error in etiquette also." And he told him how the remark slipped out about hoping that both Burnside and Meade had resigned.

"Tom, that will do more to get you promoted than anything I can think of."

"Thank you, Jason."

"You are welcome, Tom, let us get back to the others before they think we resigned."

Before the long weekend was over I had my telegraph operator send the following message to the Secretary of the Navy:

Mr. Secretary.

My aide, Captain Schneider, has briefed me on President Lincoln's behavior in his office this past fortnight. I must apologize for my constant criticism of his conduct of the war. I realize that he avoided me because I always wanted him to do more than he was capable of at that moment. His was a constant balancing act between what was right for the country and what was possible with the resources at hand. In my opinion, he always chose 'God before Country' not my 'Country above all else.' Few men would have done that. I cannot believe that I was one of the later. My eyes are now open and I will not try to 'shorten the war'. The country must go through this 'cleansing process', I regret that so many young men and women have died to date. The death of my sister, in combat, still haunts me.

Captain Schneider regrets his remarks made to you and Secretary Stanton. He is the finest officer I have ever met. He functions well above his present rank and he is now ready to assume new duties within the Marine Corps. It is my recommendation that he be assigned to the Marine Commandant.

After Tom and his family had returned to Washington and Tom returned to the Army Navy Building, I got the following response from Secretary Welles:

Admiral Caldwell.

I shared your telegram about the president to all the cabinet members and they agree 100 percent with your description of the last several months in the White House. We are all in agreement that the president has taken on way too much of the war effort. Secretary Stanton has reorganized the military to function as corps divisions instead of the western or eastern theaters of operation. The five star army and five star navy flag officer will brief the president at appropriate intervals. The president is no longer responsible for every decision at every level of the military.

You expressed regret that Captain Schneider was growing to the point that you were holding him back. I agree and have recommended the following to the Marine Corps:

Promotion to major affective January 1, 1864

Assignment to Secretary of the Navy, Army Navy Building

Area of responsibility: recruitment and training USMC

I need your selection for your new aide, in your next message.

Without hesitation, I sent the following reply:

Mr. Secretary.

Promotion of Warrant Officer Samuel Mason, present assignment Bermuda, to Captain USMC. Transfer to Army Navy Building affective January 1, 1864.

17

Winter Campaign
Washington City

Winter activity during the war was a time to slow or stop major campaigns. This time was used to train new recruits, both volunteers and the draftees. Both the north and south could no longer depend upon volunteers to fill the ranks and both sides resorted to conscription of men to serve between the ages of 25 to 45. Leaves were granted from the Army Navy Building during these times and I had gotten a 30 day leave to return to Bermuda. Granted, it was a working leave in that we needed to bring Jerome Lewis and his office into the new communication loop that we had devised for the Army Navy Building. Secretary Seward had his own 'basement' operation in the White House but he saw the advantages of our network. The problem was no cable from the United States east coast to Bermuda existed. Tom Schneider reminded me of what we did in Navel Intelligence during the Utah missions.

"Remember, Sir. We used the telegraph where the

lines were strung and in between we had the pony express deliver the message to the next line operator."

"So, what we need is pony boat express!"

"Yes, Sir. How do we do that?"

"I will talk to the Postmaster General and see what is available. We use mail steamers now. I wonder if there is anything faster?"

I walked to the White House in search of the Postmaster General. I found him in his office and said, "Montgomery Blair, just the man I need to see!"

He appeared to be startled, as few cabinet members ever addressed him in the cabinet meetings, he was just there, the chief mailman of the United States. "Yes, Admiral, what can I do for you?"

"Well, I have a question."

"I hope I can answer it. What is it?"

"I need to get messages back and forth between Washington City and Bermuda Station faster than the once a week mail steamers."

"You need a telegraph cable."

"Thanks, when can you have it installed?" He really looked startled now, his glasses nearly slid off the end of his nose.

"I mean the American Telegraph Company, not the post office!"

I laughed and said, "I did not mean that you should lay a cable, Monty."

"Seriously, Jason, you need to talk to the people over there. They are expanding in every direction. All you have to do is pay for the rent on the line and allow them to send public messages as well."

"Really, what do you suppose the monthly rent on a

cable is?"

"Thousands of dollars, I would imagine, I do not know."

"Monty, I hate to ask this, but could you come down there with me to talk to them? I am a nobody in the message world, but you are a real somebody. They might listen to you."

He puffed out his chest and said, "Finally, somebody appreciates what I try to do around here." He stood and strode out of his office and told his secretary, "If anyone is looking for me, I will be on a secret mission with the Admiral here!" He kept on walking and I had to hurry to keep up with him.

He hailed a White House carriage and we were off to downtown Washington and the American Telegraph office. He was well known there and he breezed past the hired help and we were sitting in the company president's office, a Mr. Dewitt, and were visiting like old friends.

"So, the Postmaster General here says that you install and then rent underground telegraph cable. Is that correct?"

"Yes, Admiral. But we do not do anything for the federal government, it is a matter of payment, you see. The fact is, the feds are always late or unpaid in their bills since the war started."

"This would not be for the federal government. I am president of Caldwell International, you know the holding company for American Telegraph?"

"Oh, my God. I did not put two and two together Mr. Caldwell, I am sorry!"

"It is Admiral Caldwell until the war is over, Mr. Dewitt. It is 600 miles to Bermuda, correct?"

"That is correct, Admiral."

"So what is it going to cost Caldwell International to lay 600 miles of cable?"

"Well it will not cost Caldwell International anything since you own us. I mean the cost will be our costs, I mean our cost will be paid by others that use the cable." Montgomery Blair was really enjoying this.

"Good, so we have established that it can be done. What is the time frame; weeks, months or years?"

"Certainly not years or weeks, General, but months should do it."

"It is, Admiral, and can you start tomorrow?"

"Yes, Sir. All we need is a signed authorization from you to begin."

"Have your secretary type it up Mr. Dewitt, Monty and I are going to lunch and then we will be back and we will sign it."

"We, Admiral?"

"Yes, we, Monty. The United States Post office just became our first public customer!"

He laughed and said, "Agreed, Admiral, it will be the best buy of my administration."

We had that lunch. And every Wednesday we had lunch, until Louise and I left for Bermuda and our Christmas break.

18

State of the Confederacy
Richmond, 1863

In Richmond, President Davis was considering the progress made by the army and navy in the last six months of action. Galveston, like all the other seaports of the South, was blockaded by the Union fleet. General Magruder, after collecting artillery at Houston, occupied the works erected opposite the island on which Galveston stands. Two steam packets were converted to gunboats and strong bulwarks of cotton bales made them small arms proof. These were manned by Texas cavalry men. They steamed up and engaged the Union gunboat *Harriet Lane*, while confederate troops were marching over the long railway bridge that connects Galveston Island to the mainland. The *Harriet Lane* drove off one of the gunboats, but the other ran alongside and under brisk rifle fire the Texans leaped aboard the *Harriet Lane* and killed Captain Wainwright and the crew. The *Westfield* tried to go to the aid of the *Harriet Lane* and it too was destroyed with all hands. Meanwhile the land troops had captured the city and the blockade was lifted and it looked like it would now stay in the hands of the Confederacy.

President Davis also had limited success in obtaining Great Britains assistance in the launching of privateers upon the high seas. Privateers were licensed by a government to capture merchant ships upon the sea and sell them in European ports of call. So long as the Confederacy was not recognized as a distinct nation by other governments, its privateers could not take their prizes into any port to sell them. So far, the privateers for the Confederacy were stopping and robbing US Merchantmen of everything worth taking and then burning the ships.

Confederate privateers would have had a difficult time in fitting out and getting to sea without the help of England. In April, Davis bought the HMS *Oreto* and renamed it the CSS *Florida*. When ready, the Florida was sailed to Nassau, Bahamas. She then appeared off Mobile harbor flying the British Union Jack. Commander Preble, of the Union blocking fleet, had been warned about giving England another Trent Affair. He did fire upon her and she entered the harbor safely. The *Florida* received her armament and came out again, under the command of Captain Maffit. She inflicted immense damage on the blocking fleet and sailed off into the middle Atlantic towards Bermuda. The second ship built in England was named the CSS *Sumter*, it was captained by A. J. Semmes. The *sumter* was not as fortunate as the *Florida* and it was sunk by the USS *Tuscarora*. Captain Semmes escaped and returned to England for another ship. The one built for him was the CSS *Alabama*, the most successful privateer to date for the Confederacy. The CSS *Nashville* was sunk by the USS *Montauk*.

Davis ordered that all blockades be destroyed by the Confederate Navy and privateers, starting with Charleston Harbor. A Union fleet of ironclads blocked the harbor. Captain Ingraham of the CSS *Rampage* ran out accompanied by two gun boats and scattered the ironclads and captured a Union gunboat. He then sent word to President Davis that the blockade was broken. And it was until the next day, when Admiral Du Pont, was ordered to attack and occupy the city of Charleston by Admiral Benjamin Hagood. The ironclads now formed a line of battle with the USS *Weehawken* under the command of Captain J. K. Rogers. A cumbrous "mine sweeper," in the shape of a raft, was fastened to the front of the *Weekawken* and it slowed the advance of the line. The *Weekawken* now came under fire from Fort Moultrie and then exploded a mine under the bow and put her out of action until repairs could be made. The second in line was the USS *Keokuk* and it too came under heavy fire from both Fort Sumter and Moultrie. She was struck ninety times in the course of half an hour and sank to the bottom of Charleston Harbor. The third in line was the new USS *Ironsides* and it had a remarkable escape from sinking. Her rudder was shot away and she became entangled with three other ironclads, the four of them lay in deadlock for quarter of an hour trying to free the mine that lay under them. A hundred cannon from Fort Sumter pounded the entanglement until Admiral Du Pont signaled by flags that the fleet should withdraw. The blockade fleet retired to Port Royal Harbor and for another day the blockade was lifted.

The failure of this attack was a great disappointment to Admiral Hagood. He ordered Admiral Du Pont to return and establish the blockade. He was instructed not to allow the enemy to put up new defenses on Morris Island. Admiral Du Pont's reply dwelt so much on the risks involved, he was replaced by Admiral Jab Dahlgren, he made plans for a coordinated land and sea attack on Charleston. General Gilmore, the hero of Savannah, was to lead the land attack and capture the three land forts of Charleston while Admiral Dahlgren would silence Sumter and occupy it.

The conventional plan of attack used at Fort Pulaski in Savannah did not work in Charleston. General Gilmore ordered General Strong to take the first land fort while Union gun boats pounded it from off shore. General Strong was wounded and seventy-five percent of this troops were killed in the first day of action. Gilmore was enraged and ordered the gun boats to level the fort. After 14 hours of shelling the fort grew silent and the rest of Gilmore's troop cheered. The summer temperatures were reaching 100 degrees and Gilmore said his troops could wait until the cool of the evening to occupy the fort. At dusk his troops advanced and met murderous cannon fire from the fort. While Gilmore rested, the Confederates reinforced the fort from Charleston. Gilmore was now livid and ordered the city of Charleston to be shelled at random. It threw the general population of the city into panic. General Beauregard, defender of Charleston, sent an impassioned message to Gilmore, "Never before, among civilized nations, has a commander ordered the murder of non- combatants without prior notice so that those might leave and save their lives." The battle for Charleston lasted another forty-two hours. The southern wall of Fort Sumter was in ruins. The loss of life was minimal, however. The other forts held and the inner line of defenses extending across James Island towards Sullivan's Island were impregnable. The combined attacks by union forces had failed and the victory was reported to Richmond.

Upon hearing the news from Charleston, Davis said, "It is time to start the great naval uprising of the South." He was referring to his preparation for battle order no. 211 which had been issued after the fall of New Orleans. It stated that next to New Orleans, Mobile was the most important seaport on the Gulf of Mexico. Accordingly, the fullest preparations shall be made for its defense. A naval force was formed under Admiral Franklin Buchanan, the hero at Hampton Roads. He ordered the construction of five heavy gun boats at Selma, one hundred and fifty miles up the Alabama River. The Confederate ironclad the CSS *Tennessee* was built in this shipyard. It was on station with eighteen officers and one hundred men.

Buchanan believed that he could destroy the blockade of Mobile with surprise and the darkness of night to aid his efforts. On the night of May 18, 1863, he planned to destroy the blockade, then destroy the entire Union Gulf Fleet under Farragut, capture Fort Pickens at Pensacola, then on to New Orleans and finally sail around the tip of Florida and free the entire east coast. Quite a grandiose plan for one ironclad and five heavy gun boats! But then, Franklin Buchanan was a dreamer like his cousin James. Like all grand schemes, they come to an end. The *Tennessee* ran aground in the dark and remained immovable until after daylight. With the chance of taking the blockade fleet by surprise gone, he waiting for the tide to change and refloat the *Tennessee*. He anchored under the guns of Fort Morgan at the mouth of the Alabama.

No place in the South was more powerfully fortified than Mobile. Fort Gaines was a brick fort on Dauphin Island and had a garrison of 864 men. Fort Powell commanded the principal pass to Mississippi Sound. Fort Morgan was the main fortification and mounted its guns in three tiers. The ship channel was spanned by a double row of surface mines called 'torpedoes'. Buchanan's delay of the Tennessee and his obvious intention of defending the Port of Mobile gave enough time for one of the blockade vessels to steam to the Union Gulf Fleet and warn them. The Fleet promptly sailed for Mobile with Admiral Ben Hagood on board the USS *Hartford*.

The Union Gulf Fleet consisted of twenty-one wooden vessels and four ironclads. Admiral Farragut's plan of attack was to pass up the channel close under the guns of Fort Morgan, where a free channel had been left for the blockade runners. The vessels were to sail in pairs, with the larger ship on the left to give fire support. Farragut's intention was to lead with his flag ship the *Hartford*, but at the urgent request of Admiral Hagood, he gave that perilous post to the Captain James Alden of the *Brooklyn*. They were to attack in the morning of the next day and David Farragut could not sleep that night so he sat up and wrote to his wife.

"We are going into Mobile in the morning if God is with us, as I hope He is, and in Him I place my trust. If am to die tomorrow, I am ready to submit to His will. God bless and keep you if anything should happen to me."

Before seven the next morning the fleet crossed the bar and moved up the channel in a battle line. Farragut took position in the port main shrouds on the upper sheer ratline, twenty-five feet high. He could see the USS *Tecumseh* open the battle by firing at Fort Morgan. His monitors like the *Tecumseh* and *Brooklyn* were expected to draw the fire from Fort Morgan. The CSS *Tennessee* and her five escorts came out from Fort Morgan and opened fired on Farragut's fleet. The enveloping smoke screened the ships from his view and he climbed higher on the ship's rigging. Ben Hagood was closely watching Farragut, fearful that some accident might befall him, he ordered a seaman to climb the rigging with a rope to secure him to the shrouds. The thickening smoke made Farragut go still higher. He could signal by flags to other ships in his fleet from here and he did so. He called for the ships to close up ranks. The larger ships obeyed and they poured broadsides into the fort.

Captain Carvin of the *Tecumseh*, was eager to meet the *Tennessee*. He paid no attention to fire from the fort, making straight for the *Tennessee*. A change of direction by the *Tennessee* caused him to run directly over the line of torpedoes. Suddenly there was a muffled explosion and a massive column of water leaped into the air. The *Tecumseh* lurched to port, her bow dropped, her stern titled up, the screw turning in the air and she slipped below the water carrying all hands to their deaths. Farragut was watching the disaster and signaled to look for survivors. He watched as he saw his line of battle become entangled with the line of torpedoes. He shouted below to the *Hartford* crew, "Damn the torpedoes, full speed ahead." Ben Hagood could not believe his ears, he was about to die at the battle of Mobile. What he did not know was that David Farragut, high up in the riggings had seen a clear line directly through the network of torpedoes and had signaled the other ships to follow in single line after the *Hartford*. Ben held his breath, expecting to see the noble old flagship and her heroic admiral blown to bits.

"No more decisive test of bravery is conceivable." He would later write. "Than that of the men below decks on the *Hartford*, standing in awed silence, they heard a strange, grating noise along the entire hull of the *Hartford*. They knew it was the cables attached to the torpedoes. That hideous scraping sound slid off into silence. They had missed the *Hartford*."

The Confederate commander of Fort Morgan was watching and would later declare, "The admiral clinging to the mizzenmast was as calm as he could be and his quick perception saved the Union fleet that day."

Farragut's action now placed the *Hartford* in the lead of the line of battle, Ben Hagood was shaking with fear as the huge CSS *Tennessee* bore down on them and hit them with a percussion shell. For the second time in two minutes, Ben Hagood feared for his life in Mobile. A jagged hole was torn in the Hartford's hull, but it was above the water line, she had escaped the second peril. Then Buchanan drove the CSS *Tennessee* towards the *Hartford*, intending to sink her, as she had the USS *Cumberland* at Hampton Roads. Farragut signaled to evade the charge and to sweep up the channel. The CSS *Tennessee*, having missed the *Hartford* continued down the line of battle. She raked broadsides into the rest of the entire line, but all Union vessels continued up the channel after the *Hartford*.

Fort Morgan had been passed with the CSS *Tennessee* and her gun boats retreating and holding under the fort.

Mobile harbor was now in full possession of the Union fleet, who anchored some four miles above the fort. But so long as the Tennessee waited to attack again, the victory was not complete and Farragut was determined to destroy the monster as soon as he had given his men a few hours rest. But Buchanan did not wait to be attacked, he slowly started creeping towards the Union fleet. The parapets of the three forts were crammed with soldiers to watch the destruction of the fleet.

Slowly swinging around, the Tennessee steamed out to engage the fleet. Farragut had his signal man transmit the following:"Raise anchors - attack with bow guns - ram at full speed."

Farragut reasoned that his ships guns would do little to slow the *Tennessee*, he would have to sink her by ramming. Farragut had iron plating on the bows of his wooden ships, not fully iron construction. When the USS *Monogahela* rammed the *Tennessee* , the iron prow was torn off. The *Tennessee* developed a small leak. When the USS *Lackawanna* rammed the *Tennessee*, she rolled fifteen degrees to starboard. Now the *Tennessee* was hurt. Not out of fight, she turned towards the *Hartford* and they engaged. Ben Hagood knew this time he was dead. A wooden ship cannot stand against a larger all iron vessel. He said his prayers and waited to die.

At a critical moment, the captain of the USS *Manhattan* cut across the bow of the *Tennessee* and fired the largest guns of the US fleet, fifteen inch. The *Tennessee* turned like a wounded animal to face its new threat. She turned directly into the USS *Chickasaw* and received a ram under her stern, locking the two vessels together. Ben Hagood had to smile, the Chickasaw looked like a bulldog biting a horse in the ass. The *Chickasaw* had eleven inch guns and she fired point blank into the stern of the *Tennessee*. Meanwhile the USS *Winnebago* rammed the helpless *Tennessee* amid ships and she rolled again. The *Manhattan* was now in position to fire the fifteen inch guns and the *Tennessee* was in trouble. Admiral Buchanan had his leg blown off below the knee and before he died he turned command over to Captain Johnston to try to make an escape. Escape was impossible and he surrendered.

The Union fleet now turned its attention to the three forts. They shelled Fort Powell and a white flag was raised over the fort. Fort Gaines was now addressed with similar results. Only the monster Fort Morgan remained. It was shelled for two days and it surrendered. Mobile was now a Union seaport. Admiral Farragut was transferred from the *Hartford* to accompany Ben Hagood to Washington and a hero's welcome. In this furious battle, the Union lost all hands on the *Tecumseh*, 52 killed on other ships, 170 wounded and 4 missing assumed lost at sea.

1863 was a year of bitter disappointment for President Davis and his war cabinet. Stonewall Jackson was killed after the victory at Chancellorsville by friendly fire. When Vicksburg fell to Grant and Sherman, the entire State of Mississippi was now in Union control. The disaster at Gettysburg further reduced the size of the standing army in the east. In the fall, a victory cheered Richmond, it was the battle of Chickamauga. The defeat at Chattanooga released General Sherman from Grant's Command to begin his Atlanta Campaign. The only bright spot was in December when General Bragg released General Longstreet to drive a Union force into Knoxville and trap them there.

19

CSA Embassy
Bermuda

From Bermuda, General Butler reported that the English invasion fleet that was supposed to enter the Chesapeake in support of the Confederate States of America, had sailed for home. The 8000 Marines had landed in Brunswick, Canada. The US Consulate Office was closed for thirty days and John Butler wished he could jump on a trolley and visit the Caldwells in St. George. His attention from his paper work was interrupted by the ringing of the door bell at his front office door. He walked to the door and peered through the side lights. It was Jerome Lewis, his friend from the US Consulate Office. He threw open the door and said, "I was just thinking about you."

"You were? Can you spare a few days? Louise and Jason are spending the holidays at Caldwell Place. Does the embassy have a petty cash jar?"

"Of course."

"The Inn has a reservation for you. Jason says you

can come and visit for a few days if the Confederacy is not bankrupt!"

"Are you headed there now?"

"Yes, my family is already there. I was sent to fetch you."

"Come in and I will pack an overnight bag and we can leave."

They rode the train from Hamilton, passed through the Flatts section of Bermuda, across stone work bridges and blue sparkling waters. The temperature was 72 degrees in the middle of December and John Butler thought the winters in Charleston are not that bad, but they could not
compare with the beauty of Bermuda, he would be sad to leave this place. Then he had a strange thought, "I am a bachelor, I can live anywhere I want, why not here. Jerome, what are you going to do after the war?"

"I have to decide if I want to stay with the State Department or return to the Navy as my full time career. I was a policeman in Louisville, Kentucky before I joined the Navy. So I have some options."

"Would you ever consider staying here in Bermuda?"

"As long as I was the minister here, yes. It is a beautiful place to live and work."

"I have decided not to go back to South Carolina."

"You have! I am surprised, General."

"That is just the point, Jerome. At home I would be the defeated General from the Civil War. I want to start over with a clean slate."

"Well, you could not pick a better place. Have you ever been interested in a business, John?"

"Yes, I ran a small business in Charleston before the war. I was also a General in the State Militia. It was an honorary title. I have never commanded troops in battle."

"Talk to Jason this week, John, I think he might have something for you."

"Here in Bermuda? That would be great."

"And even better if you could start before the war ended. What he has in mind would be in no way a conflict of interest for you, John."

"What is it? You have gotten my curiosity going."

"Caldwell International is bringing a telegraph office to Hamilton and St. George."

"The country is so small, why connect Hamilton and St. George."

"Not if you connect Hamilton, St. George, America, Canada and England."

"What?"

"Think about it, John. The cable is in place between Canada and England. The US is already connected to Canada to have transatlantic cable service. What if a cable was laid from Bermuda to America?"

"This is Jason's doing. He has found a make work job for me?"

"Not at all, John. He would never even ask you if you wanted to work in Bermuda. He is from South Carolina and he knows how you Carolinians think. He asked me to broach the question with you so you could turn him down gracefully. He wants you to run the Bermuda Telegraph System. The offer is genuine and it will be open for you to think about. The cable is being laid from St. George to Maryland as we speak in both directions at the same time. Jason never does things half way, John."

"My God, my prayers have been answered!"

"I take that is a, yes?"

"Damn right it is a, yes. Where do I sign on?"

"Caldwell Place in about ten minutes, looks like we are almost there."

The train pulled into St. George station and we walked down Duke of York Street to Rose Hill and up the steep incline to Caldwell Place. We were both out of breath when we hit the front doors.

"John Butler, it is good to see you again." Louise Caldwell gave him a hug and held on to his arm. "Let me introduce you to everyone. Everyone, this is General John Butler from Charleston. That man over there is Jason's Father, Robert and next to him is his brother, Robert and next to him is another Robert, Robert Whitehall." People began to giggle and Louise said, "What?"

"Too many Roberts." Said Mariann.

"Oh, that is right. If you forget someone's name just call them Robert!"

Louise never did get the rest of the introductions finished, but John Butler did not care. He was among his fellow South Carolinians and he loved it. Jason and James came into the room with a large tablet of paper and James said, "Hey, Uncle John, want to play identify that ship?"

"Hulls and masts, or do I have to identify sails? I am lousy at sails."

"So, is Dad. He cheats, so watch him."

They laid the large paper tablet on one of the serving tables in the dining hall and James began his first lesson. He drew three masts. " The first mast is called the foremast, it has three sections. The section closest to the deck is called the lower foremast, the middle is called the fore-top mast."

"Wait, why not call it the middle foremast?"

"Cause that would make it to easy for you land lubbers!" The room erupted in laughter.

"James Jason Caldwell, you will apologize to your Uncle John or go to your room!" Louise was red in the face.

"I am sorry, Uncle John, my mouth ran away with itself."

"Let me get this straight, all three masts have lower masts, right?"

"Right."

"And all of the masts have top masts, right?"

"Right."

"Then why not call the middle, the middle?"

"Cause the middle sections are named after their masts, like mizzen, main and fore."

"I get it, cried John Butler!" And everyone laughed again.

"Now, on to the hard part. The sails are called yards."

"Can someone get me a drink?" John Butler was having the time of this life. Or maybe he was introduced to family life for the first time as an adult. Jason left, fixed him his favorite, returned and handed it to him.

"You can tell where the yards are by which mast they are on. For example, main yards are on the mainmast, fore yards are on the foremast and mizzen yards are on the mizzenmast."

"Wait a minute, are you making this up as you go,

James?" The laughter got louder.

"No, honest the mizzenmast is the most important because the jigger mast can be raised or lowered."

"Good God, I need another drink!" The main dining hall erupted again.

"Really, Uncle John, it is simple, just look at my sketch!"

"Where is this Jigger mast?"

"I have not drawn it, yet!"

"Because you just made it up, right?" And the dining room was in stitches from laughter.

I glanced over at Jerome, he smiled and nodded his head yes. I said, "That is enough, James, go find your sister and tell her your mother wants to talk to her."

I gave a shrug of my shoulders and said, "When you have time, Uncle John, I would like to talk to you about a business venture that I am starting on Bermuda'.

20

Virginia City, Nevada
Spring 1864

When silver was discovered in Nevada five years ago, it was not met with the same "Gold Rush Fever" at Sutter's Mill, California. It took almost a year for the news to reach prospectors and large scale mine operators. It was known within the White House, however, and Jason Caldwell had sent his representatives to explore this business prospect. They were guided by two of his RR marines, corporals D.D. Wilson and Matthew James, now private citizens and employees of Caldwell International, now just known by its initials (CI). When the CI representatives; a mining engineer, surveyor and construction foreman, reached Carson Canyon they found 200 gold miners at work along the gravel banks of the canyon river with rockers, Long Toms and sluices. Most of the men complained about a heavy blue-black material which kept clogging their rockers. The CI engineer thought this might be silver and when he had it assayed, it was determined to be almost pure sulphuret of silver. Traveling on up the river, they came to the town of Johnstone. Here they paused long enough to purchase a few lots upon which to build later. Jason Caldwell had insisted that they not pan for gold. Or they should not stake claims for silver, instead they should build a saw mill and obtain timber for the mill. He reasoned that mining required timbers cut from trees and water. They were to purchase any water rights that they could find. Then and only then, should they begin to buy up played out gold strikes, turning these into silver mining operations.

By the Spring of 1860, those who discovered the Comstock Lode had extracted all the gold and discounted the "blue-stuff". Patrick McLaughlin sold his interest in the Ophir Mine to CI for $3,500.00. Emanual Penrod sold his share for $8,500.00. Peter O'Riley held on to his share for a few months and sold to CI for $40,000.00 in order to build a hotel. One year later the Ophir Mine produced one and one half million dollars in silver dividends for stock holders. D. D. Wilson, manager of the saw mill, sold over a half a million dollars in cut timbers for the prevention of cave ins to other mine owners. Matthew James, director of CI Water Company was selling sump pumps to keep the mines free of flooding from vast quantities of underground streams of hot water. The hot water was collected and sent to Johnstone through pipes and sold there to businesses and townspeople. The proceeds from these enterprises were placed in the Bank of California until the CI bank was built in Johnstone in 1861 and 1862 in Carson City.

There were no railroads into Nevada, CI noticed this and began a shipping operation. Freight and passengers were transported by mule teams of from 10 to 16. Ore was hauled from the mines to the mills for refining by CI, Shipping. They brought to the mines all the timbers, mining machinery and supplies. No wagon made an unloaded run anywhere. Goods and merchandise needed by small mining towns was hauled over the Sierras from California on the return trips from deposits of pure silver and gold from the refining mills. CI investments would have flourished by shipping contracts only, but it was the CI Water Company that became the real "Gold Mine."

In 1860, the flow of water from natural springs was adequate to supply the needs of the miners and small towns of Johnstone, Virginia City and Gold Hill. As population increased, wells were dug for domestic needs, and the water within several mine tunnels was added to the available supplies. As the refining, smelting mills and hoisting operations multiplied, the demand for water for use in steam boilers became so great that it was impossible to supply it without creating a water shortage. To fill this need the water company began hauling water to whomever needed. Water tank wagons became common sights as they traveled from the Sierra Nevada mountains to the Virginia ranges that lay in the Washoe Valley. The CI engineer, Herman Schussler, began working on a plan to replace the wagon trains by a cast iron pipe line. The 7 mile distance between water source and water demand could be met with a 12 inch diameter pipe which would produce 92,000 gallons of water per hour. CI Water Systems Construction division now became the leading manufacturer of water systems for towns in Nevada.

In the spring of 1861, D. D. Wilson had sent his second report back to the home office in Pennsylvania.

He had the accountants provide an annual statement of saw mill production, sales and expenses. His salary was $10.00 per day, he itemized his expense account, and indicated that his profit sharing of 2% of timber production for that year was $10,000.00. Employees were paid at $1.00 per day plus expenses and ½% profit sharing or $2500.00. The cost of timber purchased that year was $40,000.00. Equipment and supply costs were $28,000.00. Transportation costs were $11,250.00. This left roughly $440,000.00 on deposit in the CI Bank of Johnstone for payment of outstanding debts. The mill had been constructed at a cost of $80,000. The interest on the loans for operating expenses, equipment and transportation showed a balance of zero. Not apparent to a casual reader was that the interest was paid to a CI bank, transportation costs were paid to a CI firm and timber purchases were from a CI firm.

Matthew James sent a similar annual report for the water company. It had a balance of $850,000 on deposit in the bank of Johnstone to pay outstanding debts; interest, transportation, machinery purchases, pipe and supply purchases. His annual salary was also $10.00 per day, plus 2% of net operating profits or $13,000.00 His expense account was not itemized, but it was modest, it included one trip to Indiana to ask his school sweetheart to marry him, now that he was a rich man.

In 1864, when the copies from the lumber company, water company, mining and shipping were forwarded to Jason and Louise Caldwell at Seneca Hill, Pennsylvania, they were pleased. The western assets had increased from the 14 million dollars in 1860 to 44 million for 1864. When Louise reviewed the statements, she said, "Jason,

D.D. and Matthew have done another outstanding amount of work for us in the last three years. We have increased their profit sharing by 2% each of the last three years. That means they make $30,000.00 and $36,000.00 a year in profit sharing plus their annual salaries. I am pleased that you took them off hourly and gave them salaries so they stay content and with us."

"I agree, they signed contracts with us for five years. The contracts are due to be signed again. I should travel to Nevada as soon as I can find time."

"Oh, Jason, I do not know about you going all that way, just to sign contracts! The length of time that you will be away from the Army Navy Building, will they give you leave?"

"In 1862, General Dodge started building from Council Bluffs westward along the trail that I took to Nevada in October of '57. In five years he is past the point where you turn south off the overland stage route and head into Fort Bridger. I will book passage from Washington City on the train and ride it to the end of the line, somewhere in Utah. D.D. Wilson, Matthew James, Herman and the other managers can meet me there. It will take some coordination, sure. But you must keep face to face contact with your managers, wherever they may be. I will suggest that we meet in California when the Central Pacific meets the Union Pacific coming from Council Bluffs. They estimate that it will be somewhere around Ogden, Utah. As soon as that is completed, you and I can get on a train in Pittsburgh and get off in Sacramento, California."

"Why is it necessary to go before the railroad is fin-ished, then?"

I wrote to DD telling him about Congress authorizing a United States Mint for Carson City."

"What did you ask him to do?"

"To check with Herman, our mining engineer to get a new estimate on how many more years the silver will last. Last time I asked him, he said it looks like a fifteen to twenty year run. After that, the veins of the Comstock will be completely gone. I want to stop taking our silver to California, I want to start selling it to the mint right there in Carson City. They will strike silver and gold coins."

"And what about the supply of gold in Nevada, Jason?"

"That should be gone soon, we will still haul refined gold from California to Carson City, Nevada."

"But, if both the silver and gold are gone?"

"Some day that will happen, but not in our life times."

"Are you going to be sad to leave the Department of the Navy and your work there for Gideon Welles, Jason?"

"Louise, this country has held together better than I thought it would, the future for a Union with the south still does not look good. We have survived and even prospered during the national war between the states."

"Has the war brought additional profits for a company like ours?"

"Yes, I told you earlier that we would loose everything in either South Carolina or Pennsylvania depending upon which is occupied territory. At this point, neither side is going to occupy the other. They will fight until one side or the other is completely ruined and unable to continue the war effort. We have temporarily lost our holdings in South Carolina. The western assets are secure and will remain so. Nevada has applied for statehood it should be granted later this year.

"Jason, what will happen to your parents property and the rest of your family when the war ends?"

"I have talked with my father about coming back to South Carolina with me and Robert, but I doubt he will want to leave Bermuda, he can run Robert's business for him. I will make the offer to move them if they want. It is really up to them."

"Could they manage their business's from a remote location, like you do, Jason? We have excellent people that manage for us. They need to find people they can trust. You trust people, Jason."

"As we have said before, evaluate first, then trust. Then we never have to say, *what in the hell is this*?"

"What?"

"Remember me telling you about Master Chief Gunnerman, my DI in Annapolis?"

"Yes, you said he taught you a lot about how to handle people. He always assumed that you would not do things correctly, and therefore, you did not try very hard to please him."

"Yes, Louise, we assume that people will do the right thing, because they want to please us. The fear of letting someone down is much greater than the actual fact. You try harder, you correct things on the fly, when things go awry."

"Jason, that is exactly how you are with your brother and father."

"Of course, practice what you preach!"

"So, when will you leave for Nevada?"

"I need to calculate how many days of train travel, both ways. Then add a few days for interruptions and at least one day for the meeting. Then I can inform Gideon how many days I will be gone."

"You inform him?"

"Yes, we have an agreement. I work for him for one dollar a year and I have as much time off as I need. If I am gone to much, he will simply date my letter of resignation and I will be retired again."

"Sounds sensible."

"Louise?"

"Yes, Jason."

"Do you always have to have the last word in our conversations?"

"No, it just works out that way!"

Sam and I were on our way west the next week. It took us three days to get to Independence, Missouri on a nonstop sleeper. We had boarded the train at Union Station and stepped off the train whenever it stopped for mail or water to stretch our legs. Nonstop meant you could sleep on board. From this point westward the new railroad was built along side the old Butter field overland stage route. It still operated but now it ran shorter routes from the train stations to out lying areas and back again. We had an overnight at Chimney Rock and then proceeded on into Fort Laramie in Wyoming Territory. My managers were waiting at the end of the line. They had a much shorter distance to travel but it took the same number of days.

The train came to a chugging stop. Six men on horseback greeted us. D. D. Wilson was no longer the boy who was excited upon being promoted from private to corporal in '57. Beside him sat Matthew James, his side kick in the marine detachment that I commanded in western Utah Territory a few years ago. Peters and Keets sat next to them, grown men no longer shave tail marines. Peters wore a star on his vest, indicating that he was the Johnstone town Marshal as well as a CI employee. William Burns and Herman "the German", my mining engineer, looked older but they were older when I hired them to open the Caldwell venture.

"Hello Cap'n, welcome to the wild west." D. D. Wilson said.

"Hello, gentlemen. Have you got horses for us?"

"Yes, Sir. Have you got bags and bedrolls?"

"Bedrolls, you have got to be kidding, D. D."

"Yes, Sir. I just wanted to see the expression on Sam's face, Sir."

"Stop calling me sir and help me get up on this beast. Do you have any idea how long it has been since I have ridden a horse?"

"Let me do some calculations? You were last on a horse in Nebraska in 1857 or 8, correct?"

"Yes, but I was only 39 years old then. I am as stiff as a sixty year old now."

"You have had a lot of miles on the old body since then, Cap'n. I read you were in the battle of New Orleans with Admiral Farragut. How was that?"

"I was never so frightened in my life!"

"And what about Captain Hagood, he was in Mobile with Farragut, correct?"

"Ben and I see each other regularly, but he admits that sailing with Farragut is a death wish experience for sure. How about you marines? Do you ever miss being at sea?"

"The last three years have been a continuation of the mission that we took out here with you, Cap'n. We have all worked hard, fought Indians and highway men at one time or another. But I like it, I think that D. D. and the others all love it here, Sir." Matthew said.

"How is your wife you brought out here from Indiana, Matt?"

"Connie is fine sir, expecting our first any day now."

"What is Tom Schneider doing, Sam?"

"He is in the Marine Commandant's office in the Army Navy Building." Sam replied.

" Jerome Lewis is still in Bermuda. Sam and Rachel were assigned in Bermuda when I was there. When I got promoted, we moved back to Washington."

"I bet Rachel's folks liked that, Sam."

"Yes, D. D., she and the kids see them everyday."

"Kids? How many do you have?"

"Three, just like Louise and the Admiral here, they can be a handful."

The conversation kept our minds off the pain in our butts and it was no time at all until we rode into a small mountain town called "Paradise." It was a typical Rocky Mountain town with dirt streets that were more mud than dirt whenever it rained. We stopped at a livery stable and handed our horses off for the night. We grabbed our single bag and headed for the only hotel on the three block main street. Eight men walked into the lobby and rented the entire hotel's upper floor. It was not a large hotel. And it was not a large town, but it had a telegraph office, a saloon, a restaurant on the first floor of the hotel. A livery stable with black smith kept the town connected with others. A doctor's office which doubled as an undertaker kept three churches and four graveyards busy. A one room school house taught the children of the town through the eighth grade. A boarding house rented women by the hour to provide all the creature comforts of an American town in 1864.

I walked to the telegraph office and sent a message to Seneca Hill. It was the tenth since we had left Washington. I gave Louise the station number and asked her to telegraph me back. The office would deliver it to the hotel. That evening we all met downstairs for a western T- bone steak that covered the entire plate, I could not eat it all. We adjourned to the saloon for a night cap and a few stayed to play some cards. I left to read my telegram, it should be at the hotel by now. I picked up my key and asked if I had any messages. "None, Sir." Was the reply, so I thought Louise must really not have approved of this trip west. I slept, off and on, all night and arose at daybreak. I needed to read the contracts one more time before I talked to each of the men I had come to see.

My individual meetings began to take place near six o'clock because Matthew James was an earlier riser, also. We began with a verbal rundown of what had happened at the CI water companies seen I had last seen him. I asked him, " Would you like to sign another contract with CI., Matthew?"

"Yes, I enjoy company management and the freedom that you have given me to operate it as I see fit. I would like to hire additional employees that would not involve the one half of one per cent profit sharing, however.

Once the company gets to 200 employees there will be no corporate profit for CI."

"I will think about that Matthew. I can not foresee a time when we have 200 management employees reporting to you, but you never know. We already have hourly paid employees, the profit sharing is only for yearly salaried employees. And remember, Matthew, the one half of one per cent is for net profits only. CI already has a corporate profit built into it with the holding company concept set by our lawyers. Our intent is to show no profit after the employee profit sharing, that way the individual company income taxes are reduced to almost nothing. The corporate taxes are the only income taxes that will be paid to the Nevada Territory and the United States Government."

"I realize that the lion's share of my income comes from my profit shares. How can I reduce my personal income tax, Sir."

"You should talk to the company lawyer in Carson City, Matthew. He will probably recommend that you invest some of your profits to purchase stocks or bonds in other companies. You are a trusted member of CI management, but that does not mean you should not invest in other companies. I have started a new company called American Telegraph and Telephone, you should look for opportunities like that."

"What is a telephone?"

"It sends a voice over the telegraph lines. The concept was demonstrated at the 1854 World's Fair in New York by an Italian inventor Antonio Meucci. It took me until 1860 to interest him in selling his Italian patent rights. We are not interested in building the devices, we are interested in providing compatible lines over which they will operate. We have just finished laying a cable from Maryland to Bermuda for telephone and telegraph messages. All new lines installed by us in the future will be compatible for voice or telegram."

"Could I try to do that in California and Nevada?"

"Yes, either on your own or with help from CI. You could begin by stringing poles and wires to connect the capitol in Carson City with other towns and cities in Nevada. In a small area, voice communication could be possible within a year. I believe that men and women must have something that excites them in some way. Life should be a growth process, whereby a good idea takes care of itself. I can talk with my family in Bermuda via this new process whenever I like because I can afford to pay the line rental. Right now, voice communication is too expensive for the common household. In your lifetime, Matthew, I would judge that most households in California will have telephones." I could tell by the look on his face that he doubted that!

D. D. Wilson, manager of the first profit making venture in Nevada for CI, was waiting when Matthew left my room. He sat down and said, "Where is the new contract, Cap'n, I would like to read it and make some changes."

"Changes?"

"Just pulling your leg, Cap'n. I would like to read it, but you have made me a rich man beyond my dreams and I trust you. I see nothing but opportunity here in Nevada. Next year we will expand the lumber mill so that we can produce other products besides mine timbers and ship lap products. We will see a huge increase in building of towns throughout that area of Nevada."

"I agree D.D., you can get together with William Burns and build banks in each of the new towns once they reach 2000 people or so. I also want you and William to use the blueprints from the bank that was built in Carson City to build a second bank there. We will call it Nevada State Bank. Statehood has been granted by congress but no one in Nevada knows yet. I want to be the first to use the name Nevada State. My lawyers are drawing up the papers."

"When do we start, Cap'n?"

"Yesterday! D. D. Wilson, you were one of the men in my detachment that I always knew would have a bright future. Here is your new contract, read it and sign it before tomorrow. Send in the next one waiting outside, will you?"

We shook hands and he left the room and sent in the company engineer, Herman Schitzmeyer. Herman had immigrated to the United States from Switzerland. He had trained in Germany and was the finest mining engineer I had met.

"Jason, I read the papers you sent me on Meucci's paired electro-magnetic transmitter and receiver. Can you send me a pair for testing? Have you tried these?"

"Yes, they are of good fidelity but the signal is weak. We had to increase the inductive loading of the telegraph wires to increase the long distances between Maryland and Bermuda. This, unfortunately, causes a great deal of heat. The heat is fine underwater. But serious burns result when the telegraph line is strung overhead on poles, the wires burn through and break the connection. We will continue to work on the heating of the wires. We also experienced what my English engineers in Bermuda called sidetones, I call them feedback or echoes. We had several pairs of wires in the cable between Maryland and Bermuda so we just used two pairs, one to send and the other to receive. Unless this problem is solved we will need to string two pairs of telegraph wires for a telephone circuit."

"Well, it is damned exciting. Just think sending your voice over wires. It would make this meeting unnecessary in the future."

"Except, I want to look at the people I talk to. When we send pictures along with the voice, then I will telecommunicate with the western CI companies. How are things progressing on your efforts on secondary recovery of metal ores and oil deposits?"

"Here are my plans for the oil recovery in Pennsylvania. We should have a method to process silver and then gold from waste water and the slag produced by the smelting mills here in Nevada. How are you going to get the mills to give us their waste, Jason."

"We are going to use some business pressure, Herman, we are going to inform them that they can no longer discharge waste water back into the streams or on to the ground. We fear the future contamination of our water sources. We will, however, provide for the removal of this harmful, unwanted water. Matthew assures me that he can build a pipe system that will return the water from the mills directly to us. We, also, will begin to offer free dump sights where they can bring their solid waste. When each mill begins to shut down for lack of raw ore, we will buy it and begin the recovery process of the solids. We will, by then, have our own water recovery system, something that we have not attempted to build in the past. If you are certain that your process will work, you will be a very rich man by signing your new contract."

He read it, signed it, thanked me and sent in the construction company manager, William Burns.

"William, have you read Matthews plan for building a return waste water system for polluted mill water?"

"Yes, but I do not understand why we want this water?"

"Because it is full of silver that the mill did not get in their processing of the ore."

"Is the amount significant?"

"Herman, says he will recover about a million dollars a year!"

"Wow, that will pay for the pipeline in two years!"

"Make that paid out in three to five, will you, William?"

"William smiled and said, "Something about taxes, Captain?"

"Exactly, we do not want the federal government to think we are getting filthy rich, just filthy from processing all that dirty water. We will tell them that we are trying to be a good neighbor and stop the dumping of contaminated mill water into fresh water streams and rivers."

"Understood, Captain. Do you want me to sign a new contract?"

And it continued through the waiting CI managers outside my room until everyone had signed or taken his contract to consider it until tomorrow. I was hungry and I walked over to the Saloon and had a late lunch and beer recommended by Herman. It was made by some German brothers he knew who had moved from Colorado and began their own style of brewing using clean mountain water.

I walked over to the telegraph office and sent another telegram to Seneca Hill and wished that we had perfected a way to talk to Louise and the children without burning up the wires. I returned to the hotel and made ready for my return trip the next day. Sam found me and handed me three telegrams from Louise.

"These have just now caught up with you, Admiral. We moved too fast coming out here. When you sent a telegram from a location when we stopped, she must have sent a reply to you along our path, but we were already past that point. Anyway, I am glad these finally got to you."

"I thanked him and tore them open to read all about what was happening in Pennsylvania. Our communication system in the United States still had a long way to go to catch up with our transportation. I had a very good night's sleep and in the morning, I had all the signed contracts in my bag. We had decided to meet next time in California. They would ride directly west instead of coming north to meet us. Louise and I would take the train directly to Sacramento and then south to meet them. Sam and I, along with a livery stable hand, mounted our horses and set off for the railroad end point. When we reached it, we thanked the livery hand while he tied the two horses to the back of his saddle for the return to Paradise.

"What did you think of Paradise, Sam."

"Every thing being equal, I like Pittsburgh better." We both laughed and found our seats on the train.

21

Presidential Nominating Conventions
May - July 1864

The Republicans had two conventions because they split into two rival groups. The first was a group of radicals who nominated General John Fremonte for the Presidency on May 31, 1864. With the outcome of the war still in doubt, some political leaders, including Simon Chase, Benjamin Wade and Horace Greeley, opposed Lincoln's renomination on the grounds that he could not win. And if the Republicans lost the White House, the graft and corruption, that is common in war time, would pass to the Democrats. Besides the monetary issues, this group was also upset with Lincoln's position on the issues of slavery and post-war reconciliation with the southern states. When it was apparent that the Republican party would not give Lincoln another nomination, the Lincoln delegates left the convention and formed a new political party called the National Union Party. The Democrats were overjoyed, until they found the pro-war faction of their party promptly joined the new party.

The National Union Party held their convention in Baltimore, Maryland, from June 7 to June 8, 1864. They nominated Abraham Lincoln. Lincoln, dissatisfied with the radical Vice President, Hannebal Hamilen, chose a war Democrat, Governor Andrew Johnson of Tennessee. Johnson was ideally suited to run as a vice presidential candidate with Lincoln. He had strongly supported the Union, he was a southerner and he was a leading member of the war democrats. It took two ballots:

Presidential Nomination Ballot Voting 1864

	First Ballot	Second ballot
Abraham Lincoln	494	516
Ulysses S. Grant	22	0
Not voting	3	3

In the balloting for Vice President nomination:

Andrew Johnson	200	492
Hannebal Hamilen	159	9
Jason Caldwell	149	0
Daniel Dickinson	11	27

Jason Caldwell received a telegram on the evening of June 8, 1864, from the convention chairman, informing him that his name had been placed in nomination for Vice President by Montgomery Blair, to run with Abraham Lincoln on the National Union Party ticket. In the first balloting he had received 149 votes just behind the current Vice President. He did not tell him that Lincoln had chosen Andrew Johnson, and on the second ballot Johnson was given overwhelming support by the convention. Jason finished reading the teletype-writer message, tore it off the machine and walked with it to find Louise.

"Louise, where are you?"

"In here, honey."

"What do you suppose Monty did at the convention?"

"He placed your name in nomination for President?"

"No, Vice President."

"You are not even a Republican, Jason. Why would he nominate you for a Republican ticket?"

He nominated me for something called the National Union Party, it is half moderate Republicans and half war democrats."

"But it was at the Republican convention?"

"No, the Republicans nominated John Fremonte."

"Jason, quite kidding. Tell me the truth."

"The Republicans are split into two parties. We will definitely have a Democratic President in November. That is the only reason Lincoln was elected in '60, because the Democrats split into two parties."

"My brother will be happy to hear that. George McClellan will get the nomination and he has the money, thanks to you, to reach newspaper readers across the Union states. The south will not vote in this election, will they?"

"No, this will be the first time in our country's history that some Americans will not be allowed to vote in a Presidential Election."

"Jason, I have never voted in a Presidential or any other kind of election!"

"And that is not right, Louise. Why not start the movement for women's vote in the next election? Caldwell

International will fund the movement at the same level that it is funding George McClellan."

"You mean it, Jason?"

"Yes, you and I will hire some editorial writers to place ads right along side McClellan's. That way the wives can urge their husbands to vote Democratic. It will appear that George is supporting the women's movement, even if he is unaware that he is!"

"I love the idea, Jason. I will start contacting people tomorrow, I will start with Cynthia Majors.

The Democrats held their convention the weekend of July 4, 1864, and again, as they did in 1860 split along two different party lines. There was a distinct group of "peace at all costs" and the remainder of the war Democrats that did not join the National Union Party with Lincoln. John C. Breckinridge was again nominated by the war Democrats and he selected Daniel Dickinson who was unsuccessful in his bid to become Lincoln's running mate. The peace Democrats suggested that the party postpone the convention and move it to Chicago. The war democrats said they had a candidate and would not attend a "second" convention.

In Chicago, tens of thousands of Democrats from political activists to con men showed up at the convention. The Amphitheater at Michigan Avenue and Eleventh Street was restricted to convention delegates only, but they were subjected to the crowds of special interests none the less. Four years into the Civil War, most Democrats were tired. Many thought President Lincoln had gone too far, especially concerning the Emancipation Proclamation. Chicago was pro-union, but many Chicagoans had ties to the South. These pro-south representatives wanted to play on Republican corruption. They wanted to bring the nation to peace. And they selected George McClellan as their candidate on the first ballot. The real fight was for the Vice President slot. McClellan indicated his choice was Admiral Jason Caldwell and on the first ballot the voting was:

Jason Caldwell	65.5
George Pendleton	.5
L .W. Powell	32.5
George Cass	26
John Caton	16
Daniel Voorhess	13
General A. C. Dodge	9
Joseph Phelps	8
Abstaining	.5

Before the second balloting began, Powell, Cass, Caton and Voorhess met with George Pendleton and asked for several future favors. They then announced that they were withdrawing from consideration and releasing there delegates to support George Pendleton. When George McClellan heard this he sent for Jason Caldwell.

"Jason, I want to offer you a cabinet position. I will name you as my Secretary of the Navy."

"You have a much bigger problem than who should be your Vice President, Sir."

"I do? And what is that?"

"You should be offering the Vice president position to John Breckinridge. He was Vice President four years ago and he would make a much better candidate than either myself or Pendleton."

"He will not see me, Jason. I have tried. He thinks he wants to be a Presidential candidate again."

"And the same thing will happen again. You and he will spit the Democratic vote. Remember, in the last election Lincoln had two million votes, but Douglas and Breckinridge together had over three million. If you can not come to some agreement with Breckinridge, I will have to withdraw my letter of credit for your campaign."

"Why would you do that? I am going to win this thing. The Republicans are split too."

"No, you and John Breckinridge will insure that Lincoln will win. Fremonte will have little or no effect on this election. I am sorry, George, I can no longer support you." I left his hotel room and made arrangements to leave for Seneca Hill. As I was checking out, I was paged for a telegram:

JASON

DO NOT ACCEPT VP OFFER FROM MC CLELLAN. JUST LEARNED FREMONTE HAS MET WITH LINCOLN. HE HAS OFFERED TO DROP HIS CAMPAIGN IF THE PRESIDENT WILL DISMISS SOME OF HIS CABINET APPOINTMENTS. IT DOES NOT LOOK GOOD FOR YOU. LINCOLN HAS ASKED WELLES TO SIGN YOUR LETTER OF RESIGNATION. LINCOLN FEARS YOU WILL BE RUNNING AGAINST HIM IN NOVEMBER.

MONTY

As I rode the train home to Pennsylvania, I tried to

put my thoughts together. "I will be getting a telegram from Welles, telling me what he has decided to do and when. I have little personal items in my Army Navy office. Sam Mason can bring everything I need, including the morse code writers, to Seneca Hill. I will offer a job to Sam. If Monty gets caught in the political squeeze, there should be room for him at American Telegraph and Telephone in Washington City."

The train pulled into the Titusville Station and I thought what the nation needs is some good news. I had been to meet with the Caldwell employees of Nevada and had seen first hand the excitement that these Americans felt. It had come in the form of important mineral discoveries. Besides the oil wells now in Pennsylvania, new silver deposits were found in the western United States. When the Comstock Lode of silver was brought to light in Nevada, it was estimated that the silver reserves in the United States was now equal to all the rest of the world. Gold and silver was still being mined in California, Colorado, and several other locations throughout the west. The Rocky Mountain region discoveries were abundant in minerals of all types.

The last four years of war in the east should be balanced with the new wealth and welfare of the nation. Oil amounted to millions of dollars added to the national economy. The Comstock Lode alone was estimated at a quarter billion dollars. I should use this "Good news" and financial windfall to assist in the rebuilding of South Carolina. I made a mental note to write a series of letters when I got home to Seneca Hill.

SENECA HILL
Office of Caldwell International

August 1, 1864

Dear Father,

I have returned from the Democratic National Convention in Chicago. You or I have represented the Caldwells of South Carolina in the last ten conventions. We are always ahead of others when predicting the future. I can now predict that Mr. Lincoln will be re-elected. General McClellan refuses to make peace with John Breckenridge and put him on the ticket as Vice President.

I may be asked to resign from the department of the Navy. When will this happen? I do not know. But as you always say, "Advanced knowledge is like gold." And I have asked Sam Mason to pack up my things when the time comes.

I also have the information that you requested in your last letter. I will send you that in a telegram directly to Caldwell Place. Letter writing always helps me clear my head and you are a good listener. I have been giving some thought as to what we might do to help rebuild South Carolina.

My vision for Caldwell International is to expand as rapidly as possible into banking, development of our mineral based assets and ignoring our agriculture based commodities. As soon as we are allowed back into the state, we should return with all the resources necessary to assist the City of Beaufort and the State of South Carolina.

Louise sends her best.

Jason

CALDWELL
INTERNATIONAL

St. George, Bermuda

August 1, 1864

Mr. Kyle Johnston

Director Port Facilities

Port Royal, South Carolina

Dear Mr. Johnston:

Please be advised that within a few months, at the end of the war. I will be sending you an offer for the purchase of the Port Royal properties formerly owned by Caldwell Trading and Shipping. Please send notice of amount due to:

Bank of Bermuda

    Caldwell Trading and Shipping Account

St. George, Bermuda

If a purchase is not possible, please send the next years lease forms to rent the same facilities from the owners.

Sincerely yours,

Jason Caldwell

THE ARMY NAVY
BUILDING

Department of the Navy

August 1, 1864
Robert Whitehall, President
Caldwell Trading and Shipping
St. George, Bermuda

Dear Robert,

*The offer to purchase the office, warehouses and other properties
in Port Royal is enclosed for your information. Please mail it
to them for me. If a purchase is not possible, I will forward
a copy of the lease of same back to you. We can always rent
available warehousing as our needs dictate . A secure facility
must be found in Port Royal after the war for the shipment of
Oil to South Carolina. I will arrange for Seneca Oil to begin
shipments as soon as I get clearance.*

*Also, you may want to contact the C I Offices in Nevada and
get quarterly reports sent directly to you again. I have directed
the banks used in Nevada to report deposits directly to you.
Income from Nevada will now be used to rebuild our holdings in
South Carolina. Income from Pennsylvania can be used also.
As President of the company, decide where you would like to
live, inside or outside of South Carolina.*

*For the time being, there is an advantage to the Bermuda
location. Awaiting your response, I remain*

Sincerely yours,

Jason Caldwell

Trying to run a business while serving part time in the Army Navy building was not something that I would have to do much longer if the telegram from Monty proved correct. The election this year would end my service in Washington City. Then Louise, the children and I would be free to live wherever we chose. I was putting away my stationary when Louise stuck her head inside my office and said, "Have you read your morse code incomings yet."

"No, there is a stack of them here, I was about to go through them."

"I have read most of them as I took them off the writer. Louis Napoleon has landed troops in Mexico."

"What?"

"Maximilian, Archduke of Austria has been appointed by Napoleon as the Emperor of Mexico."

"I had better start with the earliest date and read all of these."

JASON

AS DISCUSSED IN OUR CABINET MEETINGS THIS SPRING AND SUMMER, THE LOSSES IN BATTLES AND BY DISEASE HAVE BEEN APPALLING AND THE QUESTIONS OF WHEN IS THIS BLOODSHED TO END? IS THE UNION WORTH SO MANY LIVES? ARE WE NOT PAYING TO HIGH A PRICE FOR ITS PRESERVATION. INDIFFERENCE IS NOW COMMON PLACE AMONG THE CABINET MEMBERS WITH THE EXCEPTION OF Welles AND SEWARD. THE REST INCLUDING MYSELF, HAVE SUGGESTED A WAY OUT. VICE

PRESIDENT HAMILEN, HAS SUGGESTED THAT HE BE AN ENVOY TO RICHMOND TO LEARN UPON WHAT MUTUAL TERMS PEACE COULD BE HAD BETWEEN THE TWO PARTIES.

THE PRESIDENT WAS ANGRY, BUT INDICATED THAT HE WOULD TAKE OUR SUGGESTIONS UNDER ADVISEMENT. MY FEELING IS THAT THE PRESIDENT WILL NOT RELINQUISH EFFORTS TO RESTORE THE UNION. HE WILL INSTEAD REPLACE ALL WHO DISAGREE. HE ALREADY HAS REPLACED THE VICE PRESIDENT BY CHOOSING JOHNSON AS HIS RUNNING MATE.

MONTY.

I placed that message in a new pile and picked up the next.

JASON:

WE KNOW YOU ARE AWAY FROM SENECA HILL ATTENDING THE DEMOCRATIC CONVENTION. BUT YOU SHOULD BE AWARE THAT LOUIS NAPOLEON HAS JUST FORMALLY RECOGNIZED THE CONFEDERATE STATES OF AMERICA AS A SEPARATE NATION; WITH THE ASSISTANCE OF ENGLAND AND SPAIN HE HAS LANDED TROOPS IN MEXICO. HE ALSO HAS CREATED THE EMPEROR OF MEXICO TO REPLACE THE REPUBLIC OF MEXICO, PRESIDENT JUAREZ.

THIS IS A IN FLAGRANT VIOLATION OF THE
MONROE DOCTRINE AND THE PRESIDENT
HAS RESPONDED. CONTACT US AS SOON
AS YOU READ THIS.

EDWIN STANTON, SECRETARY OF WAR

GIDEON Welles, SECRETARY OF THE NAVY

I did not place that message in the new pile. I ran
to find my key operator, Peter Wise. I had him send the
following response:

SECRETARIES STANTON AND WELLES:

WHAT   WAS   PRESIDENT   LINCOLN'S
RESPONSE?

JASON CALDWELL, UNDERSECRETARY OF
THE NAVY.

We waited. Four minutes later the morse code writer
began to chatter.

ADMIRAL:

MESSAGE RECEIVED AND A COPY EACH WAS
HAND DELIVERED TO BOTH SECRETARIES.
STAY ALERT FOR MESSAGES TO FOLLOW.

SAMUEL MASON, CAPTAIN USMC

Again, I sat and gazed at the morse code writer willing it to come to life with a message response. An hour
later it did.

JASON:

THE PRESIDENT HAS PREPARED A SERIES OF RESPONSES.

FIRST, HE HAS HAD THE AMERICAN AMBASSADOR IN PARIS FILE A FORMAL COMPLAINT WITH NAPOLEON. IT INFORMS HIM THAT WE ARE SENDING TROOPS TO ASSIST PRESIDENT JUAREZ. GENERAL SHERMAN WILL BE ORDERED TO BREAK OFF HIS ATTACK THROUGH THE SOUTH AND BOARD TROOP TRAINS FOR THE MEXICAN BORDER AND ADMIRAL HAGOOD IS DIRECTED TO LAND MARINES VIA THE GULF.

SECOND, HE HAS SENT ORDERS TO GENERAL GRANT TO BREAK OFF HIS SIEGE OF PETERSBURG, VIRGINIA AND BOARD TROOP TRAINS FOR CANADA. GENERAL GRANTS ORDERS ARE SUBJECT TO GREAT BRITAINS FORMAL RECOGNITION OF CSA AND HER CONTINUED SUPPORT OF MAXIMILIAN IN MEXICO.

THIRD, HE WILL BE SENDING YOU ORDERS TO COMMAND THE SIXTH FLEET TO INVADE CUBA WITH THE FOURTH MARINE DIVISION IF SPAIN FORMALLY RECOGNIZES CSA AND CONTINUES THEIR SUPPORT OF MAXIMILIAN.

FOURTH, AND I THINK A BRILLIANT STEP, HE HAS SENT COPIES OF THE MONROE DOCTRINE TO THE KING OF SPAIN, QUEEN OF ENGLAND, AND NAPOLEON III. ALONG

WITH A PERSONAL LETTER TO EACH
STATING THAT A STATE OF WAR NOW
EXISTS BETWEEN THE UNITED STATES AND
FRANCE FOR VIOLATION OF THE MONROE
DOCTRINE AND IT WILL EXIST WITH
ANY OTHER EUROPEAN COUNTRIES WHO
VIOLATE IT.

My God, I thought we are going to be at war with
Europe! I reread Sam's message. It stated be alert for
the messages to follow. I carefully read the last message
again. It jumped off the sheet at me, there is no sixth
fleet, where did that come from? There is no fourth marine division. I smell a rat! I had Peter key another message to Sam, this time partly in code.

SAM:

HAVE READ FIRST MESSAGE. I AM
PREPARING TO TAKE COMMAND OF THE
SIXTH FLEET. NOTIFY GENERAL SCHNEIDER
OF THE FOURTH MARINES THAT HE IS TO
BE READY TO SAIL UPON MY ARRIVAL IN
POTOMAC DOCKYARDS. USE FOLLOWING
SUBSTITUTION CODE FOR REMAINDER
MESSAGE.

474J48474HTYGDMMVKKFJGU998E77
E6E6FGCBBSMMDJJSSMSMSSM3M4M4M5M

REAR ADMIRAL, USN

In less than a minute I received the following in
code.

Admiral

The secretaries were worried that you might not get their little ploy. Our outgoing and incoming are being read by the ORION spy group that was sent north with General Butler after Bull Run one. I assured them you would caught on, thanks for the promotion to General. Pinkerton has identified fifteen members still active inside ORION. They report everything then can to Richmond. It is our hope that the President's outgoing to Generals Sherman and Grant will be reported to Richmond. We need to make sure this is reported to London, Paris and Madrid. Can you let this slip out in Bermuda so that London will get it? The State Department is already lodging formal complaints in the three capitals, your information will confirm it.

Tom

Peter and I were going to have a busy night. We sent telegrams to Jerome Lewis in Bermuda assuming they would be read by ORION. I wrote a rather carefully crafted telegram, again for ORION's benefit, to our embassy in Paris informing them of the plans to land a force of marines on the eastern shore of Mexico. I also sent a message to the Madrid Embassy saying that the fourth marines would invade and capture Cuba unless Spain formally announced that they were no longer were in support of Maximilian in Mexico. I sent a telegram to the Washington Post for them to run in the next available edition.

ATTENTION SAILORS ON LEAVE FROM SIXTH FLEET

REPORT TO YOUR STATIONS BEFORE O800 AUGUST

6, 1864, FOR IMMEDIATE DEPLOYMENT.

REAR ADMIRAL CALDWELL, USN

In between Peter's key tapping of various messages, I read the rest of the incomings and placed them into two piles. We sent brief returns on the second pile and then fell into our beds for the night.

Early the next morning I was on the train for Washington. I picked up a copy of the Washington Post from the train platform and the headline read.

US Gears up for war in Mexico

The reporters never got anything right. Others from the Army Navy Building were already at work leaking information to the newspapers on the cover story. The reporter for the article that I read said he had, from confirmed sources, that Mr. Lincoln would not tolerate a dictatorship in Mexico. Lincoln had already alerted the 4th Division of the Marines to return from leaves so that an invasion force could land on the east coast of Mexico. I smiled and said to myself, "No, the 4th is going with me to Cuba — try to get the lies straight, will you?"

I stepped off the train in Union Station and was met by a group of reporters. I was in uniform, so I was an easy target. If you want to get a bulls attention you wave a red flag, right! The uniform of a rear admiral is like a red flag to reporters. I tried pushing through them to meet Sam Mason, but I stopped just in time, looked

218

exhausted and said, "What is it? I have got to get to Potomac Dockyards."

"Are you the fleet commander for the sixth, Admiral?"

"The President has just issued orders to that affect."

"Can you tell us if you are going to Cuba?"

"The fleet is scheduled to perform a sweep of the Gulf of Mexico to hunt down any remaining CSS ships of the line and destroy them even if we have to chase them to Cuba."

"Will you land the 4th Marine Division in Mexico, Admiral."

"I think you have the wrong admiral, Fleet Admiral Benjamin Hagood is the supreme commander and he decides where and when the Marines with land on foreign soil. He could decide to take them to Canada, Cuba or Charleston, South Carolina for all I know." You are a liar Jason Caldwell, I thought.

The next day all of the papers, had from confirmed sources, the fact that Admiral Hagood was going to land a marine division on the east coast of Mexico while Admiral Caldwell would begin a blockade of all Canadian east coast ports until England withdrew their support of the French Army in Mexico. Sam and I sat in my office in the Army Navy Building sending messages by telegraph to nonexisting marine detachments to please hurry to the Potomac Dockyards. Gideon Welles had ordered everything that could float to begin to built steam in their boilers and make ready to sail away from the dockyards. He even had gun boats that were in for refits ready for towing so late the night of August 6, 1864 the dockyards could be emptied of all vessels. Most of these were towed around the Chesapeake for a few days and then gradually they were brought back one at a time.

The gamble worked. On August 21, 1864, the State Department reported that Madrid had contacted the American Ambassador to explain that a formal letter of Spain's neutrality in the American Civil War was on route to both Richmond and Washington. The State Department then informed Madrid that the sixth fleet would be redirected to the Gulf of Mexico. Secretary Seward walked into my office on the 22nd and said, "Jason, your sixth fleet is not going to invade Cuba."

"Good, they are needed in Mexico or Canada, I have not decided which one." I smiled and thought, "My last acts as an Admiral in the USN are deceptions and misinformation for the enemy."

No word was forthcoming from either London or Paris, so the War Department decided that Richmond had taken the bait that Sherman was in the process of moving his army to Texas and Grant was in the process of moving to Canada. Word was sent to Pinkerton to determine the actions of Confederate General Hood, the defender of Atlanta. He sent reports to Washington that indicated that Richmond believed that only a small portion of Sherman's Army remained near Atlanta. General Hood was free to leave his intrenchments and capture the Union Army that remained.

On the night of August 25th, two corps on the extreme left abandoned their intrenchments and marched to the southwest. Then other corps followed the next day to destroy the Union Army. The people of Atlanta were delighted to learn that the Union Army had withdrawn which meant the lifting of the siege of Atlanta.

General Hood did not learn of the deception until it was too late. His army was caught in the open by a superior Union force. The terrifying news spread thorough Atlanta. Hood saw the fatal trap into which he had been led and knew that his only hope was in getting out of the city at once. A portion of his military stores were loaded on wagons and the rest were set on fire. The skies were lit up by the glare of the fire and the exploding munitions. This set the entire city ablaze. Sherman sat upon his mount outside the city and viewed the lighting up of the heavens. " In years to come, my army will get the blame for the burning of Atlanta."

22

The ORION Network
Richmond, Virginia

President Davis was alarmed so much when he learned of the capture of Atlanta from the ORION network, that he and his Secretary of War, L. "Pope" Walker, hurried from Richmond to Hood's army to learn first hand the actual situation. They found most of Hood's army intact and Hood planning to attack Sherman who had moved his headquarters into the State Capitol of Georgia. Hood, Walker and Davis sat together in Hood's tent.

"Mr. President, the tables are turned. I have him bottled up in Atlanta. I have sent for addition reinforcements, in fact General Hardee has left Lovejoy Station and should arrive within the hour. When they arrive, we will surround Atlanta and starve him into submission."

"Can you keep Sherman here for at least a month, General?" Asked Pope Walker.

"Of course, why?"

"I am ordering the ORION Network to commence operation Archangel!"

General Hood had no idea what the hell, "Archangel," was. But he did not want to let the Secretary of War and head of the ORION spy network know of his ignorance. It sounded like an act of desperation to him, however. He changed the subject by telling his President, his version of what had happened in Atlanta the night of September 1, 1864.

"I have been told that Union General Slocum rode into Atlanta at daybreak on September 2nd and was met by the Mayor of Atlanta who presented him with a folded US flag. The general had the state flag of Georgia removed from the top of the capitol and the US flag raised."

"First, Mobile by Farragut and now this by Slocum. We must cut off the head of the dragon before the entire Confederacy is eaten alive."

"Yes, Mr. President, Sherman has ordered all civilians out of Atlanta, he intends to defend the city to the last person. He can not escape me, I will destroy him. His advance from Chattanooga has cost him over 5,000 dead, 22,000 walking wounded and over 4,000 missing. CSA lost 3,000 during the advance. Neither Sherman or Grant seem to understand that the Conscription Act is not a bottomless pit of humans ready to fight for their country. ORION reports that thousands are sick of the fighting and are now avoiding the draft by going to Canada."

"Yes, yes, General; but what do you think of operation Archangel?" Pope Walker asked.

"Do you think it will work, Mr. President?"

"Archangel is a bold move, not an act of desperation. If Lincoln is re-elected in November, we will put it into action."

"I have until November then to starve Sherman out of Atlanta. I can meet Sherman's support coming from Chattanooga and defeat the general commanding them, correct?"

"If an opportunity presents itself to defeat a whole Union army coming to the rescue of Sherman, that would be an added bonus. The main item of battle is to keep Sherman in Atlanta and prevent his escape. If he escapes, his army will destroy every major city in his path, look what he did to Atlanta."

Major General Hood did not tell his president that he was the one who burned Atlanta. He rode with his president to board his train for Macon, Georgia. At Macon, Davis had the train stop and he gave a speech to the awaiting crowds. "My fellow citizens of the Confederacy, General Hood has managed to trap the animal Sherman inside Atlanta. The entire city is surrounded and he can not escape. General Hardee's army from southern Georgia has joined him in this great effort to starve the Union army inside Atlanta and to advance north toward Chattanooga to meet the Union General Thomas who will try to free Sherman. Before November, the war in Georgia will be over with a great victory for us."

In a nut shell, Jefferson Davis revealed the entire southern strategy for the battle of Atlanta. A Pinkerton agent was standing in the crowd at Macon listening and he remembered nearly every word, which was promptly forwarded to Sherman headquarters in Atlanta. Hood's plan was to completely surround Atlanta when Hardee's army arrived and then set off for Chattanooga to defeat General Thomas in battle. Hardee was late. Sherman's

Cavalry rode from Atlanta to meet Thomas and warn him of the upcoming battle. Sherman's orders were; he should not engage Hood, but fall back with his forces until he could be supported by the Army of the Cumberland. Sherman gave orders for Thomas to "look after Hood." The advance party from Chattanooga was commanded by General Schofield. He fell back before the advancing Hood fighting a delaying action until the Army of the Cumberland could reach him. Schofield met Thomas outside of Nashville, a Union stronghold. The month of September passed with light fighting around Nashville, while Sherman broke out of the containment around Atlanta and defeated General Hardee's army in another months time. The end of November came with a slight victory for Hood's forces outside of Nashville. But that was the last that he would see of victory. General Thomas attacked out of Nashville with a superior force, capturing 54 cannon, 4,460 prisoners and 2000 missing confederate loses. In two days the Confederate Army under Hood fled in confusion for a second time. Thomas pursued with relentless energy and Hood and his demoralized troops forded the Duck River then the Tennessee River and then disappeared into the country side. More importantly, Sherman was allowed to take Macon. Macon was defended by Howell Cobb, former Secretary of the Treasury under President Buchanan. Cobb's 10,000 volunteers were no match for Sherman's 60,000 and they were swept aside like dry leaves before the wind. No one stood between Sherman and Savannah.

Sherman arrived in Savannah on the 10th of December. The famous "march to the sea," was over. The three hundred miles were straight through the heart of the

Confederacy, and for most of the men leaving Atlanta, it was no more than a pleasure excursion. The remainder of Hardee's forces in Atlanta had withdrawn into South Carolina.

In Richmond, ORION ordered the commencement of operation Archangel. Pope Walker was not amused by the total disappearance of General Hood and his army. This coupled with the retreat of General Hardee into South Carolina reduced his options for delaying the war. Winning the war was no longer an option. The most he could hope for was a draw and Archangel would give him this much needed delay and the opportunity to council with the new administration in Washington. Walker sent his one line, coded message, to the Grand Dragon, Army Navy Building.

Commence Operation Archangel.

23

The Election of 1864
November

The Washington Post had the following headline after the presidential election of 1864.

Democrats Split Vote Again: Lincoln Wins

	States	Popular Vote	Electoral Vote
Lincoln	22	2,218,388	212
Breckinridge	1	1,225,110	13
McClellan	4	1,812,807	24

The election 1864 was the first time since 1812 that a presidential election took place during a war. For much of 1864, Lincoln believed he had little chance of being re-elected. Confederate forces had won at the battles of Mansfield, Crater and Cold Harbor. In addition, the war was continuing to take a high toll. The prospect of a long and drawn out war started to make the idea of "peace at any cost" offered by the "copperheads" look more desirable. Because of this, McClellan was thought to be a heavy favorite to win the election.

However, several political and military events made Lincoln's re-election possible. First the Democrats nominated two candidates and split their party at the convention. And they remained split, unlike the Republicans who joined forces in September to run an affective campaign. The political compromises made at the Democratic convention were contradicting and made McClellan's campaign inconsistent and difficult. McClellan was also mystified by the number of newspapers who ran his announcements beside the following:

THE BEGINNING

ELECTION of M'CLELLAN!

Pendleton	Vallandigham
V.President	Secretary of War

A R M I S T I C E!

FALL OF WAGES!

NO MARKET FOR PRODUCE!

Pennsylvania a Border State?

Invasion! Civil War! Anarchy!

DESPOTISM!!

THE END.

THE FOLLOWING CITIZENS WOULD LIKE TO VOTE FOR GENERAL M'CLELLAN, BUT WE CANNOT

WE ARE WOMEN!

Louise Buchanan	Cynthia Majors
Carol Johnson	Mary L. Edwards
Eleanor Baker	Kay Merrywell
Emily Dodge	Beverly Schmitz
Connie Stills	Trudy Wells

GIVE US THE RIGHT TO VOTE! AND WE WILL!

At first McClellan laughed at the newspaper's co-incidence, then when it happened again outside of Pennsylvania his campaign workers contacted the news-papers involved. They reported that a Mrs. Louise Buchanan Caldwell had a standing order to place her an-nouncement whenever the General placed his and she had paid for 100 in advance.

The final straw for McClellan was Union Generals Sherman and Grant. Sherman was advancing on Atlanta and Grant was pushing Confederate General Lee into the outer defenses of Richmond. It became increasing obvi-ous that a Union military victory was inevitable and close at hand. McClellan hopes faded when John C. Fremonte announced that was encouraging his followers to vote for President Lincoln. Fremonte announced, "Mr. Lincoln has agreed to stop the corruption within his cabinet by dismissing Postmaster Montgomery Blair and his stooge

Undersecretary of the Navy, Jason Caldwell."

The Lincoln and Johnson ticket ran newspaper announcements also and Louise Caldwell was there to answer with:

LINCOLN   JOHNSON
President   V. President

DON'T CHANGE HORSES IN THE MIDDLE OF THE STREAM!

Vote for Lincoln and Johnson. A certain Victory for the Union!

PRESIDENT LINCOLN YOU FREED THE SLAVES OF THE SOUTH.

WHAT ABOUT THE WOMEN OF THIS COUNTRY?

WHEN CAN THEY VOTE FOR YOU OR ANYONE ELSE?

Only 24 states participated, because 11 had seceded from the union. Three new states voted for the first time, Nevada, West Virginia and Kansas. Tennessee and Louisiana were completely under federal control and voting took place, however, their electoral votes were not counted.

On November 24, 1864, Abraham Lincoln dismissed Montgomery Blair and appointed William Dennison as the new Postmaster General of the United States. No one was calling for the dismissal of Jason Caldwell and

Gideon Welles never dated his letter of resignation. More importantly, Mr. Lincoln did not date Gideon Welles letter of resignation. On December 11, 1864, Lincoln did ask for and receive resignations from the Secretary of the Treasury, William Fessenden, he was replaced by Hugh McCulloch. He than dismissed Attorney General Bates and replaced him with James Speed. Gideon Welles, William Seward and Edwin Stanton were now the only remaining members of the cabinet that had not been replaced.

The Grand Dragon left his office in the Army Navy building and was walking to Lafayette park to clear his head. He stopped at the third bench from the Jackson Memorial and reached under the left side to find a sheet of paper folded several times and wedged between the bench and the front leg. He pulled it out, unfolded it and read.

Commence Operation Archangel

It has come to this then, he thought. He refolded the sheet of paper and placed in the pocket of this great coat. He stood, stretched and then walked to the Hay-Adams to send a telegram. He sent a telegram to his family saying he was called away from the Army Navy Building to deliver a message and he would not be home for two days. That way his disappearance from work and his survival would not be questioned during the investigation of the horrible tragedy that befell Washington City.

He walked back to his office and withdrew a small bottle marked MEDICINE and walked to the basement of the Army Navy Building. He found the water supply tank for the boiler and poured the contents in. He immediately left the building and waited in Lafayette Park for the Archangel Squad to meet. Before long he was met by a young page from the House of Representatives, and then from the Senate. They both nodded their heads that the medicine had been administered. They waited nearly an hour before the janitor from the White House arrived. He was calm but could not stop talking about what he had done.

"Shut your mouth. We must never speak of this again. We have just killed hundreds of people." The Grand Dragon and commander of the Archangel Squad said.

They did not leave the park and go their separate ways as was planned. Each had a cover story for being out of their buildings. One was delivering a message, one was sick, another had a sick mother at home and the forth had cut his hand and was at the doctor's. They stared at the buildings wondering how long it would take for the poison gas to work. It did not take long. A muffled sound came first from the Army Navy Building and then smoke from the basement windows could be seen. The boiler had exploded. Workers came streaming out of the building to stand on the sidewalks facing Lafayette Park. Then the same sound came from the White House with the following results. The Archangel Squad left for their prearranged destinations. Similar boiler explosions in both the houses of Congress forced federal workers into the December cold of Washington City.

The next days Washington Post carried the following headline and article.

Boiler Breaks Give Federal Employees Early Christmas Vacations

It was revealed today that the steam boilers in the White House, Army Navy Building and Houses of Congress were slightly damaged by minor explosions when cleaning fluid was accidental added to the water tanks by workmen this week. The President and his staff have moved to Blair House with an extra added marine detail for security. Boiler repairs in the White House are expected to take a week or so. The after election work of the White House continues. It was reported that the new Postmaster General, Attorney General and Secretaries of the Interior and Treasury had not moved into their offices when the boiler breaks occurred.

The Senators and the House of Representative will begin their Christmas breaks early this week and the repairs to their buildings will be completed after the first of the year. Many had already headed home for the holidays. The Army Navy personnel not vital to the war effort were also given an early vacation.

Secretary of War, Edwin Stanton was quoted as saying, "We needed a break from the war but this not what I had in mind. General Sherman, upon hearing of our 'out in the cold', here in Washington, has notified me from Savannah that the weather there is warm, why not come to inspect the troops!

The Secretary of the Navy had the following comment. "The temperature in the Army Navy Building will remain pleasant as long as the Army and the Navy continue to report victories from the fields of battle and sea lanes throughout the southern United States."

Meanwhile, the officers inside the Army Navy Building are wearing their great coats and stamping their feet while continuing to manage the war effort. Undersecretary of the Navy, Admiral Caldwell had already taken his Christmas break with his family in sunny Bermuda. He will be unaware of the cold working conditions until his return.

The Grand Dragon sat at his kitchen table in Washington City reading the Washington Post and wondered why ORION had given them cleaning fluid to dump in the water tanks of the building in which they worked. He would have to walk over to the Hay-Adams and send another telegram to his control agent.

War Secretary Walker sat at his breakfast table in Richmond, reading the overnights and learned of the disaster of Archangel. Now they would have to do it the old fashioned way and a list for assassination was hand written on a piece of paper. It began:

1. Abraham Lincoln (Grand Dragon send free theater tickets to the White House)

2. Andrew Johnson (explore security at Blair House)

3. Seward's home is not secure, attack same date as Ford appearance

4. Stanton's home is not secure, attack same date

5. Fressenden is in the hospital (ORION find out condition)

6. Dennison is unmarried address unknown (find location)

7. Speed has not moved to Washington City (find

present location)

8. Welles lives in Maryland (easiest hit of the cabinet can be taken day after)

9. Usher? (ORION report current information)

On or before April 1, 1865 plan a concurrent attack on the homes of Seward, Stanton, Welles, Caldwell and the newly appointed members of the cabinet. These are to attempted only after the Dragon has been found outside the White House and eliminated.

24

Christmas in Bermuda
December 1864

Christmas has always been a special time of year for the Caldwell family, a time for gathering and celebration and we were all in attendance at Caldwell Place, St. George, Bermuda. This year Louise and I had closed Seneca Hill and given the household staff a month's paid vacation. They had agreed to return January15, 1865, and reopen the estate. My father and mother said they would like to stay in Caldwell Inn for Christmas. They had locked up their new estate on the island they had purchased in the Great Sound and had come to St. George by water taxi. Trey and Mariann had purchased our parent's house in St. David and the cottage next to it. They hired work men and had constructed a connection between the two cottages. They now had a place large enough for their children and a small household staff. James; age 7, Ruth; age 5 and Carol, age 2 had not seen their cousins for two Christmases and it was a loud and cheerful Christmas vacation. I suggested that the

Whitehalls and John Butler move into the inn so they could all be together and they agreed. My father pulled me aside and said, "You do know that John and Sallie have been seeing each other, Jason. He already lives with her in her cottage here at Caldwell Place."

"John and Sallie?"

"Yes, son! What do think of that?"

"John, has found someone? I did not know that."

"Few people did until he told Sallie he wanted to live with her, it seems he is proud of it."

"Well, if Sallie loves him, he should be. You know, Dad, Sallie is a fine person and one of the finest managers we have ever had anywhere in Caldwell International."

"Oh, Jason, I did not mean it that way. I am happy for John, just like I was happy for you and Louise. I figured you were a confirmed bachelor, what with all the ladies that came and went in your life."

"Dad, Louise knows nothing about when I was young and stupid. We need to keep it that way. I never asked her about other men in her life. It has never mattered to me."

He held me close and it reminded me of the Christmas of '62 when Louise and I went to Boston. He whispered in my ear, "Louise and Sallie are both fine women, Jason, you and John are lucky to have them in your life. I love you, son."

"What are you two up to?" Mother said.

"He told me what he wanted to get for you for Christmas, Mom. I told him that I doubted you could get into one of those new body corsets."

"Robert Hays Caldwell, you had better not even try to get me one of those foul things!"

"Well, then Jason and I are leaving for Hamilton to do some more shopping. Are you coming?"

"No, I am not!"

My father knew that I needed to get on into Hamilton and get the mail from the Army Navy Building. So we walked together, down Rose Hill and into the Duke of York turned left and ended at the Bermuda Railroad Station.

"Jason, are you all right, you look pensive?"

"I have been trying to decide if I need to stay with the US Navy until the end of the war. Or another option might be to stay until the end of Lincoln's second term. I am a confirmed Democrat, Dad, I can not go along with many of the things that the Republicans stand for."

"Stanton is a Democrat, right? How does he do it, Son?"

"Stanton is a politician, Dad, he thinks that he can be useful to the Republicans that seem to be lost most of the time."

We were pulling into Hamilton and I left him to walk to Trimminghams on Front Street and I headed for the US Ambassador's Office to visit with Jerome Lewis. "You go ahead on home when you have finished your shopping, Dad, I have no idea how long I will be with Jerome."

"Jerome, I have to make a decision. You have been my counsel for many years now. I always feel better talking to you. I am not getting anything accomplished as the undersecretary of the Navy. For the last several months, all I have done is send off fake messages to non-existing units under my fake command."

"Welcome to my life as an Ambassador, Admiral. That is exactly all I have done here and I am sick of it. When you figure out how to get us back in the war, count me in."

"Jerome, I had no idea."

"Before you decide anything, Admiral, read these incomings from the State Department. It seems that someone tried to poison the people working in the White House, Senate, House and Army Navy Building."

"What?"

"Just go through those, it is all there. Those stupid bastards nearly killed five hundred non- combatants."

I began reading and when I finished I said, "Jerome, this may be what we are looking for. Who ordered this? Are they active in Washington or were they sent to do this thing on a one time basis? We can find out. Together, we can do something about this. We are not without resources."

"What do mean?"

"Jerome, someone who would not be noticed added the poison to the water tanks, right?"

"Right."

"Then they are employees! We have confederate sympathizers or confederate agents working in these buildings, probably a group known as ORION."

"My God, you are right, Admiral. I have other messages here that mention the ORION network."

"Thank you, Captain. How would you like to help me identify the members of ORION?"

"Can you do that?"

"Of course, I am an Admiral. See the big red A on my undershirt!"

"How can I get one of those? Only, make mine a big blue C."

"Either I will transfer you within 30 days or I will resign my assignment and return to Bermuda and we can work from here."

"From here?"

"Yes, I think we will find the answer to the puzzle from the Ambassador to Bermuda."

"John Butler, he is harmless."

"He is a member of ORION did you know that?"

"God, no. How did you find out?"

"He told me in a hotel room at the Hay-Adams, only I was not listening."

"I do not understand?"

"You will, do you want to help me in this? You will have to come to Washington. You can use your diplomatic cover to get a lot of things done that you could not get done as a Captain in the USN working for me."

"If you return to Washington as a member of the State Department, it would be better, agreed."

"Agreed, oh, my wife is going to kill me, she loves it here in Bermuda."

"She and the children should stay here, Jerome, tell her you are assigned to Washington on a short temporary assignment. I will try to get you a 90 day leave of absence from Seward to work for me. In the meantime, come out to St. George and spend a few days with us, the inn is nearly empty."

"We can come for a few days, Admiral."

"Good. Let me get busy on the communications that should be sent."

I wrote, so Jerome could send the following in diplomatic pouch:

TO: Secretary of State Seward, the White House

FROM: Rear Admiral Jason Caldwell, Hamilton, Bermuda

SUBJECT: temporary change in assignment for Jerome Lewis

I would like your permission to have Jerome Lewis return to Washington with me. I will need his expertise for 90 days, after that time he could return to his duties at his station in Bermuda. Further information on this matter is available from Secretary Welles.

Awaiting your response.

TO: Secretary Welles, Army Navy Building

FROM: Rear Admiral Jason Caldwell, Hamilton, Bermuda

SUBJECT: Ninety day leave of absence from my duties as undersecretary

Certain information has come to my attention regarding the boiler breakdowns in Washington. It has come from some unusual sources in Bermuda and South Carolina. If true, the network, I refer to should be "rolled up" before another attempt is made upon the President's life and the members of his cabinet, including myself. I have managed to identify the members of this network, those working out of Richmond and those presently assigned in Washington. Additional information is available from Secretary Seward and I will forward coded messages as information becomes available.

Awaiting your response.

TO: Abraham Lincoln, President of the United States

FROM: Rear Admiral Jason Caldwell, Hamilton, Bermuda

SUBJECT: Special assignment duties

I have requested a special 90 day assignment from Secretary Welles. This assignment is critical to the out come of the war and it deals with threats to your life. I once asked you if you trusted Allen Pinkerton. Pinkerton has withheld action on ORION because he lacks information on how to identify its members. I now have that information. If Secretary Welles can not grant this assignment, then I must, in all good conscious, resign my position as undersecretary. I will then retire from military service, and proceed on the assignment as a private citizen.

In any regard, I am presently gathering data on this assignment. You have my full and undivided support of the war efforts made to this date.

I left Jerome with the mail and walked to the C S A Embassy with one of Jerome's incoming messages. I rang the bell and a woman answered the door. "Is Minister Butler in?" I asked.

"Yes, who shall I say is calling?"

"Admiral Caldwell."

"Jason, I am so glad to see you." John Butler greeted me with a genuine warmth.

"Thank you, John. Do you have news of what has

happened in Washington regarding the attempt at a mass murder?"

"Yes, come in and I will tell you what I know."

"John, I do not want you to say anything until I show you something." I removed my great coat, jacket and vest. I rolled up my left sleeve to just below my elbow and said, "Do you have one of these?"

"Yes, Jason, I do."

"It is a tattoo of the constellation O' rion. You are required by South Carolina fraternal tradition to consider me a fellow warrior."

"I always have, Jason. You are my brother in arms."

"This damn Civil War has placed brother against brother. Did you know that a group of crazy people have been trying to kill Mr. Lincoln?"

"Yes, I walked into Washington City with thirty-five of them, I told you that at the Hay-Adams four years ago."

"I was too stupid to put it together, John. I know you can not tell me anything, honor requires that you keep your word. I have figured out a few things, can you shake your head yes if I tell you some things that I fear might be true?"

He shook his head yes, sat down at this desk, smiled and waited for me to begin.

"You and I were given these tattoos when we were very young, probably after our second birthdays."

He shook his head, yes.

"It consists of a very large group of men in the south?"

He looked straight ahead and said nothing.

"It consists of a group of men only from South Carolina?"

He shook his head, yes.

"These men are presently divided between Richmond and Washington, except for you and I."

He shook his head, yes.

"John, you should know that I am going to arrest those in Washington. Pinkerton will probably keep an eye on those now in Richmond."

He shook his head again.

"John, the war is almost over, why is Richmond trying to keep this bloodbath alive?"

"That can not be answered by shaking my head, Jason. It is madness. Only those in Richmond can answer you. I quit being of any use to Richmond a long time ago. Sallie and I are going to get married and have a family here in Bermuda, the Confederacy is dead to me. You must believe me."

"I do, John. I knew your heart was not in this when we met at the Hay-Adams."

"I wish I had a list of names to give you, Jason. I do know that the assassination squad you are looking for is called, Archangel."

"Thank you, John. You have just saved many innocent lives."

I left John's office and walked back to Jerome's office. "We need to send some additional information, Jerome."

TO: Secretary Stanton, Army Navy Building

FROM: Rear Admiral Jason Caldwell, Hamilton, Bermuda

SUBJECT: Special coded message

The information that I have obtained and forwarded to Secretary Welles should not wait until my return after the first of the year. A subgroup within the ORION network has been activated by Richmond. This is an assassination squad that calls itself Archangel. They are the ones responsible for the attacks on the buildings there. I have confirmed this from two different sources. They will try again before the end of the year.

You can identify an ORION member by a small tattoo of the constellation just below the left elbow. If the tattoo has been removed, a scar will appear where the tattoo was. The O'rion tattoo consists of two bright stars, Betelgeuse and Rigel, surrounded by smaller stars to represent the "great hunter." The O'rion organization is similar to the Masonic Order and dates from similar times. It was carried to the United States in 1701 by Stephen Bull when he settled in South Carolina. The tattoo is common in South Carolina, both my brother and I were members as children. It is not common outside of South Carolina and anyone found with one in Washington should be held for questioning until I can return.

You will find at least one member working in the White House, Senate and House, and in the Army Navy Building. They would not be questioned when entering or coming from a basement, so they are probably posing as workmen, repair men or labors. Look at the employment dates for all employees, my sources say they walked into Washington after the first battle of Bull Run. They would

not have worked in Washington prior to that time. Let
me know what you find. Can you spare Major Schneider
to assist me in this assignment for 90 days?

"Did John Butler confirm this, Admiral?"

"Yes, he did. Thanks to him we have the name of the assassination squad and who their targets are."

"Who is the second source?"

"My father."

"Your father?"

"He is very proud of his family history and he has told both Robert and me stories of the O' rion Fraternity in Ireland and what is was used for in South Carolina. I have no doubt that these members are working for the Confederacy in Richmond. It will be a race to see if we can round them up before they have completed their assignments."

"Do you think the targets have any idea that they are being hunted?"

"Lincoln should, there was an attempt on his life just after the election of '60, remember?"

"Yes, we were involved in the stopping of that too."

The day after Christmas the diplomatic mail pouch was delivered to Jerome's office. It contained the following:

TO: Rear Admiral Caldwell, On leave, Hamilton, Bermuda

FROM: Secretary Seward

SUBJECT: Receipt of eyes only President, through the State Department

The White House has granted your request for reassignment. You will leave your present location on or before January 2, 1865, and report to the Ambassador's Office, Havana Cuba. Here you will meet Major Thomas Schneider and his invasion force of US Marines. You will proceed at the best possible speed available to the Gulf of Mexico and land Major Schneider's marine forces just south of Brownsville, Texas. Major Schneider has a letter from President Lincoln to President Juarez. He will be responsible for all land operations and the link up with President Juarez's army. You are not permitted to set foot on Mexican soil. Upon the safe landing of the marines, you are to remain on station for evacuation of Major Schneider after his mission is complete.

Your request for retirement from the USN is hereby denied. All officers presently serving will continue until the war ends, plus six months.

If you ignore these orders and return to the United States, you will be arrested along with all other members of the ORION network and detained at St. Elizabeth's Hospital. No further communication is desired from you on this matter or any other until your assignment in Mexico is complete.

"Jerome, did you get any mail?" I said weakly as I handed the communique to him to read.

" No, I did not. This is sent in the open, Admiral, it was sent so ORION could read it."

"We sent everything in code, right?"

"Then there will be no Archangel members to arrest in Washington. They have failed to detain anyone for questioning. What do you make of that?"

"Not sure, Jerome. I am not permitted to send anything to the State Department. I will send orders for Sam Mason to box everything in my office and send it to Seneca Hill by January 15, 1865. He then should make his way to Pennsylvania and meet with my staff there to send and receive messages in code."

"What have I forgotten, Jerome."

"Protection to Havana. We have more 'palace guards' than I need. Take six of the most experienced marines that I have. You may be arrested when you step off the ship."

"Not if I go on the Cold Harbor. I do not think Tom will arrest me, Jerome. He trusts me completely, even if the White House does not."

"The War Department does not even have even army replacements for Grant or Sherman. If Tom shows up with marines, they will be raw recruits that he has just trained through his office in Washington. May be a hundred. He will need squad leaders like the six you will take from here. It may be just smoke again for France and England to absorb through ORION. Just for the record, Jason, I will do everything I can to assist you in the next few months, this stinks!"

"Whatever it is, Jerome, they have gotten my attention. Sam will be sending telegrams to you, I will be sending ship's mail to you and you can send mail to me, I will let you know the ship's name etc. as soon as I can. It will be a slow process, I am sure."

"A suggestion, Sir."

"Go ahead."

"How many recommisioned ships do you have in St. George?"

"You mean former USS ships of the line, vintage 1799?"

"Yes, it might be a good idea to show up in Havana with everything that floats if you want to sell the concept of an invasion force instead of a mail delivery to the President of Mexico in exile."

"You mean if ORION is watching they will see a large number of ships. Oh, that is a good idea, Jerome. We have a few days before I have to leave. I can get as many vessels as I can locate. Even if I have to rent some. This is going to be fun."

"Can I come, Admiral?"

"Do you have orders to the contrary? Do you have earned leave that you can request?"

"No and yes."

"Do it!"

25

Flotilla to Havana
January 1865

On new years day 1865, seven ships left St. Georges' Harbor, Bermuda and set sail for Havana, Cuba. Our orders were clear, "leave on or before January 2, 1865. The following ships left one day early. The Cold Harbor, a Snow, had its crew and passengers; Admiral Caldwell, Mrs. Caldwell, Captain Lewis, Mrs. Lewis, General Butler, Mrs. Butler (on their honeymoon), Mr. Robert Whitehall and Mrs. Whitehall. The *USS Somerset*, a Brigg, had its crew and six marine guards from the US Council's Office, Hamilton. The *USS Nelson*, a Brigg, had its crew. The *USS Providence*, a Snow, had its crew. The *USS New Haven*, a Ketch, had its crew. The *USS Trumbull*, a Ketch, had its crew. And finally, the Brigg *USS Spitfire* with its crew left for Havana. These were all sailing vessels, none were steam powered. They made quite a sight when all yards were put to the wind. A fast steam powered Sloop of War could make the trip from Bermuda to Havana in two and one half days. We would take a week.

"Admiral, what if the Navy had taken you up on the offer to sell these ships to block Charleston Harbor, we would not be in one of the last wind driven fleets to enter the Civil War."

"You are right, Robert. The Navy got a better offer from the whalers in Nantucket. No one will ever suspect that we are the means for the invasion of Mexico. I like it!"

"Jason?"

"Yes, Louise?"

"You are sure all of us are safe doing this?"

"Unless we meet something unexpected in Havana, say a steam powered fleet of seven vessels, we will be fine. If the Navy has provided us with ships, then you and the others will have had a nice winter vacation. You can stay as long as you like in Havana and take the 'fleet' back to Bermuda. I am not the most popular person in Washington right now. I doubt Tom and his recruits even find a ship to meet us there."

"Then what, Admiral?"

"Then, Captain Lewis, we wait in Havana until the end of the war waiting for the USMC to get there. Those were our orders and by God we will obey them to the letter."

"Do not curse God, Jason, it is bad luck."

"Let us all get down to the main salon for some of Hop Sing's food and enjoy the rest of this week. We can not send or receive messages until we arrive in Havana."

We did just that, and the week flew by with everyone enjoying themselves, especially John and Sallie Butler. John had sailed on the Cold Harbor with us to Boston and he was getting his sea legs. He enjoyed telling Sallie all about the names of the masts, how they were divided, how the yard arms carried different types of sails. This was all courtesy of James Jason Caldwell's lessons of course. We hated to see Havana Harbor and a single ship USS Philadelphia anchored there. That meant that the US Marines were already in Havana. I reported to the harbor master that one Snow, the Cold Harbor, would like to dock, the other six would anchor just inside the harbor. Captain Jacob lowered a long boat for Jerome and I. Two crew members helped us row out to the Philadelphia. A Sloop of War looks huge from a long boat. Jerome hailed the Philadelphia, "Admiral Caldwell to come aboard."

"Permission granted."

A gangway was lowered but it would not reach the long boat. It was about three feet above the gunwales of the long boat. "Can I give you a boost, Admiral?" After two tries, I was boosted onto the gangway and Jerome followed. We scrambled up and onto the deck of the Philadelphia. The ship's captain saluted us and said, "Welcome Admiral Caldwell, we have been expecting you." He was smiling a wide handsome grin.

"If you will follow me, I will take you to the briefing room."

"The briefing room?" I thought. I wonder who is on this ship?

We entered a long narrow room just port side of captain's quarters and there sat Secretary Welles and Major Thomas Schneider. Without thinking, Tom bellowed, "Flag Officer on deck!" He and everyone else, except Gideon Wells, leaped to their feet.

"As you were, everyone." Welles said without looking at me. "The Philadelphia is scheduled to leave in two hours, we need to get this over with. Admiral Caldwell, here are your written orders from the President of the United States. Major Schneider, you were given your orders by the President when you met with him in the Oval Office, correct?"

"Aye, aye, sir."

I was speechless. I had met President Lincoln in July 1861 and had not seen him since, now Tom has a meeting with him? May be I was all wrong about what this mission is supposed to entail. I must have had a blank look on my face because Gideon Welles said, "Relax Jason, you are among friends, no one here believes that you are a member of a Confederate spy ring." That broke the tension and everyone burst out laughing. He continued, "You gave an excuse for the President to slap you down, Admiral, he does like you very much. Probably because you say and do whatever you think is best. If I had as many millions as you, I would probably do the same thing." Smiles instead of laughter met his last remark.

"The point is, this is a real mission, not something to fool the Confederate listeners. That is why the President sent me to see you, Jason. He wants France to withdraw their troops from Mexico and the only way that will happen is if we land troops of our own to assist the Mexican Army in the over throw of Emperor Maximilian."

"How many Marines have you brought with you Mr. Secretary?" I asked.

"I have 875 well trained and eager to show what they have learned to the Mexican Army. Can you fit that many in your flotilla, Admiral?"

"Of course, I have had no communication on how

many billets I would need, so Captain Lewis and I planned for a 1000."

"Captain Lewis, it is good to see you again. I remember what an excellent job you did with President Lincoln's protection detail after he was elected. We need someone just like you in the White House now."

"Thank you, Mr. Secretary."

"Gentlemen, I must cut this short. You have to get your marines onto their transport. You are dismissed. Jason, can you stay a moment?"

"Of course, sir." When the others had left, he said, "Jason, I think the President is wrong. ORION will not stop until he is dead. I think he knows that he will not live out his second term and he is taking unnecessary risks with his own life. The rest of us have hired extra security in our offices and our homes. You should also."

"I will, sir. And thank you for this chance to get out of the President's dog house. Tom Schneider will do an excellent job for you, sir."

"I know he will, look who trained him!" And with that said Gideon Welles shook my hand and said, "Be careful with your wife and the guests that you brought with you, Jason. A war zone is no place for women and Confederate spies."

I must have had a shocked look on my face because he said, "You are not the only one with spies working for them, Jason. Have Robert Whitehall send me the lease agreement for the flotilla so that I can process payment. I was just kidding about you not needing payment because you were a millionaire, Jason."

I thanked him and told him the guests would be staying in Havana for a few days before sailing back to Bermuda. I left the briefing room to find Jerome and

Tom. Jerome, Tom and the six marines from Bermuda had their heads together getting caught up on the time apart from each other. I heard Jerome telling Tom that he had brought the six sergeants from the US Council's Office in Bermuda, could he use them? Tom just smiled and said, "The 875 raw recruits are like babies, now they have six more fathers!" He had a big smile on his face.

"All master sergeants take one step forward, you are now first lieutenants!"

A smile was crossing my face, " I said that very thing in Utah Territory a few years back to encourage my men, I thought."

"All staff sergeants take one step forward, you are now second lieutenants! Now you six lieutenants can go and meet the 875 marines and get them transferred to the Admirals Flotilla."

"Aye, aye, sir." They all said in unison.

We met the two hour deadline for the transfer of the marines to the three Snows, three Briggs and one Ketch. We would leave one Ketch, the New Haven, for the return of guests to Bermuda when they had finished their vacation in Havana. Tom Schneider, Jerome Lewis and I returned to the Cold Harbor. We enjoyed another great meal, put the families on the docks with their suitcases to say goodbye before the fleet sailed for the Gulf of Mexico. I waved from the bridge of the Cold Harbor as we pulled away from the docks and headed for the five anchored troop transports. We pulled along side the Brigg, Somerset and Tom transferred for the sail out of the harbor.

Jerome and I were standing at the starboard rail and we could see Key West off the starboard side. "Secretary

Welles was not kidding about you returning as chief of protection for the White House, Jerome. He is worried that Allen Pinkerton's men will not keep up the same level of protection now that the war is about over. If you do not take his offer, would you consider chief of protection for Caldwell International? Gideon thinks there will attempts on the lives of the cabinet members including mine."

Jerome said, "I already have a new job. Secretary Welles hired me and the six sergeants as your protection detail two weeks ago. I do not have the heart to tell Tom that he will have his six new lieutenants for only the trip to Mexico and the unloading of war materials, after that they will return with me as part of your detail. We go wherever you go. That includes Washington, Pennsylvania or the moon. It is an honor to serve you again, Admiral."

"Jerome, is this what you want?"

"Yes, sir. I have sat on my butt the entire war. Now I feel like I am doing something important."

"What about the wife and kids?"

"The kids are old enough to return to the US after the war. The wife will stay in Bermuda with the others at Caldwell Inn."

It would be another five more days until we were close enough to land the marines south of Brownsville, Texas. According to Captain Jacob's charts, it was 1050 nautical miles from Key West to Carboneras, Mexico. We had already come nearly 1400 miles from St. George to Havana. We posted lookouts on the main masts, we should not meet any CSS vessels, they were completely bottled up now that Fort Fisher had fallen. We had heard in Havana that Admiral David Porter's squadron of warships had subjected the fort to terrific bombardment while General Terry's land troops took it by storm. Wilmington, North Carolina, was the last resort of the blockade-runners and it was sealed off. This trapped the only remaining Confederate war vessels.

A few hours off the Mexican coast, a marine who was top side, spotted the Laguna Madre a long narrow barrier island that protected the fishing village of Carboneras located at the mouth of the Conchos River. Captain Jacob found the break in the barrier island and slowly led the six ships into the intra coastal waterway. A flag man signaled the other ships in line and we anchored just off shore. A boat was lowered and the three Spanish speaking marines joined Tom to row to the village docks. They tied up the boat and walked to the nearest canteen. President Juarez had his army hidden in the Nuevo Leon Mountains but had sent watchers to the coastal villages of La Pesca, Ciudad Madero and Carboneras. Tom met them and asked for assistance in unloading the boxes of muskets and other surplus materials that were offloaded from the Philadelphia into the holds of the three Briggs. He explained, through his interpreters, that President Lincoln had sent nearly a thousand men to support the Army of Mexico and its fight against the French. These troops would remain in Mexico until the French were driven out. He explained that this was just the first of many shipments to be made by the fleet now anchored at Carboneras. He also told them that General Sherman and his army would be sent to McAllen, Texas, ready to invade Mexico, should President Juarez request them. They indicated that the French were not in this part of Mexico and the marines could march to their camp in the mountains, or they could ride to the closest encampment and get soldiers to offload the needed supplies. Tom indicated that he would need a hundred workers if they could find that many. He would wait until they returned and he waved goodbye as they rode out of Caboneras.

Tom returned to the Cold Harbor and visited with Captain Jacob and me. "It is going to be difficult to unload heavy materials into long boats and row to the docks, but I do not see any way around that. There are no French troops near here so we should be able to take our time and unload as soon as the Mexican Army sends us a hundred men."

"A hundred men? What are you going to do with that many hands that may not be familiar with ships and long boats?" I asked.

"I am going to begin training my men, Admiral. There must be some common words between the two languages that my men can learn and use in conversational work, right?"

"I suppose so." I said doubtfully.

Before the month was out, Tom had his men learning simple Spanish commands mixed with sign language. Every time an American marine used a signal for lift up, the Mexican soldiers would cry out the Spanish for lift up and then they would laugh until the marine could repeat it correctly.

"You know, Tom, this is going to work. We will return to Havana to meet the Philadelphia and transfer another shipment. Will you be alright when we leave?"

"At some point, Admiral, it is a leap of faith. If we march into a French ambush, so be it. There will be a lot of dead Frenchmen buried in Mexico."

"Be smart, Tom, if you cannot find this President Juarez, leave and return for a pickup here at this location. Always have someone you trust watching for our return."

"Aye, aye, sir." He snapped to attention and gave me a salute.

26

Advisors in Mexico
February 1865

Tom Schneider and his marines had moved inland from their landing points at Carboneras, La Pesca and Ciudad Madero. They were led by their guides sent from President Juarez's encampment in the Nuevo Leon Mountains. President Juarez had also sent 100 Mexican soldiers to help with the unloading of the armaments and supplies sent by President Lincoln. The soldiers were unarmed except for rather long knives or short swords that they carried in their belts. During the unloading process, 875 English speaking US Marines began to learn simple Spanish commands. The tons of supplies were stacked in a storehouse in the fishing village of Carboneras and Tom sent one of the guides and ten soldiers back to President Juarez to request horses, wagons and pack mules. Until they returned all Tom could think of to do was train the 90 remaining Mexican soldiers. Tom had three Spanish speaking privates within his 875 marines and he found a dozen Mexican soldiers who indicated that they spoke English.

For the next week, several crates were opened and surplus muskets from 1845 were cleaned and test fired. Each Mexican soldier was asked if he could fire a musket. Every one nodded his head yes, even if he could not. Tom formed two lines with loaded guns in each row. After the first row fired, they knelt so that the second row could fire. The exercise did not go well. The first row fell flat upon the ground at the sound of muskets firing behind them. When they realized that they were unhurt, the leaped to their feet and cheered when the second row managed to fire each of their weapons and a celebration began.

"No, no. You must reload and fire again!" This command was translated into Spanish, but most of the soldiers looked at their US counterparts to see what to do. The demonstration was simple. Place the musket butt on the ground. Reach into your kit and drop a musket ball down the mussel. Place a paper wadding in the mussel. Remove the tamping rod from the mussel and ram the wadding so that the musket ball would not roll back down the barrel. Replace the tamping rod in its holder along the barrel. Raise the musket across your arm, cock the hammer. Reach again in your kit and get a twist of gun powder, bite the end off and pour into the powder chamber.

"Be careful at point." Tom said, " the hammer is still cocked." But he was too late as several of the muskets fired some into the air and some into fellow Mexican soldiers. The first casualties of the Mexican War with Maximilian were self inflicted.

"Everyone place your muskets on the ground." Tom shouted. "Sergeant Daniels, you and rest of the marines form two lines and we will demonstrate how to fire, load and fire again."

The marines had not fired muskets in their basic training and they were no better than the Mexicans watching. "Cease firing! Get me a musket and I will show you how it is done."

Thomas Quilian Schneider was like a machine. He loaded, fired, loaded, fired and loaded again in less than forty-five seconds. He turned to the startled Americans watching and said, "This is what a French Infantry Soldier can do against us. We will all have to do this against them or we are dead."

When this was translated to the Mexicans, there was no more cheering and hugging of their compadres. Grim looks began to appear on the faces, mixed with fear for the French Infantry Soldier. The next day when the ninety volunteers were supposed to report for training, there were two hundred and eighty men, women and older children present.

"What is the meaning of this, Jose?" Tom asked his senior Mexican officer.

"Mia, Major, we are determined to learn how to fight. Yesterday only a few of us had ever fired a weapon. If you are to train us properly, everyone in the village of Caboneras must learn. The French are beginning to built forts into this part of Mexico. They must be driven out!"

"Jose, anyone who wishes to learn will begin today. Translate that for me."

Jose turned with tears in his eyes and said, "Mia, Americono Major, will teach us!" The cheering began again.

"Jose, I need to talk to you, come into my tent."

They walked off the dusty patch of ground and across a grassy area on the outside of the village where the marines had their encampment. "Jose, I will show you a map. Show me where the French have established outposts." Tom unrolled a map of northeastern Mexico.

"Here is my capital, Mexico City. It is 400 miles from here. The French puppet, Maximilian, stays here. He has sent the French troops north to occupy the our forts at Pachucal, Tampico and Tamaulipas. From Tamaulipas they sent out small groups to locate suitable places for the French to steal what they need from the villages."

"Have they come to Carboneras, Jose?"

"No, Mia Major. They keep further to the south, in villages like Hidalgo and Santa Jimenez."

"Santa Jimenez is only 48 miles from here! They will be here next Jose. We must act before they find the storehouse with the supplies. We must make them think that we did not land at Carboneras. We must attack and draw them away from here. Go see if Admiral Caldwell's ships have returned to the harbor."

A breathless, Jose, returned in an hour and he reported sails on the horizon. The Caldwell Flotilla was returning from Havana with another shipment of equipment and supplies. Tom and his aide was waiting on the docks as the first long boat tied up.

"Take us out to the flag ship, we must talk to Admiral Caldwell." Tom ordered.

"Can we unload first, Major?"

"Just sit everything on the docks as fast as you can, my men will take it to the storehouses."

On board the recommissioned USS Providence,

Tom explained what the French were attempting to do in northeast Mexico. "I would like you to take my marines from here back down the coast to La Pesca and up the river to Soto La Marina. This is south of the French at Tamaulipas. We only need one vessel, the shallowest draft. We will attack French patrols and seize the horses and wagons for transport of the supplies in Carboneras to President Juarez. I do not feel comfortable with 30,000 muskets sitting in a storehouse, we need to get them to the Mexican Army."

"I agree, Tom. I would like to mention something that might be helpful. I would not bury any dead French in this part of Mexico. I would load them on wagons and return the bodies to the New Haven, it has the shallowest draft. The New Haven can bury them in the Gulf of Mexico. Any prisoners should also be held in our larger vessels for transport to Havana."

"The idea is make them disappear! I like that Admiral. Put some fear into the French."

"And one other thing, take Jerome with you and he can report back to me after the operation is over."

"Done, when can we get started?"

"As soon as the New Haven is unloaded, we will unload her first. Have your marines here before sundown so we can land you at night."

Before sunset a thousand men showed up for transport. "Where did all these come from? I thought you were taking 800 marines?" Jerome Lewis asked.

"I am, Jerome. I have 800 marines on this operation and 75 left to guard the storehouses in Carboneras. The extra 200 are Mexicans eager to kill as many French as they can find."

"Do they realize that we will be on foot until we captures horses?"

"I will try to buy horses as we move inland from Soto La Marina. I have gold in my money belt."

"I better signal for the other ketch, USS Trumbull to accompany us, Tom."

A thousand men on two small ketches was a sight to be seen as they left the fishing village of Carboneras for a short run down the coast of Mexico. They stood shoulder to shoulder, some in United States Marine Uniforms and some dressed like Mexican farmers, because that was what they were until they had some training in how to fire a musket. The USS Trumbull and New Haven entered the river and stopped at Soto La Marina. It was a dark winter night and the village was asleep as the 1000 made their way towards Ciudad Victoria, the first French outpost past the Fort of Tamulipas. About ten miles into the march, they came upon a French encampment consisting of tents full of sleeping French calvary, their horses and wagons. A single sentry was posted but was fast asleep. Two marines crept up on him, covered his mouth and placed a knife between his ribs and into his heart. The first French death was recorded by Jerome Lewis for report back to Washington. The sleeping camp was awakened by a 1000 screaming marines, some American, some Mexican. The draft horses were hitched to the wagons. The single dead French soldier was placed in it and the prisoners were marched back towards the waiting ketches at Soto La Marina. Tom gave orders to take the rest of the wagons and horses directly to Carboneras and begin the loading of supplies. He ordered the supplies to taken to President Juarez immediately.

The company was now down to 900, 800 marines and 100 Mexican nationals. As the sun rose they came upon a small village and Tom used some of this gold to buy every wagon and horse that he could find and these were sent to Carboneras to help move the supplies to President Juarez. At around noon, a dust cloud was visible on the horizon. This meant that a large number of horsemen were probably on the road towards the Fort. Tom drew his sergeants around him and told them what he wanted them to do.

The French Cavalry officer signaled for his column to halt. Six Mexican bodies lay in the roadway, apparently dead or dying. One of the farmers raised his hand and motioned for the French to help him. The troops dismounted to rest the horses and that is when the marines raised from their cover along side the road. They rushed the column with fixed bayonets screaming, "Ferma La Fenettra." A Mexican who said he spoke French had told them it was "Surrender the fight." It turned out that it meant, "Close the window." But the result was the same, the entire column surrendered without a fight. This was more than Tom had hoped for. There was only one dead, the sentry and many prisoners. The horses were tired together in groups of three and a single rider was assigned to each group. The groups were told to ride for Caboneras and use the horses as pack animals to move the remainder of the supplies. Tom ordered the remainder of the company to begin the march back to the waiting ketches at Soto La Marina. French calvary were used to riding, not walking and they began to complain. Some sat by the side of the road and refused to move. Tom drew his revolver walked to the first french man and shot him in the head. He walked to the second french man and started to shoot him, but he jumped to his feet and said in perfect English, "We need to rest."

"You can rest on your trip across the Gulf of Mexico. I will shoot any man who refuses to march."

The french man turned to his officer and translated. French orders were shouted down the line of prisoners and we began to march again towards the waiting ships. We reached them before sundown and loaded the prisoners on one ketch and the remaining marines on the other. By sunrise the following day, Caldwell Flotilla was prepared to sail back to Havana.

27

Return to Havana
March 1865

We sailed on the morning tide. We had had no communication with what was happening in the States until five days later when we docked in Havana. The USS Philadelphia was not there. We anchored just inside the harbor again and docked the Cold Harbor. The lone seaman who could understand Spanish went with me to the US Ambassador's Office in Havana. There we learned that General Sherman had driven across North and South Carolina with only token resistance. The Confederacy was finished. Lee was now faced by two Union armies. Lee had attacked Grant at Petersburg and was defeated. Richmond was under siege. Jefferson Davis moved his headquarters west by train. February had been a very good month for the Union and March promised to be even better. The Philadelphia made Havana two days later and we began the transfer of French prisoners onto and the war materials off of the Philadelphia by lashing the Briggs to the Philadelphia and transferring boxes by sheer force. In four days we were ready to make the return trip to Carboneras.

" With this trip we will have provided over 50,000 muskets with bayonets, 60,000 side arms, 10,000 crates of muskets balls, wadding and gun powder, Admiral. Sherman's army could not have done what the USN has done in as short a time." Jerome was looking out to sea trying to spot Key West.

"It will not be long until we can stop at Key West and resupply, Jerome, the Confederacy is falling apart. It is only a matter of months, probably weeks."

"Thank you for getting me into Mexico with Tom on his mission, Admiral, I thought may be I would not see any action during the great war to save the Union."

"Yes, and when our grandchildren ask us where we fought in the Civil War, we will have to say, 'Mexico'". We both laughed and then remembered that nearly 900 US Marines depended upon the bimonthly runs from Havana to Carboneras, Mexico.

We brought food stuffs and most importantly mail. The mail pouch was stuffed with letters for the marines now in Mexico. They will appreciate getting these, I thought. There was mail from Bermuda for the crews of the flotilla and there were letters for me. The one written in Ruthie's hand was the best letter I have ever read. I folded it and placed it inside my tunic. During the next two months, whenever I was lonely, I reached inside and unfolded it and cried again.

On your last return trip to Havana, we anchored the flotilla and docked the Cold Harbor as usually but this time the US Ambassador was there to meet us. We lowered a gang way and he boarded the Cold Harbor.

He was not a navy man, because he did not ask for permission.

"Admiral Caldwell."

"Yes, Mister Ambassador?"

"You have been recalled to Potomac Dockyards, here are your orders."

"Captain Lewis."

"Yes, sir."

"Here are your orders to return to duty in the White House as soon as the Cold Harbor can untie. I am sorry, I know you look forward to shore leave and mail. The mail is here in this pouch. You and the crew of your ship are to be in Washington immediately."

"What has happened, Mister Ambassador?" I asked.

"The President and Secretary Seward have been assassinated!"

"Oh my God, Jerome, we should get the Cold Harbor turned around as fast as we can. How is the fresh water and food supply? Do we have enough for a week or more?" A hundred things ran through my mind. Then I remembered the most important thing.

"Mr. Ambassador, what do I do with the rest of my ships, they need provisions if they are to accompany me to Washington. It will take days to resupply all of us."

"We have no orders that involve your ships, Admiral."

"Fine, they can sail twenty-four hours after we set sail. Send the following message to Secretary Welles:

" Today's date, today's time, message received and understood. Have split flotilla into two parts. Flag ship and one escort to enter Potomac no less than three days. Rest to follow for needed repairs."

Jerome and I realized that we were still holding the sealed orders from the Ambassador. We tore them open and learned. During our last trip to Mexico, Richmond fell. General Lee surrendered at Appomattox Courthouse. General Johnston was in conference to surrender to General Sherman and on the evening of April 14th Archangel struck.

28

Washington City

April 1865

On April 14, 1865, the President received the news of Lee's surrender to Grant two days earlier. Johnston had not surrendered to Sherman, as yet, but his surrender was certain within a few days. He asked his secretary if the White House had received any free tickets to Ford Theater that week.

"Yes, sir. We have had several tickets sent everyday this week. Should I notify the secret service that you and Mrs. Lincoln will be attending tonight?"

"Yes, Jamison, Mary has been wanting to see 'Our American Cousin' for a month. Send in a messenger and I will see if Mr. Welles and Mr. Stanton over in the Army Navy Building would like to go. Find Secretary Seward and see if he and his wife would like to join us."

"Mr. Seward is home in bed trying to get over that bad fall he took yesterday, sir."

"I had forgotten that, Jamison, forget about the

Sewards, then.   Do we have six tickets? Mrs. Lincoln
wants to meet the star, can you send a White House card
to Mr. Booth at the theater asking him to come to the
President's box during intermission?"

"Yes, Mr. President."

"Good.   Send in the messenger, will you? Oh, here
you are. Will you run over to the Army Navy and see if
you can get a response from Secretary Welles or Stanton
on a night out at Ford's?"

"On my way, sir." Mr. Lincoln did not notice that
the messenger had a small tattoo just above the left elbow. The messenger had been employed at the White
House for four years and was trusted with messages of a
verbal nature. He walked at a normal pace until he was
out of the White House and then he ran across the street
and into Lafayette park. He carried a small piece of paper and wedged it where he usually did. He then walked
over to the Army Navy Building and went to the office
of the ORION commander, who also had a small tattoo
just above the left elbow.

"It is tonight, sir."

"Are you sure? I do not want to disturb the Grand
Dragon with another false alarm."

"Yes, sir. I heard them talking. I was sent to ask
Stanton and Welles if they would like to attend with the
President."

"We have to attack Welles and Stanton at home. Go
to both Welles and Stanton and indicate that the invitation is for them alone, not their wives. If anyone asks
you later, indicate that you got confused about the invitation for the wives."

"There was no mention of the wives, sir. I assumed

that the invitation was for them alone."

"Very good, that reduces our chances that both will accept. After you find out who has accepted, return here to me."

"I will be back soon, sir."

The Grand Dragon was sitting in Lafayette Park reading the drop message from the White House messenger and wondered if he had all the pieces in place. He had assigned the most dangerous task of cutting off the dragon's head to himself along with the assistance of a Maryland confederate, John Booth. Four members of his group would be assigned the homes of each of the cabinet members for elimination tonight. He looked up at a particular window of the Army Navy Building and wondered if his second in command would perform his tasks correctly.

The second in command waited for the messenger to return. "Sir, both Mr. Welles and Stanton indicated that they could not accept tonight, maybe another time?"

"Excellent, go back to the White House and indicate exactly what was said by each. Then add that a Major Rathman, one of the aides and his fiancee, a Miss Clara Harrison would be happy to accompany the President and Mrs. Lincoln. If he asks who this Major Rathman is, you tell him, he is the stepson of Senator Williams from New York. There will not be time to check that out by one of the secret service's men."

"Very good, sir. Do you want me to come back here?"

"No, take your place in the line of messengers and act as everything is normal. And remember to report to work tomorrow. We must remain in place for another assignment if necessary."

"Yes, sir."

It was intermission as the actor John Booth entered the hallway to the President's Box in Ford's Theater. He was immediately stopped by a secret service man and asked for identification. Booth handed him his invitation from the White House.

"Very good, sir. You may enter. You will have to give me that stage prop dagger, though."

"It is only rubber, sir. See", he bent it nearly double.

"I guess no one can get hurt by that, you can go in."

Booth entered the box and saw four people seated looking forward. The two men sat together with the wives at each end of the row of four seats. Just as he was about to introduce himself to the President and Mrs. Lincoln, the man seated next to him raised his arm and shot the President behind the left ear. Booth was dumb struck but he still carried the stage prop dagger. The plan was for the Grand Dragon to shout "assassin" and then shoot Booth before he could protest. He would then place the pistol in Booth's hand. Plans do not always work smoothly, because Booth recovered and grabbed Rathman's arm to wrestle the pistol from his hand. The pistol fell to the floor changing the plan. Rathman placed his free arm under Booth and pitched him over the box rail and onto the stage floor. He hoped that the fall would kill Booth by breaking his neck. But a sprained ankle was all that happened. Booth was in a panic, he was a known southern supporter and everyone would believe that he had shot the President, he must get away and he fled the stage and the theater. He was closely followed by two ORION members.

It was several minutes before the audience returned

from intermission and realized what had happened. The President still sat beside a weeping Mary Lincoln and a shocked young couple. An Army major opened the box door and shouted for the secret service agent.

"Mr. Lincoln has been shot by the actor Booth! Get a doctor! Hurry Please!"

"What happened, Mr. Rathman?"

"The actor, Booth, shot the President. You certainly saw that?"

"No, I heard a shot and saw you trying to get the gun out of his hand. Oh, this is terrible, look Mrs. Lincoln has fainted."

A doctor entered the box and declared that the President was injured but not dead. He stopped the flow of blood and gave Mrs. Lincoln a stimulant.

"We can move the President whenever you would like." The doctor said to the secret service agent.

"Can you help us, Major? More agents are on the way, he should be moved to a bed. See if you can find a house next to the theater that will accept the President."

"I will be right back as soon as I find someone."

The Grand Dragon ran next door to the house of a Mr. Peterson and explained what had happened. He ran back and helped move the President to a bed where he lingered until seven the next morning before he died. Major Rathman and Miss Harrison disappeared in the confusion and when White House personnel were questioned the next day by the secret service's men, no one knew a Major Rathman or a Miss Harrison.

Intermission was scheduled at Ford's for 9:45 PM. At ten o'clock four men approached the homes of Secretaries Seward, Stanton, Welles, and Blair House. The four men assigned to Seward's home had individual assignments. One man approached the front door and knocked. A house servant opened the door and inquired who he was and what he wanted at this hour.

The man replied, "I have been sent with medicine by the doctor for Secretary Seward."

He then tried to push by the servant. The slight disturbance alerted the house security. The Secretary's son was awake and confronted the man at the door and was knocked unconscious by a blow to the head from a pistol butt. By this time a security guard rushed in to help and was shot by a second man who appeared in the doorway.

"The bedrooms are on the third floor, get up there."

Two ORION agents rushed up the stairs looking for the Seward's bedroom. They threw open each door until they found Mr. Seward along with his daughter and her sailor boy friend. The boy friend immediately tried to stop them but one of the attackers held him at gun point while the other shot the secretary in the face and neck. ORION members were always told to shoot the head of the victims, never to shoot the body. Seward fell to the floor wounded but not yet dead.

At the home of Secretary Stanton, four men were assigned the same mission. One held the get away horses, another acted as a lookout and two tried to gain entrance. This time the security was better and the two trying to gain entrance were shot and killed at the front door. The remaining two escaped into the night. At the home of Secretary Welles, entrance was gained and a man sleeping in a bedroom was mistaken for Welles and killed with all four men escaping. At Blair House, the security was the best and Vice President Johnson slept through the night without incident, four riders passed on the street but did not even slow beyond a trot.

The belief that a new ORION attempt was afoot for the assassination of the leading officers of the government caused Secretary Stanton to take immediate steps to protect Washington City against further attacks. Additional guards were placed around Blair House, and St. Elizabeth Hospital where Secretary Seward was now located and clung to life. Stanton ordered the secret service to learn the truth of the plot and to bring the criminals to justice.

29

Washington City
April 15, 1865

The next day, April 15, 1865, as provided by the Constitution, Andrew Johnson was sworn in as the seventeenth President of the United States by the Supreme Court Chief Justice. He took the oath in the cabinet meeting room before a small group of cabinet members and his invited guests. Johnson was an ardent Democrat, but when the storm of secession swept over Tennessee, no man was more intensely Union than he. He was the US Senator elected from Tennessee in 1857. When Tennessee seceded he stayed in Washington and Lincoln appointed him Military Governor after the fall of Tennessee. His violent expressions against the secessionists, who he declared ought to be hanged, led to an attempt to lynch him in May, 1861. He met the mob, revolver in hand and drove them off, killing three. It was this man who assumed the office on April 15, 1865.

His first order of business was to gather his cabinet together. Secretary of State, Seward, was still in the hospital but the others met with him for his advice. The meeting began by the President saying the following to his cabinet.

"I am not Abraham Lincoln. I am Andrew Johnson. I have been your Vice President for a little over six weeks and now I am your President. Will you all give me a few days to adjust to this sudden change of events? I will, of course, accept resignations from those of you present that do not want to continue in my administration. Make no mistake, it is now my administration. I will make the final decisions after considering your areas of expertise. I will not listen to anyone who tries to speak outside of his area of expertise, however. Let me begin by going around the table and telling you each what I already know about you. Some of you, I have never met. Others, I have met before, but know little about you."

He stopped and gazed around the cabinet meeting table waiting for questions. When none came he began.

"Secretary Seward will be recovering for sometime and I will appoint an acting member to replace him until he can return to work in the White House." Heads bowed in agreement.

"Secretary Stanton, your area of expertise is the War Department and as a fellow Democrat, I expect the same level of service that you gave Mr. Lincoln. I trust you completely and probably know you the best from my time as Military Governor of Tennessee. You will not direct the secret service to do anything for you. The secret service does not work in the Army Navy Building, they work for the White House, in fact they will all be fired today for gross incompetence in regard to the ORION network. I have asked, and he has accepted, Captain Jerome Lewis, the former head of Presidential Security to begin work as soon as he can get here from Cuba." Heads again bowed up and down with exception of Stanton.

"Who will serve as security until he can get here?" asked Secretary Stanton.

"I have asked Secretary Welles to provide United States Marines as armed guards to be placed throughout the White House and the Army Navy Building. You better remember the passwords that will be given to you at the end of this meeting, because if you forget it and can not repeat it you will be shot and killed." Stanton swallowed hard and looked at the rest of the cabinet members who were all frowning. Security was no longer a joking matter.

"Secretary Welles, that brings me to you. Can you get Admiral Caldwell back from Cuba with Jerome Lewis?"

"I can send another telegram, Mr. President, Lewis is presently in charge of the protection detail for the Admiral and I think it would be a good idea for them to travel together."

"If Admiral Caldwell will accept my apology for the stupidity shown by the White House in regard to the threat from the ORION network, he may agree to accept my offer of a cabinet level position that I will request. But I doubt that a man of his caliber and great ability will want to serve in the White House again."

"Sir, I do not understand why you think so highly of Caldwell, he is a member of ORION for God sake!" Said William Dennison.

"You will refer to me as Mister President in the future, Mr. Dennison, or I will replace you with Montgomery Blair so fast it will take your breath away. You are unqualified to be Postmaster General in my opinion and I hope you decide to resign before the end of the day. Your appointment was a political mistake by Mr. Lincoln and frankly you will be an embrassment to this administration if you do not learn what the Postmaster General is supposed to be doing. I have asked Montgomery Blair to be your immediate supervisor. He will take a 90 day leave from his position as CEO of American Telegraph. If you do not meet with his approval after 90 days, you Mr. Dennison, are history. And as far as Admiral Caldwell being a member of ORION, that is ridiculous, he identified the entire network working in the White House and the Army Navy Building and your precious secret service did nothing, damn them, I think Pinkerton was a member, not Caldwell – you fool." Andrew Johnson had lost his temper, but like Jason Caldwell, he could not abide fools.

"Now where was I? Oh, yes. We are up to you Mr. Mc Culloch. You are the third Secretary of the Treasury in four years. The two before you were thieves. If I ever hear of improper conduct from your department, I will have you arrested. Is that clear?"

"Yes, Mister President."

"Good. Now on to you Mr. Speed, as Attorney General, I expect you to keep me out of jail." The tension was broken around the table and everyone laughed except Dennison he was still smarting from the dressing down from the President.

"That leaves you, Mr. Usher, I have no knowledge of you or the Department of the Interior. I have no first hand knowledge of anything that you have done in the last four years. That is my fault, not yours. Could I get a one page summary of what your department has done?"

"Yes, Mister President."

"In fact, I would like a one page summary from all of you by the end of today." He stood signaling that the meeting was over.

"Gentlemen, see the lady at the doorway for your passwords."

The President walked from the cabinet room to his working office with two secretaries in tow. One male and one female. The woman had been hired at the beginning of the day. He had told her, "You will be replacing Mr. Lincoln's secretary, a man, can you do that?"

She smiled and said, "Yes, Mister President."

"I want you to transcribe everything that is said in the cabinet meetings, we are going to make some enemies before this is over and I want a record of what was said and by whom."

When the two secretaries entered the President's working office, he said, "Please sit down I have some dictation for both of you."

"But Mister President, I do not take short hand." George Jamison said.

"Then you are excused Mr. Jamison, I am sure that you have plenty of typing back at your desk."

"Yes, Mr. President."

"Shall we begin, Mrs. Wainwright?"

"Whenever you would like, Mr. President.

"Personal to Secretary Stanton.

Item One. Jefferson Davis and his cabinet are now fugitives upon the evacuation of Richmond. It is my fear that he will try to reach Kirby Smith in the southwest, and with his help, he will attempt to prolong the life of the Confederacy. I, therefore, as commander and chief of the armed forces order General J. H. Wilson to use every effort with his cavalry to capture the fleeing President. I do not wish to discuss this order with you or have you issue it through General Grant. This is a direct order from me to General Wilson. I want you to make it clear to the General that I except Davis to be in custody before May 1st or his letter of resignation on my desk by May 2nd.

Item Two. Issue an order for General Grant to move south until he engages General Johnston of the remaining Confederate Army trying to protect Davis' escape. You are to direct General Grant that I want Johnston's unconditional surrender, identical in terms that were granted General Lee. I am tired of General Sherman's pussyfooting around Johnston. Tell Grant that either Johnston surrenders or he has orders from President Johnson to attack and take no prisoners. I desire no input from you or General Grant on this matter. I want the war ended by May 1, 1865.

Item Three. Issue an order for General Sherman to pull out of the fight against Johnston and march towards McAllen, Texas. If he meets any Confederate resistance he is to take no prisoners. If the Confederate mentality is to die on the battlefield, tell Sherman to do his best to kill every damn one of them from as far away as possible with artillery fire. Barring that, use the new long range rifles to drop the enemy where he stands. General Sherman is not to stop and bury the enemy dead, he is to let them lay where they fall. The message must be introduced that the war is over, only death remains for those foolish enough to resist.

Item Four. General Sherman is to remain within the

US boarders, but he is to send scouts into the mountains to locate Major, (make that Colonel), Schneider's marine force. President Juarez will be offered Sherman and his troops to hunt down and kill every God Damn French troop they can find. The French have been told by President Lincoln to withdraw. I will not ask them again. I will find and kill as many as I can until they get the same message as delivered to the Confederacy. The longer we wait, the more Union deaths we will encounter.

End of personal."

"Do you want me to read that back to you, Mister President?"

"Yes, please."

When she had finished he said, "A good start. Let us try another. Send a blind copy of the Stanton personal to Admiral Caldwell, acting Secretary of State, will you?"

"How do I do that, Mister President?"

"After you have typed the personal for Stanton, take it to the basement and it will be keyed to our Havana Embassy. You will only have to type it once. After the message is sent to Havana, hand carry it to Stanton and place it in his hands only. Let no one else see it. Take a receipt slip and have him sign for it. Never use a messenger for paper work inside the White House or the Army Navy Building."

"Yes, Mister President."

"When that is done come back in here and we will twist another cabinet member's tail."

She was smiling as she said, "Aye, aye, sir."

"Your husband must be a marine, Mrs. Wainwright. I like Marines."

"He would like your take charge attitude Mister President."

"Send in the messengers waiting outside with Mr. Jamison, one at a time."

"Yes, Mister President."

The first member of the messenger squad entered the President's Office.

"Roll up your left shirt sleeve."

"Yes, sir. May I ask what this is about Mister President?"

"Of course, I am promoting all messengers today. The ones with large biceps will be given a raise in pay."

"Really!"

"Yes, you qualify for the pay increase. Please roll down your sleeve and stand along the wall over there, I might need your help."

In this fashion, Andrew Johnston, seventeenth President of the United States, personally arrested three members of the ORION network not listed on the White House known list. He had to use a revolver that he had placed in his top desk drawer only on one of the three. When news of this spread throughout the White House, a panic started within the remaining members of ORION network working in other parts of the White House and they were arrested by Marine guards as they were trying to flee the grounds. At the same time, Gideon Welles, was doing the same thing with all members of the Department of the Navy. Two were arrested and when this happened a panic started in the Department of War and fleeing members were arrested as they tried to exit the Army Navy Building. The Grand Dragon was in Lafayette Park watching the events unfold and told himself, "I think I will like Canada this time of year and he headed for the train station."

Captain Jerome Lewis arrested John Stuart for the attempted assassination of Secretary Seward. His sister lived in Washington City and her house was known to be the meeting place for ORION members. When she was questioned, she was not recognized as Miss Harrison. A man who claimed to be a Simon Payne was found to have dyed his hair and shaved off his beard, but was identified as John Stuart. For the next ten days, Jerome Lewis' men searched for the actor Booth. Booth had returned to Maryland with Daniel Harrold and William Bilts in close pursuit. When Booth stopped for sleep one night in a Virginia barn, the two ORION agents set fire to it. Booth awoke with a start and yelled "Who is out there?"

"Federal Marshals, come out Mr. Booth the real assassin has been caught."

Booth's last words were, "Thank God you found me."

He was shot in the head and left for dead. His body was found by Lewis' men and taken to Washington where a post-mortem examination was made. The remains were taken to St. Elizabeth's for processing. Lewis' men continued to arrest ORION members that were known to them from the secret service's list that was four years old. Twelve were arrested in all. Only Miss Mary Stuart and the Grand Dragon survived the search for and the arrest of the assassins.

Acting Secretary of State Caldwell sat behind his former bosses desk and said to himself, "Here I go again, a fish out of water. I wonder what Ben Hagood is doing?" He had several meetings with President Johnson and he was given the job of dealing with Jefferson Davis after his capture. On May 1, 1865 he received the following telegram from General Wilson:

HAVE LOCATED SUBJECT IN QUESTION SLEEPING IN A TENT OUTSIDE

IRWINSVILLE, GEORGIA. NO SHOTS WERE FIRED. ALSO HAVE DETAINED

AWAITING YOUR INSTRUCTIONS; MRS. DAVIS, DAVIS CHILDREN, AND VARIOUS AIDE-DE-CAMPS. THEY WILL BE ESCORTED BY COLONEL PRITCHARD OF THE FOURTH MICHIGAN CAVALRY TO MACON, GEORGIA. AWAITING FURTHER INSTRUCTIONS.

GENERAL J. H. WILSON

I carried the telegram to Mrs. Wainwright and let her read it.

"When he has time, show him this and ask what we should do about the others arrested with President Davis.

"Let me see what he is doing Mister Secretary." She opened the Oval Office door and stuck her head inside. She softly closed the door and said, "He has his head down on this desk and is sound asleep, poor dear."

I smiled and said, "Come and get me when he is wide awake and wants to see me."

She nodded her head and I went back to my office.

An hour later, a refreshed Andrew Johnson stuck his head around my open door and said, "Guess what? It seems that no one can find the Undersecretary of War. Stanton is making all kinds of excuses for him. What do you make of this?"

"Mister President, either he was an ORION member or he was killed by an ORION member, what other conclusion can we make?"

"Exactly what I thought! That dumb, sumbitch Stanton had a spy working for him and did not even know it. Or worse, Stanton is a secret, southern sympathizer."

"Mister President, I do not think Edwin Stanton is either of those things. I think he was using his assistant to feed misinformation to Richmond. He thought he could control him and the reverse was probably true."

"Where do you think he is now?"

"The Undersecretary?"

"Yes."

"Canada, Mister President."

"Exactly, I judge a man's intelligence by how much he thinks like me. You, Admiral, are one smart, sumbitch!" He turned on his heel and was gone.

"Tomorrow, Andrew Johnson will be twisting Stanton's tail again and asking Gideon Welles to do many of the things that should be sent to the War Department." I thought to myself.

30

General Amnesty
Summer 1865

President Johnson issued a proclamation of general amnesty for all former Confederate combatants. Certain classes of people were not included in this amnesty. Any West Point Graduate above the rank of Colonel, those persons that had voluntarily taken part in the rebellion whose property values were in excess of $20,000.00, a former US Senator, a former US Representative and twelve other cases which totaled sixteen classes of persons excluded from the amnesty. The amnesty proclamation did provide for a special written application for Presidential pardon. Because of this, General Lee wrote the following:

> Richmond, Virginia
>
> June 13, 1865
>
> "His Excellence, Andrew Johnson, President of the United States"

"Sir: Being excluded form the provisions of amnesty contained in the proclamation of May 29, 1865, I hereby apply for the benefits and full restoration of all rights and privileges, extended to those included in its terms."

"I graduated from the Military Academy at West Point in June, 1829; resigned from the US army, April, 1861; was a General in the Confederate Army and included in the surrender of the Army of Northern Virginia, April 9, 1865."

"I have the honor to be, very respectfully, your obedient servant,

R. E. Lee

There was no letter requesting pardon from Jefferson Davis, who was a former US Senator, he was unaware of the proclamation. He and his male companions were taken to Fort Monroe to stand trial for treason. The date of this his trial was fixed several times, but postponed. The legal question of whether or not the Constitution forbade the withdrawal of a state from the Union could not be answered, the Constitution dealt with how to add states, not remove them. The acting Secretary of State said, "If Mr. Davis should make an honest effort to escape from Fort Monroe and flee to Canada as so many have done, I think he would succeed."

No one saw more clearly than President Johnson, the difficulty in fixing upon the wisest course to be pursued with the prisoner and he sent for his acting Secretary. "Jason, come sit down. What have you decided to do with Mr. Davis?"

"I would like to send him to another country to remain in exile for the remainder of his life, Mr. President."

"Sort of like Napoleon I, hope he does not escape and return like that French bastard!"

"Well, there is a problem with finding a country that will accept him. England has closed all of her ports, harbors and waters against any vessel bearing the Confederate flag or Confederate officers. I thought we had a chance with France, but now they have done the same thing. So far, eight countries have refused to grant him entrance. I do not think exile is an option, Mr. President."

"What is his health at this moment, Jason. Can he live much longer in a cell at Fort Monroe?"

"The doctors in Richmond say he is very weak and depressed, he is not eating normally and he has lost a lot of weight."

"What if we arrange for someone famous, like Horace Greeley to announce that the New York Tribune will post a bond for his release from Fort Monroe while he waits for his trial? We then delay the trial month after month until there is no need to prosecute a dead man!"

"I will have my editor friend at the Washington Post leak that very idea, Mr. President. It will an accomplished fact in few weeks."

"Jason, how is Secretary Seward coming along? I saw he was in his office yesterday with you."

"He is healing nicely, Mr. President, I will be leaving in a few weeks."

"What are your plans, Jason?"

"I graduated from the Military Academy, Anapolis in '37 so I have eighteen more months until my retirement from the Navy. I will report to Secretary Welles for my assignment."

"I have suggested to Secretary Welles that he consider you for the position of Marine Commandant, assignment Army Navy Building. It would mean that you would have to become a four star Marine General instead of your four star Admiral status. What do you think?"

"My son would never forgive me, Mr. President. He is a future Anapolis man through and through, he loves the Navy and everything it stands for, just like me. However, I am a loyal American and I will follow my orders wherever they send me and whatever they may entail. President Lincoln taught me that."

"President Lincoln was a fool for not listening to you and your advisory board, Jason. The war would have lasted about two years if he had invaded the South through their seaports with Marines. The army should have been used to hold what the Navy captured for them. You can reach Richmond by gunboat for God's sake!"

"Yes, we butted heads the entire war."

"Jason, you will be happy to know that on July 1, 1865, we passed the eight hundred thousand mark for mustered out of service, soldiers, sailors and marines. These men have reentered private life, returning to what they were doing before conscription. Only the volunteers remain on active duty, mostly in Mexico and on the Texas/Mexico border. Over a million men are now on inactive reserve in case there is a national emergency. I have you to thank for the ideas that made this possible."

"It is nice to be useful and appreciated, Mr. President."

"Do you ever think you can call me Andrew?"

"The day you leave office, Mr. President."

"I would be honored to have you as a friend, Jason. You may have heard that I have forwarded a list of names for Vice President to the Senate, I am tired of butting heads with them. They can pick the one they would like. I plan to ignore whoever they choose, that is why your name was not on the list."

You never got the last word with Andrew Johnson and I left his working office to find Monty Blair and to twist the tail of his apprentice, Postmaster General Dennison.

"Monty, what are you doing for lunch?"

"Jason, I was wondering if you would show up, it is Wednesday, you know. I understand the Hay-Adams has a wonderful New York strip steak and a fine red wine today."

"How many days before you have to go back to American Telegraph, Monty?" I said this loud enough for Dennison to overhear.

"It depends on how fast my understudy can grasp the simplest tasks, I have permission from the holding company that owns American Telegraph to remain another 90 days if need be." I saw Dennison sag in his chair.

We left Monty's office and headed for Jerome Lewis' office to pick him up for lunch. "You know, Monty, we should really stop with Dennison. Is he ready to do the job?"

"Sure, he was ready a week ago."

"Monty, I need you back at American Telegraph as CEO. The profit margin is down and it should be way up with the war over and all these troops returning home."

"I will tell the President, Jason. I was just having some fun with the political appointee!"

"I am a few weeks away from a new assignment with

the Navy, myself. I have no idea where they will send me. I have a meeting with Gideon this afternoon."

Jerome Lewis heard me say that as we found him in his office and he said, "They should let you be an advisor from either Pennsylvania or Bermuda, if there is any justice left in the world."

"Or better yet, Military Governor of South Carolina." Monty said.

"Now that would really be a disaster!" Jerome said. We all laughed and left the White House in route to the Hay-Adams for a Wednesday lunch.

After our lunch we walked slowly across Lafayette Square, we said goodbye and the two of them headed for the White House and I walked towards the Army Navy Building. I found Gideon Welles at his desk behind a huge pile of papers. He peered over them and said, "Jason, good to see you again. Are you getting tired of the White House and need a real assignment with the Navy?"

"Yes, that about sizes it up from where I stand."

"Jason, did you know that Andrew tried to get you confirmed as his Vice President before he offered you the position of acting Secretary of State?"

"I had no idea, he did say he was tired of butting heads and he sent a list from which they could choose a name."

"The Senate will never confirm anyone for any position that he chooses. They have a two-thirds majority, just like the house and they will over ride any veto that he makes. It is a standoff. Too bad for the country. He could get many things done for the country if they would leave him alone and let him do his job. I am ashamed to be a Republican. The house is considering impeachment, did you know that?"

"There are no grounds for impeachment! My God, Gideon, what has this country come to?"

"I think that is why Lincoln chose a 'War Democrat' as a running mate. He knew his days were limited and he did not want someone else to get the credit for saving the country. If Andrew would just take the reconstruction plans that Lincoln had in his office and publish them, then they would be adopted without question."

"Do you think someone like me should suggest this to him?"

"No, you have been assigned to me for the next eighteen months and you are going to be too busy to make helpful trips to the White House. Starting today, you are granted 30 days home leave and 30 days travel leave. After all, you have a home in South Carolina that you have not seen in four years." He handed me my leave papers, signed and ready for my signature.

"You will need to stop off at Seneca Hill so that Sam Mason can bring you up to date on the ORION network now active in Canada. He will travel with you to South Carolina, as your aide, as will a protection detail of marines (I have called them the RR unit)". He was smiling as he handed me those orders. He continued, "The President wants to send a message about mustering out soldiers and sailors. He has decided to do something special in your case. He thinks it would be symbolic if you personally handed the orders to the CO in Beaufort and placed him and his troops onboard the Caldwell flotilla for return to Washington."

"When you have completed that, I want a report

from you on how Bermuda has managed to have a working telephone system installed. That will require you to travel to Bermuda to discuss how this was done with the chairman of Bermuda Telegraph and Telephone company. You should not take more than 90 days on this mission, however. You will file your report from the Bermuda Conciliate's office, a Captain Milroy now has Jerome Lewis' duties there." He handed me a third set of orders.

"Your report from Bermuda should indicate how the telephone cable from Bermuda to the Maryland Eastern Shore can be extended into the Chesapeake and up the Potomac. It is time that we have secure voice communication throughout Washington City. I also have orders for you to report to the American Ambassador in Havana as soon as your report is sent, the time table of course is to be determined by you." He handed me another set of orders. My head was swimming.

"Sir, is that stack of paper in front of you all for me?"

"Yes, it is. Jason, I guarantee that these orders will take at least 18 months to accomplish, maybe longer. Some are more important than others, you can sort them out and even have some of them done by others as you see fit. From Havana you will take the Caldwell Flotilla back to Mexico and get Colonel Schneider and four of his marines and deliver them to Potomac Dockyards. After the Colonel's report he will be assigned to you to complete the expulsion of Maximilian from Mexico by force." He handed another set of mission orders from his stack in front of him and then he said, "Jason, it is up to you. You can leave the Navy at the end of the next 18 months or you can complete the missions I have outlined for you." He pushed the entire stack of papers across his desk, they rested in front of me like Mount Everest.

"If you will give me a free hand on procedure, I will complete the missions in the order that you have suggested. I will need time with my family, at my discretion. The normal letters of introduction from you and the White House to carry along to convince doubters that the mission has been authorized and a Canadian passport."

"It is all in your stack, Jason, and some other things that you might find useful, like a US Treasury voucher for purchase of needed materials while on a mission."

"I hope to survive the next three and one half years in this office, if I do not, I hope my replacement has the good sense to find men like you to command men in the service of their country." He stood and extended his hand across his desk and said, "Do you remember the day I took this job from Secretary Touche?"

I shook his hand and said, "Yes, I do, sir."

"I thought then that the wrong man had been selected for the job, it should have been you, Jason. If you complete these missions for me, I will be the most successful Secretary of the Navy since John Paul Jones was a USN Captain."

I reached out and gathered the pile of papers and said, "I will have Montgomery Blair come over and talk to you about American Telegraph installing a telephone compatible underwater cable. You do realize that there are no above water lines in Bermuda, sir. John Butler has installed underwater cable from the connection point that American Telegraph left him to connect the tiny chain of islands that make up Bermuda. Bermuda is an ideal place for such an installation because the cable must be kept from overheating and burning through the wire carrying the signals. From my house in St. George, I can talk to my father and mother who live on a tiny island inside the Great Sound, my brother who lives on St. David's island or the City of Hamilton, Government House. We ran a cable from Government House to the Royal Naval Dockyards. They think it is a private line, but we can listen to anything being said."

"Why did you have American Telegraph run a cable from Maryland to Bermuda?"

"So we could talk to anyone connected to the transatlantic cable. There are now three lines across the Atlantic Ocean, sir. You can send a telegram to London, or you can talk to them if you like."

"How do you talk to Bermuda from Seneca Hill?"

"We installed an underground cable from Seneca Hill to Erie. Once we connected to Erie we used Lake Erie and just dropped the wire in the water until we got to the canal connecting Lake Erie and Lake Ontario. From Ontario we used the St. Lawrence to connect to the transatlantic cable to Europe. I was able to talk to the Lord Admiralty before I was able to talk to Bermuda, however. As more and more telegraph cable was installed we kept bridging the open spaces until we had a Bermuda crossing from Salisbury, Maryland."

"So what I asked you to do from Salisbury to Washington is a minor thing compared to what you have already done?"

"I would think so, but I have no knowledge of how this system works, it is really the brain child of Monty

Blair. The best thing that ever happened to American Telegraph was when Monty was fired as Postmaster General by President Lincoln. I had a chance to hire him and he has made over fifty million dollars for the company at ten times his salary here in Washington."

"Then why did he come back at Andrew Johnson's request?"

"His salary continues at American Telegraph and it was only for 90 days. This is his last week at the White House, so it is important that you talk to him today or tomorrow. Shall I send him over?"

"Are you going back to your office in the White House, Jason?"

"Yes, I need a larger brief case to carry all these papers home to Seneca Hill."

"I will walk with you and see Montgomery. Why do you call him Monty, everyone else calls him Montgomery?"

"I am the only one he allows to call him that. It started as a joke. We were sitting in the Washington office of American Telegraph trying to convince them to lay a double bonded telegraph connection from Salisbury to St. George, Bermuda. The office manager had no idea that Caldwell International was the holding company for American Telegraph. Monty turns to me and says, 'Jase, this man does not who is talking to, he knows me from the White House.' He turns to the office manager and says, 'Let me introduce the Chairman of Caldwell International.' The man's eyes bugged out and said, I had no idea, Mr. Caldwell, please forgive me."

"That does not sound like Montgomery Blair."

"I know, he was putting on an act". I turned to him

and said, "Well, Monty, let's go to lunch so he can sort it out for us and we will return in a couple of hours to sign the contracts. This was on a Wednesday."

"So that is how the Wednesday lunches began between you two. That drove everyone in the White House crazy trying to figure out what you two were doing."

"We were having lunch!"

We walked into the White House and Gideon Welles said, "That reminds me of a joke. A factory worker left work one night pushing a wheelbarrow full of straw. The night watchman looked through the straw but found nothing. This happened night after night until finally the night watchman said to the worker, 'I know you are stealing something. If you tell me what it is I will not report you to the management.' The worker replied, 'wheelbarrows'.

We were both laughing as we found Monty's office and I said, "You will be getting telegrams as updates until your telephone is installed in the Army Navy Building. Thank you for allowing me to serve the last eighteen months in the Navy with dignity, I will not forget this, Gideon." We shook hands again and he entered the Postmaster General's office. I heard him say, "Montgomery Blair, just the man I was looking for."

"Call me Monty."

Well, that is off to a good start, I thought as I continued on to the Secretary of State's office. I found out later from Monty that Gideon Welles was amazed by what American Telegraph could do with a pair of copper wires. Monty gave him the cost of laying a private, government line verus a public line which was free of installation costs but carried a monthly fee, paid every month or the line went dead. Monty estimated that as soon as everyone else heard of his plan, especially the White House that additional lines would be required. He warned him that dropping the cable in the Chesapeake and Potomac was a rapid process, once you came on land, the costs skyrocketed because ditches needed to be dug and water pipes for cooling were then installed. He indicated that the trench from Seneca Hill to Erie cost over 650 thousand dollars to construct.

"You have to understand Mr. Secretary, the telephone system that we use is very costly because of the over heating of the cable. Soon, say ten years or less, it will be possible to send telephone transmissions through wires in the air and the cost will be cheaper than a telegram. I predict telegrams will decrease in popularity as the telephone becomes common place in America."

Monty explained that the Federal Government was heavily in debt because of the war. After the Revolutionary War the debt was 75 million, the War of 1812 drove it to 127 million and this war drove it to over 12 billion, the yearly interest being 140 million dollars. Monty doubted that Gideon or even the President could get an appropriation through Congress for the amount necessary to construct a private line. The cost being in the neighborhood of ten million dollars.

"How can American Telegraph afford to make such a large investment?" Secretary Welles finally asked.

"It is a cost of doing business, the monthly rent on the use of the telephone line will be 50,000 dollars."

"That is six hundred thousand dollars a year!"

"Correct, a lot cheaper than the ten million to construct a private line. You have to understand Caldwell

International is one of the largest holding companies in the world. Jason Caldwell has no idea how much he is worth, it varies daily. I would say he could buy Morgan and Chase and have money left over. A million dollars to him is pocket change."

"No wonder he wants out of the Navy!"

"If he worked really hard at business he could remove the national debt in a year, Mr. Welles. Jason Caldwell is my hero. There will never be another like him for a century."

"I am beginning to understand why people either love or hate him. The jealousy factor alone must be a constant thorn in his side."

"Think of it this way, Mr. Welles, how many Admirals do you know that take their own private fleet with them on assignments for the Navy. The lease agreement you have with him is causing him to lose thousands of dollars a day in lost revenue. He thinks nothing of it, just a loyal American serving his country."

"Thank you, Monty, I will talk to the President about what we have proposed, but I think we will be sending telegrams well into the future!"

"You can reach me at my office in town if you change your mind or need a written, formal proposal from American Telegraph."

I was still packing things from my few months as the acting Secretary of State when Gideon Welles stopped and entered the office.

"That was an interesting conversation, Monty is a remarkable man. No one bothered to spend much time with him during his first four years here. That was our loss, I see now."

"He is a very quiet man. Very confident with who he is and what he is capable of accomplishing. If I had twenty more like him, I could run a hundred companies with ease. Right now Caldwell International is trying to find college graduates that speak at least one foreign language and understand how to make a profit from a business enterprise. Do you know that Spanish or French is not required for graduation from college any more?"

"Mon Dieu, Comonques quelltelle que sollerie!"

"Very funny, you know that neither French or Spanish is required for graduation from the US Military Academy. What did you just say?"

"I have no idea, but it sounded really good. You would be surprised how many people respond with Oui, Oui and nod their heads like they speak fluent French."

"Gideon, I am going to miss not seeing you everyday. But my boss has given me this impossible list of tasks and only eighteen months to complete them."

"Jason, the telephone thing will have to wait. After talking to Monty you can cross that off the list as something to look forward to in the future. You should sort the list and complete the most important first. And go home to South Carolina, that is an order!"

"Aye, aye, sir."

31

Home Leave
Fall 1865

I was sitting on the train out of Washington bound for
Seneca Hill, Pennsylvania. I had boxed what few items
I could not carry and mailed them to my home. I had a
long train ride ahead of me so I managed to get a private
compartment with a small writing table that dropped
drown from the wall. I opened one of the two brief cases
and began reading and making notes with my new foun-
tain pen that Louise had given me from her shopping
spree in Havana. I started by reading the orders for the
Naval commander, occupation forces, Beaufort, South
Carolina. Gideon Welles reasoned the best way to remove these forces was to place them on the ships of the
flotilla and bring them back to Potomac Dockyards for
mustering out of the service. Gideon had forwarded the
original orders to a Commander Davis (no relation to
Jefferson Davis, I mused) and had placed a copy in my
stack of to make notes. That was good, it would not be
a complete surprise when a four star Admiral shows up

on his door step with orders from Washington. I placed everything related to the trip to South Carolina in one pile and made the following notes:

1) Pay taxes on 353 Bay Street, check condition of house, hire household staff, reopen;
2) Check rental properties and homes of Father and Brother;
3) Check conditions of Caldwell Properties in Port Royal;
4) Find Carol's grave in Port Royal and have remains removed to St. Helena's Churchyard for internment in family plots with markers for her husband and children. Even if the remains can not be found, they should each have a separate marker and place of honor.....

I realized that I could no longer see through my tears. "Is the war really over?" I asked no one.

I worked the entire time the train traveled the 220 miles to Pittsburgh. I realized I was hungry, locked my compartment and found the dining car. After a meal, I felt like pouring through my papers again and I returned to work while the train continued on to Erie. I would get off before Erie at a little stop called Clarks Mill, here I changed to a coach seat for Franklin and on into Oil City. Oil City was the closest train station to Seneca Hill, here Sam Mason would be waiting with a carriage to take me the rest of the way. As I stepped off the train and onto the platform I heard, "Oh, it is Daddy, right over there, Ruthie, can you see him?" That was all it took for Ruth to run head long into my knees and hold on tight, she would not let loose. James, as old as he was, jumped up on my back and held on for dear life. Louise was smiling and holding on to Carol's hand so she could make her way across the platform and place a giant kiss directly on my mouth.

"Really, Louise, control yourself, we are in public!" I said this with a giant smile because she always said this to me when we showed any affection in public.

"I do not care. You are my husband and you never have to go back to Washington again in our life times. I will kiss you whenever and wherever I please until the day you die." She was crying.

"Why are you crying, Mommy?"

"Because your Daddy is home to stay, Carol."

Sam and Rachael came forward with their children and we had a giant, group hug. Sam grabbed my two brief cases and said, "Welcome home, Admiral. I have two large carriages waiting just outside, we should get the children out of the cool air and into Seneca Hill."

"I am completely in agreement, is it a 'fires in every fireplace', time yet?"

"The household staff has planned something special for you, Admiral, try to act surprised. They really have been working to provide a proper homecoming for you."

We rode a few miles and the house on the hill called Seneca Hill came into view. Every gas lamp in the place was ablaze even the outside carriage portico was well lit. And there standing with his arms crossed waiting for us was Louise Buchanan Caldwell's brother, the fifteenth President of the United States. "How long has he been here?" I asked Louise.

"He came over from 'Wheatland' last week. He is so

excited about going to Beaufort with us, Jason."

"He is going to South Carolina? You are going to South Carolina?" This was not in any of the papers that I studied.

"Yes, he got a letter from President Johnson informing him that he could be of great assistance to you in the normalization of South Carolina and her return back into the Union. He loves Beaufort, Jason."

I felt a lump in my throat as James Buchanan threw his arms around me and gave me a warm embrace. "Jason, Jason. The war we tried to avoid is finally over!"

"Yes, it is." Was all I could think of to say.

"Daddy, Uncle James has a present for you. It is inside all wrapped up in a tiny box can we go inside and see what it is?"

"Yes, James. Help Sam with my brief cases and we will see what it is."

We all trooped in through the front entrance and greeted the household staff who were all lined up like a White House reception line. I spent some time with each one and thanked them for the years of faithful service to my family. James could not stand it another minute. "Daddy, have Uncle James tell you about his present to you."

"Jason, past presidents are not without some influence." He cleared his throat and continued. "When I heard that President Johnson was at war with his own Senate, I wrote to the Republican majority in an open letter asking for them to consider something I thought was important."

He flipped open the box James thought was wrapped and inside was the Presidential Medal of Freedom. I could not speak.

"It took two Presidents to get this done, Jason, but it is long overdue! Please accept this with my congratulations. Here is a letter from President Johnson that he would like you to read to your family."

"You will have to do that, James, I am afraid I could not make it through without embarrassing myself." I said while wiping my nose with my handkerchief.

He opened and began reading:

THE WHITE HOUSE

September 25, 1865

My Dear Friend Jason,

Your brother-in-law has managed to do something that I have been unable to do for two months. He, and he alone, convinced the United States Senate to approve my granting of the Presidential Medal of Freedom to you on this day.

In all of my years of public service, I have never met anyone more deserving of this recognition. You are the loyalist American alive today. May your retirement from government service be blessed with good health, (you already have the wealth), happiness and continued success in the things you find important to your family.

Andrew Johnson

Everyone was quiet until Ruthie said, "That was a nice letter Daddy, was it as nice as mine?"

"No, it was not." I reached into my tunic and found the letter that I had over my heart. I unfolded it and began to read:

SENECA HILL

DEAR DADDY,

MOMMY SAYS MY PRINTING IS VERY GOOD. I TRY HARD TO DO WHAT MY TUTOR SAY TO ME. DO YOU KNOW SHE HAS ONLY ONE EAR RING. JAMES STILL HITS ME. I TOLD HIM YOU TELL HIM NO NO. I ASKED MOMMY WHY YOU ARE AWAY. SHE TOLD ME THAT SOME PEOPLE DO NOT LIKE TO FOLLOW RULES. THE RULES ARE FOR SO WE CAN ALL LIVE TOGETHER. SHE SAID YOU WERE TELLING SOME PEOPLE NO NO. DO YOU MISS ME. I MISS YOU ALL THE TIME. I GIVE YOU A BIG HUG WHEN YOU ARE BACK TO ME.

RUTH LOUISE CALDWELL

I folded the letter and placed it back inside my tunic. I had read it so many times that I could read it without tears filling my eyes but most of the people in the room had never heard it and they were affected the same way I was when I first opened it months ago. I looked around the room and found many of the listeners shaking their heads, yes.

The welcoming home party continued on into the

night until the children fell asleep in chairs and I carried them to their rooms and tucked them in for the rest of the night. Louise looked on and said, " They do not need night shirts tonight, Jason. They can sleep in their underwear."

"Mrs. Caldwell, is everyone else assigned to their sleeping quarters?"

"They are, Admiral, the rest of the night is ours."

32

Mission to South Carolina
Winter 1865

The next morning found us planning our trip to South Carolina. James Buchanan, Sam, Rachael, Louise and I sat around the breakfast table drinking our last cup of coffee and visiting.

"You know, Jason, a past presidential visit anywhere is a nonevent. The last trip that I took to South Carolina was March, 1858. It was planned and announced to the newspapers, no announcement need be given in the fall of 1865. We can travel by train from Seneca Hill to the Potomac Dockyards to board the Caldwell Flotilla. The President has offered us the use of Charter Oak."

The USS Charter Oak was added to the flotilla by President Johnson. He had indicated in his letter to James Buchanan that he should use the Presidential Ship. He had also offered six members from his protection detail. We would meet the members from Jerome Lewis' office at the dockyards. They would be responsible for the safety and well being of the past president, his sister traveling with him, Admiral Caldwell, the three Caldwell Children and Captain Sam Mason. Sam's wife, Rachael and their children would remain in Washington with Rachael's parents. Naturally the President's suite was suitable for a former head of state. I remembered the last time I was aboard. I was the most junior Admiral in the Navy.

"How are the plans getting along for the protection detail, Sam?"

"We are on schedule, Sir. I think I will have a commitment from Captain Lewis for a detail of six from the White House. He will let me know, tomorrow. If he says yes, then we have commitments from two former shore patrol officers, two former city policemen, and two former rapid response unit members. I know all six and they are very good."

"We will be on the Charter Oak later this week then. I have a pile of papers to sign and a few telegrams for you to send before we leave."

The voyage south this time was consumed with the political awareness of the flotilla. We stopped at several seaports along the way. President Johnson wanted maximum newspaper exposure so we stopped in Virginia and North Carolina before getting to Port Royal. These were arranged ports of call with the White House. Telegrams were waiting at all three ports and replies were sent to the President. The final telegram telling of our arrival in Port Royal was made by Sam as the flotilla moored next to the piers in Port Royal, the Charter Oak continued on into Beaufort.

The town of Beaufort had never had a President of the United States visit until James Buchanan in March of '58. Beaufort was founded in 1712 and was built on a bay formed by the mouth of the Beaufort River. Bay Front is a street, a marina, and a place for people to gather in a large park. The founding fathers wanted the Bay of Beaufort to remain pristine for future generations. No building was permitted on the water's edge, except for the marina where vessels could dock and a ferry which operated to the barrier islands along the coast. The Charter Oak tied up along side the park at high tide, across from the marina. Thousands of people filled the park to over flowing in '58, no one seemed to care in '65. The Past President, Louise and I came down the gang plank because of the tide, followed closely by our protection detail.

In 1858, it took James Buchanan, Louise and I nearly two hours to move slowly through the crowd and into waiting carriages for the short drive to 353 Bay Street. Today, no one greeted us and we could not take a carriage to 353 Bay Street because it was occupied by Union Naval Officers assigned to Beaufort. We did find a carriage for hire and asked to be taken to the Commanding Officer's headquarters. His headquarters turned out to be my Uncle's house on Boundary Street. I wore my naval fatigues with four stars on the collar points. A dress uniform would send the wrong message, I thought. It would be better to be one of the sailors on this trip. We paid our driver and the three of us walked up the front steps of the CO headquarters. We entered the house used as an office and found the duty officer.

"Can we see Commander Davis?"

"Do you have an appointment?"

"On your feet, sailor!" I shouted. Louise jumped and James Buchanan was smiling. "Are you in the habit of addressing an Admiral in such a casual tone?"

"No, sir. I mean, I did not see your rank, Admiral."

"Get Commander Davis out here right now. Tell him

the President of the United States would like to see him!"
Now James Buchanan was chuckling, he had seen this act
before. Louise had a terrified look on her face and when
the ensign ran from the outer office. I bent down and
gave her a kiss on the cheek.

"Try to keep a straight face while I try to get your
house back for you, honey."

Both the ensign and a commander came running
into the outer office. "Admiral, sir. No one told me you
were coming. Where is the President?"

"Right here, son." And James Buchanan held out his
hand for Commander Davis to shake it.

"It is so good to meet you, Mister President. What
can we do for you?"

"You could offer us a chair to sit down."

"Of course, how stupid of me, come into my office.
Ensign Jensen, bring another chair for the lady."

We marched into his office and waited for Louise to
be seated. James Buchanan was enjoying this.

"Commander Davis, you did get orders saying that
you would be transported to Potomac Dockyards some
time this week, correct?"

"Yes, Mister President, we can be ready to depart in
twenty-four hours."

"Good the fleet is moored at Port Royal. We will see
you in Port Royal tomorrow at this time."

"Tomorrow?"

"Yes, that is twenty-fours from now."

"I meant twenty-fours from official notification to
disembark."

"How official can we make it, Commander?" I said
smiling. "You and everyone under your command will
sail tomorrow from Port Royal. It may take us more than

one day to complete our business. It seems that you have commandeered this lady's house for the past four years. May I introduce Louise Caldwell, the owner of 353 Bay Street."

The commander said, "How do you do, Miss Caldwell."

"That is, Mrs. Caldwell, commander, and this Admiral is my husband."

"Oh, dear me, we had no idea that it was your house, Admiral, or we never would have ....."

"It is not my house, commander, it belongs to the lady."

"I do not understand?"

"How soon can Mrs. Caldwell move in to 353 Bay Street so she can list any damages for payment by the US Navy."

"We can not pay any damages to Confederate property during the last four years, Admiral."

"The house at 353 Bay Street belongs to a loyal 'Yankee' from Pennsylvania, you did check the property deed before you commandeered her house?"

"No."

"Then you may have made a career ending decision, Commander Davis. However, I think this can be fixed in short order. I want you to walk over to that address and tell all the officers that they have twelve hours to pack their things and get themselves to Port Royal for the voyage to Washington. The troop ships there comfortable, ask the marines where they are to put their gear. Oh, and tell them if they have taken souvenirs from the house they will not make it all the way back to the Potomac Dock Yards. Do I make myself clear?"

"Yes, Admiral, I am on my way right now."

He left in a hurry. "Jason, that was a terrible thing to do." Louise was not amused, her brother was.

"Louise, Jason handled that just right. The fear of God will be in every sailor not to steal the home owners blind when they leave tomorrow."

"We are leaving tomorrow?"

"No, the flotilla full of US Navy personnel will leave Port Royal exactly twenty-four hours from now." Her brother said. "The Charter Oak is under my command, sorry, Jason, but it leaves when I say so."

"Aye, aye. Mister President, what are you going to do when the commander finds out you are not Andrew Johnson?"

"We never said I was Andrew Johnson, besides I have a letter from Andrew that I can show him."

The look on Ensign Jensen's face was incredulous.

"Ensign Jensen, that is kind of a tongue twister. Do you type ensign?"

"Yes sir."

"Good, type up a promotion form for me to sign. I like lieutenant much better than ensign."

"Thank you, sir."

"You are welcome, Lieutenant."

He rushed off to find the proper form and we walked out on the front porch. A boy older than James was riding a bicycle down the sidewalk of Boundary Street. I waved and called, "Son, you want to earn a dollar?"

He skidded the bike to a stop and said, "Yes sir!" He jumped off his bike and walked over to us.

"Here is a dollar. I would like you to ride down to Bay Street and tell every shop keeper that the Navy is leaving Beaufort tomorrow and that Admiral Caldwell is home and will make sure any outstanding bills will be paid. Tell them to bring the bills to this house. Oh, and if you see a carriage for hire will you bring it back here and I will pay you another dollar."

"Thank you, General, sir."

"It is Admiral, but you are close. See you in a few minutes."

We waited on the porch with our protection detail, sitting in white rocking chairs. "What do you think of the southern past time of 'sitin and rockin', sergeant major?"

"I could get used to this, Admiral." He said with a smile.

Ensign Jensen found us and I signed his promotion papers. "Make sure those get in today's mail pouch, Lieutenant."

"Aye, aye. Sir."

We were waiting for a carriage so that James Buchanan could complete his list of items that had to done the first day. Louise was about to say something when Commander Davis came walking up the street with a Navy Captain.

"Jason, I thought that Commander Davis was the ranking officer here in Beaufort?"

"So did I, James, I wonder where Davis found him?"

"Admiral Caldwell, may I introduce Doctor Belks from the Navy Hospitals here in Beaufort."

I stood and said, "And may I introduce my wife and President James Buchanan."

The look of confusion on the commander's face was evident.

"Good morning, Mister President, Mrs. Caldwell. I

have come over here with the Commander to inform you that I am not under his command, I have a command of my own and therefore I can not leave my billet at 353 Bay Street until the hospital is evacuated."

I looked at him and did not say anything, just stared at him. The seconds turned into a minute and then James Buchanan said, "Doctor, it is good to met you. I have a letter here from President Johnson, I think you should read. You will find that we are here to evacuate the hospitals. In fact we are waiting for a carriage to tour the several houses that you have turned into hospitals here in Beaufort. Perhaps you would like to give us a tour?"

"I am too busy for that, I decide when my patients can be moved, not you Mr. Buchanan. It will be weeks before some of them can be evacuated."

I had seen James Buchanan perturbed, upset and even angry at times. Usually the quieter he got the more upset he was. He rose from his rocking chair and walked directly up to the doctor until their noses were less than an inch apart. "You are saying that you refuse an order from the President of the United States." He was whispering.

"No, Mr. Buchanan, I am saying I refuse an order from you."

"And if Admiral Caldwell gives you the same order, you will refuse him?"

"Yes, sir. The Navy Medical Staff does not take orders from the military command."

"I have read your records, Doctor Belks, you have been here the whole four years of the war. That is a little unusual."

"No, sir. I was responsible for taking the largest Confederate Houses here in Beaufort and turning them into top notch military hospitals. That is why I have been here four years."

"Were you the one responsible for removing all the household contents from these magnificent homes, piling it on their front lawns, soaking it with kerosene and burning it?"

"Yes, it was the most efficient way to dispose of the contents."

"Did it ever occur to you that some of these homes are not Confederate." You could barely hear his words.

"They were all Confederate, Mr. Buchanan."

"Sergeant!"

"Yes, Mister President." He was at attention and standing beside James in one giant step.

"Arrest this ass hole. Put him in handcuffs. Take him back to 353 Bay Street and have any other officers present find every personal item that the doctor has including underwear and pile it on the front lawn, pour kerosene over it and burn it. He will leave tomorrow with only the clothes on his back. Personally take him to Port Royal and have the marines lock him in the brigg of the USS Providence to await court martial."

"Aye, aye. Sir." Sergeant Major Clyde Hawks stood a good six inches taller than the doctor and he was not gentle putting the handcuffs on him and dragging him off the porch towards Bay Street.

"Commander, you better go with them. There are other Navy doctors here?"

"Yes, sir." He said with a smile on his face.

Louise stood up and said, "James, I have never seen you like this."

"Your husband was too angry to deal with him. Jason can not abide fools and I can not abide flaming ass holes."

"What is the difference?" She managed to ask.

"A fool does not know he is an ass hole. A flaming ass hole knows he is."

I burst out laughing and it was contagious, first the other sergeants from the protection detail, then Louise and finally James Buchanan could hardly stand up. Our young man came riding his bicycle followed by a carriage. "You owe him another dollar, Jason."

The three of us sat in the carriage and the two sergeants stepped on the foot rails and we were off to visit the hospitals. The first place we stopped was "The Castle", a large four story Caldwell family town house. It was constructed of tabby, covered with stucco and it looked like a small manor house in England. The stucco had not been cleaned in four years, it needed paint on all the wood trim and shutters. The grass was not clipped and the flower garden I remembered as a child was over grown and neglected. It did not look like a hospital. I gave the driver a dollar and told him to wait we would be going to all the hospitals. He nodded and we walked inside the castle. It was damp and musty smelling. A nurse sat behind a desk and asked, "Are you here to visit, folks?"

"Yes, we are." Louise said.

"Are you relatives?" She asked doubtfully.

"We have come from Washington with a letter of evacuation from President Johnson." She replied.

"Oh, thank God. I have prayed for this day. These men need to get home to their families. I must warn you that most of the war survivors are amputees. They may be on crutches or in wheel chairs but they are still men, or some just boys, that need the support of those they love."

"Can we visit the wards?"

"Of course, follow me."

We walked up one flight of stairs and entered a large room. You could still see where the walls had been removed from several smaller rooms to make the ward. The walls were lined with cots.

"You do not have hospital beds?" Louise asked shocked.

"No, ma'am. Doctor Belks says that canvas cots can be washed after the patients die and can be used over and over again."

"That flaming ass hole." I heard Louise say under her breath.

"What was that, dear?"

"That claim is old. I have heard it before, but I do not believe it."

"You are absolutely right my dear. A bed is much better."

We stopped at the foot of cot where a young boy was recovering from his wounds. "Is he a local boy that was injured and treated here?" Louise asked.

"No, he is a private that was brought here from Columbia when Sherman came through."

"What is your name, private?" Louise asked.

"Peter Loresmith."

"How old are you Peter?"

"I will be seventeen my next birthday."

"What are you doing here if you are only sixteen, Peter?"

"I was a private with the Rhode Island 4th, ma'am."

"No, I mean why are you in the army?"

"They took me, ma'am."

"Who took you?"

"The army recruiters in Rhode Island. Two men came to my Mother's cottage and said that she would have to pay 300 dollars or sign me up. She said my Pa was already in the army. It did not matter, either pay the 300 dollars or I would be drafted."

Louise began her silent crying that I had seen only once before. Large beads of tears slowly rolled down her cheeks. She bent over and kissed the boy on the forehead and said, "We are here to take you home to your mother, Peter."

She straightened to her full height and said to the nurse, "Admiral Caldwell has transport ships in Port Royal, can any of these patients be moved by carriage tomorrow?"

"They all can be, ma'am."

"That ass hole, and to think, I felt sorry for him."

"Ma'am?"

"You are a Navy nurse?"

"Yes, ma'am."

"Then you will be leaving tomorrow, also. Where is home?"

"Pennsylvania, ma'am."

"We are from Pennsylvania! Where are my manners? Let me introduce my brother, James Buchanan and my husband Admiral Caldwell."

"I thought I recognized both of you, Franklin County, right?"

"Are you the only one on duty here?"

"Oh, no. There are several others on different floors."

"Good, go and tell them what has happened. They have a full day ahead of them packing supplies that they will need. We will have a wagon here in a hour for them to start putting everything together. You nurses will be in charge, not Dr. Belks, he has been arrested and jailed, awaiting court marshal."

"Praise the Lord, it is about time that sadist has been put behind bars. I would like to testify at his trial!"

"You shall. After you talk to your nurses come back outside and you can show us what we need to know at the other hospitals." Louise Buchanan Caldwell was now in charge of the evacuation of the hospitals in Beaufort. She stomped down the stairs and out on to the porch of the castle and found one of the protection detail. "Walk over two blocks and towards the bay and you will find a livery stable, hire a wagon and have it brought here. You can catch up with us, we will be visiting each of the hospitals."

"Yes, ma'am." He was off on a trot.

"Louise, slow down, you have a week here in Beaufort, more if you need it."

"Oh, Jason, a week will not begin to be enough. I am here until the people of this town have their dignities returned to them."

"What do you mean?"

"Jason, it is going to get worse. We are going to find things that will be beyond our understanding. Please, let me do what only a woman can do. You and James deal with the criminal actions, let me try to pick up the pieces of these people's lives."

"Yes, ma'am." I saluted and turned to find her brother.

James came walking out of the hospital with the nurse. "This is nurse Bellamy. Jane Bellamy, I know her family."

"Nice to meet you, Jane. James your sister is now in charge. She finally understands what you and I tried to avoid four years ago."

"Admiral, before we go to the next hospital. There is something I think you should see."

We now had two carriages hired for the day and the first carriage stopped at the St. Helena's Episcopal Church, my church. Nurse Bellamy stepped down and said, "Follow me." We walked through the outer walled section of the church graveyard and stopped in our tracks.

"Where are the grave markers?" I said in horror.

"They have been stacked at the rear of the church after it was abandoned as a hospital."

"My church was a hospital?" I was numb.

"It was a surgery during the war. Hospital ships brought the wounded here. In good weather amputations were done about here." She pointed to the bare ground where not a blade of grass grew.
"Why has the grass been removed?" I asked.

"It was not removed. Three head stones at a time from the graveyard were used as surgery tables. Two as legs and the large flat ones as table tops. The surgery was done, several patients at a time. The table surfaces were washed down with water to remove the blood. Human blood has caused the grass to die."

"Oh, my God." Was all I could manage to say. I felt weak.

"What about in winter?" I asked softly.

"In winter they moved them inside."

We entered the church and my childhood memories were destroyed. "How could they do this to a place of worship?" Stone surgery tables still stood where some of the pews had been removed. I walked over to them and read the inscriptions on the surfaces, they still held dark black remains of human blood. I turned and faced my wife. "You are right. We are not leaving Beaufort until this has been made right! I do not care how long it takes."

James Buchanan was silently weeping as we left the church and returned to the graveyard. "There must be a master plot plan I can get from the church sextant, Jason. I am in charge of returning all the markers to their proper places. What an outrage to the families, where were your family buried, Jason?"

"Over there by that giant live oak, a few of the smaller markers are still there."

"You are not going to like hearing the rest, Admiral."

"The rest, there is more?" I almost shouted.

"Yes, the Union soldiers that died on the operating tables were buried on top of the grave sites you see here. This was when action was slow. When the bodies were piling up from so many, the dead were piled, soaked with kerosene for a funeral phyre."

"The bodies were burned, not buried?"

"Yes, sir. Right over there in that shallow pit, where the ground is still charred black."

"I will have it filled, Jason." James said with a hollow voice.

"Certain organs and bones will not be completely burned only charred, they were gathered each day and buried in a hole on top of an existing grave."

"Were records kept of the dead? Do we have those?"

"Yes we do, Admiral. I know where Doctor Belks kept them. I will be responsible for all the records that I can find for you."

The four of us stood looking at the aftermath of the

horror that must have occurred here from 1861 to 1865. James Buchanan turned to his sister and said, "Now you understand what Jason and I tried to avoid my four years in office and what we both endured watching this last four years. I will dedicate the next four years to the people who suffered both North and South."

* * * * * * * * *

James Buchanan was a prophet. He died four years later, 1869, in Wheatland surrounded by his family and friends. He had written to Andrew Johnson and said he wished a closed casket be placed under the Rotunda of the Capital and the usual State Funeral with burial of the casket in Pennsylvania. His remains, however, were cremated in honor of the soldiers in St. Helena's Churchyard and his ashes were spread, by his sister, on the surface of beautiful Beaufort Bay.

33

Requiem Mass
Saint Helena's Church

The Episcopal Church in Beaufort, South Carolina, had a service on Wednesday, December 21, 1865, to honor those who fell during the last four years. It was a musical tribute to those who died and a solemn celebration of the restoration of the Church and adjoining graveyard. All of the markers had been replaced according the plot plan that James Buchanan had found. He faithfully went every day from 353 Bay street to the church. He supervised and paid for the restoration of the graveyard. He directed that three tablets be erected in the manner that they were used by surgeons during the war and had a bronze plaque attached. The plaque described what happened on this spot, 1861 - 1865.

The missing pews were found in a warehouse on Boundary Street and lovingly restored and placed where they belonged. The silver communion service that was donated by John Bull in 1734 was never found. Louise Buchanan Caldwell had an identical set made by a silver-

328

smith in Sheldon and donated it during the mass. Father Timothy Brightwell gave the following sermon:

> *"Enclosed in a high brick wall, she sits like an ecclesiastical poem among its grayed lichened gravestones; its slender spire piercing the green masts of the trees like a clear bugle call. Ancient live oaks, with their swaying banners of gray moss, weave myriad leafy designs of light and shadow to fling against its mellowed, pinkish walls of brick and tabby.*
>
> *When the wind blows, the palmettoes chant a requiem for those who sleep beneath the stones. The tall sycamores, green in summer, gold in autumn, silver green in spring, march two by two like loving sentinels from the east gate. In early spring, a purple flame of wisteria creeps along the walls, creating a scene of such breathtaking beauty that artists' easels set up along the path seem almost a natural part of the scene.*
>
> *We now sit in one of the oldest ,as well as the most beautiful, of the early churches in America.   Built to fill the need of a struggling young colony, it is simple in design, almost to austerity, rising four square and solid to withstand storms, wars and time.*
>
> *This old church has witnessed prosperity and adversity. She is filled with memories of joy and sorrow. She has witnessed the heartbreak of death and parting. For many generations tiny infants have been christened at her font.   Young girls in gossamer white and solemn little boys, have knelt at her altar for first communion. As I look out upon you, her congregation, I see a people who will not tolerate the death of a church or its people. Within these walls is Beaufort's unwritten story of birth,*

faith, life, war and death. It can not be erased by an invading army. It can not be wrought asunder by those who plundered its valuables. The valuables that we hold dear are each other and the families that have toiled so many hours to restore this Church.

A former President of the United States sits with us today and has transferred his membership from Pennsylvania. He and his nephew have donated countless hours to our building and replacement efforts here at Saint Helena Episcopal Church. His sister married a man from this congregation and she has returned with him to help heal those of us in need. She has paid all of the outstanding taxes on all of the homes of this congregation because she knew the need of some of us and she understood our refusal to pay a union tax collector's call for payment. She has encouraged all of us to have faith in God and in each other.

It is the pride that God gives all of us to enjoy his blessings, that we rededicate this church today and every day that we enter and kneel in prayer."

I was holding Louise's hand siting with her and her brother. Next to James Buchanan sat his nephew who had become his shadow these last three months in Beaufort. Everywhere that James the elder went, his nephew was there watching and learning. Next to James sat his sister, Ruth. She no longer complained of James' torments. James had changed. He had grown into a sensitive older boy and I wondered if we might have a future Episcopal Priest or even a statesman in our family. It would be his choice, not mine. Even our baby, Carol, had changed these past three months, or maybe we saw her differently. The entire family knew that our mission to Beaufort was about over. Beaufort would always be my birth place, a special place in all our hearts. Our lives were in other parts of the world, however. James Buchanan would return to his home at Wheatland, his nephew was old enough to visit him often, it was a short train ride from Oil City to Wheatland.

I had sent and received reports of what we had accomplished on our trip to South Carolina. In twenty-four hours, the main body of the Caldwell Flotilla had left from Port Royal. All of the Navy personnel were on board as well as the hospital staff and their patients. The Captain of the USS *Providence* had thought that a mistake had made by locking Doctor Jonathan Belks in the brigg and he released him to care for his patients. He was seen about the ship the first day and then he vanished. He was reported as lost at sea. Three of his patients died of natural causes before reaching the Potomac Docks and were buried at sea.

A week later the USS *Charter Oak* sailed for Washington with Sam Mason and the protection detail. Sam carried a number of reports and letters important to Secretary Welles who had sent me on this mission. One of the reports I had written, I decided not to send. It was heart wrenching to me personally, but it would result in no action whatsoever. I would read and reread it over the next few years of my life.

Report of General Sherman's Troop Behavior

Filed November 23, 1865

Admiral Jason Edwin Caldwell Reporting

The previous reports have dealt with the evacuation of federal troops from Beaufort County, South Carolina. I have discovered several disturbing facts about General Sherman's troop behavior on their taking of the city of Savannah, Georgia. They passed through Beaufort County destroying everything in their path. Nonmilitary, civilian homes, churches and public buildings of every description were set aflame. The hate caused by this will never dissipate from this and future generations of this locale. A typical example follows:

The people of Sheldon, South Carolina, had a historically significant church that had an interesting history. In 1780, when the British under General Prevost passed it on their march from Savannah to the siege of Charles Town, decided to leave a message for the rebels. They gathered as many of the town's people as they could find and locked them in the wood framed church and burned it to the ground with everyone inside. The Methodist-Episcopal Church of America declared it a holy shrine of martyrdom. The people of Beaufort County, including my Great Grandfather, rebuilt the church of brick so this tragedy would never occur again. And it survived nearly a hundred years until Sherman's calvary decided to use the church as a stable. They ignored the bronze plaque describing it as a holy shrine. They gutted the inside so that straw could be placed on the floor in order to stable the horses of his cavalry. Horses defecating on a holy shrine should have been enough. When the calvary moved on, they were ordered to burn the church. Anything wooden perished, every thing brick survived. It stands today, a ghostly reminder of man's inhumanity to his fellow man, a cruel act by one group of Americans upon another. The people of

Sheldon have decided never to rebuild. Each Easter they will gather and celebrate a sunrise service for generations to come. As a small boy I remember my Grandfather taking me from Beaufort to Sheldon to celebrate Easter mass within the beautiful brick walls of the church. Every Easter, that I am alive, I will take my Grandchildren to sit upon the grassy mounds and celebrate the sunrise and the renewal of the hate generated by General Sherman.

One of the reports that Sam carried had to do with Sam's present assignment as my aide decamp, it read.
Plan for Sam Mason's Mission to Canada

Filed November 23, 1865

Admiral Jason Edwin Caldwell Reporting

One of the hardest things for a fleet commander to do is the promotion of an aide back into active duty. Sam Mason has been an exceptional aide and I will hate to have him assigned back to the Army Navy Building in Washington. But it is time for his promotion and advancement within the service. I would suggest that he be given the Canada mission of trying to establish the whereabouts of former ORION members. He is returning with six members of the protection detail and he works well with them. I suggest that you assign some additional marines to make up the RR Unit and send them off on the Canadian Mission post haste.

I have ordered the return of the Caldwell Flotilla to Port Royal and will proceed with the evacuation of Colonel Schneider from Mexico in a timely manner. They should arrive in the Potomac Dockyards sometime in early December.

Another report dealt with housekeeping matters. Report of the use of US Treasury Vouchers

Filed November 23, 1865

Admiral Jason Edwin Caldwell Reporting

The banks in Beaufort, South Carolina, finally accepted my use of Treasury Vouchers for the resupply of the vessels used to transport the Navy occupation forces and the Navy hospitals here. They should start arriving in a few days for payment.

The federal reconstruction representatives assigned here are a bunch of "scalawags and carpet baggers" as one local has labeled them. They step off the train with only a single piece of luggage made out of what looks like a piece of carpet. And a new set of orders and procedures from Washington, often countermanding previous orders. I am considered another one of the "damnyankees" (one word) from Washington. An example follows:

I and my daughter Ruth entered the Beaufort County Courthouse to pay the new federally imposed taxes on my house and family plantation. I was in civilian clothes minding my own business when one of the "carpet baggers" noticed me and asked me to get in the front of the line of people waiting to pay. I refused. I waited my turn. When I finally got to the head of the line, I was missing one of the forms that I needed from the auditors/ appraisers office. In a loud voice, the "scalawag" said, "Admiral, these new taxes are for Confederates only, you are a member of the United States Navy and are exempt from such taxes." I heard a muttering from the line behind me, "damnyankee". Ruth and I sat down on the floor and I said, "I was born here, you fool, I am here to pay my taxes. We will not move until you receive our payment."

He finally agreed to take my payment. The new taxes appear to be a form of punishment, as a South Carolinian I think they are a bad idea and will only cause further delay in the acceptance of this State back into the Union.

Ruth and I spent a great deal of time together. James and James worked at Saint Helena's Church. Louise and Carol were busy with the restoration of the Church and the house at 353 Bay Street. So, father and daughter went first to Port Royal to check on the location of the grave described by John Butler's aunt. We checked with the sexton's at the Port Royal Churches and various grave-yards to find where the "defenders of Fort Beauregard" were buried. We were told that no such grave existed. I asked if they remembered the firing on Beauregard during the US Navy invasion of Port Royal. Sure they remembered it alright, "The cowards defending the fort ran at the sound of the first shot fired, no one was killed because the fort was empty!"

"Where did they go?" I asked dumb founded.

"In all directions, some went back to Beaufort others made their way to the uninhabited islands like Fripp and Pritchard."

I must have looked upset because Ruth asked, "What is wrong, daddy?"

"Your Aunt, Uncle and cousins may be alive, if I can find them."

"If WE can find them." She corrected me.

"If we can find them." I said with a smile.

The next day, Ruth and I were on the ferry to Lady's Island. We hired a "two-wheeler" and searched the little villages like "Frogmore"until we reached the ford crossing to Datha Island. We stopped and talked to people asking them if they knew of anyone who had escaped from Beaufort or Port Royal in 1861. We explained that we were looking for Robert Caldwell's daughter and her family. They all knew of the Caldwell plantation on Pollawana, but they had not heard of anyone escaping to locate there. We crossed over to Pollawana and found Tobias Caldwell and his family still on the plantation. I asked him if he knew anything about my sister, Carol.

"She was blowed up over in Port Royal, Mr. Jason. She is buried in a mass grave somewheres over there."

"Thank you, Tobias. Can I show my daughter the old deserted house where I was born? Is it still standing over in the grove of live oaks?"

"Yes, sir. Mr. Jason. It is still there. Folks round here says it is haunted, it has lights at night."

My heart jumped. Maybe that is where she is, I thought. We hurried over the sandy road until the horse was winded and we stopped before the old plantation house. No one could live here, it was deserted and beyond repair. We got out of the carriage, tied the horse to the hitching post and walked up to the front steps.

"Be careful, now honey, these steps look rotten, we do not want to fall through them."

"Lift me up on the porch, daddy."

I did and hoisted myself up after her and we stayed away from the steps. The front door stood ajar and we pushed it open and birds flew in all directions. They frightened us and we jumped. We were standing in the great foyer that my mother was so proud of when she greeted her guests forty years ago.

"Over here is the parlor, Ruth. And upstairs are bedrooms where my brother, your Uncle Robert and my sister, your Aunt Carol, used to sleep and play with our toys."

"You had toys, daddy?"

"Of course, I was little just like you when I lived here."

"I am not little. I am small for my age!"

"Yes, I keep forgetting that you are really six going on twenty-one."

"What does that mean, daddy?"

"You are six years old, but think like an adult."

"Oh, is that good?"

"Sometimes."

We finished our tour of the house, untied the horse and started back to Tobias' house on the other side of the island. We ate lunch with them and then continued on to the Fripp Island ferry. This ferry was a privately owned means of getting from Hunting Island to Fripp. We talked to the man in charge and asked about visitors that might have come and gone.

"This is a working plantation, Admiral. You remember Captain John Fripp's kids inherited it from him. There is only one main house, close to the beach. They have servants, but they are former slaves that have been with them for years. There are no white people, other than the owners. I do not think your sister and her family are here. I know you want to find them, Admiral. The truth is there were only a handful of casualties at Fort Beauregard, the survivors ran for their lives. They did not find any remains to bury, Admiral. Your sister died inside Fort Beauregard, let her rest in peace. The folks in Port Royal made up a nice story about the 'defenders of Fort Beauregard' for future generations. The truth is the Fort was not defended, it was destroyed by US Naval cannon fire."

"I think you are right, besides it is getting past time to get back to Beaufort."

"You and your daughter should hurry so you catch the ferries between Hunting, Saint Helena and Lady's Islands."

"Will do, thank you for what you said. It helped me clear my head."

As we rode from ferry to ferry, Ruthie asked, "What was Aunt Carol like, daddy?"

"Well, let me remember. Her hair was about the color of yours. She liked to talk nonstop, like you. We had left the plantation and moved to Beaufort so that Robert and I could go to elementary school. She was too young and she was upset that she was left at home. Your Grandpa hired a private tutor to come to the house in Beaufort so she could begin her lessons early."

"Just like me, I have a tutor."

"Yes, you do. You learn everything as quickly as she did. When it was time to go to first grade in Beaufort she lasted only about three days and Grandma was called to school for a visit with her teacher. It was decided that she should be moved to the second grade because she already knew how to read her letters and make her numbers."

"Just like me. When will I go to second grade, daddy?"

"You have a private tutor that lives with us. I am sorry to tell you that you will be stuck with her until you pass your exams into second level."

"What is second level, daddy?"

"The first level is beginning or elementary. Second

level is for really smart children like you. You will get a new tutor and your tutor will become your little sister's tutor."

"Oh, goodie. I would hate not seeing Miss Templeton every day."

"But you can not bother her, she will be busy with Carol."

"Carol, same name as Aunt Carol."

"You figured it out, your sister is named in honor of Aunt Carol."

"Why do James and I have tutors? Why are we at home and not in school?"

"If we lived in one house, in one location, then you would be in a school. Your daddy's job takes him all over the world. And because I love you so much, I take you with me."

We had by this time found our way to the livery stable where we had rented the carriage for the day. I paid the livery hand and we walked to the Beaufort Ferry.

"Daddy?"

"Yes, Ruthie."

"I love you."

"Me, too, 'Ruthie Two Shoes.'"

"Why do you call me that?"

"When you were a little girl, not like the big girl you are now, you kept losing one shoe under your bed or wherever and I had to help you find it. So I started called you, 'Ruthie Two Shoes'."

"Daddy, will it make you mad if I tell you that I used to hide one shoe so that you would help me find it?"

"I think I figured that out after the umpteenth time, Ruthie. And no, I will never get mad at you for wanting to spend time with me. There will be a time, many years from now, when you will meet a nice young man and fall in love with him, like I did with your mother."

"Then what happens?"

"Then, I hope the nice young man holds on for dear life, because life with you will be one hell of a ride."

"You swore, daddy!"

"I know. Do not tell your mother!"

"Where are we going for Christmas, daddy?"

"To your home in Bermuda, the flotilla is back in Port Royal and it is time that the crew members get back to Bermuda to be with their families for Christmas."

"Why do you call the ships a flotilla?"

"Because there are not enough of them to be a fleet, and they are unarmed merchant ships."

"Then why is one of them called USS *Providence*, it has cannons."

"Yes, it does. It was built for the US Navy about 70 years ago. I bought it and changed it into a merchant ship and used it for many years. When the war broke out, I loaned it back to the Navy."

"Do they pay you rent?"

"Yes, they do. You know, it seems I have had this same conversation with your mother!"

"Are we rich, daddy?"

"In more ways than you can imagine, honey. This family is truly blessed."

"Will we ever run out of money?"

"Never!"

"Promise, daddy."

"Promise, Ruthie"

34

Bermuda Mission
Year 1866

Part of my mission package from Secretary Welles was a fact gathering trip to St. George, Bermuda. He had devised a set of assignments that would allow me to return to civilian life with the ghosts removed. I realized that he had ordered me to South Carolina so that I could confront the guilt caused by the death of my sister. And more importantly, the fact that I had not resigned my commission with the U.S. Navy and joined the C.S.A. Navy as nearly 320 other officers had done in 1861. Gideon Welles had become my protector, he understood me better than anyone else now serving in Washington. He allowed whatever time I needed in each of the locations where ghosts waited for me. We were all returning to St. George on the Cold Harbor. The flotilla from Port Royal now numbered ten ships and it was time to return some of them to the Caldwell Shipping and Trading Company so that Robert Whitehall could began using them.

"A penny for your thoughts?" Louise said as she slipped her arm through mine.

"Oh, you startled me!" I said. "It is cold out here in the wind. Are you warm enough?"

"Yes. How long do you think we will be in Bermuda, Jason?"

"Until all the ghosts are gone, probably all winter and spring."

"Ghosts? I do not understand, Jason."

"A ghost is created whenever you think you have caused the death or demise of another."

"Are you talking about Carol?"

"She was a ghost, but she is gone now. Ruthie and I put her to rest the last three months."

"So that is what she was talking about."

"Did she tell you about our search for her Aunt and Uncle?"

"Yes, I guess you had to do that. What was all the talk about money?"

"She worries about family finances, Louise. She is just like you."

"What did you tell her?"

"Well, we had quite a conversation between ferries coming back from Fripp Island. She asked if we had enough to live on if I quit my job as Admiral in the Navy."

"She was worried about income?"

"Both of you have no concept of what Caldwell International is worth. I explained it this way. Suppose that ten golden eagles, were placed one on the top of another?"

"Oh, I see. A hundred dollars would be about an inch thick."

"She got that part just like you did. But not when I told her that the number of gold eagles that Caldwell International has would be 400 miles high."

"Now I am lost."

"So was she. I tried it this way. If an inch is 100 dollars, how much is a foot high?"

"1200 dollars."

"Correct, how much is a 1000 feet?"

"1,200,000.00, oh my God, Jason, a mile is over six million dollars! How high was the stack you told her?"

"400 miles."

"400 times 6 equals 2.4 billion. Oh, Jason, that cannot be right, can it?"

"That is what the company was worth last quarter, it varies from day-to-day, up and down. It will drive you and Ruth crazy if you try to keep track of it. Think of it this way. God has truly blessed this family. He made it all possible and he can take it all away in the blink of an eye."

"Then, we should do something worthwhile with some of it before God decides to blink. Jason, set up a foundation to help others less blessed than we are."

"Good idea. What should we call this foundation and who should run it?"

"The director should be James Buchanan, can you think of anyone you trust more?"

"Agreed. Now, the name." I said.

"United States Development Foundation, USDF for short. If my brother does not want to be part of this, tell him he has to until President Johnson leaves office. You trust him?"

"How can you not trust someone who thinks you

deserve the Presidential Medal of Freedom?"

"Who would be funded from the foundation and why?" I asked.

"All western territories or former states seeking admission to the Union! The federal government has indicated that they will not pay for reconstruction of what Sherman did to the south. USDF will. The first hurdle or rule for assistance will be that the government has refused to help. The second will be that no northern state need apply, only western territories or CSA states. The third rule will be that once a state is admitted or readmitted it is no longer eligible."

"Louise, you should be the director. You have it all figured out."

"I cannot. I am the executive secretary and treasurer so I can keep an eye on our money."

"That is not how it works, Louise. Once the foundation is funded, the money is no longer ours to do with as we see fit. We will create the funding each year that we pay federal income taxes at the limit allowed by the tax codes. That way we pay the foundation instead of the federal treasury."

"I like the sound of that!"

"You become more southern every year you live, you know that, Louise?"

"And you become more northern, Mr. Business Tycoon."

We laughed and noticed that the colors of the offshore waters were beginning to turn a bright blue and coral. St. George would appear in about an hour. We went below and finished our packing.

USDF was formed and James Buchanan became its

first director. He sent letters to each of the provisional governors in the former CSA appointed by President Johnson. The confusion was soon apparent. Many governors thought USDF was a department in Washington and following the USDF guidelines to the letter, they called state conventions to do three things:

First they repealed the ordinances of secession,

Second they repudiated the state debts incurred in the aid of the Confederacy and,

Third they ratified the Thirteenth Amendment to the Constitution, which abolished slavery.

Once this was done the funding arrived in Virginia, Tennessee, Louisiana and Arkansas. Tennessee was re-admitted to the union in early 1866 and was shocked to learn that they no longer qualified for USDF funding. And further shocked when the governor's letters of protest, addressed to USDF, Washington City, were returned with the letter marked, "No such agency". The "Civil Rights" bill passed by congress in 1866 gave the right to veto to all Negro men. This caused considerable concern in the northern states. The US House of Representatives was based upon the voting population. Therefore, the fourteen southern states with freed slaves suddenly increased their representation from 52 to 76 members of congress. The majority of congress was Republican, but the majority would change once the rest of the states followed Tennessee into the Union. The republican majority decided that they needed to slow down or stop the readmission of southern states into the Union until they could modify the right to vote sections of the new civil rights bill. They proposed that every person who desired to vote should be able to read and write his name before voting. A poll tax would be required. A voter was required to own property. This applied to every state in the Union. And the right to vote was to be an adoption to every state constitution. They reasoned that no southern state would grant the right to vote to former slaves. This would keep them from readmission to the Union. This backfired when all fourteen states of the former CSA added this requirement to their state constitutions. Massachusetts, Colorado, Connecticut, Rhode Island, Wisconsin and Minnesota all refused to change their state constitutions and if you were a black man living in these states, you could not vote. Black men who had fought for the north in the war could not vote when they returned home if they lived in these states.

The "radical republicans" became alarmed when the USDF taught black men to sign their names and read them. The annual poll tax was paid by the USDF. Deeds to one square foot of land were made out for black voters and paid for by the USDF. The USDF funding applied only to those states and territories seeking admission or readmission to the Union. So southern states began to seek readmission and were fully qualified to do so with USDF assistance. The quarrel in the thirty-ninth congress was bitter and when the southern members of the house of representatives were elected in the midterm elections of 1866 and came to Washington to serve their terms, they were refused upon the grounds that they had not taken their loyalty oaths to the United States. When each presented a copy of their sworn oaths, provided by USDF, a new requirement was passed by congress that no member of congress should have been connected in any way with the former Confederacy. This reduced the number by half. The remaining half were told to return home while the other half would be investigated by the reconstruction committee of Congress. The committee recommended to the congress that southern representation be limited to the 1860 membership levels until the census of 1870 could be made to determine the correct number of representatives from each of the southern states. This recommendation was passed by both houses of congress and vetoed by President Johnson. The veto was overridden by a two-thirds majority.

Thaddious Stephens, a republican member of the House from Pennsylvania, was the leader of the drastic measures regarding reconstruction. He was implacable and intolerant of opposition carrying his views into effect by the imperious force of his iron will. His real object was to preserve the republican two-thirds majority by keeping the southern democrats from being seated as voting members of the US House of Representatives. The midyear elections of 1866 had eliminated the two-thirds republican majority. Representative Stephens was seventy one years old and rapidly failing in health, but this did not stop his savage vigor, showing no mercy to the other members of his party who might disagree with him. When a fellow republican protested to him on the floor of the House, that his conscience would not permit him to support some of his radical measures, Stephens replied, "To hell with your conscience man this is your country!"

The reply to that comment was, "Your position is a concept foreign to me. I do not believe in my country right or wrong. I believe in God before country. Right is always on the side of God. It would appear to me that your radical point of view is wrong for the country and wrong for the Republican Party."

He received a standing ovation from the members present and the republicans lost several votes to the minority on each of his proposals from that date forward. President Johnson had vetoed each of the measures that the radicals put forward but he was overridden in each case. This so angered him that he decided to take his case for "God before Country" directly to the people. He decided to make a train tour, extending from Washington City to Chicago which he described as "swinging round the circle." He invited James Buchanan to accompany him. The director of USDF agreed and met him in Washington City. James Buchanan was never popular with the people after his Proclamation of 1858, and this further injured Johnson's popularity. They were viewed as two failed democratic presidents complaining directly to the people. After one train stop the two Presidents reviewed their progress to date.

"James, why is it so difficult for some of these people to see a fairly simple concept of right over wrong?"

"It is more complex than that, my friend. The republicans have convinced the populace that several thousand uneducated former slaves do not have the ability to vote properly (translated, they will not vote for them). As soon as they can convince the black men of voting age that the republican party is the only party for them, things will change in a hurry."

"Why are the republicans fearful that the black vote is a democratic vote?"

"The democrats welcomed them into the party. Republicans are uncomfortable around people of color. 'White men only' is the defacto motto of the republican party. They failed to see that after the war with Mexico, there were more men of color within the new territories and states in the west than white voters. Therefore, that is a democratic strong hold. The south is not the only democratic area of the country, look at both of us. If Louisiana is readmitted, for example, the black voters will out number the whites by forty percent."

"And these are all democratic votes!"

"Correct. The struggle between you and the congress is one of political might and keeping control."

"There is supposed to be a separation of powers between the branches of government, James. I have been unable to get anything done, I might as well resign."

"Thanks to the republicans there is no sitting Vice President, they will never confirm a democrat and you will never appoint a republican. If you resign, then the White House goes to the republicans."

"I have only the next two years then, I will not get re-elected."

"Andrew, you have to face what I had to face. You will not be nominated."

"Then whoever is nominated at the republican convention is our next president?"

"Unless the black men of this country are allowed to vote, yes. Even if the southern states are readmitted in time for the election, the congress will find a way to keep democrats from taking their seats. It is all about keeping control."

"I had such high hopes for this country, James."

"So did I. The only thing that kept me sane the four years I was in the White House was a young man by the name of Jason Caldwell, my brother-in-law."

"I wish he was part of my administration."

"He is too smart for that, Andrew. He will get more accomplished through USDF than you or the next republican president."

"You have convinced me, James. How can I get some of the things that I feel are important to USDF?"

"You are talking to its director. Give me a list."

"I want to change of cabinet members."

"You will have to convince them to resign on their own, Andrew. A dismissal requires Senate approval for just cause."

"Just 'cause I want to is not enough?" He asked with a smile on his face.

"Who are we talking about, surely not Gideon Welles?"

"Hell, no. Gideon Welles is the only republican I know that his head screwed on straight. He is best of the cabinet."

"I agree. Who then?"

"Edwin Stanton."

"Edwin? My God he is a democrat! He was a member of my cabinet."

"I know, he opposes everything I try to do inside the cabinet. Did you know he had a Confederate spy working for him in the Army Navy Building?"

"Yes, Gideon Welles thinks the spy is in Canada, of all places."

"Not anymore. Captain Mason reports from Canada that the 'Grand Dragon' passed through there on his way to England. Those English bastards supported the Confederacy for four years by building ships of the line for them, all the while declaring that they were neutral.

Those sumbitches!"

James Buchanan was smiling. Jason had told him of Andrew's colorful language when he was mad.

"The first thing that you have to do is hold your temper in public and in private meetings. Use it only to drive a point home and only rarely. That way it is tool not a character trait."

"You are right, Mr. President, I, Andrew Johnson, am properly reprimanded for my barnyard approach. I will try to do better."

"Trying is not good enough, Andrew. Doing, is what is important to you the next two years. Do what you can get done, forget trying things that do not work. Quit trying to bump heads with the congress, ignore them and get what you want through USDF. And do not give them any grounds for impeachment, Andrew. If you do, they will use it."

"Thank you, James."

James Buchanan was smiling again, he remembered Jason saying, "You will never get the last word in a conversation with Andrew Johnson!"

"No, thank you for inviting me on this trip around the circle."

"I really needed your support, James. You will not see another veto from the White House."

James Buchanan was smiling again.

35

Wheatland
1867

James Buchanan found the state of the country alarming at the beginning of 1867. Anarchy prevailed in many quarters and was rapidly spreading. When the armies of volunteers were disbanded at the close of the war, fifty thousand troops were retained for service in the south. They were insufficient to preserve peace and enforce the laws. Stanton resigned his office and was succeeded by General Schofield. Congress thanked General Sheridan for his service as military governor of Louisiana after Louisiana was readmitted. The House of Representatives impeached President Johnson because he ignored them and he was acquitted in the Senate by a single vote.

And yet the blessed work of USDF went on by itself, independent of these revolutionary proceedings. Those that now worked for USDF were mostly veterans of the war. Some had worn blue uniforms and some gray. They were coworkers, not enemies. USDF left the wrangling to the politicians and began to get things done. USDF capital began to build up the war torn places in the south. Not one dollar was ever assigned for war damages in the north. Southern states, in the next two years would all be readmitted, one by one, until all became ineligible for USDF aid. Nebraska was admitted as a state this year and USDF aid stopped flowing to Lincoln, the state capital.

James Buchanan had an interesting visitor from Washington City that year. It was Secretary of State William Seward, looking fully recovered from his brush with death and full of energy. He had been having discussions with Russia for the purchase of Alaska. Congress had called the proposal, 'Seward's Folly" and refused to even consider it.

"James, think about what this purchase will mean to the United States. Russia is the only country with territories on three continents, Europe, Asia and North America. Russia's treasury is nearly empty because of her wars with England. USDF can purchase 577,390 acres for twelve dollars an acre."

"William, I think you made a trip to Pennsylvania for nothing. You are aware that USDF owns nothing and is forbidden to keep property of its own. That is why I work out of my house. We are even forbidden to pay office rent. One of the founding precepts is that funds will never be given to the federal government for any reason."

"I understand that, Mr. President, but Alaska will become a US territory and territories are eligible for funding, correct?"

"Correct. And once Alaska is a territory we can certainly help. We are not in the business of doing things as large as the Louisiana Purchase. You are asking for a purchase nearly two and one half times what it cost the federal government in 1803. As long as I am director of USDF, I would veto such an action. You are free to speak to the incoming director, however."

"Who is that?"

"The honorable Andrew Johnson."

"When will that be?"

"Well, we thought it would be this year but the impeachment failed and his appointment date will be March 1869."

"Would it do any good to talk to Jason?"

"You can speak with him if you like, but you and I will have to catch a train to Oil City and get a carriage to Seneca Hill."

"Is Jason home, I thought he was still in Bermuda?"

"He is, you talk to him over the telegraph line."

"Several telegrams will not do anything, I need to have a conversation with him."

"You will, voice communication over the telegraph is called a telephone. Surely you have telephones in the White House by this time. Jason offered to install them free. Oh, I forgot, President Lincoln did not think much of Jason, did he? He would not listen to most of his suggestions. And he fired Montgomery Blair who is now chairman of American Telegraph and Telephone. Different management style, I guess. I found Jason to be invaluable to my administration."

"Jason worked for me, James. I know what he is capable of when he puts his mind to the task. Why was I not told about this telephone thing?"

"I think there were several things that were never forwarded to the cabinet or credit was given to someone else for the concept. Do you want to go on to Seneca Hill? We can talk on the train. I think you should know some things about Jason Caldwell and Andrew Johnson that you might find useful." James Buchanan was smiling a devilish grin.

Both men stood and James asked his butler for his carriage driver to pick them up under the portico. He walked to his desk and wrote a short note. He handed the note to the butler and said this is what we will need when we get to Oil City. Send a message to Seneca Hill through our private telegraph line will you? A short time later they were on there way to the train station.

"Jason Caldwell has decided that the well being of the country is too important to be left to those who are presently in the White House, that includes you, William, and those up on Capital Hill. This next election he will fund any honorable candidate that will run against an incumbent republican. He will spend what ever it takes to defeat the incumbents of the two-thirds majority. He is tied of the good old boy network presently at work in the White House. I pity whoever the next president chooses for his running mate and cabinet members. Jason has given orders to dig all the dirt on these individual's past and publish it in all the major newspapers from New York to San Francisco. He is tired of the scandals that rocked the Lincoln White House. He will crucify anyone doing any wrong doing. I predict that cabinet members of the next White House will come and go like a revolving door. A democrat or a republican, it will not matter, Jason is no longer a democrat he calls himself an independent."

"That is a strong statement, James. He will not be able to do a thing to change things, however."

"William, are you blind? The federal government is four billion dollars in debt! The truth is there is nothing in the federal treasury to do a damn thing. You who serve in the White House better understand that Caldwell International has no debt and a war chest of billions that it can spend on the defeat of anyone they target. It is a new age in politics in this country and unlimited funding is the new power behind the throne."

"Maybe I am wasting my time by asking USDF for aid?"

"If you think it will go into the federal treasury, you are."

"How should I approach Jason?"

"He might consider buying Alaska as a private estate, that way Russia would not have a territory holding in North America. Other than that, I cannot think of an approach."

"Be serious, we are talking about seven million dollars here."

"Jason has more than that invested in Bermuda, California, Nevada, Pennsylvania, New Mexico, Old Mexico, South Carolina and probably a few other places abroad. Seven million is pocket change to this man. He might consider a personal loan to the State Department!" James Buchanan was enjoying himself.

"I do not understand?"

"I am sure you do not. Jason Caldwell is the last of the great American patriots. He does not have a greedy bone in his body, he works hard and expects others to do the same. When they do not work as hard as he, he comes down on them like a ton of brick. I warn you, when you talk to Jason be totally honest with him. If he finds out you lied to him, look out for falling brick."

They pulled into the train station and brought two round trip tickets for Oil City, Pennsylvania. They continued to talk, but William Seward could not get his mind around the fact that a single individual had twice as much net worth as the federal debt. Then he realized that anyone with a positive bank account had more available funds than the federal government. Only red ink was used inside the federal treasury offices and the borrowing continued.

"The war has nearly ruined this country, financially. We are so far in debt that our grandchildren will have to pay it off."

"William, I think you are beginning to see the light. The south is in much better shape than any northern state, thanks to USDF and it will continue in that vein as long as Jason Caldwell is alive."

They boarded the train for the short ride to Oil City and Sam Mason started from Seneca Hill to meet the past president and his guest. Captain Sam Mason had lead a small party into Canada to find out what they could about Confederate spies, former troops or anyone entering Canada during the last two years from the southern US. The information was spotty at best. They learned that a band of former Confederate calvary was living in Canada and raided across the Vermont State line to rob banks and then flee back into Canada. The Americans mounted a joint effort with the Royal Mounted Police and captured seven bank robbers over a three week period. The raiding across the boarder worked both ways. A volunteer detachment from Boston was composed of all Irish emigrants and they kept their arms when the war ended and used them against our northern neighbor as the best way to get back at the English, who they hated. They raided continuously until the US Marine detachment under Sam Mason had a heart to heart talk with them. They had never seen a naval deck gun in action and when seventeen of them were wounded in the first burst, they were eager to talk and surrender their arms. Sam did not arrest any of them. He just said that he would return with a full complement of US Marines if they did not behave themselves. Sam was still smiling when he pulled into the train station at Oil City. His passengers were standing on the platform waiting.

"Over here." James Buchanan called to Sam. "Sam this is Secretary Seward, you probably met him when you served in the Army Navy Building."

"Mr. Secretary, nice to see you again. You look fully recovered, better than the last time I saw you."

"Thank you, Captain. Why are you at Seneca Hill?

"My military service was no longer required, so to speak. Now I am an employee of Caldwell International. I like it so far, it is close to my wife's family and we get to see them often. And the huge increase in salary has really helped my family. Admiral Caldwell offers ten times the military salary for any of his former Rapid Response Unit members that would like to come to work for him."

"How many have been employed?" William Seward asked.

"Almost all of them. They are spread out. Four are in Nevada, two in California, two in Mexico, four in South Carolina, four in Bermuda, I am here in Pennsylvania with three others. Did you bring any bags Mr. President?"

"No Sam, we are just here to use the telephone."

"I have it all set up, the Bermuda end is waiting for your call sir."

They rode in silence as William Seward began to absorb what James Buchanan had told him on the way to Seneca Hill. He was amazed when they entered the house on Seneca Hill, he had never seen a private home larger than the White House. It sat on 640 acres in front of a working oil well. There were several out buildings and small cottages scattered throughout the property.

"Let me show you how the phone works." Sam said.

"You call Bermuda by turning this crank, it generates a ringing sound in Erie, Pennsylvania. A telephone operator asks which cable you wished to be attached to."

He went through the steps and spoke into a black shinny cone shaped mouth piece. "Operator, this is a call from Seneca Hill to St. George, Bermuda. Can you patch me through? Over." Sam then pressed a button and waited for the operators reply.

"Go ahead, Seneca Hill. Over." A voice said out of the second cone placed beside the first. William Seward was impressed.

"Bermuda, this is Seneca Hill calling for retired Admiral Jason Caldwell. Over."

"Sam, how is everything at the hill. I miss not being there we are packing here to start our voyage. Over."

"Admiral. I have Secretary Seward here to speak with you. Over."

"Mr. Secretary? Over."

"Hello, Jason. Over."

"Hello, this must be important for you to come all the way to Seneca Hill to talk. Over."

"It is, Jason. I need your advice on a proposal I am making to Russia. Over."

"How can I help? Over."

"Alaska is for sale. The Russians need to raise capital. Over."

"What is the problem? Over."

"The congress thinks I am crazy. Over."

"Why would they think that? Alaska is close to the north pole and covered with snow most of the year. Over."

"Alaska is more then that, Jason. It is 577,000 square miles that stretch from the Sea of Japan into the Bearing Sea and down the Canadian western coast. It has an abundance of timber and other natural resources including furs and fishing. Over."

"And the Russians want to sell it? Over."

"Yes, for 7.2 million. Over."

"You need to convince the congress that it is a good investment. Bonds will need to sold to raise the capital for the purchase. Put me down for a million shares at one dollar a share at twenty percent. I must run, nice to talk to you again, William, call anytime." No more noise came over the line and into the cones.

"What just happened?" William Seward said.

"You just raised 1 million of the 7.2 million you need, William, and Jason just doubled his money every five years that the bond is in force. Put me down for the .2 million." James Buchanan was smiling. "Jason never makes bad investments."

"Put me down for a thousand shares." Sam Mason said grinning. "Here is the list that Mr. Buchanan asked me to copy for you. It is the Admiral's advisory committee, they are some of the richest men in America you should have no trouble selling the remaining bonds, Mr. Secretary."

"So that was the note you were writing before we left. You had an idea that Jason would help on a personal level."

"Yes, I did. But I do not speak for the richest man I know. Would you like to send telegrams to the list from here?"

"Can we talk to them?" William Seward was like a little kid with a new toy.

"Only if they have a telephone or are visiting Jason in Bermuda." James Buchanan was smiling.

Just then, a loud bell rang and the three men jumped. "That is loud!" Said William Seward.

"Yes, we have to hear it all over the house. I have asked the Admiral's wife to install a bell in each of the rooms, but she says that it would cost to much." Sam was now smiling as he pressed the answer button and said. "Seneca Hill, answering. Over."

"Sam is that you? Over."

"Yes, Admiral. What can we do for you? Over."

"Is William Seward still at the hill? Over."

"Standing right here, sir. Do you want me to put him on? Over."

Sam stood up and William Seward sat at the desk and said, "Jason? Over."

"No, this is JP. Put me down for 6.2 million shares at twenty, will you? Oh, and Mr. Seward do not contact anyone else on Jason's list until we have done some estimating here at Caldwell Place. You will be hearing from us in thirty minutes." .... Hi, Uncle James, you need to say Over when you are done speaking Mr. Morgan and then release the button."

"Mr. Morgan, I do not have 6.2 million shares left. Over."

"Damn, how many shares do you have left? .... you have to say over."

"James Buchanan has bought 200,000 shares and Captain Mason has bought a 1000 since we talked to Jason. If you want the rest at twenty percent, I guess that would be alright. Are you sure I should not contact the rest of the list? Over."

"The rest of the list will want all kinds of guarantees that you can not give them at the present. You better jump on this deal, Seward. It is now or never. .... you have to say over. Damn, Over."

"You have a deal JP. Over."

While William Seward was convincing congress to sell interest bearing bonds at twenty percent for the purchase of Alaska, Colonel Tom Schneider, his 875 marines and 50,000 Mexican troops were beginning to surround the French Army. Fifty thousand Mexican Nationals under the command of President Juarez of the Mexican republic had been trained and supplied over the last two years by the Caldwell Flotilla. The end came at Queretaro, Mexico, on May 15, 1867. Maximilian surrendered and was held for trail by a council of war and sentenced to be shot.

A general sympathy was felt for Maximilian in Europe, and many efforts were made to save him, but his execution was a military and political necessity, which he had forced upon the Mexican Government. The Mexico City newspapers reported: "If Maximilian should receive pardon and return to Europe, he would be a standing menace to the peace of Mexico. He would still call himself Emperor and have a court in exile. Some powers would recognize him in the event of a return to Mexico. A message must be sent to Europe that if you invade Mexico you will be caught and shot." Maximilian and his two top generals, Miramon and Mejia were executed on the 19th of June.

The 875 Americans serving in Mexico were evacuated by the Caldwell Flotilla under the command of Admiral Jason Caldwell. This was his last action as a flag officer of the United States Navy. He retired from the Navy on June 30th.

36

The Election of 1868
November

The Washington Post had the following headline after the presidential election of 1868.

Third Party Hurts Democrats: Grant Wins

	States	Popular Vote	Electoral Vote
Grant	26	1,766,352	214
Seymour	8	945,703	80
Dickenson	0	699,581	0

The election of Grant was greatly assisted by the addition of a third party. Instead of taking away votes from the Republican Party it split the democratic vote tally again, but this time the republican candidate's vote total (1,766,352), was greater than the democrats and independents vote total of (1,645,284). This had not been the case in the last two elections where Lincoln's totals were less than his opposition. And the unlimited funding policy of the independents made in roads into the senate and house of representatives where independents were elected from Maine, New Hampshire, Vermont, California, Nevada, Nebraska and New York. This was the first time in our history that independent party candidates were elected to a federal office. The two-thirds majority of the republicans was gone as democrats were elected from the newly admitted and readmitted states.

The celebration of the inroads made by the independents and democrats did not last long, however. President Johnson refused to sit in the same carriage with the President-Elect on inauguration day. When a compromise solution was found whereby two carriages would be used side by side down the Pennsylvania Avenue, President Johnson refused to appear in the parade at all. General Grant rode to the capitol in an open carriage, with his favorite staff officer, General Rawlins. General Grant was devotedly loyal to his military friends and he continued to do this his first year in office. He appointed military friends to his cabinet. When they were attacked in the newspapers as not having any practical experience in there present positions and that some of them had rather colorful backgrounds, President Grant was shocked. The criticism heaped upon his cabinet was taken personally and he tried to defend them. The newspapers had a field day and it appeared that Grant was either a fool or unqualified to be president. Grant was loath to believe wrong of his cabinet and he continued to protect them until a delegation from congress indicated that his cabinet would be impeached unless he replaced them. He slowly began the process. His selection process was, of course flawed and he selected replacements as unqualified as the first round of selections. A complete list of the cabinet members during the Grant administration follows:

Secretary of State – E. Washburne, of Illinois replaced by Hamilton Fish, of New York.

Secretary of the Treasury – G. S. Boutwell, of Massachusetts replaced by W. A. Richardson, of Massachusetts replaced by B. H. Bristow, of Kentucky replaced by L. M. Morrill of Maine.

Secretary of War – J. A. Rawlins, of Illinois replaced by W. T. Sherman, of Ohio replaced by W. W. Belknap, of Iowa replaced by A. Taft of Ohio replaced by J. D. Cameron, of Pennsylvania.

Secretary of the Interior – J. D. Cos, of Ohio replaced by C. Delano, of Ohio replaced by Z. Chandler of Michigan.

Secretary of the Navy – A. E. Borie, of Pennsylvania replaced by G. M. Robeson, of New Jersey.

Postmaster General – J. A. Cresswell, of Maryland replaced by J. W. Marshall, of Connecticut replaced by J. N. Tyner, of Indiana.

Attorney General – E. R. Hoar, of Massachusetts replaced by A. T. Ackerman of Georgia replaced by G. H. Williams, of Oregon replaced by E. Pierrepont, of New York replaced by A. T. Taft of Ohio.

The prophecy of James Buchanan had been correct the cabinet offices became revolving doors whereby men entered, determined to work for the new president only to find their backgrounds reported in newspapers from New York to San Francisco. A member of the senate committee to approve cabinet selections was asked by the newspaper reporters why the senate approved members without a background check. His reply was, "We will not in the future, we will read the newspapers, they are doing the background checks for us."

This caused a series of articles that attacked the senate and its members as being unqualified to even run a simple background check on its members or future members of the White House Staff. The senators ducked for cover and were careful of what they said in public.

"Where is all the money coming from to make these hundreds of backgrounds checks?" The president asked his newest Attorney General. "You are a lawyer, Mr. Williams? Is that correct?"

"I was when I awoke this morning, Mr. President. This will all blow over in a few weeks."

But the pressure did not blow over, it lasted the entire first four years of the Grant administration. After the senate, the house was given a through background venting and the embrassment continued. When the newspapers uncovered a price fixing scheme by two close business friends of President Grant the spotlight was again upon the White House. A wall street firm of Smith, Gould and Martin convinced the president that the US Treasury should stop selling gold. This caused the price of gold to increase from 140 dollars a troy ounce on September 22, 1869 to 164 dollars on Friday, September 24, 1869. Jay Gould had planned to sell his gold at 200 dollars. His associate Jim Fisk sold at 164 and cleared eleven million dollars in profit. Near the middle of "Black Friday" a source in Nevada starting selling gold at 165, then 155 then, 145 and finally at 133, until the panic stopped.

That same source notified the papers of the price fix and Jay Gould was arrested by New York Police. The White House took the blame for the scheme and a new Secretary of the Treasury was appointed.

Many businesses failed during the Grant administration and city fraud continued unabated. An example was the city of New York. The newspapers reported the "Tweed Ring" had defrauded the city of millions of dollars. William Tweed was superintendent of the street department and was known by the locals as "Boss Tweed". A political organization known as "Tammy Hall" ran the entire state of New York for their own financial gains through building contracts and the funneling of public funds into their own accounts. Tax payers were defrauded a total of 160 million dollars before the newspapers reported the scheme to the public and arrests were made.

Some of the failures were not due to graft, fraud or other criminal acts, but by acts of God. Sunday, October 8 th, the great fire of Chicago destroyed nearly a third of the city. Fifty-seven of the insurance companies involved were bankrupt. The country lost many of its leaders during the first four years of Grant's administration. Robert E. Lee, President of Washington and Lee College chocked to dead on a piece of fried chicken at his home with eating dinner. Edwin Stanton, Secretary of War under Lincoln and appointed to the Supreme Court by Grant died of natural causes. Admiral Farragut passed away suddenly followed by Secretary Seward and Generals Thomas, Meade and Morse. Chief Justice Chase, Presidents Fillmore, Johnson and Buchanan died of strokes.

The Grant administration was unpopular with many newspapers. The New York Tribune founded by Horace

Greeley was a leading critic. Greeley was a founding member of the Republican Party. He opposed Grant's programs and plans for reconstruction at every turn. He encouraged another republican, Senator Sumner from Massachusetts to introduce an amendment to the constitution, by which a President should be ineligible for a second term, and many of those known as active republicans openly declared that if Grant were nominated for a second term they would not support him.

Greeley became the embodiment of the opposition to the administration and at a convention held in Cincinnati the "liberal republicans" nominated him and Gratz Brown, Governor of Missouri as his running mate. They openly invited the democrats to join them in the defeat of Grant for a second term. The democrats met in Baltimore and adopted Greeley's platform. They made an honorary nomination of John Quincy Adams as a symbol of their disgust for anything republican but pledged to support the campaign of Horace Greeley for President.

37

West to California
Summer 1869

Jason Caldwell sat in the dining car of the Union Pacific West bound having breakfast in Ogden, Utah. He was reading the Washington Post and shaking his head. "The democrats have given up the race for the White House, Louise. They are supporting Greeley for President. The race will be between two republicans, Greeley and Grant. Neither has a clue what the country needs." He was still shaking his head.

"When will we arrive in San Francisco, Jason?"

"In a few days. We are stopped here until the east bound Central Pacific can be turned around."

His complete answer was interrupted by a call for, "Telegram for Mr. and Mrs. J. E. Caldwell."

"Oh, Jason, that cannot be good!" She rose and waved for the telegram, tore it open and read it quickly. A look of relief spread across her face.

"Well, what is it?"

"It is from your son. I will read it to you. 'Mother

and Father – I have been informed that I have passed my exams into second level by my tutor. She got a telegram from the Pennsylvania State Board of Education. Have a good time in Alaska. Your loving son, James.' Oh, Jason, my brother would have been so proud of him." She began to cry softly at the loss of her only sibling.

"Louise, they got to spend a lot of time together these last few years of his life. Back and forth from Oil City to Wheatland. He did not suffer, he was unconscious from the stroke and went peacefully into heaven."

"It is unusual for an entire family to be with you when you breath your last, I guess." She said. "Do you think he knew we were all there and I was holding his hand when he passed?"

"Of course, my dear."

A porter came walking through the dining car announcing that all bags had been transferred to the Central Pacific and we would be leaving in twenty minutes. We would need to walk back into our coach compartment and tell Miss Templeton and Carol that we are moving across the platform onto the train headed for San Francisco. As we walked across, we heard, "Captain Caldwell, we are over here." There was D.D. Wilson and his wife who would be traveling to Alaska with us.

"Where are James and Ruth, Louise?" asked Corene Wilson.

"James stayed in Seneca Hill with his tutor to take second level examinations, we got a telegram from him a few minutes ago that said he passed and to have a good time in Alaska."

"Did Ruth stay with him. You said in your last letter that she has refused to leave his side since your brother died."

"Yes, it is the oddest thing. They used to torment each other all the time, but they changed the three months that we were assigned in South Carolina. We all did, even Carol here."

"Hi, Mrs. Wilson." Carol Caldwell had a soft, light-full voice like her mother's.

D.D. Wilson had been a private and then a corporal in the rapid response unit under the command of Captain Caldwell. By the time his first tour of duty was complete he was sure that he would like to return to Utah Territory and work for the Caldwell Shipping and Trading Company owned and operated by his Captain. He always called him Cap'n Caldwell even after the captain became a one star through four star Admiral. D.D. had met Corene (no last name) when an Indian tribe was driven from western Utah by the United States Calvary. Corene had been taken as a child from a family of settlers and adopted by the Indian Tribe until she was 15 years old. After she was abandoned by the Indians, she walked to the nearest settlement called Paradise, Utah, and worked as a maid in the hotel. She worked to regain her English speaking skills and was progressing at a reasonable rate until she met a group of men staying at the hotel. The group of eight had rented the entire second floor of the hotel. One of the men could not take his eyes off of her and it bothered her. She had learned living with the Indians the warriors took what they wanted and if you smiled at an Indian Brave he would claim you for his lodge. She tried to avoid the man, but everywhere she turned there he was smiling at her.

"Why are you following me?"

"Hello, my name is Dewayne David Wilson. But everyone calls me D.D., what is your name?"

"You do not need my name, sir."

"I do if we are going to get married, it is required on the license."

She burst into tears and the story of her abduction from a white family of settlers burst from her like a broken dam from too much flood water. She stood shaking in the hall way and D. D. placed his muscle bound arms around her and held her like a new born baby. "Tell me your first and last name and I will find out where your family is located."

"My name is Corene something, I do not remember my family name, I was so young when I was carried off by my people."

"My people?"

"Yes the tribe was called 'My People' that is all I ever heard them called."

"Well, Corene, it would seem fair to call you Corene Peoples. If I am to write to you I have to know the name and address. Do you live at the hotel?"

"Yes, in the attic."

"In the attic?"

"Yes, all of us do."

"Who else lives there?"

"The maids and the footmen. We pull a curtain across the attic to make two sleeping spaces."

"Come with me Corene."

"Where are we going? I cannot leave work. I will be fired."

"How much do you make here?"

"Twelve dollars a month, sir."

"I think you need a new job, Corene Peoples. We are going to the bank."

They found the only bank in Paradise and walked into the manager's office. "Hello, we are here to open an account."

"Very good, sir. Under what name is the account to be registered?"

"Miss Corene Peoples and Mr. Dewayne Wilson. A joint account. Here is a hundred dollars to open it and we will be back tomorrow with another 500. Each month we will make a twelve dollar deposit until the account is closed. Is that agreeable?"

"Very. Wait here until I return for the papers to sign."

"Dewayne, I cannot read or write English. I can only speak it." She was blushing.

"Do not worry about that Corene, it is easy." He grabbed a blank sheet of paper from the manager's desk and a carbon lead pencil. He wrote C o r e n e. He handed her the sheet of paper and the pencil. You try to draw over what I just did. Follow it closely. She did and then he said, "Now, move to the side and repeat what you have just done, do it slowly." He watched her do it perfectly. Without thinking he gave her a hug and said, "Corene you are a natural writer! Now your last name and they repeated the process until Corene Peoples could write her name with ease and confidence.

"Thank you, Dewayne, no one has ever shown me how to write before."

"It is really easy. And you are smart as a whip, Corene Peoples. Do not let anyone ever tell you otherwise."

The manager returned and the papers were signed

with easy and Dewayne David Wilson was in love for the first time in his life. "Mr. Sellers, do you know of a nice little house for rent in town?"

"Why, yes the bank has a house by the Church. But I am afraid that it is very expensive."

"How much is it?"

"Ten dollars a month." D. D. tried to keep a straight face, he spent more than that on a Saturday night.

"Can you deduct the ten dollars from Miss Corene's new account every month?"

"Of course. Because we know we will be paid every month, the rest of this month is free."

"Is the house furnished?"

"No, it is completely empty ready to move in."

"How much if you furnish it?"

"We could do that, but again, it would be very expensive, probably another 15 or 20 dollars."

"We have to decide on an amount, Mr. Sellers, why not make it an even 30 dollars a month with the first month free?"

"Mr. Wilson, you have a deal." Corene Peoples' head was spinning.

"We are going to walk down to the church and see your new house, Corene. Mr. Sellers, it was good doing business with you." D. D. handed him 10 gold eagles. "I will be back tomorrow with 25 double eagles, Mr. Sellers."

They left the bank hand in hand and found the house by the church and D. D. Wilson carried Corene Peoples over the threshold and sat her down in an empty house he had just rented for her. "There is no lock on any of the doors, Corene. I will have the general store put locks on before I leave tomorrow."

"You are leaving me?"

"Only for a few days, Corene. I live close to Virginia City down in Nevada and I have to return and hire a manager to replace me for a few months. You do not like long engagements, do you, Corene. A few months should let you know if you could learn to love me. I will not marry someone who I do not love and who does not love me."

"You love me?"

"Yes, Corene, it happened like a thunderbolt. You are the most beautiful person I have ever met."

"Oh, Dewayne, you are a crazy man. We have not even kissed yet."

He made a giant step toward her and swept her into his arms and kissed her on the mouth until she could not breathe. "Dewayne, I cannot breath."

"Use your nose. That is why God gave you one and he kissed her again, longer this time."

The next morning he signed his next five year contract without reading it. Caldwell Shipping and Trading would just have to get along without him for a few months until he could convince Corene to quit her job at the hotel and move to Nevada with him. It took only five months for Corene Peoples and D.D. Wilson to decide to get married in the church next door. They had been living in sin for the entire time but Corene had no concept of white man's sin or even a God until D. D. had mentioned that a God had given her a nose.

* * * * * * *

"So what do you two think of the offers?"

"I am sorry Cap'n I was a million miles away thinking of how Corene and I met."

"D. D. everyone in the hotel knew how you felt about Corene, with your mooning over her every minute." Cap'n Caldwell was smiling and Corene was blushing.

"Run the offer by us again, I will pay attention this time." The four adults sat in the dining car as the train pulled out for San Francisco.

"It is a straight forward deal, D. D.   I had the CI lawyers prepare a deed for the saw mill in your names see, Mr. and Mrs. Dewayne David Wilson.   Matthew James and his wife, Connie, will get the water works in Johnstone."

"I do not understand, the mill belongs to CI."

"Not any more." Louise said.

"You are giving it to us?"

"Yes, you and Corene have worked very hard these past few years. We would still like you to stay with the company and take care of the lumber yard for us. The housing you have built around Virginia City has produced a wind fall profit for CI. You will continue to get your annual salary and profit share in the lumber yard. But you and Corene own the mill outright, it is yours."

"I do not know what to say, Cap'n."

"Start by calling me Jason."

"Yes, sir. Cap'n Jason." Corene started to laugh first and then we all did.

"D. D., you know the best builders in Virginia City. Louise and I want to build on the tract of land that CI bought near Johnstone when you first came out west. It is now close enough to the town that the Indians have moved on west and they would not burn or plunder a ranch house and the barns."

"Ruth and James are avid horse riders. Louise and I are going to build a horse ranch and give it to them when they reach twenty-one years of age."

"I know just the man for the job, Cap'n. Do you have a set of plans?"

"No, we do not know what is required for life in Nevada. You wear a cowboy hat and a side arm, D. D. I could never get used to that."

"Sir, Corene is a drafting expert. Leave it to her. Corene get your note pad out of your purse and have Louise tell you what she wants."

"Cap'n, tell me what you would like the outside to look like."

"I would like the base of the house to be mountain stone about three feet high with the rest whole logs that we will buy in Alaska on this trip. How does that sound to you D. D.?"

"If you do not find anything that you like on this trip, I know someone who owns a saw mill that can get you a good deal on ponderosa pine logs. They are beautiful, sir."

"Agreed. Where do you get doors and windows?"

" We have mills in Nevada now. We used to have to bring everything from California. Caldwell Shipping is not doing much 'out-of-state' business anymore."

38

North to Alaska
Summer 1869

And so the days into San Francisco were spent de-signing the horse ranch in Nevada and watching D. D. and Corene, still mooning over each other. Miss Templeton had Carol do her lessons until we arrived at the station in San Francisco and transferred our bags to a hotel. We would buy tickets on a steamer, the Victoria, which left San Francisco and headed north to Vancouver island. In two days we were all berthed on the Victoria and entered the Straight of Juan de Fuca, leading to the inland passage to Alaska. Arriving at the Island of Victoria we turned and passed Port Townsend the port of entry for Puget Sound. We continued along the inside passage. It was summer time but the nights were cool and we bundled up to go on deck. We passed Canadian Indian villages and white trading posts until we came to the city of Vancouver. It looked like any city in the United States in the 1870's. We kept steaming up the straight of Georgia and into the Queen Charlotte straight which lead to Queen Charlotte Sound. Instead of re-entering the inland passage, the captain headed across the sound and stopped at Prince Rupert for fuel.

Alaska territory was less than eighty miles and we started our search for the purchase of timber in Ketchikan, Alaska. D. D. and I visited several saw mills and were not impressed by what we saw.

"These mills are primitive by our standards, Cap'n, we are interested in whole logs for your house, but we need them milled and keyed so that you do not have to clinch between the logs. They should fit together like a child's set of building blocks. I would not import any of the timber from here. The Nevada stands of timber are better."

"You gentlemen should stop at the old Russian capital, Sitka. Sitka pine and spruce are the finest logs in the world, prized for ship building." The foreman of the mill told us.

The four women, Corene, Louise, Miss Templeton and Carol explored Ketchikan on their own. When they returned they had found many interesting things to buy. Green jade and other gem stones were in many of the shops and Louise loaded down with everything she could find as gifts for the family and friends. We re-boarded and headed for Sitka. Sitka had some of the tallest and straightest trees I had ever seen.

"The foreman was right, Cap'n, Nevada has nothing to compare with this. How in the hell are we going to get them back to Nevada?"

"What a shame, D. D., Caldwell Shipping can tow float the logs as far as San Francisco but our building site is on the eastern side of the Sierra Nevada Mountains.

There is no way we can haul such huge logs over the mountains. We will use plan B where Louise and I will come to Virginia City and hand pick the Ponderosa from the Caldwell stands of timber. It is the best we can hope for. What a trip this has been for us D. D. Did you ever imagine that Alaska was so beautiful!"

"If it were summer all year long, Corene and I would move here, sir."

"So would I, but Louise will never leave Pennsylvania for more than a few months a year. I will be lucky to get her west to Nevada and east to Bermuda to spend time in our other homes."

"Why not build a lodge on the property in Nevada?"

"You mean an inn? Like we have in Bermuda."

"No, a lodge. This is a western thing. Wealthy people go away for a month at a time and stay in a resort lodge. Lake Tahoe may someday be a popular place for tourists."

"You think so? Have Corene draw a dashed outline on the map of the tract in Johnstone and letter it 'future resort lodge'. That way we have our bases covered it James or Ruth want to build."

39

Building in the West
Fall 1869

In many ways the acceptance of Alaska as a United States Territory on July 27, 1868, and the completion of the transcontinental railway on May 10,1869, eliminated the intense rivalry between the northern and southern section of the United States east of the Mississippi River. The Union Pacific and Central Pacific rail lines met in Ogden, Utah. Begun in 1863, in the midst of the war between the states, little was accomplished during the first two years. The eastern division of the road was from Council Bluffs, Iowa, to Ogden under the command of General Dodge, a distance of 1,032 miles through the great plains. The western division was begun from San Francisco to Ogden, a distance of 882 miles through the Rocky Mountains. The west was defined as everything west of the Mississippi, an area twice as large as everything east. Alaska alone was as large as the United States before the Louisiana Purchase. Business organizations and construction firms now looked westward. They began to join Caldwell International in its development of the natural resources found here.

The Southern Pacific Railroad built spur lines north to connect with the transcontinental at Reno, Nevada, and it was now possible for Jason and Louise to ride by horse drawn carriage to Oil City, buy a ticket to Pittsburgh and then transfer to the Union Pacific westward. At Reno, they could change trains and head south by spur lines into places like Carson City, Virginia City and even Johnstone. The only train gap was from Seneca Hill to Oil City and Jason considered building a short spur from Seneca Hill to Oil City until Louise heard about it and vetoed it as out of hand.

"We are not so spoiled that we need our own railroad, are we, Jason?"

"No, Louise, I just thought ...."

When the Wilsons and Caldwells returned from Alaska, they arrived at the port of San Francisco. They boarded a train headed east until it arrived in Reno. They transferred to the spur lines and took a short ride into Virginia City, Nevada. They stepped off the train fully refreshed after traveling thousands of miles. "What a great country this is!" remarked D. D. "No horse and buggy rides anymore."

"Except between Oil City and Seneca Hill."

"Get over that, Jason, there is no need for a railroad from our front door."

"Yes, Louise."

"Louise, Corene needs to show you all the building that Caldwell International has done here." He was trying to get Cap'n Caldwell out of hot water. "The guest house for CI visitors is really nice, it is a smaller version of what Corene has designed for you. I will get a carriage and you can rest up before we drive out to look at the tract of land where the new Nevada Horse Ranch will be built."

Louise, Jason, Carol and her tutor had decided to take a short nap before D. D. and Corene returned for the trip over to Johnstone. They were asleep when D. D. came back and he let them all sleep. He returned to the carriage and told Corene that he was not going to wake them. Louise, particularly, was exhausted, he had never heard her be short with the Cap'n before.

"What do you mean short? Louise is shorter than Jason."

"Short is a way of saying that she is not angry, but has run out of patience with him. No, that is not right either. Let me see. What does 'short' mean?"

"Does it mean that she is abrupt with him because she is tired, but she really loves him like I love you?"

'That is it, Corene. You are getting better and better at this English thing."

She answered in her native American Indian language. "Itsewa sandusai ectimasici loughe." She was smiling.

"Yah, yah. I love you too." He leaned over and gave her a kiss.

The Caldwell party slept for ten hours without waking. It was four in the morning before Jason stirred from his slumber. It was pitch black outside and inside the CI guest house and Jason could not sleep. He pulled himself out of bed and lit a lamp. He rummaged around in a piece of luggage until he found Corene's sketches and began to study them. He walked throughout the house lighting lamps until the entire house was brightly lit. He realized that Corene had designed the guest house, her style was unmistakable. She had a natural talent and it included more than just the ability to sketch a picture. She was technically competent to design the houses that he had planned for the next subdivision of Virginia City. Confederate officers and soldiers who could not afford their property in the southeast were beginning to move west. Why not Nevada? He would have Corene design an advertising campaign for the southeastern United States and run advertisements in the newspapers.

"Jason, why are you still up? Come to bed."

"We have been asleep about ten hours. I woke up and could not get back to sleep so I was looking at the sketches that Corene made for you. She is really talented, Louise."

"Let me make some coffee and we can look at them together." Louise left for the bedroom and returned in a robe.

"It is freezing in here." She began to boil water on the kitchen stove while Jason spread the drawings over the kitchen table. He pulled a chair out for Louise and she handed him a cup. He felt of her head and said, "You have a slight temperature. Maybe you caught cold."

"Jason?"

"Yes Louise."

"I love you and I am sorry."

"For what? You are right, a railroad track to our front door would look a little silly!"

"I was not talking about the railroad track. I have been terrible to you and Carol for a week now. I do not know what is wrong with me? I am tired all the time. It is an effort to put one foot in front of the other."

"The doctors are better in Pittsburgh than they are out here in Virginia City. To be on the safe side, I will ask Corene who they use and we will have the doctor come here today as soon as it gets light."

"Oh, Jason, do you think that is necessary?"

"Yes, I do. You are my entire life when it comes to happiness."

Jason left at first light and walked the mile and a half into Virginia City. He got Corene and D. D. out of bed and told them Louise was sick. Corene dressed and went and got a doctor. We introduced our selves and we rode out to the guest house.

The doctor listened to her heart beat and said, "It is strong and regular, no problem there." He listened to her lungs breathe air in and out and said, " You have 'walking pneumonia'. That is very rare for summer or fall time."

"We have just returned from Alaska, doctor." I said.

"Did you encounter any snow or wild changes in temperatures?"

"No, snow. But wild changes, yes."

"Mrs. Caldwell, you need bed rest and sleep. Do not stay in bed more than eight hours at a time, otherwise you will lose your strength and you will take twice as long to recover. This is not serious, I will give you some medicine from my bag. I will write out the directions for your husband. I will come out every other day to check on your progress. Drink lots of hot liquids and get some bed rest. You should be over this in a few weeks."

"In a few weeks, I have to get back to my children in Pennsylvania!"

"Listen to the doctor, Louise. I will telegraph Sam and Rachael Mason and have them bring the children to us. That will be seven tickets. I will ride back into town with you doctor, if that is alright?"

"I have no other stops to make this morning, Admiral."

We left the Caldwell Shipping and Trading guest house and rode the few minutes back into Virginia City. "I really appreciate your coming so early this morning, doctor. I did not want to wait until we got back east to see about treatment."

"Keep her out of cold drafts and wild shifts in room temperatures. We do not want her catching a cold or something else on top of what she has. If she starts to run a higher temperature, that means the infection is getting worse. Pneumonia is caused by a bacteria that settles in the lungs. Modern medicine has nothing that kills bacteria except alcohol and we can not get that into the lungs. The Indians have a cure for this type of thing and we should have Corene Wilson look at her also."

"Are you serious?"

"Corene has been a 'God Sent' these last few years she has lived here. She helps me with all my difficult cases and I trust her."

We stopped at the telegraph office and I sent the telegram to Sam and Rachael Mason explaining what had happened. I walked over to see if I could find D. D. Wilson at his office. He was there and I brought him up to date.

"Let me go get Corene and her medicine bag Cap'n. She can help, she is a wonder." He rushed out of the office and I sat with tears running down my cheeks. I had insisted that we make this Alaska trip and to build in Nevada. I wanted so much not ever to have come on this western trip.

"Are you ready to go?" D. D. was back with Corene and we jumped into the wagon and drove off for the guest house. Corene boiled a pot of water until it was steaming and added what looked like some bits of tree moss and other dried green stuff. She stirred the mixture and poured it into a wash basin.

"Come over here Louise, I know you do not feel good, but this will help."

She lowered Louise's face over the bowl and covered her head with a towel. "Breathe deeply, Louise. Deeper I want to hear you pant."

"Good God, this smells awful, Corene."

"Good, then I mixed it correctly."

She waited a few minutes and boiled another pot of water. This time she added some alcohol from a bottle she had and repeated the process.

"We need to do this every day until the doctor says her lungs are clear, Jason. Stop crying, she will be alright, I promise."

I did not realize that I was teary again and I blew my nose and said I must have caught a cold.

"Stick his head under here, Corene." We heard this from under the towel and we all laughed in spite of our concerned feelings for Louise.

A few days later the Mason's arrived along with James and Ruth. They got off the train in Virginia City and D. D. brought them out to the guest house. Louise was sitting in a large overstuffed chair with her feet up on an foot stool when her children ran into the house and threw their arms around her. She was too tired to stand and greet them. We were all teary except Carol, who announced that she and Miss Templeton were going to take a ride into Johnstone and see what the town was like. They called it a 'field trip' to gather information for a story that Carol was assigned to write about life in the wild west.

"I do not think it is very wild anymore, Carol. You should have been here with your father and me ten or twelve years ago." D. D. was beaming. "Miss Templeton, you and Carol will need an escort I will contact Marshall Peters over in Johnstone and he will meet us halfway and take you the rest of the way. Alright, Cap'n?"

"Alright, Corporal Wilson." And I saluted, the first I had given in years.

He snapped me a return and turned sharply on his heels and marched towards the door. "I guess we are going, Daddy."

"Good bye, Carol. Have a nice time and do not forget to write." I always said this when one of the children had threatened to run away from Seneca Hill.

D. D., Miss Templeton, and Carol left in the wagon that had brought the Mason's. They rode into Virginia City while we made Sam and Rachael comfortable. D. D. needed to send a telegram to the Marshall's office in Johnstone. Sam stored the luggage and came back into the kitchen where we all gathered and were talking.

"Alaska was sooo beautiful, Rachael. Maybe like what California looked like two hundred years ago when the Russians were driven out by the Spanish." Louise said. "But you know, Jason, up and back no time to play, work, work, work." She was smiling.

"I thought you did not like it there, Louise. The reason we made a business trip was to see what the territory was like and if we should sell our Alaska bonds for a profit or not."

"Sam and I are holding on to ours." Rachael said.

"The other thing was to see if we could buy some heavy timber, cheaper there than off the sides of the mountains here. We were disappointed to find out that we could not. But it does not matter now, I think the building plans are on hold."

"What do you mean?" Louise was staring hard to me, I had seen that look before.

"I mean, we may have the cart before the horse. Look at how beautiful this house is here. What do we need with a bigger place to live. This is perfect. Just add a horse barn behind us. Corene should be using her talents for commercial uses." I spread out the sketches and plans that Corene had drawn. "Look, my finger is on the dashed outline marked future resort lodge. This is where she and D. D. should start building."

"Jason, I think you may something here." They all said at once.

"And after we get the Johnstone Lodge up and running with paying costumers we will get back to Virginia City and Corene's plans for moderate income housing additions."

40

The Light Shines Forth
Nevada, 1869

While we were planning our next financial mission. Miss Karen Templeton met Marshal Eugene Peters half way between Virginia City and Johnstone, Nevada. A man on a white horse rode towards them with the morning sun at his back. He had a large light gray Stetson cowboy hat that cast a shadow across his face. His shinny silver star twinkled in the sun light. He carried the largest revolver that Karen had ever seen strapped to his waist and right thigh. He pulled his horse from a trot and said, "Mornin' D. D., this the Cap'n's kid and the school mar'am?"

"I beg your pardon? I am Carol Caldwell's tutor. I am not a school mar'am."

His manner changed completely, he dropped his western speech patterns and sounded like he was from Pittsburgh when he replied. "Too bad miss, we need a school teacher in Johnstone. We had three, but one took off for California – better pay I suppose."

D. D. looked back and forth between the two of them. "Oh, oh. I see some mooning going on here." He thought. The Johnstone Town Marshall, a former marine in the United States Navy, dismounted and gave his horse to D. D. He climbed up on the wagon seat and sat beside Karen Templeton. "Be careful with that horse D. D. he has not been completely broken yet and he likes to pull to the right a little. He will throw you off if he can. I will bring them back after the little one has seen her father's tract of land and we have seen the town of Johnstone."

"Thanks, Marshall, we really appreciate this."

"Anything for the Cap'n, D. D., you know that." He flicked the reins and they pulled away towards the town of Johnstone. The Marshall had not seen or smelled anyone as sweet as Karen Templeton since he left Pittsburgh to join the Marine Corps.

"I am sorry if I offended you. I have not been back to Pittsburgh for fifteen years and I have lost my manners living way out here. Let me introduce myself, I am Marshall Peters from Johnstone, but before that I was a sergeant in the rapid response unit for Captain Caldwell. I was the sharp shooter for the detachment. The captain always called me 'dead eye'. It was just a joke. I was no better a shot than anyone else in the detachment. The captain always made us feel good about ourselves. He would watch us and find something unique about each of us. He would build us up and give us something to be proud of. I would not have found this job as town marshall if everyone around here did not think that I was this special 'sharp shooter' from the USMC."

"What does the USMC stand for?" Carol asked.

"That is United States Marine Corps, little missy. What is your name, little honey?"

"It is Carol Caldwell and I guess it is okay for you to know my name since you used to work for my daddy."

"I still do. I am head of Caldwell International Security for the Nevada Region. And what is your name, big honey?" He was looking directly at Karen Templeton, boring into her eyes, but strangely she was not embarrassed or uncomfortable.

"My name is Karen Templeton. Are you married?" She blurted out.

"No, never found the right woman, until this morning."

"What is the school house like in Johnstone, Marshall?"

"Maybe you better call me, Eugene. I am a town marshall and my first name happens to be Marshal spelled with one L. It got really confusing when people began calling me Marshal marshall. My middle name is Eugene."

"Johnstone town marshall, Marshal Eugene Peters, sort of has a ring to it." Karen was smiling and she had a beautiful smile.

"The school house is closed for the summer. But I have a key. I have a key for every building in Johnstone just in case of fire or emergencies. I will let you in when we get there."

The three of them rode on in pleasant conversation until they came over a hill and there stood the pride of Nevada, the cleanest town west of the Mississippi. It had about 8000 people according the town marker as they drove by. It had several churches and one large red brick school house with a white bell tower. They pulled up in front and tied the horse to a hitching rail. Eugene pulled a large ring of keys from his pocket and searched for the right one.

"Here it is, Karen, right where it should be." As he began to place the key in the door, it opened and one of the teachers was startled to see the town Marshall standing on the front porch.

"Marshall, what are you doing here?"

"I had planned to show the school house here to Miss Templeton and her student, but since you are here I think you could do a better job, Mrs. Wentworth. I will be back in a few minutes."

"It is not much of a school, Miss Templeton. We have eight classrooms but only two teachers left after this spring. I have no idea where the Mayor, who is also the school board chairman are going to get six more teachers? I really do not." She was almost in tears.

"Now, now. Mrs. Wentworth, the Caldwells may be here when school starts in the fall and if they are I will bring Carol and her sister Ruth and I will teach one of the grades. Do not worry, the Admiral will not desert his town in their hour of need."

"The Admiral is here?"

"Yes, ma'am. My daddy is an expert at hiring people for jobs, just tell him what you need." Carol was beaming. Ruth always got all his attention. Now she would be able to have a really good conversation with him about something important.

They were walking from room to room through the school house when Eugene found them. He was with a another man, a short balding man with eyeglasses perched on the end of his nose. "I am the Mayor of Johnstone,

Miss Templeton, I understand that you are a teacher."

"Yes, she is. She was just telling me that Admiral Caldwell has arrived in Virginia City and plans to come here. She also said she would be able to substitute for us if she was here in the fall." Mary Wentworth blurted out.

"Is that right?" Both the mayor and Eugene said at the same time.

"I believe that we should talk with the Caldwells to find out what their plans are for this summer and fall before we make any decisions." Said Karen Templeton.

"I will speak to my father." This was from an eight year old girl who sounded like she was much older.

"Thank you, Carol. Your father would do anything that you ask of him."

"He would?" This sounded like an eight year old.

"Of course, you have him wrapped around your little finger. You are very special to him."

"I am?"

"Trust me, Carol. If you asked your father and your mother to remain in Nevada until fall, they would do so."

"And I could go to a real school with desks and everything?"

"Yes, Carol with real desks and everything."

Karen Templeton was on one knee looking directly into Carol Caldwell's eyes when she spoke to her. She glanced up and looked into the eyes of Eugene Peters and saw the man with whom she would spend the rest of her life. His eyes were full of tears but he was smiling and she could see that he was very happy.

The rest of the day passed in a blur and they were back at the guest house before the sun was down. Carol was the first one down off the wagon and ran for the front door. "Mommy, mommy I got to see a real school house with separate rooms for every grade, with desks and chalk boards and a room with books, thousands and thousands in just one room along the walls. I have never seen so many books and we got to meet one of the teachers there, a Mrs. Wentworth and she asked if I would be coming to school there in August with Miss Templeton as my teacher and I said, yes, and then we ......"

"Carol, slow down. What happened Miss Templeton?" Louise Caldwell did not look happy.

"Carol should tell you about her day, Mrs. Caldwell, after she calms down. She is very excited about what she has seen in Johnstone today. Frankly, I am amazed at what we saw. Johnstone looks like it belongs in northwestern Pennsylvania, not in Nevada. When you get stronger, you will see what I mean. It is what I have been looking for all my life. I have been offered a public school teaching job there and I am considering it. I have until August first to make up my mind."

"Is this something that you would consider? I thought you were happy with us?" Louise had a panicked look on her face.

"I will know in the next month or so."

"You are staying here two more months? What about Carol's education?"

"It is summer, Mrs. Caldwell, children need some time to unwind and relax. I know I do. I will be leaving in the morning to find a place in Johnstone. Eugene will be here to pick me up."

"Who in the hell is Eugene?" I asked, after listening to the conversation.

"Eugene Peters, he is the most interesting man I have

ever met, Admiral."

"Marshal Peters?"

"Yes."

"That must have been some field trip." I said.

"Probably the most important in my life, time will tell." She left the room to pack.

"Carol, take a breath, come sit down on your mom's lap and tell us what you saw today."

The story took nearly an hour to tell and when it was over the parents looked at each other and said, "We had no idea you wanted to go to a public school, honey, we will need to see this school and talk to the people in Johnstone. We live in both Pennsylvania and Bermuda during the school year and a private tutor seemed the best solution." Her mother said.

"Just go into Johnstone and talk, you will see what I mean." Carol had big clear, icy blue eyes like her mother and she could melt you with them if she tried and she was trying.

I glanced at Louise and she looked exhausted. "Go and get Miss Templeton, will you Carol. I want to talk to your mother." I must have had that look, because she jumped down and ran to find her tutor.

"Louise, we are not moving to Nevada so that Carol can go to public school. I have an idea, let me see how far I get with it."

"Oh, Jason. I feel the same way."

"Admiral, you wanted to see me?"

"Yes, Karen, sit down will you?"

"I have made up my mind, Admiral."

"I know you are leaving us tomorrow and we will be glad to see you go."

"You will?"

"Of course, it sounds like you were really smitten today. I understand completely, it only took one look at Louise here for me to decide the same thing." Carol was still standing beside her mother's chair and she was wide eyed.

"We want to help you, Karen. You have been a loyal tutor through three of our children. We will continue to pay your salary until the school starts here in August. And we would like to come to some arrangement for you to tutor Carol every summer that we return to Nevada."

"I am not going to go to school with Miss Templeton in August?" Carol interrupted, she had tears in her eyes.

"Yes, you are. If that is what you choose. You can stay here with D. D. and Corene. They do not have any children and I would think that they would love to have you during the school year. Your brother's school in Pennsylvania does not begin until September and that is when the family will leave so that your brother James can enroll in his second level private school. Ruth will have to decide if she stays here in Nevada or returns with us to Pennsylvania. I want you girls to understand that public school is not good enough for most students to get into a college, you will need special tutoring from Miss Templeton here, but it is more important that you get what you want, is that right?"

"Oh, Admiral. Oh, Daddy." They both started at once.

"What is it, Carol?"

"I do not want to live here without my family."

"You next, Miss Templeton."

"Do not take Ruth out of private school, sir, she is

very bright. She will be able to get into any college that she chooses."

"But not if she goes to public school?"

"No, I am afraid not. Colleges take only the brightest and best prepared students."

"And what about Carol, here. Is she as bright as Ruth?"

"She is different, sir. She can be anything she chooses to be."

"But not if she goes to public schools?"

"If you go to public school with me, Carol, you will be unable to get into any college."

"Oh, why not?" Carol had tears in her eyes.

"Your father is right, Carol. You will need private tutoring to get into a high quality second level school and into college beyond. You will waste your chance at a bright future if you stay in Nevada public schools."

"Can I spend some time with you and Eugene this summer?" Carol was accepting the hardship of life when a loved one moves on without them.

"Of course you can. Did you not hear your father say that I was employed all summer? Oh, and Admiral, I would like for Carol to spend the time this summer learning what a teacher does to prepare for the next school year. Would that be alright?"

"Perfect solution, Miss Templeton, I am glad you thought of that. Would you tell the chairman of the school board that I think I know where he can hire several teachers for next fall?"

"That would be wonderful, Admiral. These children in Johnstone deserve a quality education too."

"They will if you are a member of the staff, Karen.

God bless you and take care of Marshal Peters, he is so lonely." Louise said.

Miss Templeton left our employment and a young woman came to live with us that Carol could not stop comparing with Karen Templeton. Not in a negative way, but in a very constructive, positive way. I heard her say, "Boy, Miss Carlton sure knows more about history than Miss Templeton did. She wrote comments all over my paper! I will have to rewrite the whole thing. Miss Templeton never found as many mistakes as Miss Carlton, she is really a good tutor!"

Louise took her 'treatments' from Corene everyday until she finally said, "Enough, I am completely cured!" We rode into town and visited Doc Williams and he agreed. We continued on into Johnstone and it was a nice little town that looked a little bit like western Pennsylvania except for the huge ponderosa pines. We walked the tract of land we had purchased and relocated the site for the Johnstone Lodge. The views in every direction were wonderful, mountain lakes, streams full of trout, dense forest and peaceful quiet. "When I die, Jason, bury we here."

Acknowledgments

The publication of this second book by Authorhouse required many hands. My thanks, as always, to the following:

Acquisitions editor, Cindi Henson, in Indianapolis -

Copy editor, Connie Ryan. Thankfully, one of us knows where a comma goes -

Cover design, Silvia Panigada, in Bloomington -

Courtney, Scott, Angela and Jamie for their wise counsel and zealous representation and -

Teri Watkins for her many hours of emails and telephone conversations with me over the last two books.

Printed in the United States
153426LV00003B/1/P